CAUGHT

INVERTARY BOOK 7

JANET ELIZABETH HENDERSON

I would like to dedicate this book to one of my readers—Mary Willard.

Mary, very kindly read through a draft of Caught before it was published and she picked up on a mistake that had made it past my editor and proof-reader. A mistake that would have not only confused all you long term Invertary fans, but would have ruined the next book in the Benson's Boys series! I can't even begin to say how grateful I am to Mary for spotting what my tired brain missed.

So, here's to Mary. This one is for you!

CHAPTER 1

Mitch Harris, American music manager, confirmed bachelor and mocker of marriage, fell in love at nine fourteen p.m. on the twelfth of July, in a small Highland town. The emotion hit him like a tornado, whirling him around until he didn't know up from down. It levelled all his previously held beliefs, leaving only the foundations of his character under the debris of his life.

The force of the emotional blow brought him to his knees —literally. He crouched on his heels and hung his head while he struggled to breathe.

"If you're going to puke," his best friend, Josh, said, "go outside and aim for the bushes. These shoes are new."

Mitch looked up at the woman standing beside the town's mayor on the platform at the front of the crowded room. He felt lightheaded.

"Get a grip." Josh tugged him to his feet. "People are watching."

With a shaky hand, Mitch adjusted his tie and leaned back against the wall. He'd been late arriving at the town meeting, and there was standing room only in the pub.

Dougal, the town's unofficial mayor and pub owner, had decided to have the emergency meeting in his pub because he thought it was a dumb meeting and also because he was running a special on burgers.

"Who is she?" Mitch found it difficult to get the words past his rapidly drying mouth.

"Jodie Miller. Owner of the new spa. She's the reason for the meeting, dumbass."

Jodie Miller. Even her name was perfect. Mitch focused on the woman whose very presence was stealing the air from the room. She wore head to toe black—jeans, tank top and black high-heeled boots. Her long, straight black hair was tied in a high ponytail. Her skin glowed, her lips were full, her legs were long, her curves were lush and her dark eyes blazed.

"Okay, Archie," Dougal called from his position at the microphone. "You got your meeting. The floor is yours. State your concern clearly and concisely."

"Try saying that five times fast," Josh mumbled.

Archie McPherson, one of the old men who got together to play dominoes daily, strode to the microphone set up in the middle of the room.

"My concern is this." Archie attempted to stare Jodie down. She was clearly unintimidated. "The spa is sexist. We want the issue sorted before it opens, otherwise we're prepared to picket the building until you lot see reason. This is the twenty-first century; you can't have a business in town that only allows one sex into it. We want equal access for all the sexes."

"Exactly how many does he think there are?" Josh muttered.

Mitch didn't answer—unlike everyone else in the room, he wasn't watching Archie. He was watching Jodie. And he saw the second her eyes flashed with ire.

"Let me get this straight," Dougal boomed, louder than usual over the sound system. "You think the men of this town should be allowed to get facials and pedicures?"

Dougal looked a little bewildered, which, considering he was dressed in his usual ensemble of Elton John-style glitter and neon-coloured clothes, was in itself bewildering. The man looked like he knew his way around a bottle of nail polish.

"Damn straight we want equal access." Archie waved a fist. "The men in this town deserve access to every business. We're fed up being second-class citizens. Women's lib has gone too far and now men are being oppressed. We won't stand for it anymore. It's discrimination."

There was a loud cheer, mainly from the more drunken members of the audience, which made Mitch wonder if the pub was the best venue for a town meeting.

"It isn't discrimination, it's codswallop." Margaret Cameron shot to her feet. "Don't even get me started on how far women have still got to go to get equal rights. Men are oppressed?" She scoffed loudly. "In your dreams. And another thing: you don't even know what a pedicure is and yet you have a sudden need to get one? Who do you think you're fooling, Archie McPherson? This has nothing to do with the spa and everything to do with sour grapes over women winning access to the bowling club in the eighties. You need to get over that before you make a complete fool of yourself."

The women sitting at Margaret's table nodded along with her. The group of retired women were wearing matching t-shirts with Knit or Die emblazoned on the front and Women Rule on the back.

"I do too know what a pedicure is," Archie shouted back. "It's nail polish on your toes. So there."

"Well." Margaret put her fists on her hips and glared. "If

you're so keen on equality, how about letting some women play dominoes with your all-boy crowd?"

The Domino Boys gasped in outrage. For a second Mitch stopped staring at Jodie to check if one of the geriatric men was having a heart attack. It was a false alarm.

"Aye." Archie's eyes narrowed until they were hidden by his bushy white eyebrows. "We can do that, if you let men into your knitting club."

It was the women's turn to gasp. Dougal held up his hands as Jodie folded her arms and began tapping her toe. Mitch wondered why no one else in the room could see her impatience and recognise it as a danger sign.

"Enough," Dougal snapped. "Archie, make your point then sit down. Margaret, if you have something to say, wait until the mic is free."

Margaret sat down in an obvious snit, while Archie flashed a smug smile at her before looking back to the platform. "The men of this town are fed up with being second-class citizens. We won't stand for being shut out of a new business."

"No more bossy women!" a younger guy at the back of the room shouted.

"Men need to be on top again!" one of his mates shouted, and they all snickered.

"Rab McKintyre, that's enough out of you." Dougal pointed at the ringleader, and the guys glared back at him.

"I was in the pub last week when Dougal banned that moron," Josh said. "If this wasn't an official public meeting, he wouldn't be allowed in. He's a grade-A asshole."

Mitch really didn't care about the local trash; he was more interested in using telepathy to get Dougal to end the damn meeting so he could introduce himself to his future wife.

"You got anything else to say, Archie? Because I want this

meeting done," Dougal said to the old domino player, although he was still keeping a close eye on the troublemakers at the back of the room.

"No, nothing new to add. Just that we want the same rights as the women in town. The Highlands is no place for segregation. We want all businesses to be forced to be inclusive."

"And to serve whisky with every transaction!" Findlay shouted.

There was a resounding cheer from the men in the room. Mitch had missed this during the months he'd been away, taking care of business. There was nowhere on the planet as insane as Invertary.

"If Caroline was here," Josh said of his wife, "she'd have this mess sorted out by now. She sure as hell wouldn't let people shout out of turn."

Caroline was the town council member that no one dared mess with. Unfortunately, she was also four months pregnant, while running after a wild two-year-old, and was too tired to make the meeting.

"Order. Order," Dougal shouted, and was ignored. Yeah, they definitely needed Caroline, before this degenerated into a fistfight.

Mitch watched as Jodie looked up at the ceiling for a minute, as though searching for patience. Coming to a decision, she snapped to attention and grabbed the mic from Dougal before he could say anything else.

"Knock it off," she shouted at the crowd. There was instant silence.

"Whoa," Josh muttered. "I can see why Caroline likes her."

Mitch was barely listening. His whole world had reduced to the woman glaring from the stage.

"So, you men want to use my spa?" Jodie's voice was deep, rich and kind of husky. It was the voice of a sexy radio presenter, whispering through the dark hours of the early morning. It was a voice that would haunt Mitch's dreams for the rest of his life.

"You think the spa should be an equal opportunity business?" Her arched eyebrow should have been a warning to the crowd. They were too far gone to notice.

"Fine," she said. "You win. It will now cater to men."

There were cheers, grins and congratulatory pats on the back. She ignored it all, and Mitch wondered why no one else could see the huge warning sign flashing over her head. She was toying with them, and it was the biggest turn-on Mitch had ever experienced. She was sexy, smart and slightly evil. Mitch had always thought he'd want a nice, demure woman for a wife, but one look at Jodie Miller and he knew he'd been wrong. He needed someone like her, someone strong, wicked and sexy as hell.

"At this point in time," she said, "I'm only offering one service for men—waxing."

Jodie paused to let her words sink in. If Mitch wasn't paralyzed by the thought that he'd found his soulmate, he would have cheered her genius.

"What the hell is waxing?" a male voice shouted.

Jodie's smile was feral. "It's when we pour hot wax onto your body, then rip it off to remove the hair."

There were gasps from the older men before they turned green at the thought.

Wicked glee made Jodie's eyes sparkle. "The technique is particularly good for getting rid of unwanted pubic hair."

"I think I'm going to be sick," Archie said.

"So," Jodie shouted above the shocked complaints of the old men, "if you want your body waxed, step on up. Oh, I should also say that this service will be provided by my new apprentice." She glanced around the room before grinning. It was pure evil and sent shivers up Mitch's spine. "Betty, come on up here."

There were shouts of outrage and one glee-filled cackle as eighty-nine-year-old Betty MacLeod climbed the stairs to the platform. She was wearing her usual tartan tent and hairnet. Even in his lust-filled stupor, Mitch noted that she at least had her teeth in.

"I'm sure no introductions are necessary." Jodie wrapped an arm around the shoulders of the town's most reviled gnome. "Betty is now in charge of the male side of this business. If you would like your body waxed, please make an appointment with her."

"Hot damn." The tiny cuboid-shaped woman fist-pumped the air.

"There you have it, gentlemen," Jodie said. "You won your protest. The spa now caters to all of the sexes."

Jodie stepped away from the microphone, dusted her hands and relaxed back into her chair with her long legs crossed.

The crowd erupted. Dougal tried to calm the outrage and quieten the shouts of protest. An argument broke out between the Domino Boys and the women of Knit or Die. Mitch looked past all of it to the spectacular woman who had just stolen his heart with her intelligence, sexy body and wicked smile.

"She's the one," Mitch said, never taking his eyes off Jodie.

"Who?"

"Jodie."

"One what?"

Seriously, some days it was clearer than others that Mitch had all the brains in their partnership. "My woman. My future wife. The mother of my children. That one."

There was a moment of silence before Josh opened his mouth and inserted his feet—as usual. "Have you totally lost the plot? This is about the stabbing, isn't it? You haven't been right since it happened. I'm pretty sure you're suffering from PTSD. You need professional help, dude. Caroline looked this up and she has a list of psychiatrists waiting for you."

"There's nothing wrong with me."

"I've spent my life listening to you tell me that you're staying single forever, and now you're suddenly talking about marrying a woman you just saw for the first time. You can't tell me that's normal. There's something seriously wrong going on in your head."

"I wanted to stay single because I hadn't met Jodie. Now that I have, I'm going to re-evaluate."

"Dude, I feel I should point out that you still haven't met Jodie."

"Will you stop calling me dude? What are you? Twelve?"

"Yeah, I'm twelve, and I'm still the mature one in this conversation. Think about that for a minute."

"Look." Mitch was fast losing patience with his friend. "I told you years ago that I'd know the woman for me when I saw her. That's her."

"I'm pretty sure we were teenagers when you said that and we might have been bombed at the time. You also told me your wife had to be shy and malleable." Josh stretched out an arm and pointed at the platform. "That woman is nowhere near malleable."

Mitch grabbed Josh's arm and pushed it back down. "I never said malleable."

"Whatever," Josh said. "Seriously, I think the anaesthetic from your surgery after the knife attack might have messed with your brain. I've heard that can happen. Sometimes the effects don't manifest until months later. Like now. Like picking a woman at random and deciding she's the one. Dude, you can't do that shit."

"Why the hell not? You did."

"I did not. You vetted Caroline for me before I even met her. I thought I was getting into a business arrangement. I didn't think I'd fall for her as soon as I set eyes on her. It might have been an instant reaction, but it was a vetted one." He pointed at Jodie again. "You don't know anything about her. You haven't even had a background check run. At least I did that. Explain to me what's happening here, because one look at that woman and you're acting like a teenager with his first boner."

"Did you even hear what you just said? Nothing about that is normal. You are the last person I'd take advice from about my love life."

"Love life? Dude, you're having a psychotic break. This is all happening in your head. You haven't even met the woman."

"I don't need to meet her to know she's the one," Mitch said, again in awe. "My heart knows it."

There was a sharp smack to the back of his head. "What the hell?" He glared at his best friend.

"Snap out of it. I didn't just hear you say something sappy like 'my heart knows it.' That was just me hallucinating from lack of food, because Caroline has me on another diet. It had to be a hallucination, otherwise I would have to call in some professional help to deal with your issues. There's no such thing as love at first sight. You're in lust, dude. You're thinking with your dick, not your brain."

"It amazes me that you can make a lifetime career out of singing about love, yet know absolutely nothing about it." Mitch waved a dismissive hand. "I'm going over there to introduce myself to my future wife."

"You're about to make an ass of yourself. I know that look on your face. I've seen it before. I'm calling Caroline. She'll talk some sense into you." He dug out his phone. "I'm pretty sure this is PTSD talking. Caroline told me this might happen. I should have listened."

"Whatever." Mitch left Josh to whine at his wife while he went to introduce himself to Jodie.

It was going to be the most important conversation of his life.

JODIE WAS FAST LOSING PATIENCE. With two weeks until the spa and restaurant opened, and about a million things to do, she did not need the extra hassle of dealing with a bunch of bored old men.

Betty had produced a notebook and pencil from one of the pockets of her tartan mu-mu. She licked the tip of the pencil before glaring at the crowd.

"Right," she shouted. "Who's going tae sign up first? James, your eyebrows could do with a waxing."

Jodie couldn't help the smile that tugged at her lips. Betty was a hoot. Jodie had no idea why the townsfolk called the old woman Satan. She was just high-spirited and had a strong personality. Jodie snorted at the thought. Men were always so intimidated by strong women. Okay, so Betty's moral compass might need a readjustment, but apart from that, the woman was pretty damn impressive. When Jodie grew up, she wanted to be just like her.

"Settle down," Dougal shouted, before banging the wooden lectern with a gavel.

Jodie was distracted from the crowd's outrage by the vibration of her phone. Pulling it from her pocket, she wasn't surprised to find a text from her brother, and business partner, Deke.

Did you sort it?

Jodie looked around but no one was watching her. I think so.

A few seconds later, Deke replied, I hope so, Jo. We can't afford this kind of attention.

Talk about stating the obvious. It would be better for all concerned if their new business ran under the radar and they were just left to get on with it. One of the reasons they'd picked Invertary was that it was a tiny, quiet town—close enough to Fort William for them to draw in business from there, but far enough away from everything else to ensure a modicum of safety.

She scanned the crowd, relieved to see their focus was firmly on Dougal. With the exception of one set of eyes. Jodie's breath stopped as she spotted the man staring at her from the back of the room. As soon as her eyes hit his, it was as though an electric current shot through her body. She couldn't look away. His gaze was filled with hunger, need and knowledge. It was as though he knew her intimately. As though he could see something inside of her that no one else could see.

Jodie felt heat rush up her neck to her cheeks. Her heartbeat accelerated. She suddenly became aware of sensation racing across her body. The air around her had become charged. Her skin tingled and became hypersensitive. The clothes brushing against her skin felt abrasive. She licked her suddenly dry lips and knew that, even from that distance, the move had the mystery man's full attention.

In the more rational part of her brain—the part that wasn't suddenly flooded with endorphins just by looking at the guy—she recognised that she'd experienced this phenomenon before. Once before. It was the day she'd set eyes on her ex-husband. Alarm bells were sounding in her head, telling her to run and not make the same mistake twice, reminding her how this same struck-by-lightning feeling had turned out the last time. Unfortunately, her body didn't want to listen to those alarms. Her body was leaning towards the man who had her in his sights.

The air seemed to pause between them. Noise faded. People disappeared. There was only the two of them. And then he took a step towards her. Jodie's heart accelerated, but she didn't take her eyes off him. She watched him move with the easy grace and contained power of a big cat. A cheetah, she decided. He had a predator's confidence that made the crowd part before him. He was stalking his prey. He was stalking her.

He wore a charcoal suit, white shirt and pale blue tie that had been loosened and hung crooked. Wavy, honey-coloured hair was finger-tousled. His eyes were dark, framed by thick lashes. His lips were sensual, his bone structure defined. He was lean and muscular, with broad shoulders and plenty of height. Slowly, he climbed the stage towards her—keeping his eyes locked on hers, as though he was afraid she'd bolt if he broke the connection. He came to a stop in front of her, and at once Jodie felt at a disadvantage sitting in his presence. She stood, but the height difference meant he still loomed over her. A wicked smile, that promised sensual delight, curved his lips and let her know he was aware of her reason for standing. His eyes, caramel-coloured, she now knew, sparkled at her.

"Have a drink with me." His American drawl was warm honey.

"Are you asking or ordering?" She was surprised that her own voice wasn't a croak. Instead it came out as a seductive tease.

He closed the distance between them until she could feel the heat coming from him. "Sugar, I'll beg if you want me to."

And just like that, the old Jodie she'd buried along with her marriage, raised her head and came to life all over again.

A rush of adrenalin flowed through her and the spontaneous streak she thought had died, seized control.

"Lead the way," she said.

"Now that, I'm happy to do."

His large hand engulfed hers. The touch was hot, a brand to her senses. And Jodie, who never followed anyone, let herself be led across the bar by a stranger.

CHAPTER 2

Mitch's senses felt as though they'd been supercharged. Everything within him was tuned to Jodie. The soft touch of her slender hand in his, the subtle scent of her fragrance, the rapid beat of her pulse under his thumb as he caressed her wrist—it all wove together to form a maelstrom of sensation that engulfed him. Through it all, his heart pounded out one word—a rhythm that was driving him insane—need, need, need, need… He was a monster, consumed by desire, driven by lust and out of his mind with need.

He led Jodie through the busy bar to the quieter restaurant area on the other side of the building, passing the stairs to the hotel rooms above the pub. The chatter of the townsfolk and the soft thud of music was nothing more than white noise. All of Mitch's attention was centred on the woman at his side.

As they reached the dark wooden stairs, Jodie tugged on his hand to make him stop. Mitch turned to her, keeping hold of her hand, afraid she might run.

"Name." She turned her face up to him. "I don't even know your name."

Just the sight of her flushed cheeks and desire-darkened eyes was a sucker punch that nearly brought Mitch to his knees. As though acting on its own, his hand reached out to cup her cheek. Her skin burned under his palm.

"Mitch Harris."

She nodded and a tremble went through her. Mitch knew it wasn't from nerves.

"Do you feel it too?" Her words confirmed his thoughts.

"Yeah." There was an electrical storm building between them. Mitch had never experienced anything like it.

Jodie took a shaky breath before letting it out slowly. "This is crazy."

"Yeah," Mitch whispered.

It wasn't only crazy, it was inevitable. Before even he knew what he intended, he was backing her into the alcove under the stairs. Her fingers flexed in his but she didn't stop him. Her eyelids lowered and she pulled that lush bottom lip between her teeth. Mitch barely contained a groan at the sight. He released her hand to cup her face—one palm on her cheek, another curved around the nape of her neck. Her back was pressed to the wall, her breathing was fast, her heartbeat loud.

He stared into eyes that were mesmerising pools of desire and slowly lowered his mouth to hers. He gave her every opportunity to protest, to tell him no, to tell him he was going too fast. Instead, she licked her lips and held her breath as she stared at his mouth. He felt her hands slide under his jacket and her fingers curl into his shirt, holding him in place.

"Yes?" He breathed the word against her lips.

"Yes." It was barely a sigh.

This time Mitch did groan. A split second later, his lips touched hers. Lightning struck. A jolt of pain that turned to pure, unadulterated pleasure. His lips brushed hers, once, twice. Satin-soft and full. Temptation in flesh. Jodie's fingers tightened against his back, tugging him closer still. Body pressed against body. Hard against soft. Heat melding into heat. Heartbeats merging.

Mitch's tongue slipped out to caress the spot she'd bitten earlier. Soothing. Tasting. A tiny gasp opened her mouth for him. Mitch took the invitation and swept his tongue in to meet hers. There was a groan. Her? Him? He couldn't tell. He was flying. Free-falling through time and space with Jodie. Mitch angled his head and took the kiss deeper. Her taste was sugar and sin. An instant addiction. Mitch tugged the pony-tail holder out of her hair and wove his fingers into the silken mass, holding her head exactly where he needed it to be.

The world had gone. There was nothing but Jodie. Nothing but this. Them together. His whole body vibrated with need for this woman. His woman.

"Get a room!" someone shouted. It sounded as though it was coming from far away.

There were giggles. And then other noises began to intrude—voices, glasses clinking, the low thrum of music. The world came into focus and he was suddenly, and rudely, aware of where they were standing.

Reluctantly, Mitch fought his way up from the daze of seduction that had engulfed him, to lean his forehead against Jodie's. They clung to each other, gasping for air. Mitch struggled to think straight, when all he wanted to do was carry on where he'd left off and never stop.

"Do you have one?" Jodie's voice was husky with need and Mitch felt a surge of pride and possession the likes of which he'd never felt before.

"Have what?" he managed to say.

She nudged him back so that she could look up into his eyes. Man, she was beautiful.

"Do you have a room in this hotel?"

The question stunned Mitch before a surge of hope hit him hard. "Yeah."

She nodded, as though to herself, as her eyes closed briefly. When she looked back up at him, there was only resolve in them. "Let's have our drink in your room."

Mitch forgot how to breathe. He had to fight the need to rush her straight up the stairs. He took a minute, needing to be certain this was what she wanted.

"You're sure, baby?"

"Yeah." She let out a long breath. "This is nuts, but..." She hesitated, searching his face for confirmation. "But I need this."

A whole brass band blasted in the back of Mitch's mind. "I need you too." It was no less than the raw, brutal truth.

His body was tense with the effort it took to control himself and the situation. Mitch took a step back, reached for her hand and headed for the stairs. He tried not to rush, not to push, but the drumbeat of his heart wouldn't be silenced. It was a scream throughout his body—need, need, need... It was as though he was possessed. If this was lust, then he'd never experienced it before. This was something else, something that knocked him on his ass, stole his sense and made a slave of him.

As he glanced at the woman beside him, he knew exactly what to call this new experience. There was only one word for it. One word that could describe the power of what he felt for Jodie.

It had to be love.

JODIE WASN'T sure how they made it to Mitch's room, but suddenly they were there and he was unlocking his door. It swung wide, showing a tasteful room decorated in cream with a red tartan accent. A room dominated by a huge bed.

Mitch tugged her hand to get her attention, making her realise she'd been staring at the bed. "You don't have to come inside. We can go back downstairs, order some food, get to know each other."

She was pretty sure he broke out in a sweat just making the offer. No, Mitch Harris wasn't going to get out of this now. She'd been his prey downstairs. Now it was his turn to be hers.

She reached up, cupped the back of his head and tugged his mouth down to her. With a growl of approval, he wrapped his arms around her. Their kiss was a desperate battle. Not for dominance, but for fulfilment. Something inside Jodie could only be eased by Mitch. She knew it as surely as she knew her own name.

She was vaguely aware of the door slamming shut before her back pressed against it. Lips. Tongues. Teeth. Hands clawing at clothes. Her tank top was yanked over her head and went flying. Mitch's shirt buttons popped off when she ripped it open. Her teeth sank into the tense muscle over his heart.

"Hell yeah." His head fell back.

Jodie smiled against his skin, the salty taste of his flesh an aphrodisiac. She hooked her ankle behind his knee and toppled him to the floor. They landed with a thud. Jodie sat astride the man.

"Bit of warning next time?" He didn't sound like he minded the harsh landing.

He did an ab curl, reaching behind her and unclasping her bra. Jodie arched her back, grabbing handfuls of his hair and guiding him to her breast. She felt him smile against her nipple before he sucked it deep.

"Yes!" Jodie felt herself go liquid.

Strong hands pressed against her back kept her upright as her eyes closed. All she had to do was concentrate on the feeling of him suckling her. It was heaven.

"Harder," she ordered.

He did as he was told, adding a tiny nip of his teeth. Fireworks went off behind her eyelids, and she felt like she was floating away. She wasn't even aware she was moving until her back hit the thick carpet. She forced her heavy eyelids open to see Mitch scramble out of his trashed shirt and knotted tie.

Yum. Jodie reached up to run her nails down his abs. Each ridge perfection. Her fingertip traced over a puckered scar low on his abdomen, but there was no time for curiosity, because he was kissing her. His kiss went on forever, until her lips felt bruised and swollen and the room began to spin. Then he moved down her body, trailing tongue and teeth. Tasting, biting, kissing. Her fingers dug into his shoulders, but it wasn't enough. She needed more of him.

She wrapped her legs around him, pressed up off the floor and flipped them so that she was on top. Her breasts were instantly in his hands as they explored each other. He was a work of art. Every promise his body had made while fully clothed, was kept now that he was naked. She looked down at his trousers. Nearly naked.

Jodie leaned back on her heels, making him whine in complaint. She smiled and knew it was wicked. Fast fingers unfastened his trousers and unzipped him. She hooked her thumbs into the waistband of the trousers and his underpants and dragged them both down to his thighs.

He sprang free. Long, thick, hard. A delicious temptation. She bent her head to taste him. One lick was all she managed before Mitch's hands clamped on her hips and she was moving again. She found herself on her back on the soft bed. Mitch kicked off the rest of his clothes and pounced on her, making fast work of removing her jeans and panties. They went flying over his shoulder, his eyes never leaving her body.

Before he could climb onto the bed with her, she was on her knees. Her arms wrapped around his shoulders, her mouth on his. She swallowed his groan of approval as his hands explored her body. They soothed, teased, tantalised until she was breathless for more. He crawled onto the bed, pushing her down beneath him. Jodie slung a leg over his hip as her hand worked between them. She held him. Hard. Yet silken soft.

Damn, she needed him.

She pressed her hips up and angled him into her. His arms and legs locked, keeping him above her, just out of reach.

"I want to taste you first," he said. His eyes so dark they were almost black.

"Later." She tumbled him onto the bed beside her and straddled him.

A second later she was sinking onto him. His hands clasped her hips. His neck arched. A low, guttural cry came from his throat. And then his heels dug into the bed and he pushed up into her. Jodie lost all sense of time. Her world had reduced to this man and how he made her feel.

He cursed, threaded his hand through her hair and pulled her down for a punishing kiss. His other arm kept her in place as he pummelled into her. It was too much. Jodie felt everything within her coil tight and then explode. She shattered above him as Mitch chased his own release.

As they floated back down to earth, Jodie found herself lying on top of Mitch, her cheek to his chest, his heartbeat a drum in her ear. His big hand soothed up and down her back.

In that moment, Jodie wished it wasn't just a one-night

stand. She wished Mitch wasn't a tourist who'd go back to America as soon as his vacation was over. She wished he was hers and they could keep exploring each other until exhaustion claimed them completely—say, in twenty or thirty years.

The desire to keep him was so strong that she almost forgot she'd learned her lesson where men were concerned. They might say they liked a strong woman, but once the dust settled, they just felt intimidated. And Jodie was tired of being to blame for someone else's damaged self-esteem. She was better off on her own. It was good Mitch didn't live in Invertary. It was good that there was a limit on their time together. She was perfectly fine with the fact he'd be gone soon. Honest.

Jodie shifted her position and licked across his chest. There was no doubt in her mind that she'd miss him once he was gone. But first she would enjoy their time together. No matter how short.

CHAPTER 3

Jodie woke with a start and the words "Oh hell no!" screaming in her head. Even though it was pitch black, she knew instantly where she was and what she'd done. Even if she hadn't, the fact she was lying on her stomach in the middle of the bed with a large hand on her backside would have been a clue. Slowly, silently, Jodie turned her head to see Mitch lying on his back beside her, one arm thrown over his eyes, the other resting on her back as he cupped her rear. He was breathing deeply, steadily, sound asleep. Relief flooded Jodie, followed closely by resolve—she had to get out of there.

Jodie inched out from under Mitch's hand and let herself fall off the edge of the bed onto the floor, making sure she landed softly. The shade curtains were drawn, but the bedside clock told her it was almost seven a.m. On hands and knees, she crawled around the bed, trying to find her clothes. Her hands hit jeans and she pulled them to her. Her heart was beating so loudly that she could hardly hear Mitch's breathing over the noise. Her phone was in the pocket of her jeans. She switched it on. The light from it helped her to find one boot and her underpants before it cut out again. Several more times hitting the on button, while wishing she'd downloaded a flashlight app, let her find her tank top. There was no sign of her bra or the other boot. She would just have to sacrifice them to the god of stupid, slutty women who slept with strange American men.

Slowly, she pulled on her jeans. The material made a loud, rasping sound that she'd never noticed before. It rang out like an alarm in the darkness. She wobbled as she tugged them over her thighs. Inside her head she cursed the invention of skinny jeans, swearing that if she got out of this situation she was going to hunt down the inventor and make them pay. It took ten years to inch the damn jeans up over her hips. Even then she didn't dare pull up the zip.

In the blackness, she bent down to grab her tank from the floor and hit her head on the coffee table. The dull thud echoed through the room. She froze, standing there topless, with her throbbing forehead resting on the table, her backside in the air, waiting to be caught. Mitch turned, but kept sleeping. Jodie waited, counting his breaths until she was sure it was safe to move and then stood. Wearing one boot was pointless, but it didn't seem right to deliberately leave it behind. She tucked it into the back of her jeans so that her hands were free.

Using the light from the phone, she tiptoed to the door. Mitch made a noise as she turned the handle. Jodie quickly killed the light and rushed through the door—straight into the closet.

She hung her head in disgust.

And that was when her phone went off. In Jodie's panicked state, she couldn't remember how to switch the sound off. She wedged the phone between her thighs to muffle it, and waited until whoever the hell it was stopped calling.

She'd aged fifty years by the time her ringtone—Gaga's "Bad Romance"—stopped playing. Quickly, she grabbed her phone and switched it to silent. The screen told her she'd missed a call from her brother. As she stared at it, a text came through. The vibration echoed through the closet, making the sound seem much louder than it should have been to her oversensitive ears. Jodie stared up at the dark ceiling and silently begged God to put her out of her misery. It didn't happen, so she read the message that was so important Deke had to once again conquer his fear of texting. Or as he put it, "real men don't text, they pick up the damn phone and make the call."

Where the hell are you? You need to get back here. We have a problem.

Jodie typed fast. Bk sn. Stp frkn.

The reply took a minute to come back, as Deke insisted on typing every single word properly.

Stop freaking? Some dickhead painted the building with graffiti.

Jodie jerked up straight. Graffiti?

They spray-painted crap about the spa being women-only.

Jodie closed her eyes. The town meeting had stirred up the underbelly. Prbly kds. At least, she hoped it was. They really didn't need this sort of attention. Tell cops?

I'll call them. It would look suspicious if we didn't. And use proper bloody English. Words have vowels. Sentences have joining words!

Jodie leaned her head against the hanging shirts and took a deep breath. A bad idea, because the scent that was uniquely Mitch engulfed her and made her thought process wobble. This was not happening. She was not thirty-six and stuck in a hotel closet while having a text argument about grammar with her younger brother. It was all a dream brought on by too much stress and not enough sleep.

Fine, you deal with the cops, Jodie typed fast, making sure she used full words. I'll be back soon.

Where the hell are you, anyway?

None of your business!

Jodie switched the phone off. She'd had enough of her brother for one morning, and she had more important things to deal with. Like getting out of the closet, and room, without alerting her one-night stand. She reached for the door handle just as it turned. It slowly swung open, revealing a very naked Mitch in a dimly lit room.

"Baby," he drawled sleepily, "you're in the closet."

Jodie did the only thing she could under the circumstances: she straightened her shoulders and rose above the situation—at least, that's what she was aiming for.

"I didn't mean to wake you. I was just leaving."

Mitch looked behind her at the closet full of clothes. "To Narnia?"

Jodie scowled at him before striding into the room, aware of how ridiculous she must look.

Mitch rubbed his chin, obviously uncaring that he was stark naked. "You've got a boot hanging out the back of your jeans and your tank is on inside out." He seemed bewildered.

Jodie ignored the comment, because really, what could she say to make her situation seem less ridiculous? Nothing, that's what.

She strode straight to what she hoped was the correct door, put her hand on the handle and worked at being gracious. "Thank you for a lovely night. I hope you have a nice visit to Scotland and safe travel when you fly back home."

Mitch's lips twitched as though he was fighting back laughter. He sauntered over to her and casually leaned a shoulder against the door to stop her escape. He crossed his arms and ankles. Her eyes flickered down over his body before fixing on his face. How could he stand there so relaxed about being naked when she was freaking out because she was braless? Just looking at him made her hormones riot. Her brain was demanding she leave with at least some dignity intact, while her body was screaming, "Come to Mama!"

"I'm hoping you had a better time than just lovely, Jodie," he drawled. "I know I did."

Her traitorous cheeks began to burn, but she still managed an icy stare. "Do I need to stroke your ego before I go, Mitch?"

Mitch grinned widely and looked down his body. "She named you ego," he said to his cock. "If she's naming you, it must mean she wants to keep you."

To her disgust, Jodie had to fight a smile.

"We had a great time." Mitch's hazel eyes captured hers. "Stay for a while. Have breakfast, get to know me."

The man was walking, talking temptation.

"I can't, Mitch. I'm in the middle of setting up a new business and there's a lot to get done before we open. Plus"—she took a deep breath—"this was a one-night thing. There's really no point in getting to know each other. You have your life in America and I have my life here. I think it's best if we walk away before it gets too complicated, each of us with a fantastic memory."

His smile was dazzling. "Jodie, baby, I live here. In Invertary."

Her brain stuttered. He couldn't mean…? She looked behind him at the dishevelled room. "You live in a hotel?"

He ran his fingers through his hair. "I've been meaning to look for a place, but I travel a lot and haven't gotten round to it yet."

"You live in Invertary? Permanently? This is your permanent home?"

"Yep, this is my permanent home."

"But you're American." She felt her cheeks flush again and wished she could gain control of her traitorous body.

"Don't tell the locals. They think I'm one of them." He stepped forward, backing her up until she was pressed against the wall beside the door. He placed his hands flat against the wall on either side of her head. His body didn't touch hers, but she could feel the heat coming off him. His musky scent surrounded her. It was drugging her senses, making her feel dazed.

"But I haven't seen you around." Jodie just could not stop the idiocy coming out of her mouth.

This could not be happening. He was supposed to be a tourist. There should have been no repercussions from her one night of sin. She should have known better; Catholic school taught her that there were always consequences—especially when you enjoyed committing the sin in the first place.

Mitch pointed at the puckered red scar low on his right side. "I've been recuperating. I had a run-in with the pointy end of a knife. Then I had to travel for work. I only got back into town yesterday."

Jodie felt the colour drain from her face. Now she knew exactly who this guy was. "You're Josh McInnes' manager."

"Guilty as charged," he said, clearly amused.

He leaned forward and placed a tiny kiss on the corner of her mouth. She felt it zing through her body and knew she was in trouble. The man was fast becoming her addiction. She held up her hands to ward him off and her palms met his solid flesh. Then, of course, her traitorous fingers kneaded muscle.

"Stay and have breakfast with me, Jodie." Oh, that voice could lead anyone into sin.

And she had to resist. "I can't. This was a one-night thing. I didn't follow you to your room wanting a relationship. I came up here because I thought it would only be one night. That's all I can do. It's all I want to do. If you want something else, then you'll have to look elsewhere. I was inoculated against relationships when I got divorced."

"Okay, you don't do relationships. What do you do?" His fingertips trailed, feather-light, down her neck to her shoulder. She shivered under his touch.

"What do you mean?" Her voice was husky, her brain already losing in the fight between hormones and sense.

"This thing between us. It's combustible. I've never experienced anything like it." He stared at her for a moment as though reading her face, and then gave her a small smile. "Neither have you. I don't want it to stop."

No! Don't stop! her body screamed at her. It wanted to rub against him like a cat in heat.

"I don't do romance, relationships, marriage, togetherness —any of that stuff." Oh, why didn't she sound convinced?

"I'll take whatever you'll give me. I'll take whatever I can get." His voice, though soft, was steel, and she knew he wasn't going to let this go—let her go. The crazy thing was that instead of making her want to run, his determination only made her want him more.

"You mean friends with benefits? Is that what you're talking about?"

"If that's what you want." He inclined his head and placed a kiss on her neck at the curve of her shoulder.

Jodie felt her body melt.

"No strings?" She fought to get the words out.

"No strings," he confirmed as he kissed his way up to her earlobe.

A little moan escaped. She wasn't proud of the fact, but she couldn't stop it. His skin was hot under her hands and his lips were driving her mad.

"So, we'll just get together to, what? Have sex?"

"Whatever you want, Jodie." His voice was pure seduction. Low and sensuous. It promised dark nights and endless pleasure. "I'll give you whatever you want."

Her eyes closed as her body began to writhe against him. She wanted to give in to temptation. She wanted everything he promised. She wanted him. Even though her fear of getting entangled in another relationship was strong. Even though she knew she'd never survive another heartbreak. His was a teasing seduction that slipped past her common sense and dared her to indulge.

"No relationship." Her surrender came in a rush of words. "No dating. We don't tell anyone. It's just between us. No expectations. No long-term planning. No public displays of affection. No soppy, romantic gestures. Either one of us can call a stop to things without the other questioning it. And when it stops we part on good terms."

"Agreed." The word was a rumble against her ear as his hands threaded into the hair at the back of her head.

She was dizzy from his touch. Desperate for more. The world was shifting beneath her, but she felt safe in the cocoon of his arms.

"This is a purely physical thing. Nothing more." Yeah, that probably would have sounded more convincing if she wasn't so breathless with need. "Are you sure you want to get into this knowing that?"

"I just want you, Jodie. Any way I can have you." His words were a vow and then his mouth slammed against hers and Jodie's brain conceded defeat to her body. In the back of her mind, that little Catholic voice was reminding her that every action came with a consequence, and she wouldn't like it when the consequences of this decision caught up with her.

Like she'd done right through school, Jodie ignored the voice in her head.

Consequences be damned.

CHAPTER 4

"No points for originality," Brenda Smith said as she considered the graffiti spray-painted across the front of the old church building. She looked up at the stony-faced man beside her. "Do you think they drew the penis because they couldn't spell the word?"

Deke looked down at her, quite a way down, as even in heels Brenda barely came up to his shoulder. "I don't think that's the word they would have written."

"I've always wondered about the words we use for penis." And she wasn't lying. There was a lot Brenda wondered about. This was just the tip of the iceberg. "'Cock' sounds so aggressive and 'dick' makes me think of thick, as in dumb. And—"

Deke groaned. He seemed to do that a lot around her. "Please, stop talking."

"Fine." She pressed her lips together but couldn't keep it in. She just couldn't. He was a guy. The chances of him knowing the answer were high, so she had to ask. She had to. "Why do American men call it a Johnson?"

"Kill me now," Deke said. His soft green eyes met hers

and, as usual, her heart stuttered. His eyes were just too pretty. Especially in that oh-so-masculine face. In fact, his eyes were the only soft thing about Deke Miller. "Do I sound American? Why don't you ask one of the Americans in town? We're overrun with them. You shouldn't be stuck for choices."

Brenda was silent for as long as she could manage it. Which wasn't very long. She couldn't help it. She was curious by nature. It was one of the reasons she'd managed to get into so much trouble in such a short life. Okay, well, maybe twenty-seven wasn't so short. If she lived until she was ninety, then she wouldn't even have made it through a third of her lifespan yet. Which meant that there were still two-thirds left to screw up. Yay for her.

"Brenda!"

The name snapped her back to the world outside her head. Deke was staring at her, clearly irritated.

"Did you say something?" Brenda gave him her winning smile.

"I said why don't you get back to sorting out the spa and I'll deal with this mess?"

Yep, she should probably do that. Scurry away. No doubt Deke would feel a lot more relaxed if she wasn't standing so close to him. She'd noticed, in the two weeks since she'd arrived at the spa, that whenever she got within two feet of the man, he stepped away from her. It had become a bit of a game. She'd deliberately get too close to see if she could get him to back into furniture. It was the small things in life that amused her.

"You're doing it again." The words broke through her thoughts.

She frowned up at the man. Honestly, it was hard not to drool around him. At over six foot tall, he towered over Brenda. He was broad and muscled and had the roundest backside. It made a woman want to pat it every time she passed him. Okay, maybe not all women, maybe just Brenda. His hair was military short, a covering of fluff over his scalp that teased you to touch and see if it was soft or bristled. And although he'd been out of the Army for a couple of years, he seemed to dress as though he was still in it. In the time she'd been living at the spa, she'd only ever seen him in combat trousers, boots and various army-green t-shirts.

He also seemed to be waiting for a reply. "Doing what?"

"Zoning out."

"I don't zone out. I think. Don't be fooled, Deke. Just because this hair is blond doesn't mean the head is empty."

He looked at her like she was the crazy one. Just for that, Brenda took a step closer to him. And sure enough, he retreated. It took all of her self-control not to giggle.

"I'm happy to wash the wall," she told him.

The spa was pretty much set up. That side of the business was opening before the restaurant because Deke and Jodie thought staggering the starting dates would mean fewer problems to deal with. For the past two weeks, Brenda had helped unpack and set up the spa equipment that Jodie had ordered. She now had a beautifully equipped treatment room ready for all her massage clientele, and very little to do until opening day.

"No. I'll deal with this." Deke looked immovable. Which made her want to move him. So she took another step towards him and watched his retreat.

His brow furrowed, as though he suspected she was doing it deliberately but wasn't quite sure enough to call her on it. Brenda widened her blue eyes and aimed for innocence. She was a short, curvy blonde with blue eyes, which meant her innocent look had a ninety-eight per cent success rate.

"Okay then," he said. "Why don't you go set up the staff

housing? Benson Security is finishing up the alarm installation today, which means you lot can move in tonight."

"I suppose I could do that." She took another step towards him and watched him back up. Inside she was laughing hysterically. Deke was so much fun. "Are you sure you don't need any help in the kitchen? I hear you're interviewing more wait staff today. I could sit in on the interviews."

"Why the hell would I want that?"

"Because you scare them off."

"If they're too soft to deal with me during a half-hour interview, they'd be no good during an evening service."

He had a point, but according to Robin, who worked front of house, Deke ran the kitchen like he was still in the Army. Carly, the pastry chef, said that half the time he told her to do something, she had to resist the urge to salute.

"Still." She stepped closer, making him step back—into a bush. "I could help."

Deke moved to the side of the bush and folded his bulging arms over his green tee. "I don't need help. Go sort out the staff house. I need to go." He spun round, almost tripping over the same bush he'd just sidestepped.

Muttering under his breath, he practically ran for the restaurant. Giving her a front-row seat for that fabulous backside.

"You are so mean to him," came an amused voice.

Brenda looked over her shoulder to see Robin. Out of all the women Jodie and Deke had hired for the business, she'd known Robin the longest. They'd crossed paths a couple of times over the years. Although last time they'd met, Robin was going by the name Joanne.

"I'm just playing." Brenda wished she wasn't, but that was the state of things. A girl like her wasn't attractive to a man like Deke. No matter how much she wished she was.

Robin came up beside her and together they stared at the awful writing on the wall.

Men Rule! Women Suck—followed by a huge, badly drawn penis.

Brenda knew the words didn't have anything to do with them. It was fallout from the town meeting the evening before. Still, she couldn't stop the feeling of dread that went through her at the sight.

"I was hoping this would be my last stop," Robin said, as though reading her mind.

"This will pass. It's just kids messing around." She hoped her words were the truth. "Benson Security are finished securing the old manse. We can move in today."

"That's good." Robin didn't sound particularly excited, and Brenda couldn't blame her. Both women had lost count of how many houses they'd called home over the years. "It will be nice not to be under Jodie's feet. The manse is big enough so that we won't feel like we're on top of one another."

What she didn't say was that none of them dared to move out into a house where they lived alone. There was safety in numbers. Another reason they'd been camping in Jodie's apartment above the business for the past two weeks. The thought of taking a room at the hotel, or renting a house far from the spa, was just too stressful.

"He's got a thing for you, you know?" Robin's words made Brenda's head turn.

"No he doesn't." But her heart raced at the thought.

"When he knows you aren't looking, he stares at you. He looks kind of like a lovesick puppy."

Brenda forced a laugh that was far more light-hearted than she felt. "Deke Miller isn't the type of guy to go for women like us. He's just being protective. It's what he does. It's hardwired into him."

Robin bumped shoulders with her. "Trust me, his looks aren't protective. They're hungry."

"I wish!" Brenda linked arms with her friend and headed for the manse at the back of the property. "I think the fact he retreats whenever I'm close to him says more than a few wayward looks. He's terrified of me."

"Not you, sweetie. He's terrified of hurting you."

Brenda sighed. "Story of my life: the men who should have been terrified of hurting me weren't, and the man who shouldn't be terrified is."

"Maybe you could convince him to get over his fear." Robin gave her a wicked smile.

"I'll get right on that," Brenda said. "If I ever get to spend more than five minutes with him without him running away."

No, Brenda wasn't going to delude herself. Men like Deke couldn't see past the fact they thought she was broken. They treated her like spun glass. Terrified to get close in case she shattered. Still, that didn't mean she couldn't have her fantasies.

"Tell me again about the way he looks at me," she ordered Robin.

The women were laughing as they approached the old Victorian building that would be their new home.

JODIE DIDN'T MAKE it back to the spa until mid-morning. She ran upstairs to her apartment, showered and changed, before going back downstairs to meet with her brother and Benson Security.

The renovation work on the old church, in order to turn it into a boutique spa and restaurant, was nearly complete. The church had been built in the hills outside of town, and although it hadn't been built with views in mind, it still had a great overview of Invertary and the loch behind it. The church itself was really a mix of three different buildings. There was the old stone church at the front, with its grey brickwork and stained glass windows. Then there were two more add-on sections attached to the original church. One to the rear and one off to the side. The one to the side had been built in the same style as the church, even going so far as to include a sloping roof and mini bell tower—that was the part they were using as a restaurant. The section at the rear had been built with no style in mind. It was basically a concrete cube wedged onto the main church. It housed a couple of consultation rooms as well as their offices.

Although the church only had one level, the ground floor, the ceilings had been high enough to enable a second level to be built into it. They'd turned the new level into a large apartment for Jodie. There had been space enough to build two apartments, but Deke said that was too close to his sister for his liking. Instead, he'd had the old garage at the back of the property turned into a little house.

Deke was waiting for her at the bottom of the stairs, a steaming mug of coffee in his hand.

"You want to tell me where you were all night?" Deke asked casually, between sips of his coffee.

"Nope." Jodie headed towards the manse. The old Victorian building used to be the vicar's house. It was set at the back of the property, hidden from the road. In fact, unless you knew it was there, you would never guess that the land around the church hid such a large house.

"I see you've got the builders water-blasting the graffiti off," Jodie said. "Thanks."

"They'll sandblast it, if the water doesn't work."

"Good to know."

"Want to tell me who you were with then?"

She didn't even answer that question. Deke put a hand on

her arm to stop her, and she did, with a sigh. She looked up into her younger brother's face and saw only concern.

"You need to talk, I'm here. You want me to hit someone, just ask. You deserve to be treated right, Jo. I know the dickhead ex messed with your mind and your confidence. I'm here if you need anything. Okay?"

Jodie freaking loved her brother. How he turned out to be such a great guy after everything they'd gone through, she didn't know. She wrapped her arms around his waist and hugged him tight, revelling in the comfort.

"You're a good guy, Deke."

"Feel free to spread that around." He kissed the top of her head then disengaged. Obviously he'd reached his limit for showing affection for the day—possibly even the month.

"You also know I can take care of myself." She felt the need to remind him—after all, she had more martial arts experience than he did.

"I know, but good guys offer." He winked at her, making her roll her eyes at him. "Come on," he said. "Let's see what Lake wants. I'll be glad when the security system is up and running. A loud alarm might have cut last night's art attack short."

"I saw what was left of the drawing. There was nothing artistic about it. I know guys are obsessed with their junk; the least they could do would be to learn to doodle it accurately. What is it with guys and their penises, anyway?"

"Not you too." Deke groaned. "I don't want to talk about penises with you or anyone else. Got it?"

"Fine, Mr. Touchy, what did the police say?"

"That it's probably local hooligans who were wound up by last night's meeting and thought they'd get in on the protest."

"I didn't know Invertary had hooligans."

Deke's lips thinned. "Apparently we import them at this

time of year. There's a whole bunch come in from the local towns for the fishing tournament. Matt says things will quieten down in a couple of weeks, although he doesn't think we'll get any more trouble in the meantime."

"I hope he's right."

They found Lake Benson in the large kitchen at the back of the old Victorian manse. The building had been designed with the needs of a functioning parish in mind; therefore, the social areas of the house were cavernous rooms.

Lake was talking to one of his guys when they walked in. Grunt was a scary American guy who'd married a local woman. They were expecting their first child. He was massive, stony-faced and rarely spoke. He was one of the scariest men Jodie had ever met. If she hadn't seen him with his wife she wouldn't have let him near her business. But around Claire he was a pussycat. He doted on her, pandered to her every whim and fawned over her like she was his princess. The first time Jodie had seen the transformation happen, she'd literally stood there with her jaw hanging open until her brother had elbowed her and told her to get a grip.

"Deke, Jodie," Lake said by way of hello.

Grunt grunted.

Brenda walked into the kitchen, mug in hand. She smiled, spun on her heels and left again.

"They're meeting," Jodie heard her say. "Trust me, you don't want to go in there. The air is thick with testosterone. If we breathe too much of that stuff in, we might grow chest hair."

"And then Betty will have to wax us," Robin said. "Let's get coffee at the spa."

"Good thinking," Brenda said, and Jodie smiled at the exchange.

"What's up?" Deke said as he refilled his mug from the

warming coffee pot on the kitchen counter. "Any problems with the system?"

Lake got up, stuck his head outside the back door and whistled. A minute later, Officer Matt Donaldson sauntered into the room.

"Do I look like your dog?" he asked Lake.

Jodie and Deke shared an anxious glance at the sight of the cop. Matt nodded hello to them, then helped himself to coffee.

"What's going on?" Deke asked Matt. "I thought we'd dealt with the vandalism this morning."

"This is about something else." Matt helped himself to coffee.

Jodie focused on remaining calm and not showing any reaction to the sombre attitudes of the men in front of her. She felt as though she had been called up before the princi-pal. A feeling she'd grown used to during her school years, when she'd attracted trouble like a magnet. She thought of Mitch. Not much had changed over the years—she was still attracting trouble.

Lake stared at them for a moment and Jodie knew he was taking note that neither of the Millers were intimidated by the amount of testosterone in the room. Deke because—well, he had his own excessive amount, and Jodie because she knew she could hold her own with any of the men.

"This isn't run-of-the-mill accommodation for staff," Lake said. "The security system is state of the art. There are panic buttons in every room and a secure outside phone line that's buried deep in a metal tube. The basement is set up to function as a panic room. The windows are triple-glazed, tinted to stop people from peering in and are near impene-trable. The property is landscaped to hide the house from the road, while making sure that no one can get close to the building without being seen. This is a safe house."

There was silence after Lake's revelations. Jodie wasn't sure what she was supposed to say, and there was no way she'd give information out freely—especially with a police officer sitting there.

"We'd like to know what the purpose of this house is," Matt said calmly, and every muscle in Jodie's body went taut.

"It's for the staff," Deke said, equally calmly.

Matt watched him for a moment. "See, here's the thing. You two were here when we had gunmen attacking the castle in an attempt to kidnap my sister."

There was a low, menacing growl. "My wife," Grunt said.

Jodie took one look at the terrifying man-beast and mentally amended her assessment that she could hold her own with him in a fight. Grunt was in a category all of his own. One reserved for mythical monsters and Viking marauders.

"Before Claire's attempted kidnapping, we had a film producer who went nuts and trashed an RV," Matt continued, as though his brother-in-law hadn't suddenly turned feral. "Before that, we had an American mob wannabe here who blew up the old mine and almost killed my wife in the process. Before that, Caroline McInnes had to deal with a stalker who crashed her wedding. And before that, Lake here took out his wife's ex-boyfriend after the idiot set fire to her shop."

Jodie stared at the man before she blinked at her brother. "I'm thinking we should have picked a different quiet little town to set up shop in."

"No kidding," Deke mumbled.

Matt sat back in his chair. "You can understand why we might have become a bit worried when we realised you were building Fort Knox in our midst. You are looking at the sum total of law enforcement in town." He pointed to his own chest. "I'd very much appreciate it if the chaos and mayhem were kept to the minimum, but after last night's episode, and the security level around here, I'm beginning to get a tad worried that there's something going on I should know about."

"You said the graffiti was most likely dumb teenagers acting out," Deke pointed out.

"Aye, but the security system isn't in place to keep out dumb teenagers," Matt said. "Something else is going on. Do I need to interview your staff and ask them what it is?"

Jodie felt Deke stiffen beside her, but he gave no outward indication he was feeling anything but calm and unbothered. She forced a smile, one she hoped looked relaxed and genuine. "We're just running a spa and restaurant. The security may seem over the top, but we're used to London. It's second nature to us to take these precautions."

"I came from London," Lake said. "Your precautions aren't the norm."

Jodie shrugged. "I was married to a professional footballer. His fans were nuts. He attracted lots of unwanted attention. This is the sort of security I'm used to."

Matt looked sceptical. "My cousin Flynn was a professional footballer and his idea of security is tying an empty beer can to his doorknob to alert him to intruders."

Jodie knew Flynn. Her ex-husband had spent some time with the same club as the guy. He'd seemed a decent guy and had talked often about his home town of Invertary. It was one of the reasons she'd looked the place up when they were scouting for a quiet location.

"Flynn obviously isn't as paranoid as my ex-husband was," Jodie said. "Some celebrities need more security than others."

"Josh McInnes is about as famous as you get," Matt said, "and you make his security measures look like amateur hour."

"Maybe we should talk to him." Jodie smiled. "Give him some tips."

There was a stare-off for a couple of minutes as Jodie and Deke declined to offer up any further information. Eventually the men got fed up with the Miller sibling silence. Matt and Lake shared a look that said they weren't pleased with the situation and then the men stood.

"If you're doing something illegal." Matt put his empty cup in the sink before the three men headed for the door. "I will find out."

"I should hope you would," Jodie said.

Lake's lip twitched in an approximation of a smile. "I wanted to do this the easy way. Now I've got some digging to do. We'll talk again."

"Leave our staff alone." Deke's tone was pleasant, but his meaning wasn't. It was clearly a warning. "They don't need you two hassling them when all they want is to do their jobs and live their lives."

The three men stared at them, but none of them promised anything.

"Thanks for sorting out the alarm system." Jodie stepped into the silence before her brother started talking with his fists. Okay, that was unfair. She was the sibling known for flying off the handle. Deke was all about cool control. Still, he would have given too much away if he kept pressing the men to leave their staff alone.

Lake nodded, Grunt grunted, Matt frowned and then they were gone. Jodie turned to the window to watch them walk down the path back to the carpark area.

"They won't find anything when they dig," Deke said beside her. "It isn't possible."

"I hope you're right," Jodie said.

As she watched, the men greeted someone just out of

sight and stopped to talk. The new figure took a step to the right and suddenly came into view—Mitch.

"What is he doing here?" Jodie felt her hackles rise. He was carrying a takeout bag from Dougal's pub and was heading towards the spa.

Deke cast her a curious glance before his attention shifted to Mitch. "You mean Harris? Why would you worry about—" He shook his head. "I'm guessing he's the reason for the mystery night away."

"Butt out," Jodie snapped.

"I didn't say a word." Deke calmly sipped his coffee.

"He isn't supposed to be here."

"Does he know that?"

"He will in about five seconds." With that, Jodie stomped off to deal with the next in a long line of problems—Mitch Harris.

CHAPTER 5

"You signing up for a waxing with Betty?" Matt said.

"Full body. What else?" Mitch was pretty sure there wasn't a man alive that would go anywhere near Betty when she had a pot of hot wax in her bony hands. He nodded towards the spa and the men water blasting the stone walls. "Trouble?"

Matt looked over his shoulder at the building behind him and frowned. "Don't know yet, but we're looking into it. Right now, it looks like some of our antisocial element decided to express their sexism with bad art and cheap paint."

Mitch felt everything within him still. "Those guys last night? The ones at the back of the room?"

Matt's gaze sharpened. "I wasn't there. Which guys?"

"Young. Dumb. Dougal called one Rab."

Matt's lips thinned. "I'll have a wee word with those idiots right now. Every year they come in for the fishing tournament and spend most of their time drunk and causing trouble. I may talk to the council about banning them from the tournament for good. Maybe even the town."

"That doesn't sound legal. Can you do that?" Mitch asked.

"Watch me," Matt said. "They're too bloody stupid to question a banning anyway."

Mitch eyed the clean-up. "Is Jodie in danger?"

Three sets of keen eyes focused on him, then took in the bag of takeaway food Mitch had picked up at the pub. Smiles were slow and knowing.

"We'll let you know if your woman needs legal counsel," Lake said.

"Not my woman." And Mitch hated saying those words. "We're just friends." From Jodie's behaviour, they weren't even that. He was pretty sure the woman had relegated him to the role of sex toy and nothing more.

Lake cocked an eyebrow and Mitch felt the need to add, "Close friends. Really close friends."

Grunt decided he wasn't interested in the conversation and took off—not a surprise. The rumour around town was that Grunt felt physically ill if he was away from Claire for more than an hour at a time.

"Friends?" Matt asked Lake. "I'm his friend and he never brought me a meal from the pub. What about you?"

"Nope. I'm feeling a little neglected here."

"Me too." Matt nodded.

"Knock it off," Mitch grumbled. "Is it a crime to take a meal to a beautiful woman?"

Matt didn't even try to hide his amusement. "Are you courting Ms. Miller?"

"Mind your own business." Mitch was surrounded by gossiping old maids masquerading as grown men.

Matt gaped at him. "Bloody hell, she knocked you back, didn't she?"

"Okay," Mitch snapped. "Time for you to go do some actual police work. I'm done here."

"No way." Matt stared at Mitch, then turned his gleeful expression on Lake. "She totally knocked him back."

"Looks like that to me," Lake said. "Why else would he be chasing after her?"

"With food," Matt added and Lake nodded.

"I'm not chasing Jodie," Mitch said, although he knew better than to rise to the bait. "We're friends. This is a friendly gesture. That's all. There's nothing to see here. You two clowns can move right along." He made a shooing gesture that had no impact on them. "Whatever." Mitch left the idiots to it and strode towards the spa. He'd taken two steps when he ran into Jodie—literally.

"Jodie." He hated that he sounded breathless just saying her name. He cleared his throat, ignoring the chuckles from Dumb and Dumber behind him. "Sorry about that. I was distracted." He flashed a full-wattage smile at her and got an angry frown in return.

She put her hands on her hips. "What are you doing here, Mitch?"

Okay, so not the reception he'd been looking for, but he wasn't going to be deterred. He held up the bag. "Brought you lunch."

"We own a restaurant."

"Yeah, but it isn't open yet."

Jodie's face darkened further as her voice lowered. "We have an agreement. You turning up in the middle of the day to hang out isn't part of it."

"I beg to differ." Mitch lowered his voice too. "You said you wanted a friends-with-benefits arrangement. Well, we had the benefits. This is the friends part."

"You know fine well what I meant when we were talking about that." Her cheeks flushed with anger and Mitch thought she looked like Snow White with her ruby lips, black hair and porcelain skin. So sue him, he was American.

Disney was in his blood. She glanced behind him and stepped in closer to him. "We agreed to sleep together. Nothing else. I thought I made myself clear."

"Yeah, you did. Friends with benefits. Your words. Not mine. And I'm here to feed you, friend."

"You know I only meant the benefits part!"

"Maybe you should have proposed a booty call arrangement instead, then. 'Friends with benefits' implies there is a friendship on which to lay the benefits. No pun intended. With this arrangement, you can't have one without the other. I'm a lawyer, Jodie. We live by the detail in an agreement. We agreed to friends with benefits. I'm just holding up the deal we made."

"I want to change the deal. I want a booty call arrangement." She was no longer whispering, but Mitch was too irritated to care.

"Not going to happen. I like the deal we made and I don't want to negotiate new terms. You're stuck with me, baby. If you want the benefits, you have to take the friendship with them."

"Then I don't want the benefits." She lifted her chin. "I can get benefits anywhere. I don't need to get them from you."

Mitch took a step towards her until their bodies were touching. "Baby, you know damn well you can't get benefits like that with anyone else. Don't kid yourself."

"You arrogant, egotistical…" Her eyes sparkled with rage.

Mitch had heard enough. He clasped the back of her neck and pressed his lips to hers. She gasped and Mitch took advantage by slipping his tongue into her mouth. For a second he thought she'd shove him away and clock him one. Instead, she went liquid in his arms. Mitch felt hope surge. You didn't get chemistry like this more than once in a lifetime, if that. There was no way she could get benefits like this anywhere but with him. The kiss was hot and heavy, and neither of them ended it until they were panting for air and their bodies were on fire.

Reluctantly, Mitch released Jodie. She looked dazed for a second before she realised her hands were no longer on her hips but clenched in his shirt. She stepped back from him and glared. Mitch cocked an eyebrow at her in challenge.

"Still want to renege on our deal?"

"I have no problem doing without your benefits, Mitch Harris. Just watch me." With a frustrated growl, Jodie snatched the bag from his hand and turned on her heels.

"Totally knocked him back," said Matt behind him.

Mitch ignored the idiot. The conversation had not gone as he had planned. He couldn't let Jodie stomp off in a bad mood, not without resolving things between them first. He grabbed Jodie's arm to stop her running and he honestly didn't know what happened next. One minute he was about to say something, the next minute he was flying through the air. He landed with a thud on his back on the ground in front of the woman.

The world seemed to lose focus for a minute as Mitch tried to get his head around what just happened. That's when the laughing registered. He blinked several times and Jodie's face came into focus above him. She wasn't smiling.

"Don't grab me," she snapped.

And in that instant, it all became clear. "You threw me over your shoulder."

"It's reflex." She stepped over his body and headed to the spa, still carrying the bag of food he'd brought with him.

A moment later, the door slammed loudly and then two grinning faces blocked out the sky.

"What just happened?" Mitch said.

"You had your backside handed to you by a girl." Matt held out a hand. "I wish I'd had my camera out."

Mitch wasn't too proud to take the hand. When he got to

his feet, he dusted his suit off. The damn thing was only fit for the cleaners and he was certain there was a lump the size of an ostrich egg on the back of his skull.

"I think you should probably turn your attention to someone else," Matt said. "Jodie is clearly too much woman for you."

"Go to hell." Mitch started walking down the driveway, back to his car.

"Oh, Mitch," Matt called in a high-pitched voice that was supposed to mimic Jodie but sounded more like Miss Piggy. "I don't want to be your friend. I only want to use you as a sex toy and to throw you around like a rag doll when you piss me off."

Of course they'd heard the whole thing. His day was now complete. Mitch flipped off the town's entire police force and drove off to the sound of Matt and Lake laughing. If Jodie Miller thought handing him his ass would damage his pride, then she'd never dealt with a lawyer before. It took a whole lot more than that to deter Mitch Harris. Perversely, instead of bruising his ego, he found he was kind of proud of her. His woman had skills that were damned impressive. It only made him want her more.

Unfortunately, his little visit had made things worse between them instead of better. He needed a new plan of attack. Which meant he needed help.

With a sigh, he hit the button on the steering wheel that activated his phone and said Lake's name at the prompt. It rang twice before Lake answered.

"Benson."

"I need a full work-up on Jodie," Mitch said. "I want to know everything about her. Especially what she likes and needs."

There was a pause before Lake spoke. "Matt's standing

right beside me. Should I tell him he has a budding stalker on his hands?"

"Stalker?" Mitch's eyes rested on the blue loch as he frowned. "This isn't stalking; it's called being prepared. Are you trying to tell me that if you had a daughter, you wouldn't do a background search on her boyfriend? And what about Kirsty? I'm sure you researched her at the start of your relationship. This is exactly the same."

"What's he saying?" Matt said in the background.

"He's trying to convince me he isn't stalking a woman who knocked him back."

"Knocked him down, more like," Matt said.

"It isn't stalking!" Damn it to hell. "It's not like I'm hiding in the bushes to take photos of her. I just want some info. Are you going to do this for me or not?"

"Nope," Lake said. "Stalking is a crime. You should know that you're now officially on Matt's watch list."

With laughter ringing in his ears, Mitch hung up on his so-called friends. It was a sad day when a guy couldn't get some help to wear down the woman he loved.

CHAPTER 6

Jodie lasted four long days without Mitch. No, scratch that. It wasn't Mitch that she missed, it was the damn benefits that came attached to him. No strings, she scoffed as she snuck up the back stairs to the hotel rooms above the pub. The man came with so much string he could be one of those huge balls that people visited on American road trips.

And yet here she was, like an addict, desperate for her next fix, because all she could think about was sex. With Mitch. The rat-bastard.

He'd forced her to skulk around in the middle of the night. It was his fault she'd lied to Dougal. She'd rented a room at the hotel, telling the owner it was for a new member of staff who was coming in from Edinburgh in the morning. Part of that was true, she did have a staff member arriving, but there was no way the woman would stay in the hotel. Nope, Jodie had told the lie just so she could get her hands on a key card to the outside door. And why did she want her own key? So she could sneak about the hotel, in the middle of the night, to get her fix!

It made her so mad that she'd cracked before Mitch. She'd

expected him to come crawling back to her. She'd daydreamed of him apologising for even suggesting that they take their relationship out of the bedroom. Her dream had been so vivid that she'd actually heard him say, "I was wrong, you were right. Please treat me as your sex slave. I won't ask for more."

But no. He'd out-stubborned her. And here she was, standing outside his hotel room, ready to swallow her pride and tell the man what he needed to hear, in order to get into his pants.

She was a pathetic excuse for a slut and she was totally letting down all slutty women everywhere. Unfortunately, she was also desperately horny, and every woman knew that horny trumped guilt and common sense any day of the week. Jodie let out a heavy sigh as she stood staring at Mitch's door. The hotel corridor was quiet. Everyone was asleep. Most likely Mitch was too. She took some small pleasure in the fact she was about to disturb him. The addictive bastard deserved it.

It wasn't just being horny and desperate that had driven Jodie to sneak into the hotel. She'd become so irritable and short-tempered that her staff had cornered her and begged her to sort whatever was bothering her out. That was how bad things had become—she was scaring her staff.

Argh, she was being pathetic. No woman had ever died of sexual frustration. Had they? She was tempted to pull out her phone and google it, but she knew she was just delaying the inevitable. She wanted Mitch. That was all it came down to. She was weak and she wanted Mitch.

With utter disgust at herself, Jodie knocked on his door.

MITCH COULDN'T SLEEP. It was impossible. Every time he closed his eyes, he saw Jodie. And seeing Jodie led to remembering how she felt, and that led to yet another cold shower. He'd had so many cold showers over the past few days, just from imagining Jodie's touch, that he was beginning to wonder if he should ask Dougal for a cut in his room rate, seeing as he didn't use hot water anymore.

He'd been so sure that she was as addicted to him as he was to her, sure that she wouldn't be able to resist being with him. And he'd been wrong. Arrogance, that's what it was. He'd been arrogant and now he had the blue balls to show for it.

Mitch let out a sigh. There was nothing for it but to grovel. First thing in the morning, he was heading over to the spa and he was going to do whatever it took to get Jodie back in his life. He'd been impatient. He'd wanted her so badly that he'd pushed too hard. She wasn't ready yet, he knew that now. He could slow down. He could. Slow was way better than stop. He hated stop almost as much as he hated cold showers.

A knock at his door got him climbing out of bed. If it was one more guest in the hotel looking for free legal advice, he was going to pummel them. Josh was right—he needed a house of his own. One that was far away from the cheap-assed Scottish public. He scoffed at himself. Look at him, thinking of settling down with his own place. At the ripe old age of thirty-eight, he was finally growing up.

Mitch threw open the door, without looking through the peephole first, and instantly froze.

She was here.

He glanced around, half expecting a hallelujah chorus to pop up behind him. Nope. Just an empty room with a bed—and Jodie in front of him.

Mitch didn't wait for her to talk. All he cared about was that she was there. He reached out, grabbed Jodie's hand and pulled her into the room.

"About time," he said before his mouth was on hers.

He felt her hands slide up his body and his t-shirt disappeared. He was frantic for her. Jodie's hands pushed his pyjama pants down over his hips and he felt them pool at his feet. Mitch was just as desperate to get her naked, she was topless within seconds and he moaned at the feeling of her bare breasts rubbing against him. His lips stayed on hers, kissing her with desperation rather than finesse. He felt her kick off her shoes and shimmy out of her jeans and then they were both naked.

"Up." It was an order barked against his lips.

Mitch clasped her waist and lifted her until she was trapped between the wall and his body. Her long legs wrapped around his waist. Her fingernails dug into his shoulders as she fought for control of their kiss. She didn't need to fight, Mitch gave it up willingly. All he wanted was Jodie. He didn't care how he got her.

"Now." Her hips shifted and he felt himself slide into position at her entrance.

Every fibre of his being demanded that he ease inside, where he belonged. But his mind suddenly had another idea. His brain fought out from the lust-induced daze it was swimming in and demanded that he sort out the terms of their relationship while he had the upper hand.

His dick twitched with annoyance, but for once, Mitch was more interested in what his brain had to say.

"Mitch, now!" Jodie wriggled against him, trying to get him to impale her.

Mitch gritted his teeth and didn't give in to her demand.

"I want to be inside you just as badly as you want me to, baby. But first we need to sort a couple of things out." Yeah, it was physically painful to say those words.

"What?" She smacked her hands down hard on his shoulders and her thighs clenched. Damn, this was the worst kind of torture.

"I want the friends part of our deal." There, he'd said it. Now if she'd just agree, they could get back to the important stuff.

No. That was his dick talking. His brain knew the friendship was the important stuff. It also reminded Mitch to make an appointment with a shrink first thing in the morning to find out if he suffered from schizophrenia, as he was pretty sure normal men didn't have arguments with their dicks.

"You have got to be kidding me," Jodie screeched. "Stop messing around. We'll talk about this after we're done."

He shook his head, even though it pained him to do it. Again, his dick was telling him, after the deed was a much better time for discussion.

"No can do." Mitch fought for control using sheer will. "You'll wriggle out of the conversation. So we sort this now, or you can leave and we'll sort it another day. Your choice."

Please choose now! his dick silently screamed.

Oh, now she was mad. Her eyes turned mean and her legs tightened. "You're telling me that you won't have sex with me? While we're naked? While you're less than an inch away from completing the deal? You're telling me this now?"

"No. That's not what I'm saying." He shook his head vehemently, which made his body sway and his dick rub against the part of her that it really wanted to get into. Mitch struggled to focus on what was happening above his neck. "I just want a commitment before we go any further. The deal was friends with benefits. I want the friends part. Starting now. I want you to agree to the friends part before we go any further."

"This is blackmail!" She was outraged, and he didn't blame her. "What kind of idiot wants more than sex?"

Mitch thought it was wise to treat that as a rhetorical question.

"So, what?" Jodie glared at him. "You want to hang out? Talk about our days? Watch TV together?"

"Yes, Jodie, that's what friends do." He was beginning to wonder if he was going to be her first ever friend.

"Why the hell do you want that?" She looked so incredulous that he almost started laughing.

Almost. It had been his life experience that when you were on the precipice of having sex with a woman, laughing wasn't the best move.

"I like you. I want to get to know you. Suck it up, Jodie. Make the deal and move on." This was going down in history as the least romantic conversation ever.

She looked like her head was about to explode. "Fine. We can be friends."

He should have been elated that she'd given in, but instead he felt slightly terrified. She had the same look on her face that she'd had the night she dealt with the protesting old men.

"What are you planning?" he said.

"Nothing. I'm giving you what you want, so that I can get what I want."

Yeah, he didn't believe that for a minute. "We're talking friends. No ignoring me in public. We hang out. We do stuff together. We talk. You get that, right?"

She rolled her eyes dramatically. "I know what friendship is, Mitch."

"And you're agreeing to it?"

"You're really beginning to piss me off now." Her nails dug into his shoulder.

"So we have a real friends-with-benefits deal?" Which in his mind meant they were dating, because seriously? What was dating if not hanging out, getting to know each other and having sex?

"Yes," she snapped. "Now can we stop this ridiculous conversation and get on with things?"

"You're so romantic. It makes me feel special."

She grabbed handfuls of his hair and pulled his mouth down to hers. Her kiss was a punishment. One that made every cell in his body come alive. His brain sighed and passed over control of his body to his dick. He'd won. He had what he wanted. He was in a relationship with Jodie. So what if he was a little wary about what she had planned? He'd deal with that bridge when he got to it.

"Mitch." She pushed her hips up towards him.

"Bossy woman," he said with a grin.

Then he kept his part of the deal and slid home. Taking them both to heaven along the way.

The repercussions of blackmailing Jodie into being friends kicked in the following morning. Mitch had been asleep when the coward had slunk out of bed and his room. When he woke, it was to thumping on his door. He glanced at the clock and realised Jodie had made him sleep through yet another morning run. The woman was hard on his desire to stay fit.

He opened the door to find Dougal standing with a package. "Do I look like a delivery boy?"

Mitch rubbed his eyes as he looked the hotel owner over. He looked like a Las Vegas lounge act. Maybe a Liberace tribute? One that looked like gay Santa and sounded like a foghorn.

Mitch took the package from the frowning man and swung the door shut. It was way too early to be dealing with Dougal.

Sitting on the edge of the bed, he opened the package. It was a plaque. He read it twice before he started laughing.

Friends are like stars, it said. You can't always see them but you know they're always there.

There was a Post-it note attached to the plaque. It read, This is good advice. Let's only see each other in the dark. It's enough that I know you're there. It was signed with the letter J.

Mitch picked up his phone from the nightstand and dialled Jodie. He'd stolen her number from her phone while she'd been asleep the night before. Yep, that was how dysfunctional this relationship was. Yet he was strangely pleased about the state of it.

"Who's this and how did you get my number?" Jodie snapped.

"Good morning, love. I see you're still as paranoid and unfriendly as ever."

"Mitch." It was said on a sigh. Not the happy kind of sigh, more the long-suffering kind.

"I got your gift. Thanks. Personally, I didn't think we were at the gift-giving stage of our relationship, but if you think we've reached that level then I'm happy to catch up."

"We don't have a relationship." It sounded as though the words were forced through her teeth.

"Really? What is a friendship if not a form of relationship?"

Her reply was a low-level growl.

"Anyway, I wanted to call and tell you that the gift is lovely and that friends don't sneak out on friends during the night. Seriously, Jodie, do I have to teach you everything about how friendship works?"

His answer was a dial tone. Mitch was grinning when he hit the redial button.

"What?" she snapped.

"Friends don't hang up on friends, Jodie."

He got the dial tone again. With a laugh, Mitch tossed his phone onto the bed and headed for the shower. There was only one thought in his head: Let the games begin.

. . .

JODIE RESISTED the urge to throw her phone at the wall of her office. Bloody infuriating blackmailing man.

"Problem?" Brenda asked from where she was sitting on the other side of Jodie's desk.

Jodie looked over at the blonde she'd come to consider a friend.

"Men." Jodie felt that explained everything.

And apparently it did, because Brenda nodded. "Do you want to talk about it?"

Jodie thought about that for a minute. Did she? Really what she wanted to do was throw someone around on the workout mat in the basement, but Brenda looked like she might break if Jodie tried that with her. So talking it would have to be. She leaned forward and rested her elbows on the desk.

"It's like this," Jodie said. "I have a friends-with-benefits arrangement with a guy in town."

"Okay." Brenda seemed eager to help, so Jodie carried on.

"And everybody knows that friends with benefits is just code for sex and nothing else, right?"

"Totally. It's like when some guy invites you over to Netflix and chill, you know that really means he's calling for some booty."

Jodie stared at her. "I'm not even sure what any of that means."

"It's okay," Brenda said. "I spent a lot of time these past couple of years watching the E! channel and pretty much every reality show that's ever been made. I'm totally hip with the lingo."

The twinkle in Brenda's eye told Jodie she was being had. "You're messing with me, right? Nobody says 'hip with the lingo.'" She paused. "Do they?" Holy crap, she was getting old.

Any minute now she was going to ask what young people today were into.

Brenda waved a hand. "Of course I'm messing. Carry on with your story."

Jodie was beginning to question the wisdom of confiding in Brenda. "As I was saying, Mitch and I have a friends-with-benefits agreement and he threw a hissy fit to enforce the friends part. I mean, who does that? What man in his right mind, when offered string-free sex, demands strings? He threated to cut off the benefits unless I complied with the friends part." Jodie wasn't proud that she blushed. "I caved and now I have to be friends." She felt like she was being forced to have a root canal. "I have to hang out with him. He wants to talk."

"Oh my." Brenda put a hand to her heart. "If he gave you an ultimatum and you gave in, those benefits must be amazing. How hot is he in bed? On a scale of one to ten. One being 'I will kill you if you ever touch me again,' and ten being 'I would totally be your sex slave.'"

Jodie just stared at her. The woman was completely missing the point. She'd been bullied and coerced into being friends with Mitch. That was just wrong. Plus, it seemed a little desperate on his part.

Brenda nodded as she held up a hand. "Say no more. He's a twelve isn't he? I get it." She fanned herself. "I remember sex," she said wistfully. "At this rate all I'll have to keep me warm until I hit old age are the memories."

"What are you talking about?" This was why Jodie never sat around chatting with the girls. Half the time she didn't have a clue what they were going on about. "You're almost ten years younger than me. Of course you'll have sex again."

"No, I can't see it in my future. The problem is that men can't get past my history. Well, the good ones, anyway. The bad ones like the history because it makes them think they can abuse me. The good ones run screaming. Either because they think I have too much baggage and they don't want to deal with me, or because they're afraid I'll fall to pieces if they say or do the wrong thing. I am doomed to be single for the rest of my life." She frowned. "Is it possible to become a born-again virgin? Can your hymen grow back? You know, the way piercings close over if you stop wearing earrings."

Jodie stared at Brenda again, because, well, honestly, she had no idea what to say. Fortunately, Brenda didn't seem to need an answer.

"Carry on." Brenda waved a hand. "Mitch, who's great in bed, wants to be your friend, and you don't want to because…?" Her eyebrows arched as she gave Jodie a pointed look.

"Because friendship leads to dating, and dating leads to relationships, which might lead to marriage, and I don't want to get married again. I don't want to be in a relationship. I don't want to date. I just want to get physical and get out of there. Men are too much work and, frankly, I'm exhausted. I don't have the energy to deal with one again."

Brenda seemed to be thinking hard. "You're barely in your mid-thirties. Maybe you just need some iron in your diet."

Jodie groaned and let her head hit the desk in front of her. "You aren't listening to a word I say."

"Sure I am." She felt Brenda pat her head. "You like Mitch, you want to get to know him and you're terrified you'll get hurt again."

Jodie's head came up to see a sympathetic smile. "That isn't what I said."

"It's what you meant. Your ex screwed you over, huh?"

As usual, at the mention of her ex-husband, Jodie felt her body begin to tense. It started at her toes and worked its way up until it settled in her brow and brought on a migraine.

"He wanted someone more feminine." She didn't know why she was sharing. It wasn't even something she let herself think about. "No, not feminine exactly—weaker, maybe. He said he didn't feel like the man in our relationship." She looked at her friend, feeling the same mix of tension, guilt and bewilderment she normally felt when she thought about her ex. "I don't know how to be anyone but me."

"Of course you don't. He was obviously an insecure loser. There's nothing wrong with you the way you are. You're lovely. Don't let your ex-husband mess with your future."

"I scare men off. They say I'm too bossy, too strong, too forceful." And it hurt, damn it. Why were all the qualities that men admired in other men so awful if they found them in a woman?

Brenda's smile was slow and mischievous. "You don't scare off Mitch. In fact, he's trying to get closer to you."

"Only so he can change me. Or worse, tell me over and over again what's wrong with me."

Brenda shrugged. "Then you kick his backside out the door and find someone who doesn't define his masculinity by the woman in his life."

"It's that easy?" Yeah, she wasn't so sure.

"At least you've got a man who wants you. I can't even get the one I like to spend five minutes in the same room as me." Brenda's face went a deep shade of red, as though she'd unwittingly shared too much.

Jodie mentally went through the list of workmen who'd been hanging around the spa over the past two weeks, wondering which one had caught Brenda's eye.

She was just about to guess a name when her brother stuck his head into her office. When he saw Brenda, he gave her an awkward nod and Brenda leaned towards him slightly. Jodie looked between the two of them and everything fell into place. Brenda was right. She was stuffed.

There was no way Deke would get past her history to make a play for her. He had too much baggage of his own to even try.

"Tara's here with your nail technician. Fiona, right?" Deke said, keeping his gaze firmly away from the curvy masseuse.

"That's the one. I thought she was arriving this evening." Jodie stood up and headed for the door.

"I'm not sure this was a good idea," Deke said. "I don't think Fiona's ready for a placement here."

"What makes you say that?" Jodie, with Deke at her side and Brenda following along, went to the side of the building and the carpark.

"She wouldn't get out of the car until I left," Deke said.

Jodie's heart sank. Fiona was the one person she hadn't interviewed personally. Tara had done it for her and Jodie had made the decision based on her old friend's word. Jodie pushed open the door to find a little red Kia parked out of sight of the front of the building. Tara was standing beside it, looking harried, and Fiona was curled in on herself in the passenger seat.

"Tara?" Jodie said as she walked up.

"Honey." The older woman engulfed Jodie in a bear hug. "She'll be fine once she gets used to the place."

Jodie looked at the slight woman who was studying the dashboard while she rocked in place.

"How long has she been out of her situation?" Jodie said.

Tara shifted nervously. "About six months."

"It must have been bad for her to still be in this state," Brenda said from behind her.

Jodie looked over her shoulder and noted that Deke had stayed in the doorway out of sight. This was not good.

"I don't think this is going to work," Jodie said. "The spa might be women only, but we have a restaurant and there are guys around most of the time. She's bound to bump into someone. This place is meant as a last stop for women who've dealt with the worst."

"She'll be fine." Tara opened the passenger door and ignored the fact that Fiona cringed away from her. "You'll be fine, won't you, Fiona? Fiona worked in the best nail salon in Edinburgh for years. She's perfect for you here."

"I don't doubt her skills." It was everything else that had Jodie worried.

"Come on." Tara reached in for Fiona. "Let's introduce you."

Trembling, Fiona climbed out of the car. She cast her eyes around for Deke and seemed to calm when she couldn't see him. She gave Jodie a tremulous smile.

Jodie felt for the woman, she really did, but she also had a business to run. "Fiona, honey, tell me honestly. Can you cope with being here?"

Fiona opened her mouth to speak, but then her eyes hit something behind Jodie. She went deathly pale and started to shake.

"Hey, baby," said a male voice behind Jodie. "I come bearing gifts."

Mitch.

Jodie turned to order him back from the group.

And that was when the screaming started.

CHAPTER 8

Mitch wasn't happy. He paced the spa's reception area as he waited for Jodie to come inside and explain what the hell was going on. One minute he'd been grinning at the thought of another battle of wills with Jodie and the next thing he knew, Deke was dragging him into the spa. All while Jodie and an older woman tried to calm a hysterical young woman.

He hadn't wanted to go into the spa. Something was seriously wrong. The woman had taken one look at him and completely lost her mind. She wasn't just hysterical, she was terrified. Of him. And that was a feeling Mitch never wanted to experience again. Ever. Damn, it made him feel dirty inside just thinking that he was responsible for making a woman react like that.

The heavy door slammed open and Jodie barrelled into the room, followed closely by her brother. Neither of them were smiling.

"Mitch," Jodie said. "What are you doing here?"

She stood in front of him, arms folded, legs apart, eyes dark—ready for a fight.

He held up the bag he'd picked up from Fort William that

morning. "I was being a friend. Dropping by like normal friends do. Bringing a gift—seeing as we're doing the whole gift thing now." Mitch took a step towards her. "Want to tell me what happened out there?"

Her eyes cut to Deke, who was standing at the edge of the room, his pose identical to his sister. Something passed between them. Mitch wasn't sure what, but he'd been a lawyer and a businessman long enough to know that there was something heavy going on and these two were right at the centre of it.

"You surprised us. Fiona is…sensitive." She sounded casual, but she couldn't look him in the eye. "She scares easy."

That set off alarm bells in his head. "That wasn't someone who was a little bit surprised and called out. That was a woman who was about five minutes away from needing sedation." Mitch looked between the brother and sister. He didn't like what he saw. They were tense. Closed up. Anxious. "Something's going on here. Something bad. No woman should be terrified like that. I think we need to call Matt in."

"No!" Jodie gave her brother a look that bordered on panic. "We've got this under control."

"Right." Mitch ran a hand through his hair. "Did you call a doctor? That woman needs help. I've never seen anything like it before. She took one look at me and lost it entirely." The words slowed on his tongue. Things he'd seen and heard over the past week began to click into place. The isolated house, hidden from the road. The security system Lake and Matt had been talking about. The terrified woman. The panic in everyone's eyes. The fear at the sight of a strange man. "This is a refuge for battered women, isn't it?"

Jodie opened her mouth and he could tell by the look on her face that she was going to deny it.

Deke spoke first. "Yes."

"Deke!" Jodie railed on her brother.

Deke threw an arm out. "You think he isn't going to ask questions at the police station? Matt and Lake are already suspicious and digging into our story. We don't need to pour fuel on the fire." The look he gave Mitch was pure steel. "You can't talk about this."

Mitch's agile mind was working at full speed, taking in more information, following more clues and coming to more conclusions. "This isn't an official refuge, is it?"

"No." Deke walked to the fridge behind the reception desk, pulled it open and took out three bottles of beer without asking if they wanted one. He opened all three and shoved two over the counter towards them.

"You have beer in your reception area?" Mitch grabbed the beer and slipped onto one of the high stools at the counter.

"It was for the work crew. The health drinks are for the clients," Deke said.

Jodie stayed rooted to the spot. It was clear she was still trying to figure out whether they should give any information to Mitch at all. It stung a little that they didn't know each other well enough for her to trust him.

He looked at Deke. At least her brother was willing to open up to him. "How'd you get into this?"

Deke let out a heavy breath. "Long story. The most relevant part is what's happening now." He glanced at Jodie, obviously hoping she would step up and explain. When she didn't move, he carried on. "There are women out there who aren't safe in the official system. These women need support and help to disappear. They need somewhere they can live and be safe."

"And that's what you're providing," Mitch said. "Housing, jobs, safe environment and a new identity."

"Yeah." Deke drained his bottle and smacked it onto the high reception desktop.

Mitch wasn't dumb; he could join the dots better than most people. "You're part of a network that helps that happen. Like the old Underground Railroad system in the US."

Deke nodded. "But more so. We don't just provide safe passage for these women; we provide a safe haven when they reach their destination."

Mitch's mind was running with possibilities. "You'd need some way to monitor information. A way to keep track of who was where and if they were still being hunted."

"We have a secure website."

"And if one of the women is found, you move her on." It wasn't a question. Mitch knew it was the only way the system could work.

Deke didn't say anything and Jodie hadn't moved from her spot. Mitch didn't know what to make of that, so he kept his attention on Deke.

"What happens if one of you is pressured into giving out information on the whole operation?"

"There are fail-safes. The first being that we don't know about the whole thing. We know about the people on either side of us on the line. That's it. We know where the women came from and who to contact to move them on. We don't know where they go from here. If someone wanted that information, they'd need to work their way down the line and pressure each person in turn."

"And by that time the whole thing would have shut down," Mitch said. "What about legal action? Cop involvement?"

"Most of the women already tried the usual system," Deke said. "Their men found them, sometimes multiple times, and their lives became worse. For other women, things started out too bad for the system to cope with. Or they got out of their situation in a way that meant going to the authorities would not be good for them."

"You mean they killed to get out," Mitch said and Deke nodded.

"Don't you dare judge." Jodie stalked towards him. "You have no idea what those women had to deal with."

Mitch held up his hands. "No judgment. Just a helluva lot of questions."

"We deal with women who need to stay hidden," Deke said. "Women who still have a threat hanging over them. Whether that's from the authorities or from their past partners, it doesn't matter."

"What about the woman outside? The one I terrified." He hated saying that. Hated that he'd caused that reaction just by being a guy.

There was silence while Deke and Jodie looked at each other. It lasted so long that Mitch thought they weren't going to answer his question.

"Her husband is a cop," Jodie said at last.

Mitch felt like he'd been punched in the gut. "He wasn't charged?"

She shook her head. "His friends stood by him. There were explanations and alibis. There might have been suspicion, but his circle closed tight around him and made it impossible to pin anything on him. He even went as far as trying to have her committed to a mental hospital as proof she was making up stories. It was his word against hers, and she didn't stand a chance. She was in hospital after he'd almost killed her and a nurse who knew about our network helped her escape. Her husband went looking for her and when he couldn't find her, he took it out on her sister. The sister is in a coma."

Mitch sucked in a breath. "No charges?"

"No witnesses." Jodie walked over to them and grabbed the bottle of beer. "The nurse at the hospital, the one who treated our woman, recognised the sister's injuries. They were almost identical to Fiona's. The nurse was too scared to go to the police and tell them she thought the same guy had beaten both sisters, so she told her network contact instead. The only option for Fiona is to hide."

Mitch let out a string of curse words. Deke opened the fridge, took out another couple of beers and put one in front of Mitch.

"She's still dealing with the situation," Deke said. "It was too early to bring her into a situation like this. The woman who brought her, Tara, is going to take her somewhere where she can get help. Somewhere with a counsellor and no men around. It will help her to deal with what happened to her."

"But the husband still gets away with what he did." The words stuck in Mitch's throat.

"That's why we need places like this," Jodie said. "There will always be guys who get away with it. There will always be women who have to live with the threat of them coming after them again."

Mitch clutched his beer bottle tight. "The system is flawed."

"You're the lawyer," Jodie said. "Feel free to work to change it."

"Now I understand why you don't want the cops here," Mitch said. "It would send up red flags that Fiona's husband would recognise. It would endanger her."

"And the rest of the women here," Deke added.

"You haven't been in town that long," Mitch said. "You could trust Matt with this. He's one of the good guys."

"He's a cop," Deke said, as though that explained everything.

"Yeah, but he's been known to colour outside the lines. He would keep this out of the system. He would help you to protect the women."

"It's a risk we aren't prepared to take," Jodie said. "Matt has his job. His loyalty lies there. He might be a good guy, but we don't know him and he's part of the system that is hiding Fiona's abuser."

"How do you two expect to protect these women alone?" Couldn't they see that they were in over their heads? A state-of-the-art security system wasn't going to keep out someone if they were determined to get in. Especially if that guy didn't give a crap about the consequences of breaking in.

"We're set up tight," Deke said. "Jodie and I can take down any guy who comes around, and if there was a full-out attack, we'd call the cops. Hell, we'd call everybody. But the chances of the women being found are slim. By the time they get to us, they've gone through several safe houses and identities. Their trails are cold. We have a couple of women who've been running for years. We hope this will be their last stop, that they can set up home here and get on with their lives."

"You guys are hoping a lot of things," Mitch pointed out.

"What are we supposed to do, Mitch?" Jodie's anger burst out. "Stand back and abandon them? Leave them to fend for themselves? Watch their partners find them and kill them? These women don't have anywhere else to go, or anyone else to trust, except for the people who've been through it themselves."

Mitch stilled, every cell of his body alert. His focus completely on Jodie. "You?" The question was quiet because he was certain he already knew the answer, and it sickened him.

"No, my ex-husband didn't hit me. He wouldn't have dared. There was no way he could take me in a fight." Her look was pained. "And that's why he left me. Apparently strong women emasculate men. Who knew?" Her droll tone was a challenge.

One Mitch wasn't going to rise to. "Baby, I'll tussle with you anytime and I don't care if you win."

Her eyes narrowed. "Oh, I'd win."

For some reason, that look and those low words made all his blood rush south. Deke cleared his throat and when Mitch glanced over at him, the guy was trying not to laugh.

Mitch gave himself a mental shake. "If you weren't beaten, how did you get involved in all this?"

"I've volunteered at refuge centres for years. That's how I found out about the network." There was something in the flat way Jodie delivered the information that made Mitch think there was a whole lot more to the story than she was letting on.

Mitch turned to Deke and cocked an eyebrow at him. Deke didn't seem to have the same problem his sister did with sharing information.

"We grew up in the refuge system." Deke could have been talking about the weather.

"You grew up in refuges?" Mitch stared at the two of them. They were acting as though that wasn't a huge piece of personal information to just drop on a guy.

Jodie was staring at him intently. "Don't make a big deal out of this, Mitch."

"Don't make a big deal?" Yeah, he sounded like a demented parrot. But this was a big deal. Suddenly Jodie's reluctance over getting into another relationship made perfect sense. She'd grown up around a man she couldn't trust, then lived amongst women who only knew men who abused their partners. Add to that a failed marriage to a guy who sounded like a total loser and getting close to her was going to be the emotional equivalent of climbing Everest.

"He's doing that thing," Jodie said to her brother.

"Oh yeah." Deke took a drink from his beer, but he was clearly amused.

"What thing?" Mitch knew he probably shouldn't ask, but the words escaped anyway.

"The thing people usually do when they hear this stuff," Jodie said. "If it's a woman we tell, she suddenly starts looking at Deke as though he's five years old and needs to be rescued."

"I get lots of cooing, petting and pitying looks," Deke said. "Don't mind the petting so much, but the pitying looks and the cooing get on my nerves."

"At least that's better than the other reaction you get," Jodie remarked.

"Oh yeah, the one where she runs a mile because she figures being a violent arsehole is hereditary. That one is great for your self-esteem." Deke took another drink from his beer bottle.

"And if it's a guy," Jodie said, "he starts thinking I have monumental trust issues that only he can overcome. I become a challenge to his manliness."

"Trust me, baby," Mitch said, "my manliness is pretty secure and doesn't need a challenge. This isn't about me. It's about you. And you do have trust issues."

She let out a heavy sigh as her brother chuckled. "No. I have common sense. That's a totally different thing."

"You had a bad marriage and now you're scared to try again. That's a trust issue. And that's without even getting into the things you dealt with as a kid." Why Mitch was fighting about this with Queen Oblivious, he didn't know.

"My pitiful marriage has nothing to do with not wanting a repeat performance. I don't want to get into a relationship because I'm done with that phase of my life. I'm happy on my own. It's got nothing to do with trust. I've been there, done it, got the t-shirt. Why is it that men think every woman wants to get married? Why is it normal for a guy to want to remain single and sow his wild oats, but if a woman wants to do the same there's something wrong with her? Something like trust issues." The crazy woman actually made quote signs with her fingers around the words "trust issues," as though he was the one talking madness.

"I can't speak for all women, or all men, but I can tell you from personal experience that you have serious trust issues. That's why you've been avoiding me and shutting down any talk about our relationship."

"We. Don't. Have. A. Relationship."

"See what I mean?" Mitch gestured to her as though she were evidence. "You get touchy when I even mention the word. That isn't normal."

"And yet you still want to hang out with me. I wonder why. Could it be because you think you can somehow fix me? Maybe you plan to mend my warped thinking by sexing it out of me?"

"Jodie, I had to blackmail you into hanging out with me. If it was left up to you, I'd get relegated to the role of sex toy and we'd never see each other in daylight."

Her hands went to her hips. "And what is wrong with that, exactly?"

"It's wrong because it's a choice you're making out of fear. You break out in hives at the mention of the word relationship. Let's face it, 'friends-with-benefits' is just another way of saying you're dating and you can't handle it."

"We. Are. Not. Dating." Her eyes blazed.

He pointed at her. "There it is again. Trust issues."

"Okay, it's time for you to go." She took a step towards him.

"Jodie, think about it for a minute. You're reacting emotionally. Try to be logical." Mitch knew the second the words were out of his mouth that it was the wrong thing to say. The fact that Deke made a clucking noise confirmed it.

"I'm being emotional?" Jodie practically screeched, and Mitch winced. "I need to be logical? Fine. How's this for logic? I've had enough hanging out together for one day. Consider the friends portion of today's arrangement over. Bye-bye, Mitch, your hotel room is calling you."

She grabbed his arm and hauled him towards the door.

"Jodie, you're being unreasonable." Mitch seemed determined to dig himself into a hole then shovel the dirt in over his head.

"Unreasonable? Try this for reason and logic. This arrangement of ours doesn't involve heart-to-hearts. I'll be in touch next time I need to scratch an itch, or want someone to watch a movie with me. Until then, have a nice life."

The next thing he knew, Mitch was standing outside.

"You agreed to be friends," he shouted at a closed door.

"Friends know when they've overstayed their welcome," the door shouted back.

Mitch could have sworn he heard Deke's muffled laughter.

"Friends don't kick each other out when the conversation gets uncomfortable," Mitch shouted.

"Friends kick each other's backsides when they need it, and I'm beginning to think you could seriously use a good backside kicking."

Okay, he knew a threat when he heard it. It was time to leave. "This isn't over. We're talking about this. I'll be back," he shouted at the damn door.

There was no reply, only the rumble of male laughter. Mitch had no recourse but to head back to the hotel—taking the gift he'd brought Jodie with him.

CHAPTER 9

"This is your idea of a night out?" Robin sounded more incredulous than impressed.

"Sh," Brenda said. "You're ruining the mood."

"What mood? We're sitting in the dark, on deck chairs, hidden behind a bush, while we perv on Deke. This isn't a night out. It's stalking."

"It isn't stalking if you don't follow them. We're just sitting in the garden watching the view." Brenda's eyes were glued to the wall of windows on Deke's small house. On the other side of the glass, a shirtless Deke was sweating hard from his workout. His muscles glistened as they flexed. It was better than any movie she'd ever seen.

"We're sitting in the garden, in the dark, perving on our boss."

"Not my boss." Brenda didn't work in the restaurant. She was free to perv on Deke as much as she liked.

"You promised me a night out before the spa opens tomorrow," Robin said. "This isn't a night out."

"You know"—Brenda kept her eyes on Deke, worried she'd miss something—"I never took you for a whiner."

"You said we'd see a movie." Robin continued to whine, apparently unconcerned that she was doing it.

"You have popcorn. You have live action. What more do you want? This is Invertary. There's no cinema. This is as close as we'll get to movie night. Would it help if I did dialogue?" She lowered her voice and pretended she was Deke. "That's it, feel the burn. Two more reps. Look at those muscles. I'm an action hero star."

"No. That doesn't help."

There was just no pleasing some folk. Brenda ate another handful of popcorn and kept her eyes on Deke. This would fuel her fantasies for at least the next month.

"Why don't you just throw yourself at him?" Robin said, shattering her moment.

"Because he wouldn't catch me. I'm too damaged for him."

"Rubbish. He's just nervous. I'm sure he'll be fine once you get him started."

Brenda gave her a sideways glance. "You don't have much experience with men, do you?"

Robin shrugged. "I killed the last guy I slept with. That kind of puts men off. So no, I don't have a load of experience."

"You killed him accidentally," Brenda pointed out. "You only meant to drug him enough to get him so you could leave him without him beating you to death."

"I don't think the cops see the distinction," Robin said.

"It's not like you're a black widow or something. It was just one teeny wee accidental poisoning." Her attention went back to Deke. "Oh, look, he's towelling off." She sighed at the sight of the fluffy white towel rubbing over his pecs. In her dreams she'd offer to towel him down after his workouts. She could be his assistant. Yeah, he definitely needed a workout assistant.

"Who's that?" Robin whispered.

"The love of my life," Brenda said on a sigh, her focus firmly on Deke.

"No." Robin grabbed her arm, her fingers digging in enough to be painful. "Not Deke. That guy."

Brenda's head twisted to see where Robin was pointing. A guy in a hooded top and black biker's jacket was creeping around outside the rear entrance to the spa. He shook something in his hand and they heard the telling sound of a little ball rattling in a spray can. Invertary's worst artist was back.

You couldn't see into Deke's house from the back of the spa, but from where the women were situated, between the two buildings, they could easily see both Deke and the stranger. Without coordinating it, Brenda and Robin turned to look behind them to see if the manse was visible. It wasn't. They both relaxed—slightly.

"He's up to no good," Brenda whispered.

"You think?"

"Is this the time for sarcasm?"

"Sorry."

They watched as the guy turned the handle on the back door of the building. The door was locked but the alarm didn't go off.

"Jodie's forgotten to set the alarm again," Robin whispered.

"We need to tell Deke." Brenda looked at the wide expanse of lawn between them and Deke's house. Running over to get him wasn't going to work. She'd be completely exposed. "Do you have your phone on you?"

Robin shook her head. That wasn't good. Brenda had left hers in the manse too. Her eyes caught on a shadow at the corner of the building leading towards the front of the spa. Another man.

"We need to do something," Robin said. "There's more than one of them."

And the one at the back door seemed to be breaking in.

"Okay," Brenda said. "I'll get Deke. You get ready to distract the bad guys in case they spot me."

"Wait." Robin grabbed her arm in another death grip. "How are you going to get him? They'll see you."

"I'll crawl round the outskirts of the lawn." Brenda pointed to the low hedges marking the edges of the manicured grass.

Robin considered her for a minute before pulling the blue and red silken scarf she had on as a belt, from her jeans. "Tie this around your head to cover your hair. That blond acts like a beacon."

"Good thinking." Brenda wrapped the scarf around her head and tucked it tight. She looked down at the red t-shirt and blue jeans she wore. "Hey, the scarf matches." She beamed at Robin.

"I really want to shake you right now," Robin whispered. "Get going. I'll be the lookout."

Brenda silently fell to all fours and started to crawl around the edge of the lawn. She tried to make as little noise as possible and was grateful for the music coming from Deke's house as it covered some of the sound. At one point, she had to get down on her belly and slink past the low bush, like a commando going under one of those net thingies on an assault course. She kept sneaking glances at the two men through gaps in the bushes as she made her way to Deke's house. By the time she'd run out of cover, both men had gotten past the door and were in the building.

The time for subterfuge was over. Brenda jumped to her feet and ran for Deke. She didn't bother with the door. She just pounded on the wall of glass lining the room he was working out in. His head snapped up. The weights he was using to do bicep curls fell to the floor with a thud and the glass wall slid open silently.

"What the hell, Brenda? You nearly gave me a heart attack." He was irritated enough not to notice they were standing close enough to touch.

Oh, he was gorgeous when he was annoyed.

But Brenda didn't have time to admire him up close. She pulled her eyes from his glistening torso and got to the point. "Two men just broke into the spa through the back door."

Every glorious muscle in his body went taut. He reached out, grabbed her arm and yanked her inside.

"Stay," he ordered before pushing a panel at the side of the door. Part of the wall popped out to reveal a lock box. Deke pressed in a number and came out with a handgun.

Brenda felt lightheaded at the sight of it in his hands. For some reason an armed Deke was way hotter than an unarmed one. There was a very good possibility Brenda might have some psychological issues that were unresolved and needed looking into, because all she could think of was how much hotter he would look in uniform. Any uniform. She wasn't fussy.

"Stay here. Lock the door after me. Call the cops." He gave her a serious stare. "Am I clear? Are you holding up okay?"

"Yes. I'm fine. I have no plans to faint anytime in the near future. Go play Rambo. I'll call Matt."

He shook his head slightly and disappeared into the darkness. Brenda locked the door behind him, grabbed the phone off the kitchen counter and dialled the police, all the while listening for the sound of gunfire.

JODIE LOOKED at the clock on her living room wall. Exactly five minutes had passed since the last time she'd looked. She was stressed. The spa was opening in the morning and she was tense. She wanted to work her tension out with Mitch, but after the stupid things that came out of his mouth that afternoon, she couldn't let herself do it. So she'd resorted to going through her Pilates routine—twice.

With her iPod secured to her armband, her earbuds in and the music cranked up high, Jodie tried to lose herself in the routine. Even with Beyoncé's latest album blasting in her ears, she couldn't concentrate. She had a horrible feeling that when she was finished with the yoga that was supposed to distract her from Mitch, then she would just run to the man anyway.

This wasn't good. He was worming his way into her life. She needed to put a stop to things before he gained any more ground. She should never have agreed to the friends part of their arrangement. That just gave him permission to turn up when he felt like it and make her do things with him. Things like having dinner and watching a movie. Things that would make her comfortable with his presence. Then the next thing she knew, she'd be in a full-blown relationship and she wouldn't even know how she got there. He was sneaky. He was wearing her down with stealth attacks and she was going to put a stop to it. Starting tomorrow, she was going to keep Mitch Harris and his many needs, at arm's length.

A hand slapped down on Jodie's shoulder and, being Jodie, she didn't scream, just reacted. She had the guy on the floor, her knee in his throat and a fist poised to take out his nose, before she could blink.

"Deke!" Jodie retreated from her brother with a frown. "What do you think you're doing sneaking up on me like that? You could have been hurt."

"What do you mean, could have been?" Deke didn't move from the floor as he lifted his head slightly and rubbed the back of it. "You know, I could have totally gotten out of that hold. All I had to do was kick up with my legs and wrap them round your neck and I'd have had you pinned."

"Like hell. I would have broken your nose and stamped

on your crown jewels at the first sign you were going to move."

"And I thought my sisters were bad," a man said from the door.

Jodie turned to find the local cop staring down at her. If she hadn't relaxed at the sight of Deke, she would have disabled Matt too. She was out of practice and being slower to react was not good. She made a mental note to schedule time with Deke in their basement training room. In fact, she wondered if Grunt would be up to sparring with her instead. There was a tiny part of her that wondered how she'd fare in a contest with the man.

Jodie straightened and gave the police officer her full attention. "What can I do for you, Matt?"

Deke hauled himself up off the floor. "Two guys broke into the spa. They ran off when I ran in. Brenda called the cops."

Jodie's eyes snapped to her brother. "Are you okay?"

He gave her a look that told her he thought she was a sissy for asking.

"Fine. Is the spa okay?"

"It's fine. They'd started to spray-paint the hall wall, but I got there before they could write anything. There's an orange stripe running up the hall, but we can paint over it tonight. Apart from that, and damage to the back door lock, everything is fine." Deke was still rubbing his head as he sat down on one of the stools at her breakfast bar.

"Was it the same guy who spray-painted the walls outside?" Jodie asked Matt.

Matt's face was totally blank. "Well, the paint colour is different, and from the angle of the mark on the wall, I'd say this vandal was left-handed while the one outside was right..." He stopped his impersonation of a CSI episode to glare at her. "How the hell should I know if it's the same guy? Do I look like Sherlock Holmes?"

Jodie was about to tell him exactly what he looked like, which wasn't flattering, when Robin and Brenda rushed up the stairs and into her apartment. Brenda's eyes flew straight to Deke.

"Oh good, Jodie didn't kill you." She rushed to his side, but Deke was faster. He was up off the stool and around the breakfast bar before Brenda had crossed the room.

"Of course Jodie didn't hurt me," Deke said from the safety of the other side of the wide counter.

Brenda looked a little deflated at the sight of Jodie's brother running away. The coward.

"That's good." Brenda plastered an obviously fake smile on her face. "And you didn't have to shoot anyone, either. I'd call that a win."

"Shoot?" Matt stood up straight. "You have a gun? What kind of gun? What permits do you have? Where is it now?"

Jodie grabbed her bottle of water from beside her workout mat and plopped into one of her armchairs. So much for a nice, peaceful night to help her deal with the stress of starting a new business.

"The gun's somewhere safe," Deke told Matt.

"I want to see it. And the permit. And the place you keep it locked up, because you'd bloody well better be locking it up." Matt folded his arms and glared at Deke.

"No problem." Deke turned to her because he was obviously done dealing with the cop. His eyes swept over Brenda in a way that must have made her feel invisible. "You forgot to set the alarm again."

Jodie winced.

"That's the second time, Jo," Deke said, and Jodie noted that Brenda and Robin were suddenly fascinated with anything else but the conversation the siblings were having.

Deke didn't miss their behaviour. "It's more than twice?"

Way more, but Jodie didn't feel much like confessing. "I'll make sure it doesn't happen again."

"You'd better," Deke said. "We have an alarm for a reason, Jo. If you don't make the effort to set it, then it's pointless. You know…"

Jodie wasn't sure where that was heading, but she did know it was into lecture territory. She held up a hand. "Don't you dare mansplain to me. I said I'd remember, and I will." Hopefully. Jodie wondered if she should have a reminder tattooed on the back of her hand.

"Back to the break-in," Matt said. "I've taken Brenda's and Robin's statements. They were taking a turn around the garden when they spotted the men." Matt gave them a level look. "Sounds very Jane Austen to me. Especially since there were two deck chairs and a bucket of popcorn set up facing Deke's living room windows."

Deke folded his arms, looked at the ceiling and seemed to have a conversation with himself. Brenda had turned a luminous shade of red.

Robin thrust her chin up and looked at Matt. "Invertary needs a multiplex. If we didn't have to drive into Fort William to see a movie, we wouldn't have to make our own fun."

"Take it up with the council," Matt said before turning to Jodie. "Did you hear or see anything suspicious?"

"No." Although she would have thought almost taking her brother's head off when he interrupted her, would have been answer to that very obvious question.

Matt sighed. "There isn't a whole lot I can do. It's obvious you've stirred up some trouble in town…"

"So this is our fault?" Oh, there was no way Jodie was standing for that kind of attitude. "We're to blame because some lowlife men decided to target us?"

"I wasn't going to say that," Matt said with no small amount of suffering. "I was going to offer to get Lake to post a man here to keep an eye on things."

"No!" Deke and Jodie said at the same time, making Matt's eyes narrow with suspicion.

"What they mean"—Brenda stepped into the awkward silence—"is that they are two complete control freaks who are more than able to monitor their business all on their own. Do you really want to start a turf war by sending another alpha in here? It could get really messy with everyone peeing in corners."

Robin suddenly suffered from a coughing fit that didn't fool anyone.

"Thanks, Brenda," Jodie said sarcastically.

"You're welcome." The crazy woman beamed.

"I'm sure Lake wouldn't mind helping out," Matt said. "That's what we do in this town. Think about it. In the meantime, I'll make sure to keep an eye on the place, but there's only one of me and a limit to what I can do."

"We appreciate any effort you make," Jodie said.

"Aye." Matt put his hat back on. "I'm getting that. I'll see myself out." He turned on his heels and headed down the stairs.

"Peeing in corners?" Jodie asked Brenda.

"Spying on me?" Deke asked Brenda.

Brenda looked between the two of them while she was clearly trying to come up with an answer. Her shoulders slumped. "Nope, I've got nothing." She grabbed Robin's arm. "Come on. I'm hungry. We didn't get to finish our popcorn." And the two women left.

"What do you think?" Deke asked, keeping his voice low. "Local yobs or past trouble catching up with one of the women?"

"I don't know. I'll give Tara a call once she's back in Edinburgh with Fiona, see if she knows anything we should be worried about."

"I don't like this."

"Me neither," Jodie said. "Me neither."

CHAPTER 10

By the time Mitch arrived for the spa's grand opening the following morning, the driveway was filled with men. Most of them old. They carried banners and signs. Mitch read a few and cocked an eyebrow. Equality for all men. Men are people too. Stop Sexorcism Now!

Mitch spotted Matt, dressed in his police uniform, standing at the side of the crowd.

"Sexorcism?" Mitch said by way of hello.

Matt looked disgusted. "I'm pretty sure they meant sexism. Although with this lot, it could mean something else. Like they don't want anyone casting out horny ghosts."

The two men looked at each other and grinned.

"Ghostbusters," they said at the same time, then shared a high five.

"The original and best," Matt said sagely.

They watched as the crowd were led in a chant by Archie McPherson and the rest of the Domino Boys: "What do we want? Equality. When do we want it? Now!"

"Not very creative," Mitch said.

"Aye, it would have been more accurate if they'd shouted they wanted manicures."

"I thought this was sorted last week when Jodie opened the place up as unisex."

"Apparently the men want more than a waxing." Matt looked disgusted at the thought.

"Aren't you going to get rid of them?"

"Nope, they legally have the right to protest."

"Even on private land?"

"Unless they're disrupting business or intimidating anyone, they have the right to stay."

"This isn't disturbing business?" Mitch waved an arm at the crowd.

"Nobody has had any problems getting in or out of the building. The Domino Boys even made sure they left space for parking. They retained the services of Lawrence to keep them within the law."

The two men looked over at the town's new lawyer, who seemed bewildered at the mess he'd helped cause.

"Is that a pie stall?" Mitch said as the crowd moved and he caught sight of a sign on the other side of the carpark area.

"Morag McKay arrived about ten minutes after the protest started. She closed her bakery to set up here. Morag wouldn't miss an opportunity to make some fast cash. Then, when she got here, some idiot told her that the spa offered therapeutic massage. Of course, all Morag heard was the word massage, so she called in her cronies to protest against having a brothel in town."

Mitch had to resist the urge to pinch himself just to make sure he was awake. "She went from therapeutic massage to brothel?"

"Aye. Her thought process is a mysterious thing. Of course, she felt the need to inform me that she now plans to protest. She said she was giving me a chance to shut this 'den of iniquity' down before she took matters public. Then, before I could even tell her she was off her trolley, she was over there giving the newspaper an interview."

"Is it just me, or is Invertary getting worse? Is there such a thing as collective insanity?"

Matt's lips thinned. "Oh, it gets even better. In the middle of all this crap, Betty MacLeod is touting for business."

Matt pointed to the stone portico over the main entrance to the old church. Mitch took a couple of steps to the left to see what he was talking about. There, beside the door, was a deck chair with a notebook, pen and bullhorn sitting on it. Beside the chair was the life-sized cut-out of Lake Benson that had gone missing years earlier. Lake was shown wearing only underpants, his hands on his hips. Someone, Betty presumably, had taped a sign to his bare chest. It read: Sign up for the Lake Benson Wax Special.

Mitch was mesmerised by the sight. "Does Lake know he's promoting Betty's new venture?"

"I haven't told him, but I did take photos."

As they watched, Betty waddled back to her spot, put a paper bag filled with pies on the chair and lifted the bullhorn.

"Roll up, roll up," she shouted. "Make your waxing appointment today." There was a pause where she rummaged around in the bag, came out with a pie and took a bite. When she'd finished chewing, she shouted again. "Archie McPherson, you're a hairy bugger. Get over here and let me sort you out. You look like Bigfoot. You'll never catch women looking like that. You could plait the hair growing out of your nose." She took another bite of pie while she seemed to think that over. When she'd finished, she turned to face the spa doors and shouted through the bullhorn, "Jodie, can you wax nostrils?"

"We should sell tickets," Mitch said.

"I'm glad you get a kick out of it," Matt said. "You don't need to stand here all day monitoring these lunatics."

A disturbance attracted their attention back to Morag's pie stand. Three women in matching polyester coats had turned up and were unfurling a banner. They stood beside the stand, holding the banner high. It read: Keep Invertary Prostitution Free.

A fourth woman held up a placard that said: This Spa Sells Sex.

As the men in the crowd read the placard, there was a murmur of excited interest.

"Crap," Matt said. "I'm going to have to borrow Betty's bullhorn to tell all these idiots that the spa isn't a brothel. Now they'll be campaigning harder to get in there, just to see if it's true."

There was a roar of laughter at the back of the crowd and Mitch spotted the young guys from the town meeting, Rab something and his friends. They were making lewd gestures and pointing at Morag's signs.

Matt made a growling noise in the back of his throat. "I need to run those idiots out of town. I think a couple of them broke into the spa last night, but I've no proof."

Mitch's spine snapped straight. "Is everybody okay? Did they do much damage?"

Matt gave him a cheeky sideways glance. "Don't worry. Deke scared them off before they did any damage. The woman of your dreams is fine. And aye, before you ask, Josh filled us all in on how you're suffering from lust at first sight."

"Rat bastard," Mitch muttered. He was going to get that tattooed on his best friend's forehead one of these days.

"So," Matt said gleefully, "she still knocking you back, then?"

Mitch eyed his friend and wondered what penalty Scottish law had for assaulting an officer.

"THIS IS A BLOODY DISASTER," Deke said quietly to Jodie as they watched the crowd through the window in the spa reception area. They were standing shoulder to shoulder, aware that there was a client waiting for her appointment on the sofa behind them and trying to keep their conversation low enough so as not to freak the woman out. "We set up a safe haven for abused women and it's surrounded by men. It's like we're under siege. At least Fiona is long gone. She'd be cowering in the panic room if she was here." He eyed Jodie. "You read that email from Tara?"

Jodie felt her stomach flip. "I know that one of the Hampstead Heath staff was assaulted last week."

Deke's face said it all. This wasn't good news for anyone. An attack like this one could mean someone's husband or boyfriend was on the hunt. Still, there was no way to be sure. Not until they heard from the woman who'd been assaulted, and unfortunately, she was still unconscious.

"Brenda went through the Hampstead Heath centre." Deke's voice was without emotion, but his body practically vibrated with pent-up rage. "She spent months recovering in the flat the group has over the drop-in centre."

"Don't panic yet. Nobody knows the flat is there. I've seen it. It's like Anne Frank's house; the entrance is hidden behind a secret door." Jodie had briefly run a self-defence class at the centre when she was living in London. Another thing her ex hated about her. Not the volunteering, the fact Jodie had taught women how to disable a man, instead of teaching them how to do a home manicure.

"Yeah, but someone on the staff would know about her, right? She was in a rough state when she was there. Someone had to have brought her food, supplies, checked on her. That sort of thing. What if the attacker beat that out of the London staff member?"

He had a point. Unfortunately, there was no way to know for sure if the attack was connected to the network, or what information the woman may have divulged. Jodie lowered her voice further, aware that people were moving around in the reception area behind them. "Do we tell Brenda about the assaulted worker?"

"I'll keep an eye on her, but I don't think we should tell her. We'll see what Tara finds out from the hospital once this woman wakes up. Why worry Bren if this has nothing to do with her? She's happy here and settling in well. I don't want to ruin that for her."

Jodie wasn't so sure that was the right course of action. If she'd been in Brenda's shoes, she'd want to know if her ex was on the hunt for her as early as possible. But then, she wasn't Brenda. Jodie hadn't taken a beating that almost killed her. No, if Brenda's ex came at Jodie, he'd be the one who ended up in hospital.

"Okay, we wait for Tara, but we tighten security."

"Yeah." Deke's deadly tone said it all.

They both knew there was nothing like too much caution when it came to protecting the women. Their own experience growing up in refuges had taught them that if a man wanted to find you, if he was willing to do anything to do it, to tug at any tiny thread of a lead, no matter how small, then there was a good chance he would find you. Jodie tamped down the memories from her childhood that came rushing to the forefront of her mind. It wasn't that she denied their existence. It was just that they had no place in her life as it was now. She'd learned a long time ago that those memories had no power over her, and she wouldn't allow them to drag her back down to a time in her life when they did.

"Did Tara mention if there was anyone who could replace Fiona?" Deke asked.

"There's no one in the programme with the skills we need, and we're not in the position to train someone up right now. I'll have to advertise locally and cover the manicures until we get a replacement." It wasn't Jodie's favourite thing to do, but she could cover in a pinch. Her speciality had been sports massage—it was how she'd met her ex-husband—but she'd taken classes in all sorts of beauty techniques over the years. She'd always been preparing for the day when she opened her own business. Now that day was here.

And it was a freaking disaster.

She looked out the window at the raucous crowd. The men had turned their protest into a party and were clearly having a nice social time of it. Good to know they were having fun at her expense—at the expense of the women who really didn't need any more crap in their lives.

"Robin is threatening to make poison-laced brownies to feed the crowd," Deke said. "I'm tempted to let her. I thought you dealt with this protest crap at the town meeting."

"I did deal with it at the meeting. Unfortunately, male stupidity often takes more than one confrontation to be squashed. It's been my experience that men aren't so great at listening to a woman the first time she says something."

Deke ran a hand over the top of his head. Even though he was a couple of years out of the Army, Deke's hair was still far too short for him. It made his features seem sharp.

"Are you going to launch into another feminist rant?" he said.

Jodie narrowed her eyes at him. "I don't rant. I educate." Something she'd been doing to her younger brother for most of his life.

"We can't let this carry on." Deke gestured to the crowd.

"How do you propose we deal with it? The police can't do

anything. The protestors are legally within their rights to drive us mental. We're just going to have to sit it out."

"For how long?"

Jodie had been the one to go out and talk to Archie McPherson. "Who knows? Until they get bored or something more interesting comes along."

Deke let out a stream of curses. "There must be something legal we can do. We need to talk to a lawyer."

"Considering these guys hired the only lawyer in town, that would mean going into Fort William, or calling around until we find someone willing to come up here. It could take weeks to sort out the help we need and they will probably have run out of steam by then."

Deke's eyes went to the edge of the crowd. "There is another option."

"What other option? Because I'm telling you, if there was one, I would have thought of it." Jodie was getting irritated with her know-it-all brother. She'd spent the last two hours racking her brain for a solution to the problem—at the same time as trying to be as pleasant as possible to her customers. At least the women who'd booked appointments thought the protests were a bit of a laugh. That was a small mercy.

Deke's face was deadly serious when he faced her and Jodie instantly knew she wasn't going to like what she heard.

"Mitch is out there and he's a lawyer."

Jodie was right. She didn't like it one bit. "No. No, no, no, no. No."

"This isn't about you, Jo. It's about the women we're trying to provide a safe home for. You need to set aside your issues and ask Mitch to help."

"Are you insane? I'm trying to deal less with him, not more."

"I know, but this thing is bigger than your issues with

Mitch. You need to go out there and recruit him to the cause."

"Why do I have to do it?" And yes, she was whining.

"Because"—her brother's smile morphed into a wicked grin—"he'll probably want payment for helping, and I don't think it will be of the monetary kind. I'm also thinking that he won't want that payment coming from me."

"There are days when I just plain hate you." Jodie glared at him.

"I understand. It's the burden I bear for being right all the time. The masses just don't understand a brain like mine. It can make people resentful." He placed a hand on her shoulder. "Don't worry, sis. I won't judge you because you're threatened by my brilliance."

Jodie reached out, grabbed his nipple through his shirt and twisted. Hard. Deke smacked her hand away and placed his hands on his chest, to shield his nipples.

"What are we? Kids again? Knock that crap off, Jodie." Yeah, they weren't talking quietly any longer. And now, thanks to Deke squealing like the annoying pig he was, they had an audience. Unfortunately, Jodie was just irritated enough with her brother to be past caring that her client, Margaret Campbell, and her masseuse, Brenda, were staring at the two of them.

"I'm so scared," she told Deke. "What will you do if I don't?"

Deke seemed lost for a minute before he looked smug. "I won't cook for you."

Well, damn. "Fine. No more childish attacks when you annoy me."

"You mean when I'm wise and completely right in what I have to say." He ignored Jodie's glare. "Now go out there and talk to Mitch."

Jodie wanted to stamp her feet and wave her arms like a

toddler having a tantrum. Sometimes it seriously sucked to be a grown-up.

"You can do it," Deke mocked as he patted her on the back.

"Excuse me," Margaret called. The older woman ran the craft shop in town and headed up the local knitting group. Although Jodie was still irritated with Deke, she gave what she hoped was a welcoming smile to her customer.

"I couldn't help overhearing," Margaret said. "Mainly because I was listening in. Are you and Mitch having a lovers' quarrel? I know you don't have family here, except for him." She pointed at Deke, who grinned. "If you need a motherly shoulder to cry on, I'd be happy to help out."

Now Deke wasn't even trying to hide his laughter. Jodie elbowed him in the side while she kept her professional smile in place.

"Mitch and I aren't a couple, Margaret. We're just friends." She almost choked on the word and had to bite back the sudden urge to confess that even their friendship was happening under duress.

"Oh, but it sounded like you were nervous about talking to him. Like you'd had a falling out." The mischief in Margaret's eyes told Jodie that she was enjoying her meddle.

"Mitch is a lawyer." For once, Deke was trying to be helpful instead of being annoying. "Lawrence is on the side of the protest. We thought of asking Mitch to get rid of the mob."

Margaret's eyes narrowed. "If you want rid of the Domino Boys, say no more. Me and the girls will handle it for you."

"The girls?" Jodie asked, very much against her better judgment.

"The knitting club. Knit or Die."

Yeah, that's what Jodie was worried about. "Please,

Margaret, don't trouble yourself. We can handle this situation. You just enjoy your time here at the spa." Jodie gave Brenda a pointed look, hoping that the woman would take the hint and whisk Margaret off for her massage before she could meddle further.

Brenda missed the look because her attention wasn't on Jodie. It was on the protests outside. Jodie followed her gaze and saw that Morag McKay had centre stage. She'd gotten hold of Betty's bullhorn and was demanding that they close the spa for good. Only she didn't call it a spa.

"When did we become a brothel?" Brenda seemed highly entertained by the new turn of events.

Jodie answered, because Deke seemed to be looking anywhere but at Brenda. "The day I hired you, apparently. Morag thinks the word massage is code for sex."

"I wish!" Brenda snorted as she cast a sideways glance at Deke.

That look sent Jodie's antennae tingling. There was definitely something sparking in the air between the two of them, no matter how hard Deke was trying to ignore Brenda.

"I can't remember the last time I had sex." Brenda sounded wistful. Her brow scrunched as she worked it out. "Nope, my memory doesn't go back that far."

"Me neither, pet." Margaret gave Brenda's hand a sympathetic squeeze. "It's been so long I'm not even sure all the parts still work."

"I did not need to hear that!" Deke covered his ears as he stared at Margaret in pure horror.

"Men," Margaret said. "So bloody sensitive."

"I remember sex," Brenda said on a sigh. "It was good. Better than ice cream."

"Better than cake," Margaret agreed.

"Way better than new shoes," Jodie said and the women looked at her. She shrugged. "I like shoes."

"I think I'm going to barf," Deke said.

"Maybe we should rethink this no-men-allowed thing." Brenda flashed a wicked smile in Deke's direction. "It would help me meet some nice men. Who knows, maybe one of them would ring my bell for me."

Deke's face was pure thunder as he glared at the woman. Brenda seemed gleeful at his reaction.

"I wouldn't mind giving Josh McInnes a massage," Brenda carried on, feigning ignorance at the death stares coming from Deke. "In fact, I'd pay that man to let me massage him."

"That is just wrong," Deke snapped. "He's a married father with a pregnant wife."

"I didn't say I'd massage him," Brenda told Deke with fake innocence. "I'd just rub his shoulders a little. And maybe his back. Last time I saw him, his backside looked tense too. He can't go on tour with a tense backside now, can he?"

"Not funny. Not even a little."

"I have to say," Margaret said, "I agree with Brenda. There's nothing worse than a tense bum."

The two women giggled together like a pair of teenagers.

"All I can say is that I'm grateful this is a women-only spa. It will spare us the lawsuits over the staff assaulting customers," Deke said.

"This isn't a women-only spa," Brenda took great delight in reminding Deke. "The men can come in for a wax treatment."

"I don't think any of those men fancy having Betty peel them like an orange." Margaret shuddered at the thought. "I'm not sure letting Betty loose with hot wax was a good idea, Jodie. Witches have rituals that involve candles. It's highly likely that any man she waxes will come out of her treatment room sporting bald patches in the shape of pentagrams."

"Come on, Margaret." Brenda linked her arm with her

customer and started walking them in the direction of the treatment rooms. "Let's get you started on your massage, and we can have a good gab while we do it. Maybe you know of some nice single guys in town who wouldn't mind getting to know a hot masseuse with a little baggage."

"Oh, pet, we all have baggage." Margaret patted Brenda's arm before she looked back at Jodie. "Don't worry about the protest. I'll take care of it."

Jodie and Deke watched the two women disappear down the corridor.

"Why am I not reassured?" Jodie asked.

"We can't let Brenda go on a manhunt." Deke completely ignored the more important issue—that the crazy women in town were going to "help" them out. "She's been through a lot. There are a lot of creeps out there. It's too dangerous."

Jodie almost sighed at the sound of so much male delusion. "Don't worry, I'm sure Margaret will steer her towards some decent guys."

Deke wasn't happy with that at all and his bad mood turned on her. "You need to get out there and deal with Mitch. Unless you want to wait and see what the knitting women do. Maybe they'll knit gags for the men? Or tea cosies big enough to cover their protest signs?"

Jodie stalked to the heavy wooden door. "Tell me again why I thought it was a good idea to go into business with my little brother?"

"Because you'd be lost without me."

"You are so delusional," Jodie said before she let the door slam behind her.

CHAPTER 11

Mitch was trying to figure out the best way to get into the women-only building—without having to sign up for a body wax—when the door opened and Jodie walked out. She scowled at the crowd, breezed past the local reporter who was trying to get an interview and headed straight for him. It was as though all his Christmases had come at once.

"Baby." Mitch held up the gift bag he'd yet to give her. "I was just coming to see you."

"Baby?" Matt was clearly amused. Dumbass.

"Don't call me baby." Jodie sounded tense. Although he couldn't blame her. She had a lot going on.

Matt's gaze swung back and forth between Jodie and Mitch. "Are you two together now?"

"No," Jodie snapped and Mitch felt his ire begin to grow all over again.

Matt coughed, "Knocked back," behind his fist. Jodie wasn't amused. She frowned at Matt before talking to Mitch. "Can we have a word in private?"

"Sure," Mitch said, and then, just to be evil, he added, "baby."

He could have sworn he heard a teeny little growl coming from Jodie. They headed over to the bushes at the side of the building, far away from curious ears. Jodie kept an eye on the crowd as she folded her arms. Her chin came up. Whatever she had to talk about, she really didn't want to do it.

"I need your help." The words were forced through clenched teeth.

Now this was interesting. Mitch stepped forward into her space and watched her lips thin. Nope, she wasn't happy about this at all.

"I'm sorry, Jodie, did you just say you needed help? My help?"

She looked like she was ten seconds away from going postal on him. Even knowing that, Mitch couldn't quite hide his glee at the turn of events.

"You heard me," she snapped.

"Yes, yes, I did. What can I do for you Jodie, baby?" he said as sweetly as he could manage.

That earned him another growl. She looked like she was torn between giving him the details and stomping away from him. Mitch knew it had to be important when she stood her ground.

"I need a lawyer."

Mitch's amusement faded. With everything Jodie was dealing with, and hiding, this was no longer a laughing matter. "What's the problem?"

Her shoulders relaxed when she saw he was no longer amused. The sight of her relief made him want to pull her into his arms and reassure her that she could rely on him. He knew better than to act on his instinct.

"Lawrence is the only lawyer in town." Jodie's eyes darted to the Englishman who still appeared bewildered by the mess in front of him. "We need to get rid of the protestors." She paused for a second before her eyes came back to him. The worry in them took his breath away. "The women are getting stressed."

Mitch's mind was already going over possibilities. He wasn't legally registered as a lawyer in Scotland. That didn't mean he couldn't pull strings for her. He had connections and influence.

"Consider it done."

The look of utter relief that flashed in her eyes almost undid him. He was tempted to leave it at that, knowing he'd earned brownie points with her. But he wasn't known as a shark negotiator for nothing and he couldn't let an opportunity pass to push his advantage with Jodie. Especially seeing as she was almost freaking impossible to get close to.

She nodded her thanks and turned back towards the spa. Mitch's hand shot out to stop her. He should have known better. Lightning fast, her hands grabbed his arm, her leg curled around his and he was toppling backwards. His last thought before he hit the ground was: Not again.

As his head began to throb and the crowd cheered, Mitch looked up at the woman standing over him. Her hands were on her hips, her eyes were blazing and her cheeks were flushed. She looked completely unrepentant.

"Will you stop doing that?" he said with a moan.

"Will you stop grabbing me?"

Mitch thought about that for a minute, at the same time wondering how many times he'd have to hit his head before he sustained a concussion.

"Probably not," he said at last, trying to be as honest as he could.

Jodie huffed her exasperation as she held out a hand to help him up. He gratefully took it. Not because he needed the help, but because it meant he got to hold on to Jodie.

"Everything okay?" Matt said as he sauntered over.

Good to know that when Mitch was being assaulted, his good friend Matt would hurry to intervene.

"Everything's fine," Mitch said sarcastically.

It went over Matt's head. "That's what I thought." He stepped away, but turned back with a grin. "FYI, half the crowd got that on film. You should be a YouTube sensation by dinnertime."

Mitch looked down at his suit. Another one to send to the dry cleaners and hope they got the grass stain out of the back of the jacket.

"This is your fault," Jodie said. "You keep grabbing me. Stop it."

"You like it when I grab you." He waggled his eyebrows at her to make his message clear.

"Boundaries." She pointed to him. "You can grab me in the bedroom without getting damaged, but you can't grab me anywhere else unless you want to suffer the consequences."

"Boundaries." Mitch looked at the sky for a minute, hoping to find some message of encouragement written in the clouds. He was disappointed. "Let's talk about boundaries, then." He looked back down at Jodie. "My help comes at a price."

She muttered something that sounded like "Typical, here we go," all the while trying to incinerate his head with the power of her thoughts.

"What's your price?" she spat.

"I want to redraw the boundaries of our agreement. I want to stop this friends-with-benefits crap. I want you and me. In a relationship."

Her jaw dropped and she stared at him as though he had lost his mind. "Are you kidding me? It's only been days since you forced me to be your friend." She said it as though he'd made her eat worms. "Isn't that enough?"

"Nope." He reached for her hand and was surprised when

she let him take it. "I'm not asking for forever. I want you to admit we're in a relationship. I want you to admit you're dating me. And I want you to do it publicly."

"Right now, I want your head to explode. We don't always get what we want."

"You have a violent streak that's miles wide, don't you?"

"And yet you still want to have a relationship with me? Fact it, Mitch. The only reason you're pushing this is because I'm a challenge to you."

"You're definitely a challenge. But not in the way you mean."

"If I'm that bloody difficult, why are you so intent on dating me?"

"You may be difficult, but you aren't boring. You're smart, and courageous, and compassionate. You fight for what you believe in and you defend people who need it. You're freaking hilarious, mostly when you don't mean to be. You ooze passion; it touches everything you do." He stepped even closer until their bodies were touching, wishing he wasn't still carrying the damn gift bag, because he'd have loved to cup the back of her head with his free hand and kiss her senseless. "You have mad fighting skills and you are seriously dangerous with them. It turns me on to think you could knock me on my ass."

Her eyebrows shot up and Mitch shrugged. "I'm weird like that. Plus, you're great in bed. You're stubborn. You're kind. You're totally unique." He leaned forward and whispered against her ear, "And just looking at you makes my heart hurt. You are so freaking beautiful."

He heard her suck in a shaky breath. Mitch leaned back to look down at her. She was everything to him and he would do everything he could to make her see it.

"All I want is a chance. And I'm not above playing dirty to

get it—even if it means risking brain damage every time you strike out."

"Reflex," she said in a strained tone. "Stop grabbing me and your tiny little brain will be safe."

"I'll bear that in mind." Mitch ran his thumb over the back of her hand. So soft on the outside, but made of steel inside. "If it doesn't work out with us, then so be it. I don't plan on turning into a demented stalker anytime soon. But I want a chance. That's my price for sorting out this mess for you. You. Me. Public relationship. One chance to prove there's something worth fighting for between us. So what do you say?"

Jodie snorted, making it clear she already thought he'd crossed the line to demented stalker.

"Oh. And I get to call you baby."

"You do that anyway," she said.

"What's it going to be? You going to pay the price?" He wasn't going to admit that he'd sort out the protestors for her anyway. If letting her think it was conditional on her answer would give him a chance with her, then he'd take it.

"I have to tell people we're dating?" She sounded so disgusted at the thought that Mitch laughed.

"I'm going to let that slide past me and not take it for the ego blow it is."

"Whatever." She bit her bottom lip. A sure sign she was tempted. Mitch felt elation begin to build, but he tamped it down. With Jodie there was no predicting how things would go until they were set in stone. "I can call it off at any time?"

"Yeah."

"No repercussions?"

"What do you think I'd do, Jodie? Tar and feather your car?"

Her lip twitched as though she was fighting her amusement. Still she didn't agree. The woman defined stubborn.

"I still get sex?"

"People in relationships often do."

"Smart arse."

"I don't know if it affects your decision any, but you're standing here, pretty close, holding my hand. The crowd already thinks it's a done deal."

Her eyes snapped down to where she was indeed holding his hand, then to the side, and she saw that the chanting had stopped and they had the rapt attention of everyone present. Her hand flexed in his, telling him Jodie hadn't even been aware she'd been holding him. Jodie let out another strangled growl before she glared up at him.

"I will make you pay for this."

"I wouldn't expect anything else."

She looked like she was about to have a root canal on a tooth that was giving her migraines. Mitch took a moment to thank God that his self-esteem wasn't dependent on the reactions of the woman in front of him. If he didn't know she was attracted to him and enjoyed how they were physically, he'd be wondering what the hell he was doing.

"Fine." The word came out as a strangled noise.

"That isn't enough. I need to hear the words. We're together? A couple? Public?"

"Are you trying to see how angry you can make me?"

Mitch fought the laugh that was threatening. It was clear Jodie had reached her limit and he was in danger of physical retribution if he let it loose.

"So it's a deal. In that case"—he pressed against her—"kiss me like you mean it, baby."

"I really want to kick you, not kiss you."

"I know, but kissing me will be a statement to everyone watching without you having to take out an ad in the paper."

"I hate you right now."

"I understand."

He waited, aware that the crowd were watching their every move. Her eyes flickered to his lips and her frown softened. Man, but she tore him up inside. With a strangled groan she reached up, grabbed a handful of his hair and tugged his mouth down to hers. He'd thought she'd peck him on the lips and be done with it. Not Jodie: she threw down a challenge in her kiss. It was tongues, lips and teeth. An angry and passionate explosion. When she pulled back, it was Mitch's turn to stand there dazed.

"I hope you enjoy your little victory," she said. "Because I'm going to make your life hell for it."

"Bring it on, baby."

"Get rid of this crowd, Harris."

"Your wish is my command."

"I'll deal with you later." It was delivered in a tone that made him shiver.

And Mitch couldn't wait.

CHAPTER 12

Brenda led Margaret Campbell into the treatment room set up for massage therapy. It was beautifully decorated in tranquil pastel shades of green and blue, with large potted plants to break up the space. It was one of the most tasteful spas that Brenda had worked in.

"Do you mind if I make a couple of calls before we get started?" Margaret asked as she dumped her handbag on the upholstered chair.

"Sure," Brenda said. "Would you like me to get you a nice cup of green tea while you wait?"

"Please tell me green tea isn't made with grass," Margaret said.

Brenda burst out laughing. "No, it isn't made with grass. Why would you think that?"

"I saw something on telly about all that health fad stuff. They were doing yoga and drinking grass."

The penny dropped. "Wheatgrass. Very different from green tea. Trust me, if you like normal tea, you'll like green tea."

Margaret gave her a sceptical look. "If it's just the same as normal tea, why don't we just have normal tea?"

"Green tea is heathier. Less caffeine. Lots of antioxidants."

"Health fad stuff," Margaret grumbled.

Amused, Brenda went to fetch the tea, but added a plate with a couple of French fancies on it to take the sting out of the healthy tea. When she came back, Margaret sat in the rose-pink armchair pressing buttons on her phone.

"My son-in-law, Lake, showed me how to set up a conference call on loudspeaker so I wouldn't have to ring all the women in my knitting group individually. It saves a lot of time, especially as some of them can't shut up. A five-minute call can take an hour."

"Sounds like a good son-in-law." Brenda put the tray down on the table beside Margaret and saw her face light up at the sight of the yellow and pink iced cakes.

"You're a doll," she said before a voice came over the speaker.

"What's up?" someone said, then more chimed in, saying hello.

"Right, we're all here," Margaret said. "We have an emergency."

"What kind of emergency?" one of the women asked. "Is it something we need the police for? Because I can call in Matt."

"No, we don't need your son, Heather," Margaret said. "I'm at the spa and he's standing outside the building. If I need him, I can just shout out the window."

"Why are the police at the spa?" another woman asked. It sounded like she was eating.

"Because of the demonstration." Margaret listened to the sharp intake of breaths.

"Those bloody idiots didn't go ahead with that plan?" the same woman said.

"Aye, that they did, Shona." Margaret pulled a stool over and put her feet up. "They're camped outside right now. They've got banners and everything. And Morag MacKay has set up a pie stall."

"I wondered why the bakery was closed today," a different woman said. "I was hoping it was a death in the family —hers."

"Jean!" someone snapped, and Brenda hid a smile behind her hand.

"Don't tell me you aren't all thinking the same thing," Jean said.

"Anyway," Margaret cut in, "Morag got here, saw there was a demonstration and jumped on the bandwagon."

"She wants men in the spa too?" Heather sounded confused.

"No. She's protesting there being a brothel in town." Margaret covered the phone and whispered to Brenda, "I suppose it's too late to put a shot of whisky in the tea?"

Brenda just looked at her.

"Aye, I thought so. Not sure it'd come under the banner of 'heath food,' anyway." Margaret sounded so disappointed that it was hard to tell if she was still joking or not.

"We have a brothel? I didn't know that." Brenda recognised the voice as Jean, and she seemed quite excited by the prospect.

"Morag is talking about the spa," Heather snapped. "You know what Morag is like. She probably heard something she didn't like and assumed it was sex-related."

"Maybe if Morag got some, she'd stop being so obsessed with making sure everybody else didn't get any," Shona said.

"She thinks the spa is a brothel because they offer massages," Margaret told them. "I'm waiting for a massage right now and I can tell you there is nothing sexual about it."

Brenda started laughing. "No offence, Margaret, but if

something sexual was going to happen, I'd hope it was with Josh McInnes or maybe Mitch Harris. A, because they have the right equipment and B, I have a thing for an American accent." As well as for Scottish chefs who didn't know she existed.

"Don't we all," Shona said on a sigh.

"Who's there?" Heather asked.

"Oh, ladies, this is Brenda, my massage therapist." Margaret grinned at Brenda. "Say hi to the women of Knit or Die."

Brenda did as she was told, then leaned against the set of drawers behind her. "Do you want me to leave until you've finished your call?"

"No," Margaret said. "We're talking about sorting out the men and getting rid of the protest. You can stay for that."

"We are?" Shona sounded hopeful.

Margaret nodded, although none of her friends could see the move. "That's why I'm calling. Jodie is upset about the demonstration. She's worried the men will put people off the business. She was even talking about asking Mitch for legal help to get rid of them."

"She doesn't need Mitch," Heather said. "My boy can run them back into town."

Boy? Brenda mouthed to Margaret.

"Heather's son is the town's entire police force," Margaret explained.

"He'll sort that mess right out," Heather said.

"Jodie already tried that. The protests are legal and Matt can't do anything. That's why I called you lot. We need to mobilise the resistance."

There was a squeal. "I've always wanted to resist something," Jean said. "Can we wear berets?"

Margaret made a circular motion at her temple, letting Brenda know that she thought Jean was off her head. "You can wear what you like. What we need to do is hit back at the men where it hurts. If we distract their attention away from the spa then they'll leave the place alone. They want a war of the sexes, then I think we should give them one."

"I love it!" There was a loud whoop of delight.

"We need to target all the predominantly male events and areas in town." Heather was obviously the practical one.

"Aye, like the Domino Boys' meeting room at the library," Jean said.

"They don't meet there anymore," Heather said. "The guy who replaced Caroline doesn't provide chocolate biscuits. They're meeting in the pub."

"Okay." Margaret took a deep breath. "I can't talk right now. I have to get my massage done. I thought we could meet up at dinnertime."

"Not at the pub," Shona said. "All the men will be in there, stuffing their faces and patting their backs over a day spent protesting."

"You're right. We'll meet at my house," Margaret said. "I need you to bring all the spare knitting you have lying around with you to the meeting."

"Spare knitting?" Heather said.

"Trust me," Margaret said. "I have a plan."

The women said goodbye and Margaret hung up. She took a sip of her tea, made a face then plonked the cup back on the tray. She then set about demolishing the cakes.

"Do you knit?" she asked Brenda.

"Never learned."

"Do you want to learn? The Knit or Die club is looking for new members. Younger blood."

"I'll have a think about it."

Margaret considered her for a minute as though she was trying to figure out if Brenda was stringing her along or not.

"How about you become an affiliate member in the meantime?"

"Affiliate member?" The over-the-top innocent look on Margaret's face was a sure giveaway that she was up to something.

"We're all getting on a bit. I just celebrated my sixtieth. I'm not as flexible as I used to be." She looked Brenda directly in the eyes. "It makes it difficult to break and enter when your knees creak. And if any of us had to climb a fence, or a drainpipe, there's a good chance we'd pull something doing it. We could use some muscle." Brenda's jaw fell and Margaret rushed on. "For the war, you understand. We don't go around breaking into places willy-nilly. We only do it when the cause demands it. And really, is there a bigger cause than equality? Ours, not the men's. Men are equal enough."

Brenda blinked several times before she grinned widely. Moving to the Highlands was turning out to be the best decision of her life. "You're in luck. I have mad breaking and entering skills. I can pick pretty much any lock." She didn't tell Margaret that she'd learned the skill in order to get out of the closet her ex-boyfriend used to lock her in after he'd beaten her. As far as Brenda was concerned, you had to take the good out of any given situation. So her time with Clive had been horrific—at least she'd picked up some skills from the experience. Okay, not all of them were useful—like how to curl up in a way that minimised the damage from a fist and how to alphabetise your pantry (a major obsession of Clive's). Now that she thought about it, maybe there wasn't much of a positive side from her years with Clive.

Margaret whooped, bringing Brenda out of her contemplation. The woman's eyes lit up. "I knew you'd be perfect for our group."

Brenda liked that. It sure would be nice to fit in somewhere. "Can I bring a friend?"

"More the merrier." Margaret stood. "I knew instantly that you'd fit right into Invertary. It takes a certain type of person to really make a go of it in this town."

"Friendly?" Brenda guessed.

"Bonkers," Margaret said. "You have to be stark raving mad to fit in here."

Brenda handed Margaret a robe and pointed to the dressing room. With a spring in her step, Margaret went to get changed. Brenda figured she was excited about planning her war. And when she thought about it, Brenda was kind of excited too.

CHAPTER 13

Jodie didn't drink. Mostly she thought alcohol tasted like cat pee smelled. It left her feeling morose. The alcohol, not the cat pee, and seeing as she was morose enough without the help, she decided to drown her sorrows the way she usually did—with chocolate.

She sat on the flat roof area that acted as her terrace, her back to the outside wall of her living room and her legs stretched out in front of her, with a large box of chocolates beside her. She'd tiled the roof in terra cotta and blue, dotted plant pots around, hung shade sails and furnished it with quality wooden tables and chairs. With trees on the property trimmed, it was possible to make out the loch in the distance, as well as the lush green hills surrounding the town. Up here, away from everything, she could take a moment to breathe. Something she very much needed after the day she'd just suffered through.

"Is this a private pity party or can anyone join in?" The deep drawl shivered through Jodie.

So much for her peace and quiet.

Jodie turned in her seat to see Mitch standing in the patio

doorway. He was dressed in worn jeans and a U2 tee from their Joshua Tree tour. She owned a version of that tee herself.

"How did you get in here?"

"Deke sent me up."

Rat bastard brother. She'd deal with his interference later.

"What are you doing here?" And yes, the words did come out in bitch tone.

"I brought you the gift I've been trying to give you since yesterday." He held up a pretty pink gift bag. "You would have gotten it earlier, but you were too busy throwing me around like a rag doll."

Jodie scowled at the bag. "Couldn't you have just left it on the doorstep?"

"Nope. We're having some quality time together. This is what people in a normal relationship do, Jodie. They hang out."

"By people in normal relationships, you mean the ones who actually want to be in those relationships and aren't blackmailed into it by pathetically desperate men?"

She was hoping to get a rise out of him, but instead he just laughed.

"Here." He handed her the bag.

With a grumble, she took it. "Are you trying to buy my affection?"

"Absolutely, and I can tell by your accommodating disposition that my evil plan is working." Mitch nodded towards the bag. "Open it."

"Bossy man." But she was too curious not to peek inside.

Her heart stopped. There was a pair of shoes in the bag. A pair of designer crocs. They were red with tiny ladybirds attached to them and a flower motif running over the toe section and around to the heel. They were over the top, whacky and totally amazing.

"You got me shoes?" she said, a little breathily. She was a girl. Shoes had superpowers over her. She couldn't help it.

He shrugged, but his eyes twinkled with amusement. "You're on your feet all day. These are supposed to be comfortable."

Jodie felt a strange falling sensation. He'd thought of her comfort. She kicked off her flip-flops to put on the new shoes. They fit like a dream.

"How did you know my size?"

"You left your boot in my room the first night you stayed over, Cinderella."

That reminded her: "You still haven't returned it."

His smile was devilish. "The prince gets to keep the shoe."

"You're no prince, and the shoe gets returned to the woman he falls—" She cut off the thought when she realised who got the shoe. He cocked an eyebrow at her. "Never mind," Jodie said. "Keep the boot."

"Coward," Mitch muttered. He turned his attention to her feet. She was wiggling them to show off her new shoes. "Shoes look good, babe."

Jodie turned up to him and opened her mouth to tell him he could go now he'd made his delivery. Instead, he leaned over and kissed her. It was soft, slow and sweet. About half a point away from being a perfect ten. And he only lost that half point because he shouldn't have been there in the first place.

Jodie's eyes had floated shut at the touch of his lips to hers. When she opened them again, it was to see him smiling softly in front of her. The sight annoyed her. He would be so much easier to resist if he wasn't so gorgeous.

"Beer?" he whispered.

"Fridge," she answered before she remembered she didn't want him there.

"I'll grab one and then we'll hang out."

"Seriously? Do we have to?"

With a deep chuckle, he sauntered towards the kitchen, all lean limbs and toned muscle. And yeah, she noticed the fit of his jeans, too. They were butter soft and faded just enough to be sexy as hell. Jodie pulled the box of chocolates closer and picked her favourite. One bite of hazelnut praline and she was in heaven. So much so that she'd almost forgotten Mitch had invaded her home until she felt him slide down the wall to sit beside her.

His eyes were warm when they shifted between the chocolate and her mouth. "Got some for me?"

"Don't even think about touching the chocolate," Jodie said. "I will toss you off the roof if you try it."

"You have a mean violent streak, Jodie. I like it."

"I also have the skills to follow through on it."

"Yeah?" His lip twitched before he tipped back his head and drank some of the beer.

Jodie gave him some consideration. Was he mocking her? Thinking she was making false threats? It was time to knock that notion right out of his tiny head. "I'm a level one expert in Krav Maga."

"I've reached level five in Grand Theft Auto."

"Krav Maga isn't an online game, idiot. It's an Israeli martial art. Level one expert is the equivalent of having a black belt."

"I was joking. I know what Krav Maga is. I watch The Simpsons. I saw the episode where a girl kicked Bart's butt." He considered her for a minute. "Is it wrong that knowing you can kick my ass makes you even hotter?"

Jodie was beginning to wonder if Mitch wasn't a few sandwiches short of a picnic.

"Nice up here," he said when he'd finished his beer.

"It was." Jodie ate another chocolate and tried to inch

away from him. He was sitting so close that he was pressed against her from shoulder to thigh.

Mitch foiled her plan by wrapping an arm around her shoulders and pulling her into his side. Jodie probably should have protested, but she was holding a box of chocolates and protecting them took priority.

"How's Fiona?"

The question surprised Jodie. Mitch's only experience of the woman was when she'd screamed the place down at his arrival. She couldn't believe he'd remembered her name.

"She's getting the help she needs."

She glanced up at Mitch and saw a muscle throb at the corner of his jaw. "Wouldn't mind five minutes alone with the guy who got her into that state," he said, and Jodie felt that strange falling sensation all over again.

"Get in line."

The sun was setting over Invertary. The predominantly white buildings were painted in shades of red and gold by the fading sun and the cool green of the hills turned a warmer, deeper shade of emerald.

"It's a good thing you're doing here, Jodie."

"Don't get any highfalutin ideas. We aren't running a charity. The women have jobs and pay their way, like they would anywhere else. We're hardly saints."

"I heard how little you're charging for rent on the manse. Most places would call it subsidised living." He seemed amused by her efforts to set him straight.

"Some people would call it good business. You have happy staff, you have hardworking staff. Which translates into more profit. Trust me, we might care a whole helluva lot about what we're doing, but we're under no illusion that it's purely altruistic."

"Whatever you say."

"Man, you're annoying." As usual, her comment had little

impact. "What's happening with your efforts to get rid of the protestors?"

"Oh yeah, the other reason I crashed your pity party. I'll give you an update for a kiss."

She didn't move. She could be patient and wait until he came to his senses.

"After the update, then," he said when he'd eventually found his sense. "I managed to shut Morag down. She didn't have a permit to sell food on your land. Either she sells from the road, which would need a police permit, and Matt isn't feeling too favourable towards that idea, or she protests without the pie stand."

"She's going back to the bakery, isn't she?" The one thing Morag loved more than protesting anyone who didn't reach her standard of morality, was making money.

"Yep. When I explained the situation to her, she suddenly realised that there was nothing illicit going on in the spa. Seemed she was misinformed." He obviously thought this was funny.

Jodie didn't. Anything that would bring the wrong sort of attention to the spa wasn't funny. It was one thing to advertise your business; it was another thing entirely to become a humorous end piece on the six o'clock news—which was what she feared would happen if the protests continued. The men who were looking for Jodie's employees wouldn't notice an ad for a spa, but they sure as hell would notice the evening news. What if one of the women was caught on camera? She couldn't even think about that. She'd promised them they would be safe in Invertary and she'd do everything within her power to make sure it happened—including making a pact with the devil beside her.

"What about the men?" she said.

"That's a bit trickier." He placed his empty bottle on the tile beside him. "We have to prove they're disturbing your business to get rid of them entirely. There hasn't been any monetary disruption or any sort of harassment of your customers, which means they're within their rights to sit out there and shout crap to amuse themselves. I did manage to use the trespass laws to stop them from setting up on your property, but the chances are that tomorrow they'll just protest from the sidewalk outside the gate."

Jodie began to feel a little helpless. Not something she was used to or enjoyed. "Fantastic. That's no improvement at all."

"I'm going to pretend you didn't just say that. Instead, I'm going to pretend that you said, 'Wow, Mitch, you are so cool. Thank you for getting rid of Morag and pushing the men off my land.'"

"It's not that I'm ungrateful." Jodie felt bad at her ungracious attitude.

"But…" Mitch prompted.

"I just want them gone."

Mitch patted her thigh. "Never fear, baby, Mitch is here." He gave her a smug smile. "Turns out that the fact you live above your business is a stroke of luck. We can use the harassment laws to knock this on the head. It's against the law to try and force someone to do something near their dwelling. Matt is going to have a word with the Domino Boys and point out that I will have them charged with harassment if they turn up here again. I suggested that if they really wanted to get in the spa, they might consider starting a petition instead of camping outside the building."

Hope blossomed in Jodie. She was beginning to think he might actually be able to work the miracles he claimed. "They're gone, then?"

"There's no knowing what goes on in the heads of the Domino Boys, but fingers crossed they won't be coming back." Dark eyes captured hers as relief and joy swept through her. "Now. Time for my thank you kiss."

A spike of heat joined the relief and joy. "Well, you do deserve one, even if you're forcing me to give it to you."

The heat in his eyes was scorching. "I'll take it any way it comes, baby."

With feigned resignation, Jodie put down her chocolates and straddled Mitch. She casually rested her arms on his shoulders and played with the hair at the back of his head. His big hands clasped her hips, but he didn't make a move towards her. He just sat there, passively, waiting for her to do all the work. The thought of having him at her mercy made Jodie shiver.

She took her time studying him. He really was the most gorgeous man she'd ever set eyes on.

"You're too pretty for your own good," she told him.

"It's the cross I bear."

Impossible man. Jodie closed the gap between them and gently rubbed her lips against his. That was all it took to flick the switch inside her that put the world on mute and let her focus on the man beneath her. By the time she'd swiped her tongue over his bottom lip, and nibbled on the fullness of it, Mitch had lost his ability to sit passively. One big hand flattened on the middle of her back and the other curved around the nape of her neck, as he pressed her into him. A second later, he'd taken over the kiss and Jodie felt herself float away.

CHAPTER 14

Deke hid in the shadows as he watched the group of women, all dressed in black—some of it sparkly—sneak along the street towards the Scottie Dog pub. You didn't have to be a genius to spot that they were up to no good. And they were making a hash of it.

Deke had followed Brenda and Robin from the spa when they'd snuck out earlier. It wasn't like the women were on a curfew or anything. They lived there and could do whatever the hell they liked—even if it was the middle of the night. Nope, he'd followed because the ruckus they'd made "sneaking out" had woken him, then worried him. After hearing about the trouble at the Hampstead Heath drop-in centre and that Brenda had been there, Deke had taken it upon himself to act as her invisible bodyguard.

Which was how he found himself lurking in the doorway of the building opposite the pub, watching four retired women and two members of his staff case the joint. They were doing this while carrying huge multi-coloured bags, all of which were emblazoned with Knit or Die in bright white. Deke stared in awe. They'd dressed in black and were carrying luminous bags. There really was no understanding the minds of women.

There was a light on in the entrance to the hotel above the pub and one or two of the hotel rooms had lamps burning. Other than that, it was dead. Which was a good thing, because Brenda was currently picking the lock on the back door. Deke rubbed a hand over his face. This just got worse and worse. He was pretty sure that Jean was playing Candy Crush on her phone while she waited for Brenda to pop the lock. He wondered if these women even knew the meaning of the word covert, never mind the fact they should be tucked up in bed dreaming up new sweater patterns instead of embarking on a life of crime, which they clearly weren't cut out for. As Brenda's self-appointed bodyguard, he was going to have a long talk with her about her nefarious skills and the fact she was using them to not only put herself in harm's way, but to encourage the insanity of the grey-haired knitting brigade.

"Got it!" Brenda said loud enough for him to hear on the other side of the carpark.

Deke bit back a groan as the women high-fived each other. He watched as Jean ran into the bar, then stage-whispered to the waiting women that she'd turned the alarm off. Obviously Dougal hadn't changed his code since Jean helped out behind the bar.

With resignation, Deke pulled his phone out of the back pocket of his cargo pants. It was time to call Dougal. His thumb hovered over the screen while he watched several flashlights dance around inside the pub. He shook his head. They might as well have turned on the lights. He hesitated, ready to dial, then made a decision. He slid the phone back into his pocket and went to see what they were up to. There was no reason to bother the pub owner if he didn't have to. Deke could shut this down all on his own.

He jogged across the parking lot, noted that the women had left the back door wide open and closed it quietly behind him as he entered the pub. There was enough light coming through the huge windows that there was no need for a flashlight. He followed the path the women had taken through the building to the pub area. Although, if he didn't already know where they were, he could have just followed the chatter and giggling.

"Jean," Margaret Campbell said. "You do the whisky bottles. You know the ones they like."

"No problemo," Jean said.

Deke walked silently up the corridor to the bar, turned the corner and stopped dead. He had to blink a couple of times to make sure he was actually seeing what was in front of him and not hallucinating.

Margaret, aided by Robin, was covering three barstools in what looked like huge, multi-coloured knitted tea cosies.

"Make sure it's tight. We don't want them coming off easy," Margaret instructed. "And make sure the bit with all the beads is on the seat. They won't be able to sit on it then." She cackled like a demented witch.

"Where's the CD player?" Robin said.

"I'll show you in a minute," Jean said from behind the bar, where she was wrapping whisky bottles in knitted pink outfits. Each bottle had a dress and a hat. One had a handbag.

It was at this point Deke thought he was probably still in bed dreaming this shit.

"No need. Point the way and I'll get their new music hooked up in no time." Robin jogged off in the direction Jean pointed.

Deke knew he should step in and put a stop to things, but truth be told, he was fascinated. He could honestly say he'd never seen anything like it.

"I still think we should have covered everything with

powdered dye," Jean said as she adjusted a hat on a bottle of fifty-year-old malt.

Margaret shook her head. "We couldn't do that to Dougal. There was no way of knowing what the dye would get onto."

"I was okay with that," Jean said as Robin came back and gave them a thumbs-up.

"That's only because you're still upset about breaking up with him. You need to get over that."

Robin's head shot up, her eyes wide and focused on Jean. "You were going out with Dougal? I thought he was gay."

"No." Jean shook her head. "He's metrosexual. That's why he wears pink."

Deke had to bite the inside of his cheek to stop from laughing.

"But," Robin said, "he looks like Santa. Wasn't it upsetting bonking Santa?"

"Naw," Jean said with an evil smile. "Let's just say every day was Christmas."

Okay, that was it. Deke couldn't take any more. He stepped out of the shadows.

"Time to knock this on the head," he said.

The women jumped. Then they screamed.

"Abort!" Margaret shouted. "It's the fuzz!"

Robin had a hand over her heart as she squinted through the darkness towards Deke. Her shoulders slumped with relief. "It isn't the police. It's only Deke."

"Deke!" Margaret put her hands on her hips and glared at him. "You almost gave me a heart attack. You can't sneak up on a woman like that."

"Margaret, you're breaking and entering. This shit is illegal."

"Don't you swear at me," she said. "I'll wash your mouth out with soap."

Yeah, he wasn't even going to go there. "Pack it up, ladies. Your fun is over."

"You're not going to make us undo all this, are you?" Margaret pointed at the woolly barstools.

Deke looked at the woollen monstrosities and then at the clock over the bar. He did not have time for this crap. A man needed his sleep.

"No," he said. "But this ends now. Time to clear out and get home. Or I'll call Matt and Dougal."

"Fine," Margaret grumbled.

"Killjoy," Robin mumbled.

Deke stared at his maître d'. "Would be good if you were around for the restaurant opening day instead of locked up in jail."

"You would say that," Jean said. "You only want us to stop our assault because you're a guy. The enemy. This is a war of the sexes, son, and you picked the wrong team."

There was so much wrong with that statement that Deke didn't even know where to begin. "Out. Now." He pinned Robin with his stare. "Where's the rest of your crack team?"

"Men's room." She pointed down the corridor.

Deke headed in that direction. "You lot had better be gone by the time I come back through here."

There was more grumbling, but Deke was out of the room. He was knocked off his feet in the corridor as Heather Donaldson ran straight into him. The mother of the town's only cop screamed loudly. Her cry had Shona, another middle-aged knitter, rushing out of the men's room. She caught sight of Deke and turned to run back in. Deke was fast, grabbing her jacket to stop her.

"Get out of there," Shona shouted into the toilets. "We've been busted."

"Run," Brenda shouted back. "Save yourselves!"

Deke looked down at the two women in front of him.

Their faces were flushed and they seemed more relieved than worried that it was him standing in front of them instead of Dougal or Matt.

"Does your son know you're a criminal in your spare time?" Deke asked Heather.

"I have the right to remain silent," she said. "I have the right to an attorney…"

Deke held up a hand. "First, you've been watching too much American TV. That doesn't work in Scotland. Second, I'm not a cop. Your son is the cop, and if you and your cronies aren't out of here in the next ten seconds, I'll be calling him."

"Consider us gone." Heather grabbed Shona's arm and ran for the bar.

Deke watched them go. Five down, one to go. He pushed the outer door of the men's room and stepped inside.

CHAPTER 15

Jodie was glad Mitch had ignored her when she'd told him to leave her apartment. Her perfectly awful day was beginning to look up. It was suddenly a beautiful night, and if she was lucky, she could persuade him to help her break in her patio, instead of moving things into the bedroom. She liked the thought of making love to Mitch while looking up at the stars.

With teasing thoroughness, Mitch took control of Jodie's kiss, clasping her hair to hold her mouth at the angle he wanted her. Jodie writhed in his lap, pressing her sensitive breasts into his muscled chest. She could feel him, hard and ready beneath her and wiggled her hips. She was rewarded with a groan that she captured with her lips. He tasted of beer and peppermint and Mitch. It was divine, and Jodie needed more. Her fingers found their way to the bottom of his t-shirt and began to tug it up his body.

Strong hands clasped her wrists to stop her and their kiss ended. Jodie looked down at Mitch. His eyes were dark and heavy-lidded. His breathing laboured. His lips bruised by her kisses. Oh yeah, she definitely needed more of him. And she needed it now.

"Stop," he said.

It took a minute for the word to register.

"Stop?"

"Yeah." He rested his forehead against hers and closed his eyes.

Jodie waited for the rest, but nothing was forthcoming. "Why stop?"

He sighed, lifted his head and looked into her eyes. "We're in a relationship now, yeah?"

As much as it galled her to admit it, she had agreed to his terms, so she nodded.

His lips twitched up at the corners. "I can see you're still thrilled about that."

"Did you expect anything else? You blackmailed me into this. Now the whole town is probably talking about what happened outside the spa today. They think we're seeing each other."

"That's because we are seeing each other, baby." This was said with more annoying lip twitching.

"Whatever." Jodie huffed in exasperation. "Why are we stopping?"

"Because…" He paused, which made her think she wasn't going to like what he said next. "We went about this relationship thing backwards. I think it would be a good idea to cool off the physical for a while so we can get to know each other."

Yep, she was right. She didn't like that one bit. Plus, it didn't sound normal, reasonable or healthy.

"I don't need to get to know you. I've been clear. I'm only in this for the sex."

"You were clear, but things changed when we kissed outside the spa today. Now we're a couple, and I think it'd be a good idea if you knew the guy you were dating, don't you?"

No. She didn't. "I know what I need to know. I know that you're handy in a legal crisis. You give good gifts. And you're great in bed. What else is there to know? Now can you stop being annoying so we can go to bed?"

He looked up at the starry sky for a moment. Jodie got the distinct impression he was praying. She hoped it was for some sense, because his current thinking was seriously twisted.

"Look." He tipped his head back down towards her. "Why don't we talk for half an hour and see where it goes?"

"We just talked. I don't see why we have to do it again. We talked about you getting rid of the protestors. We talked about shoes. We've talked enough."

He stared at her for a minute. His face was hard to read, but he was clearly displeased. "You are murder on a guy's ego," he muttered, then took a deep breath. "People who date spend time together while they aren't having sex. They talk. They get to know each other. We're dating. I want the stuff that happens outside of the bedroom too. So, starting from now, we're going to put sex on the back burner while we hang out."

"What?" Yeah, she was screeching. She wasn't proud. "No sex? What the hell is the point of having a boyfriend if you don't get sex?"

"Babe, I haven't been your boyfriend. I've been your sex toy."

"I thought you liked being my sex toy."

"I did. I do. But I have other needs."

Now she was confused. "What other needs?"

"The need to get to know you."

And they were back to that again. "Seriously? We're doing this? You would really rather talk than get naked?"

To her relief, he at least looked conflicted. "Yeah," he said at last.

"This is pathetic. Other men, real men, don't want to sit around talking. Real men don't whine about their women not meeting their emotional needs. In fact, no man in the history of the universe has ever said 'let's talk' when a woman offered him sex. Until now. With me. I must be so special."

Mitch's smile was devilish. "I'm a lawyer, baby. A boardroom negotiator. You can't manipulate me into taking you to bed just to prove I'm a real man. I am totally secure in my maleness. We're going to talk."

"What if I don't want to talk?"

"Half an hour, Jodie. You can do half an hour, then as a reward I'll take you to bed and I'll do all the work. Agreed?"

She bit her bottom lip. "Promise?"

"Promise." He sounded solemn, but his eyes were laughing at her.

"Fine." She waved a hand. "Let's talk."

She stared at him. He stared back. No one spoke. Jodie drummed the fingers of her left hand on the bicep of her right arm.

"You want me to start?" Mitch said.

"It's your bloody idea!"

"I'll take that as a yes."

They stared at each other some more. Jodie was beginning to get majorly agitated. The kind of agitated that could only be assuaged by pacing and ranting.

"Well?" she demanded. "I hope these silent minutes count towards the half-hour mark."

"Give me a second. This is harder than I thought it would be."

"That's probably because you didn't think about it enough to begin with."

He cocked an eyebrow at her. "Not helping."

"What do you want? Topics? Fine. Let's discuss the weather. Or Scottish independence. Or women's rights. Or who makes the best fries, Dougal or Deke. I'm sure we'll know loads more about each other once the conversation is over."

Mitch said nothing, so Jodie carried on.

"Or what about first-date topics? Favourite colour. Favourite music. Favourite pets."

Still nothing. For a guy who wanted to talk, he wasn't making any effort.

"Or how about we discuss past sexual partners? I hear guys love to talk about that."

"Okay." Mitch placed a hand either side of her waist and lifted her off him. He stood, grabbed her hand and hauled her to her feet. "Conversation over. Which way is the bedroom?"

"At last. Some sense." Jodie dragged him down the short hallway off the living room.

Jodie kicked open her bedroom door and flicked on the recessed lighting. She loved this room. It sat in the peak of the old church roof, with slanting ceilings, exposed beams and a stained glass window that let in multi-coloured light. Like all the stained glass in the building, it was one mass of geometric patterns rather than depicting religious scenes. Jodie had always considered this a good thing. She didn't think she'd be comfortable sleeping under a biblical tableau —or doing anything else under it, either. Not that she thought God had anything against sex—He did invent it after all—but she was a Catholic schoolgirl at heart and programmed to feel guilt at the sight of religious artwork.

Jodie watched Mitch's gaze flick around her bedroom, which she'd decorated in multi-coloured hues to match the window. The walls were whitewashed, the warm wood exposed on ceiling and floor, but the rest of the room was an eclectic assembly of colourful materials.

"Jodie Miller, you are such a girl," he said with a grin.

"Well, duh." Jodie pulled her shirt over her head, revealing the lavender tartan bra she'd bought from Kirsty Benson's lingerie store.

"You've got a girly side." Mitch wasn't going to let this go, she knew it.

"Mitch, I run a spa. That's about as girly as it gets. Now get undressed."

He put his hands on his hips and glared at her. Although she noted that his eyes warmed when she'd gotten rid of her trousers and was only standing in front of him in matching lingerie.

"Mitch, naked. Chop, chop." She waved a hand at his clothes.

"You know, this relationship is not going the way I'd planned."

"Join the club." Jodie climbed onto her bed. "I didn't even want a relationship. I'm here under duress."

Mitch shook his head, but she was glad to see his t-shirt was gone and he was unbuttoning his jeans. That was more like it. What she didn't like to see was the look of determination on his face.

"I will get to know you," he said. "I will break through the wall and get to the soft, girly centre."

"You make me sound like a candy bar."

The smile was back. Mitch divested himself of his underpants, which made Jodie smile too.

"You taste like a candy bar."

"Yeah?" Jodie leaned back against the many pillows that covered her bed as Mitch crawled up the length of her body.

"Yeah." His voice was a husky rumble as he buried his face

in the crook of her neck. Jodie's arms and legs automatically wrapped around him. She smiled as Mitch kissed her throat, the hot weight of his body pressing into the length of hers.

"Why are you still wearing this?" He tugged her bra strap off her shoulder.

"I thought you'd enjoy removing it."

That earned her the nip of his teeth on her shoulder. She shivered at the feel of his bite.

"Give me one thing." He kissed his way up her throat to her ear. "One thing that's about you. One thing normal people tell each other while they're dating. Give me one thing, baby, and I'll unwrap you and show you my appreciation."

Jodie's breath caught in her throat at the thought of Mitch's appreciation. She knew exactly how good that could be. Somehow, being close to him like that, wrapped around him in her bed, made it easier to give him what he wanted. She cleared her throat.

"My favourite colour is blue." She felt him still, before his arms squeezed tight around her. His lips never left her throat. "The kind of blue you only ever see on the ocean after a stormy day. That deep blue-green that's impossible to find anywhere else."

Mitch flicked the clasp of her bra open before slipping the strap off her shoulder.

"My favourite food is Indian. Especially pakora. No, onion baji." She wasn't sure why she kept talking when she'd already given him one thing. All she knew was that it felt easy like this. Her reward was the feeling of his smile against the curve of her breast as he lowered the cup of her bra.

"I love spring rain, when the air is fresh and there's the promise of bright, warm sun after the downpour."

Mitch's teeth rasped her nipple and she clung to him, one

hand moving to the back of his head, where she could keep him pressed against her.

"I always wanted to go to Paris in the springtime." Her mind was torn between the words spilling from her lips and the delicious feeling of his mouth suckling her. "I could walk down the Champs-Élysées and pretend I was an actor in a classic Hollywood movie. Something with Audrey Hepburn and Cary Grant."

Mitch's free hand caressed down her side, over her hip until he cupped her backside. He pulled her up tight against him. Jodie's head went back as that wonderful dizzy sensation flooded her brain. The one where she felt like she was floating, only tethered by Mitch's touch.

"One day," she said breathily, "I want to learn to sew and make all my own clothes."

That earned her another grin against her skin. His head went back and Jodie moaned at the loss of his mouth from her breast.

"You are such a girl."

"I like football," Jodie said. "I genuinely believe in girl power and I am convinced women should be in charge of all governments."

His grin got wider, and Jodie searched his eyes to see if he was laughing at her. She didn't think he was, but she wasn't sure.

"Strong," he whispered, closing the gap between them so that she felt the words against her lips. "Girly and strong. A formidable force, my Jodie."

My Jodie.

She stopped breathing at his words.

And then Mitch opened his mouth over hers and she gasped in a breath. A breath filled with the taste and the scent of Mitch. The man who thought she was his. For the first time in her life, Jodie was frozen with indecision. She didn't know whether to fight, run or surrender.

The fact she didn't know what she should do terrified her, just a little. Because deep in the back of her mind, she was worried that Mitch might be making a place for himself in her heart. A place where she might one day call him hers.

CHAPTER 16

Deke pushed through the second heavy door into the gents' toilets of Invertary pub and stopped dead. He didn't freeze in place at the sight of the urinals, which were now wrapped up tight in knitted blankets, or because the doors to the stalls had been blocked by tightly woven woollen webs, or because there was writing on the mirror that said the men had been yarn-bombed. No, the reason he couldn't take another step forward was because the small window high on the back wall was now filled with a curvy backside clad in formfitting black jeans. Legs were kicking off the wall, leaving scuff marks, in an obvious attempt to gain purchase. It was a futile effort. There was nothing for the high-heeled sandals to grip to.

There was grunting. Some cursing. Irritated groans of frustration. Brenda was stuck. When the shock wore off, Deke did what anyone in his situation would have done—he pulled out his phone and snapped a few photos. Then he left the toilet, exited the pub and rounded the building to look up at the other half of Brenda.

She was hanging limply out of the window, a couple of

feet above Deke's head, and from her muttering, she hadn't yet realised he was there.

"Of course I know how to break and enter." From her tone, it was clear she was mocking herself and the words she'd given someone earlier. "I'm an expert. Although I'm used to breaking out of places, not into them. Don't worry. I'll get us in and out of the pub."

"This a private conversation?" Deke said.

Her head snapped up. Her blond cloud of hair looked like a halo around her head.

"This isn't what it looks like."

Deke pinched the bridge of his nose. "It looks like you're stuck in the gents' toilet window. Of the pub you broke into."

Her head went back down, so she was hanging upside down again. "Okay, then it is what it looks like." Her head came up again. "I feel I should point out that this situation in no way affects my performance at work. The fact I failed in my escape doesn't mean I'm a bad employee."

Deke gave his head a little shake. "What?"

She looked earnest. "I don't want you to think that I do this sort of thing all the time. I don't want you to regret employing me. This has nothing to do with work. At work, I'm professional. Ask anyone. Well, not anyone in Invertary, seeing as I'm new here." She sucked her plump bottom lip into her mouth for a second. "And you probably can't ask past employers, seeing as that would leave a trail. A trail would be bad. But if you could ask anyone, they would tell you that I am all about being professional at work. So you don't have to worry."

Deke stared at her in bewilderment, which Brenda obviously took to mean that he needed more convincing.

"You don't need to worry about me doing anything illegal at work." Her eyes went wide. "Or outside of work. This is a one-time thing. And it isn't really a criminal activity. It's more like an activist activity. You know, like the people who break into cosmetics companies and free bunnies?"

Deke's lip twitched. He was fighting it, the laughter bubbling up inside of him, desperate to come out. She was so damn cute and so freaking deluded, which was sexy as hell. Everything about Brenda was sexy as hell. If she wasn't one of the traumatised women they were helping out, he'd have been all over her in a heartbeat. As it was, he knew she was off limits. Way off limits. The last thing he wanted was to upset Brenda by coming onto her.

"Deke," Brenda said, cutting into his thoughts. "I need help. The window frame is cutting me in two."

Deke glanced around for something to stand on so that he could help lift her out. There was nothing. Then it occurred to him that she was going headfirst out of a window that was eight foot above the ground. There was nothing for her to hold on to. Nothing to break her fall. It was the craziest thing he'd ever seen. The thought of what could have happened to her melted his humour, replacing it with anger.

"What were you thinking? You could have broken your neck."

She looked down at the concrete ground beneath her. "I panicked." She looked back up at him. The wide eyes were back. "I have a tendency to do things first and think about them later. It's a personality flaw." She paused, obviously thinking about what she'd just said. "Although not at work. I always think things through at work. I'm all about responsibility at work." She waved an arm. "This is off-hours me. I store up the crazy for my downtime."

"I get it. You're a model employee. One that just happens to have been caught red-handed during a break-in."

"There's no red on these hands. I didn't steal anything. In

fact, I left stuff behind." She smiled widely. It was kind of crooked and totally charming. "I'm like Santa."

Deke wondered if Brenda's form of logic was contagious. "I'm going inside, see if I can pull you back into the room."

Her face paled. "Wouldn't it be better if you pulled me out this way? Facing you."

"There's nothing to stand on out here and the window isn't as high up in the bathroom."

She visibly swallowed. "How about you go back inside and bring out a chair to stand on? That would work. Right?"

"Out here there's a good chance that when I yank you out of the window we'll both topple to the ground. Less chance of an injury inside."

"But..." Her voice was rising with each sentence, the panic clear.

"But what?" Deke was losing patience. "It's two in the morning. I'm tired. Spit it out."

She opened and shut her mouth a couple of times and Deke frowned at her. Her shoulders slumped.

"It's embarrassing that you're going to be up close and personal with my rear end."

Deke ran a hand down his face. "I'll keep it professional."

She made a strangled squeaking noise. Deke turned on his heels and grinned all the way back into the building. He grabbed a chair from the bar on his way to the restroom. When he got there, Brenda was muttering to herself again.

"It couldn't have been my hand that was stuck, oh no, it had to be my backside. I have great hands. I could be a hand model. Why couldn't he get up close and personal with my hands? Why does it have to be my bum? In these jeans? The jeans that add an extra ten pounds to my backside. The jeans that are too tight and give me a muffin top. The jeans that have a tiny hole in the seat. Deke Miller is going to be face to face with my huge bum. Kill me now. Just kill me now."

Deke made no effort to hide his amusement now that she couldn't see him. He put the chair under her and looked up. Her backside was just above his head. She was wrong about the jeans. They were perfect.

"You about done talking to yourself?" he said.

She let out a little scream. "A bit of warning," she snapped back at him.

"Would you have rather I just grabbed you and pulled?"

The crazy woman was thinking about it. Deke climbed up on the chair and surveyed the situation. She was wedged in tight. In fact, the space was so small that she must have angled her shoulders to get out in the first place. Deke wasn't sure he'd be able to get her back in. Not without help.

"I think we need to call for help," he said.

"No!" Her backside jiggled. "It will be fine. We don't need anyone else."

He wasn't so sure. "We'll try." He examined the situation. "I'm going to lift your hips up. Once I've got you off the windowsill, can you push back? Then I'll hold your weight as you angle your shoulder through. How does that sound?"

"Like hell," she muttered. "Great," she said louder.

Deke put a hand on each of her hips and she jerked at his touch. He snapped his hands away instantly. Damn it to hell, he knew touching Brenda was a bad idea. There was no way these women could have dealt with the traumas they went through and not have an aversion to men touching them.

"I'm sorry." He kept his voice as soft as possible. "I know you don't like this, but I can't help you without touching you."

There was silence for a second. "I don't mind you touching me, Deke. You just surprised me."

Her words were a hand that clenched around his heart. She was making the effort for him. Trying not to freak him out with her insecurities and issues—just like his mother used to do. He'd watched his mum swallow her fears over and over as he grew up, all because she wouldn't upset her children. It cut deep that he was causing Brenda to do the same.

"Bren, you knew I was going to hold your hips. How can it be a surprise?"

"My mind was on something else."

Deke didn't have time to delve into the strange workings of Brenda's mind. It was late. He was tired. And this needed to be over. "How about I get some women to help?"

"Deke," she said, "I'm fine. Well, I'm not fine. I'm being sliced in two by this window frame. But I'm okay with you holding my hips." She paused. "Just don't look too closely at my backside, okay?" There was a pause before she started muttering again. "First thing tomorrow, I'm going on a diet."

She was a nut. There was nothing wrong with her backside. It was heart-shaped and lush. Deke snapped his eyes away from the sight and concentrated on the task in hand. No! Not in hand. His hands weren't going anywhere near that backside.

"Okay, on three. I lift. You push. Got it?"

"Got it." At least she sounded determined.

Deke grasped her hips. This time she didn't jerk at his touch, but he could have sworn he felt a shiver. He clenched his teeth at the thought of causing her discomfort, and focused on what needed to be done.

"One, two, three." He lifted her hips off the windowsill.

Brenda pushed back enough for him to wrap an arm around her waist and take her weight. Her behind was pressed against his chest. Her heel caught his leg.

"Sorry," she said.

The woman had worn heels to a break-in. She was a total, utter nut.

"Right, I've got you. I'm going to hold your weight up off the frame. You need to push back and angle your shoulders through. Don't worry about falling. I'll hold you. Just don't push back too hard. I'm standing on a chair and I don't want to topple." He also didn't want to lose his grip on her. If he did, her ribs would slam into the frame and she'd suffer bruising and pain.

"No problem. Soft backward push and a twist. I can do this."

He wasn't sure if she was talking to him or to herself again. Deke held on to the frame with one hand to balance them as he kept the other arm wrapped around her.

"You ready?" he said.

"Just psyching myself up."

Deke looked heavenwards and asked for patience.

"Right, I'm going to push." She suddenly barked out a laugh. "This is like Lamaze."

"Brenda. Focus."

"Right."

He watched her shoulders, knew when she was going to lever up, and braced. With him holding her weight, it wasn't a big deal getting out of the frame. She wriggled a bit and then slid back through. He felt the relief travel through her body. He wrapped both arms around her middle and looked up at her. She was grinning widely. It was like sunshine. For a second he lost track of the fact he was standing on a chair with Brenda balanced in his arms.

"Thanks." The word travelled through him, jolting him back to awareness.

"I'm going to lower you down slowly," he said gruffly.

She nodded and wrapped her fingers around his forearm. Deke slowly slid her down the length of his body to the floor. It was a twisted kind of agony, feeling the soft curves of Brenda's body against his taut muscle.

As soon as she got to her feet, he released her. She swayed

slightly before standing firm. Deke jumped off the chair, which meant he was standing close beside her. She barely reached his shoulder—even in her ridiculous heels.

"You're a star, Deke." She rubbed her stomach.

He watched the movement and frowned. "You okay?"

"Bruises, I think." She shrugged like it was nothing, which made his jaw tighten. She was no stranger to bruising, and he hated that.

She peeked up at him, large blue eyes through black lashes. "Is this the part where you make a citizen's arrest?"

Deke knew what he should do. He knew the right thing to do. The responsible thing. He also knew he wasn't going to do any of it.

"No."

Her grin was dazzling as she bounced on the spot. A little bundle of hyperactive glee.

"I'm not going to ask if you're sure, because I really don't want you to change your mind." She reached into the front pocket of her jeans and produced a scrap of paper. She handed it over to him. "This is the code for the alarm, so you can reset it."

Deke was seriously going to have a long talk with Dougal in the morning. Seemed like the whole of Invertary had the code to his alarm system. Brenda glanced around the toilet, sucking that bottom lip back into her mouth. Deke tried to look away, but it was just too much effort. She looked back up at him.

"You aren't going to undo the knitting protest, are you?"

"No." He had way better things to do with his time in the middle of the night than unravel the knitting mess the women had made. Things like sleeping. Or standing under a cold shower until he forgot the feeling of Brenda's body pressed against his.

"Great." She bounced again. "I should go, then." She pointed at the door.

"I have my car. I'll take you back." There was no way he was going to let her wander through town in the middle of the night alone, especially when he knew for a fact her ride had already left. He'd be having a word with Robin about that in the morning too.

"Oh, okay. Thanks." Brenda looked less than thrilled that she still had to endure his presence.

Deke tried to not let her obvious discomfort bother him as he grabbed the chair, put it back where he'd found it, set the alarm and locked the pub doors. With all the noise they'd been making, he half expected to find a crowd waiting for them outside the building. There was no one. Just the black, silent night and the lapping sound of the loch. They climbed into his old Land Rover and headed up the hill to the other side of town. Brenda sat beside him, her arms folded and her focus firmly on the passing scenery. He knew it must have been hard for her to be in a vehicle alone with him. All he could do was keep his distance and get them back to the spa as fast as he could.

It only took a few minutes before they were pulling into the driveway. Deke passed his house and drove straight to the manse. Robin had left the porch light on for Brenda, but there was no sign of her. Something Deke didn't like one bit. She should have been there, waiting, watching out for her friend.

Brenda opened her door, but turned back to face him. "Thanks, Deke. Really." Her face was soft and Deke wanted nothing more than to bury his nose in the crook of her neck and breathe her in.

Instead he nodded once, sharply. She turned to climb out of the car.

"Don't diet." His words came out low, surprising him as

well as Brenda. He knew she'd heard him because she froze. "You've got a great backside." Shit, he had no finesse whatsoever. There had to have been a better way to put that.

Slowly, Brenda turned back to him. Deke wished she wouldn't. He wished she'd get out and pretend he'd never opened his mouth.

"Deke—" she started, in little more than a whisper.

"Don't," he cut in. "That was over the line. Blame it on sleep deprivation." He bit the inside of his cheek to stop from telling her again that he was serious. She shouldn't do anything to take away from her curves. They were perfect.

He stared straight ahead, hoping she'd get the message and leave things be. Instead, he felt her move beside him. Deke stiffened when her hands curled around his forearm. When he looked her way, he found she'd twisted back around in her seat and was leaning into him.

They stared at each other for an eternity, the air in the car suddenly thick. Man, she was beautiful, with her heart-shaped face and ivory skin. As if in slow motion, her hand reached up to cup his cheek. Deke stopped breathing. He held her gaze as she closed the gap between them and then her lips were on his. Soft, full lips that gently teased at his mouth with sexy little kisses. Deke wanted to turn into her, clasp his hand in her hair and take the kiss deeper. Instead, he clenched his hands on the steering wheel and let Brenda kiss him. Her lips were satin smooth, and there was a delicious hint of strawberry. It was the most perfect kiss he'd ever had.

With one last brush of her lips against his, Brenda moved back. Her hand left his face and she looked up at him with a dark, heavy-lidded gaze. Deke watched her, afraid to say anything, afraid to move. In case he ruined everything. In case he scared her away.

Quietly, she turned and climbed out of the car. As she

went to close the door, she hesitated, then those killer eyes hit his.

"I liked your hands on me earlier, Deke. I liked it a lot."

He'd lost the ability to breathe.

"In fact," she said with a cheeky smile, "I wouldn't say no to having them on me again. Or your lips, for that matter."

Deke was stunned. Helpless to respond in any way. She wasn't freaked out? She wasn't scared? She'd liked him close? She wanted more? His head was reeling at the revelation.

With a coy little smile and a mischievous sparkle in her eye, Brenda shut the door and practically skipped up the drive to the house. Deke watched the door close behind her. He sat in his car for a long time, until he realised his fingers were still wrapped tightly around his steering wheel. He flexed his hands as he released his grip, and then he smiled.

A slow, wide smile.

CHAPTER 17

It was late morning before Mitch made it back to the hotel. Yet another morning run he'd skipped to be with her. He'd have to start running at night if he wanted to stay in shape, and he needed to stay in shape to deal with Jodie. He would have hung around and made her suffer through breakfast with him, but he figured she had made enough progress for one night. Plus, he was meeting the guys for their weekly breakfast.

When Mitch pushed through the door to the pub, he found the place in chaos. Dougal was behind the bar, his face red and his arms gesturing wildly. The Domino Boys were standing beside their usual barstools, which had strange knitted covers. The old men didn't look happy. Standing beside them was Matt Donaldson, dressed in full uniform and writing in his notepad. Mitch nodded hello as he headed for the booth they usually had breakfast in.

"What's going on?" Mitch slipped into the space beside Lake Benson.

It was Flynn Boyle, ex-footballer and current veterinary student who answered. "The pub was broken into last night."

"No kidding?" Mitch looked at Lake and noticed that both his friends were more amused than worried. "What'd they take?"

Flynn's grin was wide. "It wasn't what they took. It was what they left that's the problem." He pointed towards the knitting-covered barstools. "That's the least of it. They covered the men's room in wool. The urinals look like they've been knitted, and the doors to the stalls are blocked by woollen webs. Not only that, but Archie's favourite whisky bottle is now wearing a woolly hat and dress."

"It's not like he's going to drink at this time in the morning," Mitch pointed out.

"Missing the point," Flynn said. "That point being that there is knitting everywhere and there is only one knitting group in town that think they're a bunch of terrorists. To make matters worse, I recognise the knitting on Archie's stool. It was a blanket Aunty Heather was making for Katy."

Mitch's jaw dropped. "Matt's mom broke into the pub?"

"Aye." Flynn started laughing. "My cousin is going to have to arrest his mum for yarn bombing."

Josh arrived, pushing a pushchair with his two-year-old in it, as Flynn burst into hysterics. "What's yarn bombing? What did I miss?"

He parked the pram beside him, so that Jessica could grin at the table.

"It's when you cover something in knitting," Lake said, getting shocked looks from the rest of the men. He shrugged. "Kirsty's mother runs the damn group. Margaret said yarn bombing is either public art or subversive protest—depending on who does it."

"I'm guessing this was protest," Mitch said.

"Either that or they thought the urinals were feeling the cold." Flynn started laughing again.

Josh pushed into the booth beside him. "Jessica is joining

the breakfast club today." Josh unsnapped the harness for his toddler. He was wearing one of the Breakfast Club t-shirts he'd had made for everyone. He was the only one who ever wore it, much to his disappointment. "We're giving Caroline a break. She's tired again. Pregnancy sucks. Doesn't it, princess?"

"Sissa!" the monster shouted as she clapped her hands.

"Not sister, little brother." Josh was insistent he was having a son, even though he had no proof.

"Sissa!" she shouted, ignoring her dad.

"You tell him, princess." Mitch grinned at his goddaughter.

"Tunc Itch!" Jessica shouted.

"Uncle Mitch," Mitch corrected automatically, but grinned widely. "Hand her over. She needs to spend some quality time with a real man."

"Dumb ass," Josh muttered before lifting the toddler free and handing her to Mitch as though she were a football.

Jessica promptly smacked a chubby hand on either side of Mitch's face and smacked a kiss to his nose. "Tunc Itch!" she shouted again. "Tunc Itch pretty."

"Handsome," he corrected. "Uncle Mitch is the most handsome man in the world."

Josh scoffed. "Yeah, but her dad has been voted sexiest man alive three years running. Beat that, Tunc Itch."

Dougal bustled up to the table to take their order. From the fact his red face matched his red tartan waistcoat, you could tell he hadn't quite calmed down. "Sorry for the delay, boys." As usual, his voice was loud enough to be heard on the Shetland Isles.

"Heard you had some trouble," Mitch said. "I wasn't here last night. Did they disturb the hotel guests?"

Dougal's face was thunder. "They were stealthy. Someone picked the lock and then they turned off the alarm. Deke called this morning to tell me that Jean still had the code from when we were together."

"You haven't changed your alarm code for over three years?" As owner of Benson Security, Lake was clearly disgusted at Dougal's lack of security mindedness.

"Well, I didn't think anyone would use it for nefarious purposes," Dougal said.

"You and I are going to have a little chat about security," Lake said, and it sounded like a threat. "You need an upgrade. If the knitting group can get in, then anybody can get in."

"I don't need a system that's more complicated than this one," Dougal said. "I already struggle with the one we have. I work on the principle that if someone wants in then they're going to get in. Let's face it, lads. What's the worst anybody can do if they break in? It isn't like I'm keeping the crown jewels in here."

"You need to think about keeping your hotel guests secure," Lake pointed out.

Dougal's face paled. "Can you get me a quote on a new system by this afternoon?"

Lake nodded. "Remember, any system is just as good as the people using it. If you don't change the codes, or give them out to anybody who comes in here, the system won't work as it should."

"You aren't going to let that go, are you?" Dougal said with a sigh.

"Nope." Lake sipped his coffee.

Dougal took a deep breath, pulled out a notepad and eyed the rest of them. "Might as well get the orders in. At least the women didn't mess with the kitchen. Only the gents' toilet and the Domino Boys' regular spot. They did something to my stereo, too. It won't play any music. We're trying to fix it. Add to that, the fact I've got two of my waitresses in the toilet cutting wool off everything, when they should be out here taking orders and I am about two seconds away from losing my mind. I'm telling you lot right now—and you can pass it on to Kirsty's mother—they're banned from this pub."

Shock rippled through the group. It was rumoured in Invertary that you had to have started a zombie apocalypse to get banned from the Scottie Dog. Although there were those losers from the town meeting that Dougal had banned. Mitch eyed the owner thoughtfully and wondered if he was souring in his old age.

"Don't do something in haste that you'll regret later," Josh said.

"Aye," Flynn said. "There's a good chance they'll paint the building pink if you ban them."

"They wouldn't dare," Dougal boomed.

Flynn pointed to the corridor leading to the restroom, where two young women were heading for the rubbish bins with arms full of knitting.

"I get your point," Dougal said. "There's no telling what those maniacs will do. I'll think on it. But this was out of order. It wasn't me who decided to protest the sexist spa. I don't care if the men aren't allowed in it."

"So that's what this is about," Josh said.

"What did you think it was about?" Mitch said. "You thought they just had too much knitting and decided to redecorate for Dougal?"

Josh checked to see if his daughter was watching before he flipped Mitch off.

"Right." Dougal clearly had had enough. "What will it be?"

"Cooked breakfast," Josh said instantly.

"Not for you, laddie," Dougal said. "Your wife dropped off a list of foods you're allowed to eat. There's nothing fried on it."

Mitch and Flynn started to laugh loud and long, while

Lake actually broke out into a grin. Josh glared at them before turning back to Dougal.

"I think I can decide for myself what I can and can't eat. I'll have the fried breakfast."

Dougal shook his head as he smoothed a hand over his ample belly. "No can do. Caroline would kill me. You can have muesli, fruit and ice water. What do you three want?"

Josh opened and closed his mouth a couple of times before he pulled out his phone. "This is not on. She's gone too far this time."

The men lost interest in ordering food as they watched Josh take his life into his hands.

"Baby," he said once Caroline answered. "You can't go telling Dougal what I can and can't eat." A pause. "I know I have a concert tour coming up and need to look good on stage." Another pause. "Yeah, I know I need to be fit for it too. I work out. I eat healthy. Mostly." He took a deep breath. "No, I don't want to die before the kids turn ten."

Mitch started laughing again and Josh stamped on his toes.

"Listen, baby," Josh crooned. "It's only one breakfast." He turned away from the table. "I'll do another workout session to make up for it," he said, lowering his voice.

Even Lake started chuckling, while Flynn was laughing so hard he had tears running down his cheeks. Not wanting to be left out, Jessica clapped her hands loudly and whooped.

"Okay," Josh said on a sigh. "Love you too." With a look of utter dejection, he handed the phone to Dougal. "She wants to talk to you."

"You are so whipped," Mitch said.

Flynn mimed being pressed under a thumb. Josh mimed an altogether different gesture back at Flynn.

"Caroline," Dougal said. "How are you? How's the baby?"

He listened for a minute, then grinned at everyone. "Of course. No problem. You go rest now. Bye-bye."

He flicked the phone off and handed it back to Josh. His eyes were filled with glee, which made Mitch instantly suspicious.

"Caroline said that it isn't fair for Josh's friends to torture him when he has to get ready for his concerts," Dougal informed them.

"Maybe not fair," Mitch said. "But a whole lot of fun."

"She said," Dougal continued, "that I should consider the list applicable to anyone eating with Josh. She was sure you'd all want to support him, seeing as you're his friends." Dougal snatched the menus up off the table. "No need to order after all, boys. I'll have your muesli, fruit and ice water sent over when it's ready." With a laugh, he headed back to the bar.

"Ha!" Josh pointed at them. "See? It isn't so easy dealing with Caroline, is it? Maybe now you won't be so quick to take the piss."

"Piss!" Jessica shouted.

"Hell," Josh said.

"Hell!" Jessica shouted.

Flynn slapped a hand over Josh's mouth. "Quit before it gets worse."

"My turn." Lake motioned for Jessica. "Hand her over."

Mitch did as he was told. "Tunc Ake!" Jessica shouted with glee, but Mitch was pleased to see that Lake didn't rate a kiss.

Lake reached into his pocket, brought out his keys and handed them to the tot. He'd taken to adding tiny toys to the bundle so Jessica would be surprised each time she had them. When she saw the tiny dinosaur, she squealed with delight.

"Soft touch," Mitch mocked.

"Isn't it about time you had one of your own?" Josh pointed at his daughter, just in case there was any confusion as to what he meant. "You and Kirsty have been together three years. You're not getting any younger. Plus, I want lots of kids the same age as mine so they'll have playmates."

Mitch stared at his friend. "It's all about you."

"You know it."

"Kirsty can't have kids," Lake said without expression.

All humour died.

"Hell, sorry, man," Josh said.

Lake gave a slight shrug. "Don't worry about it. We're okay with it. We're going the adoption route."

"Good luck," Flynn said. "If there's anything we can do to help…"

"Yeah," Mitch said. "We have contacts and we can vouch for you during the vetting stage."

"Appreciated." Lake nodded, putting an end to the topic as Matt walked over to join the group. He pulled up a chair and sat at the end of the table.

"So," Flynn said, "you off to arrest your mum?"

"Not until I've had at least three coffees and half a bottle of scotch." Matt took off his hat and handed it to Jessica, who squealed with delight. "What the hell were they thinking?"

There was silence, as the group took Matt's question to be rhetorical.

"At least Jena wasn't with them," Matt said. "This seems to be only the core group."

"If Jena had been with them, the damage would have been way more extensive than a wool-covered toilet," Flynn said.

"No kidding." Matt had his hands full with his DIY-obsessed and utterly accident-prone wife. He looked at Mitch. "Did Jodie put the women up to this?"

"Nope," Mitch said. "She called me in and I talked to you. Her route was legal. This has nothing to do with her."

Flynn held up a hand. "Wait a minute. I'm missing something. Why would Mitch know what Jodie is thinking?"

Josh and Matt shared a knowing grin that made Mitch want to knock their heads together.

"Mitch and Jodie were all over each other outside the spa yesterday." Matt's big mouth was about to get smacked if he didn't shut up.

"Mitch fell in love at first sight," Josh said, making Mitch plot yet again for ways to get rid of his best friend. "But Jodie only wants to use him for his body."

"He had to blackmail her into a relationship." Matt gave Mitch a superior look. "If you have to force the woman to do more than sleep with you, you're wasting your time."

"Are you nuts?" Flynn was clearly outraged. "Why would you want to complicate what you have by asking for more? You have the perfect situation. What's not to be happy about? You get great sex and no relationship hassle."

Matt pointed his mug at Flynn. "I'm telling Abby you said that."

"You do that and I'll set the terrorist on you," Flynn said of his six-year-old adopted daughter. "Abby knows she's my world, her and the kids. But if she wasn't, I'd want what he has." He pointed at Mitch. "Why the hell are you whining? You've got it made. You get to have sex. I have twin baby girls who're up all night long, a six-year-old who's awake all day and a wife who's exhausted. There is no sex in our house. None. There may never be sex ever again. Which nobody told me could happen before I married the woman and knocked her up. Is it too early to start drinking?" He looked over at the bar as his cousin smacked him on the back of the head.

"Mitch wants what you've got," Josh said. "He wants marriage and babies. He's in love and he's clucky. Everyone around him is spawning and he wants in on the act. He's getting old. As we speak, his ovaries are shrivelling."

Mitch took a sip of his coffee while he told Josh what he

thought of him with a hand gesture—after he made sure his goddaughter wasn't watching, of course.

"I never said I wanted kids," Mitch said. "I just want Jodie."

"Mitch can have what I've got." Flynn thrust an arm under Mitch's nose. "Smell that? That's baby puke and breast milk. This is my life. Don't even get me started on nappies. I know what those kids eat and I still can't figure out what they poop. And the smell? It's worse than a locker full of guys after a match."

"It'll get better." As the proud father of a two-year-old, Josh was the self-appointed parenthood guru of Invertary. "Trust me. There will be sex again. Look at Caroline; she's five months into cooking Josh Junior. She didn't get in that condition by magic."

"Which is way off topic," Matt said to Josh before turning back to Mitch. "The topic being that Mitch here has the hots for a woman who doesn't want him. Anyone else seeing the irony here? What was it you said when I got together with Jena? Oh yeah: 'Love is jail time for men.'" He held up his coffee mug in a toast. "Here's to Mitch. May his incarceration be a long one."

"Ha ha, very funny, let's all laugh at Mitch." Mitch sat back in his chair, folded his arms and settled in for the long haul. Who knew how long it would take these idiots to get this out of their systems.

"That's a great idea, let's do that," Flynn said. "I remember what you said when I decided to marry Abby." Flynn affected an American accent. "'I stopped drinking the water in this town years ago. There's something in it that makes the men sign away their freedom and shackle themselves to the first woman who falls at their feet. Many women have tried to pin me down. I'm unpinnable.'"

"Pinbible!" Jessica shouted, just to remind them she was there.

"Absolutely right," Flynn told the toddler. "Mitch is totally pinnable." He held his hand up to Jessica for a high five, which she did before collapsing into giggles in Lake's arms.

"Assholes," Mitch muttered low enough so that Jessica couldn't repeat it.

"So, seriously," Matt said, "you and Jodie. Is this a real thing? Should we be planning a wedding?"

Yeah, he was still being mocked. Mitch smiled at his friends and then suddenly didn't find anything that funny anymore. He leaned forward and put his elbows on the table, his smile gone.

"You can joke all you like," he said. "But, yeah, one of these days there's gonna be a wedding." If he could break through the barriers his stubborn woman had erected and convince her to take a chance on him. If being the key word.

There was silence as his friends gaped at him. Who knew honesty would shut them all up?

"Well, crap," Flynn said at last. "That took the fun out of things."

Mitch sat back in his seat. His work was done.

As Dougal brought their order over, the sound system jolted to life and the Eurythmics' "Sisters Are Doin' It for Themselves" blasted out.

"I'm going to murder those women," Dougal said as he slapped their food down on the table.

CHAPTER 18

Jodie couldn't believe she was actually going through with this. Mitch had spent the afternoon harassing her into having a proper date night with him. Of course, he didn't want to book a restaurant in Fort William for their date—oh no, he wanted to have dinner in the pub, where the whole town could see them together. Jodie had asked him why he didn't just make her wear a sign around her neck saying Property of Mitch. He didn't think she was funny. Which was a good thing, because she didn't think anything about this was funny.

"Are we going in? Or are we going to stand out here all evening?" The blackmailing, bullying, annoying American was amusing himself. As usual.

"I'm working up to it." Jodie stared at the heavy wooden doors of the Scottie Dog pub and silently chanted, You can do this, you can do this…

Mitch leaned a shoulder against the building and put his hands into the pockets of his suit. The guy had about a million suits, all perfectly cut and form-flattering. If she hadn't seen him in jeans, she would have sworn he came out of the womb in a tiny mini-suit.

"I don't understand this," Mitch said. "You're the scariest woman I know, and yet you're freaking out about dinner in the pub."

"It isn't just dinner. It's show and tell with me as your bring-along."

Jodie looked down at her clothes. She felt overdressed for Invertary's only pub. She'd dug out one of the outfits she'd worn to celebrity dinners with her ex-husband the soccer star, and now she was regretting it. She should have worn jeans. Instead she had on wide-legged, mustard-coloured silk trousers, a black camisole with subtle lace inlay and ribbon straps, to-die-for black Manolo pumps and a chunky gold cuff bracelet. She'd worn her hair in a sleek, high ponytail and added large gold drop earrings to the mix. With her black clutch, she was ready for a night on the town—London town. Not Invertary town. What the hell had she been thinking?

"You look gorgeous," Mitch said as he pushed away from the wall. "Sexy." He sauntered the few steps between them and dipped to kiss her shoulder. "And hungry." He grinned at her. "Can we go in now?"

Jodie resisted the urge to kick him. She didn't want to damage her shoes. "You are going to pay for this."

"I know." He put a hand on the small of her back and practically pushed her towards the doors.

"I don't just mean financially."

"I know." He didn't sound worried about her threats.

As soon as they entered the pub, the room went quiet and every eye turned towards them. It wasn't any worse than the media events she'd attended with her ex-husband. Only that wasn't the life she lived anymore and she was out of practice at dealing with the attention. Mitch urged her forward again and Jodie suddenly had the urge to grab his arm, fake-panic and yell that she needed rescuing because she was being held hostage. A wicked grin broke out just at the thought.

"Whatever evil little scheme you're hatching, don't even think about it." Mitch's voice was a low rumble against her ear as they wended their way through the tables.

Now she really was tempted. To the point where she was becoming jittery just at the thought. She might have acted on her plan, but their corner booth came into view and her steps stuttered to a halt.

"I'm going to kill them," Mitch said.

When she glanced up at him, she saw his attention was on the bar at the far side of the room. She followed his gaze and saw Josh, Lake, Matt and Flynn grinning at them. They lifted their drinks in a silent toast. Jodie ignored the idiots and looked back at their table. Mitch's so-called friends had dressed up the booth for their date.

There was a black tablecloth decorated with red hearts. A large vase of red roses. Heart-shaped pillows on the bench seats. A bottle of cheap sparkling wine in an ice bucket. On the wall at the back of the booth, someone had stuck a lot of red paper heart cut-outs around a banner that read, Mitch and Jodie forever, in gold glitter. In Jodie's place setting was a tiny stuffed bear holding a chocolate heart. In Mitch's was a box of condoms.

Behind her, the pub, and especially the idiots at the bar, were waiting for her reaction. Jodie climbed into the booth, took the chocolate from the bear and gratefully ate it. She then gave a royal wave to the room. Because why the hell not? She was rewarded by a round of applause.

To her surprise, Mitch looked genuinely uncomfortable as he stood beside the table. "I can get us another booth," he said. "I'm sorry about this, baby."

Jodie felt a strange clenching in the region of her heart. "Sit down, Mitch. Let's get this over with."

She watched him relax at her harsh words. The guy was a masochist. The more she fought him and complained, the more fun he seemed to have.

As Mitch slid into his seat, Jodie reached for the condoms and grinned when she read the package. "They got you extra-small. Do you want me to go over there and put them right on the topic, or will you just whip out your penis later to compare with your buddies?"

Mitch cocked an eyebrow at her, but he was smiling while he did it.

Dougal came bustling up to the table, clearly amused.

"You waitressing again?" Mitch said. "I thought the war of the sexes ended with the yarn bombing."

Dougal sighed. "It isn't over. The Domino Boys are plotting something stupid. I know it's stupid because they stop talking whenever I get near them. Usually, they tell me their plans, so this one must really be daft. Anyway, I'm here because you're VIP guests."

"I can see that." Jodie looked around the booth.

Dougal winked at her. "Only the best for our Mitch." Then he told them the special—coq au vin and baby roast veg. Seeing as Jodie didn't want to prolong the evening by studying the menu, she ordered the special for both of them and Dougal bustled away to sort it out.

"Good job I wanted chicken," Mitch said drolly.

"At least you get what you want. I wanted a quiet evening at home, reading."

"Get over it."

Jodie glared at him and watched his eyes darken. Her anger totally made him hornier. She was dating a weirdo. No. Not dating. Not willingly, anyway. With a groan, she pushed all thoughts of their relationship out of her head. It was too hard to think about.

"Why are we here again?" she said. "If this is to prove to the town that we're in a relationship, then it's done now. We don't need to stay for food. You can go work and I'll go home."

"We're here because this is what couples do. They go out. They talk. They get to know each other. Suck it up. It's like you've never been in a relationship before. What did you do with your ex while you were dating?"

"I massaged his injuries and we had sex. Sometimes we ordered in Chinese."

Mitch stared at her for a beat. "That's it?"

"Serge wasn't much for going out."

"He never took you on a date?"

Jodie thought hard, but couldn't remember a date night before they'd been married. After they were married she'd been roped into going to the events Serge couldn't get out of, like the sportsperson of the year dinner, that sort of thing.

"It was hard for him," Jodie said. "He got mobbed wherever he went, and he had a stutter and an accent, which meant he didn't like to talk in public and he was more of a homebody." Or a gym body. Their house had been half home, half gym.

"Tell me how you two met again?" Mitch seemed mystified by the relationship.

"I worked as one of the sports masseuses for his soccer club. He wasn't like the other players. He was shy, quiet and a little bit intimidated around women. The celebrity side of the sport was hard for him, but he was a great player."

"If he was such a great guy, why did you two split up?"

There it was, the embarrassing sixty-thousand-dollar question. Jodie consciously ordered her muscles to relax. Mitch would have found out at some point. It wasn't exactly a secret; Flynn had been on the same team as her ex and knew why they'd split. Then there was the unfortunate tabloid article, where one of his friends had blabbed about him to the press.

"He divorced me because he said I emasculated him." There, it was out. She was not going to hold her breath and worry what Mitch thought about her marriage. She wasn't. Not. At. All.

The silence lasted long enough for Jodie to wonder what was going on. When she looked up at Mitch, she saw he was mad.

"He divorced you because he was intimidated by you?"

It took a minute for Jodie to realise he was angry on her behalf, not angry because she'd intimidated her ex. The realisation almost robbed her of speech, but Mitch was waiting for an answer, so she made the effort to get it together.

"It was more than that. He said he didn't want to be married to a woman who could take him in a fight. He said that I had no need for him, that I was perfectly capable of running my life and everybody around me without his help. He said that I was too aggressive in bed and that I was too opinionated out of it. He said he wanted a wife who was more feminine."

Mitch's eyes blazed. "That son of a bitch said way too much and all of it was bullshit." Mitch reached over the table to take her hand. "If you were too strong for him, then all that means was he was too weak for you. There is nothing wrong with you, baby. Nothing."

In that moment, if they'd been alone, Jodie would have totally thrown herself at him. Apart from her brother and her mum, no one had ever said anything like that to her before and from the look on Mitch's face, he meant every word. But Jodie had been fooled by sweet talk before.

"You say that now, but experience has taught me different. In the beginning, guys think I'm a novelty. As time wears on, they see me as a threat to their manhood. That's usually the part where they run off and find a woman who crochets doilies and bakes cupcakes. Not that there's anything wrong with that. If a sister wants to do any of those things, good on her. It's just that, in my experience, men tend to prefer those types of women to, well, my type." There. It was out. The big, ugly truth. She might be girly, but she wasn't a damsel in distress who needed a big, strong man to rescue her. Truth be told, if any rescuing was needed, she'd probably be the one to do it, and men, generally, didn't like that one bit.

"Morons," Mitch growled, and his hold tightened on her hand. "I love that you're smart and capable and could kick my ass in a fight. I even love that you're slightly evil. It makes for an interesting time of it. Don't let the losers get you down. For the record, I am nothing like your asshole ex. My self-esteem is not reliant on you crocheting doilies. Whatever the hell those are."

Jodie couldn't help the laugh that bubbled out of her. Her stupid heart wanted to believe every word he said. An emotion she hadn't felt for so long that it took time to recognise, bubbled through her. It was hope.

Suddenly choked up, she had to clear her throat to talk. "Good to know."

"I need to talk to you," someone said, breaking the moment she was having with Mitch.

Jodie looked up to find Betty standing beside their table. Mitch released her hand, sat back and folded his arms as he stared at Betty in bewilderment. Jodie wasn't far behind. The old woman's head was blue. Not just the wispy white hair that was more threadbare than anything else, but her actual scalp. It looked like she was wearing a luminous blue swimming cap.

"What happened to your head?" Jodie said when she'd found her voice again.

Betty patted her thin hair like a beauty queen fluffing her do. "Brilliant, isn't it? That's what I need to talk to you about. The waxing thing is a non-starter. The men in this town are too damn scared to sign up. Bunch of whiny wee bairns. I need to branch out and add to my skillset. I thought I'd be your hair dye person."

Jodie opened and shut her mouth a couple of times, but no words came out. Mainly she was stunned into silence by Betty's blue head.

"I noticed you didn't have a dye person," Betty said. "I've filled the gap. No need to thank me." She rummaged around in the deep pocket of her tartan mu-mu and came out with a tatty piece of paper. She put it on the table in front of Jodie. "That's what I expect to be paid."

Jodie ignored the paper, her focus still on Betty's head. "There is no way in hell I'm going to let you near my customers with a bottle of dye, nor will my customers."

Betty's eyes narrowed. "Why bloody not?"

"Seriously? You look like you dipped your head in a bucket of paint."

Betty put her hands on her hips. "This is all the rage. I looked it up on the interweb. You need to get with the times, lassie."

"You need to get some serious psychiatric help. You look like you're turning into a Smurf. Grumpy Smurf. That's what I'm calling you from now on. You are not dyeing hair in my spa. Never. Ever. Not going to happen."

Betty's eyes narrowed more, to the point where they were almost obliterated by her eyebrows. "Are you sure you want to take me on in a fight, lassie?"

"Bring it on, old woman. Just remember that whatever you do, I'll do to you one hundred times over. You should know by now that you don't intimidate me. Plus, unlike the other people you pick on, I don't mind crossing all sorts of lines to get even. Think about that for a minute. If you can still think with all that dye seeping into your brain."

There was a glare-off as the two women stared at each other. At last, Betty let out a snort of anger.

"Fine. No dyeing hair, but you need to find me something else to do. This waxing job is boring my knickers off." With that, she stomped away.

Jodie sat back in her chair and shook her head at the ceiling. Why me?

Suddenly a big hand cupped the back of Jodie's head and pulled her forward. Then Mitch's lips were on hers. The kiss was deep and passionate. When his lips left hers, she was breathing hard.

"That was fucking sexy," he said as he stared into his eyes.

Mitch sat back on his seat as Dougal came up to the table. Jodie felt a little stunned. Dougal put their meals in front of them.

"Dinner's on the house," he said. "Can't remember the last time someone scared Betty off. I think it was in the fifties."

"What are you talking about?" Jodie said. "Lake sorts her out all the time."

"Lake contains her," Dougal said. "But he never takes her on in a fight. Never." He patted Jodie on the head, like she was a puppy. "You are a wonder. Just don't turn to the dark side, lassie. We've already got Betty for that."

Jodie eyed the room of grinning faces and one or two people gave her a thumbs-up.

"This town is nuts," Jodie muttered and tucked into her food.

CHAPTER 19

Brenda shuffled from foot to foot on the path outside Deke's small house. She knew from talking to Jodie that it used to be a garage, but they'd had it converted to a tiny house. If Brenda had been in charge of the conversion, the end result would have looked like something out of a fairy tale, with climbing roses and singing birds. Deke had gone for a more modern, and realistic, approach. One entire wall of his house was made up of smoky glass, and a steel frame cube had been added to the back as a conservatory. The result was a glorious mix of Victorian carriage house and industrial workspace. Somehow, it fit perfectly together.

But the design of the place wasn't what was held her attention. No, her attention was firmly focused on the blazing lights inside the house and Deke's shadowy form as he wandered around the place. Unlike the other night, Deke had shut the blinds and there was no perving over his body for Brenda. Probably a good thing. Brenda's heart was racing enough without adding to its stress.

She glanced at the time on her phone. It was ten o'clock.

Too late to visit, but it had taken her this long to work up the courage. Brenda adjusted the wicker basket as her hands began to get clammy. She was here. She might as well knock on the door. What was the worst that could happen? Scratch that. The worst was her going down in a fiery ball of humiliation and shame. It wasn't a good idea to think about the worst. No, it was better to spend her time thinking about that wonderful kiss they'd shared. Surely he would want more of that. She knew she did.

With a deep breath, Brenda forced her legs to walk the last few steps to the door. Her hand knocked before she gave herself a chance to change her mind. It then took all of her self-control to stop from running like the coward she was before he opened the door. She was on the verge of diving for the bushes when the lock clicked and the door swung open, revealing a decidedly surprised Deke.

"Brenda." He took a step towards her, still with one hand high on the door. His eyes scanned the area behind her. "What's wrong?"

"Nothing," she said hurriedly. She held out the basket, aware that her hands weren't anywhere near steady. "I brought a thank you gift, for not turning me into the police last night."

Oh how she hoped her smile covered the fact her knees were knocking and she'd broken out in an icy-cold sweat.

His eyes flicked to the basket before returning to her face. "You brought me a thank you gift? At ten o'clock?"

"Is it past your bedtime? I hear the older you get, the earlier you go to sleep."

"No, it isn't past my bedtime, but it's a bit late to be dropping off a thank you gift."

"Surprise?" She gave him what she hoped was a sunny, and in no way insane, smile.

He wasn't reassured. Mainly he looked confused. He was

so cute when he was confused. But then, he was seriously cute all the time. Brenda especially liked the little frown he got when he was concentrating on a recipe he was working on. It made her want to jump into his arms, wrap her legs around his hips and kiss away the lines between his brows. Then she would lie back on the kitchen counter while he spoon-fed her whatever he was concocting. It would be a sensual tasting, one where he'd soon get fed up with the spoon and use his fingertips to paint her lips with the sauce from the pan...

"Brenda!" The word snapped her back to the present, where she was currently standing outside her hunky boss's door, staring at him with stars in her eyes.

"Yes?" she said, although she was wondering if he was technically her boss, as he ran the restaurant and she worked solely in the spa.

"You didn't hear a word I said, did you?" He looked so exasperated that she wondered how long he'd been talking.

"Uh..." Brenda knew there was probably something clever she could say, but for the life of her there was nothing forthcoming. At last she remembered the basket in her hand. She held it out to him. "Here you go. For you. Thank you for not sending me to jail."

With a slow shake of his head, he took the basket from her hand. It looked small and girly in his grasp. Or maybe it was that he looked even bigger and manlier. She wasn't sure. Maybe it was the shoulders or the well-rounded biceps that made everything seem smaller. His arms were huge. Brenda wondered if it would take both of her hands to circle one of them.

"Massage oil?" The incredulous question snapped her attention back to his face. His eyebrows went up. "You brought me massage oil?"

"I'm a massage therapist. It's not like I'd bake you cookies or cook you a meal to say thank you. You're a chef, for one thing, and my cooking is awful, for another. No, I had to stick with what I know best." She tried hard not to let herself get lightheaded at the thought of what she wanted to do. "I thought I'd give you a thank you massage."

"A massage?" He looked between her and the basket in his hand. "You want to massage me? As a thank you?"

"Yes." She didn't understand why he was struggling with the concept. She was a massage therapist. Massaging was what she did.

Deke just stared at her until Brenda began to shuffle on the spot.

"It's a bad time, isn't it?" Brenda said when things passed the point of awkward. "I'll come back tomorrow." She paused when his expression remained unfathomable. "Or not. I don't need to come back at all. Ever. Maybe I should get you tickets to a football match as a thank you instead? That's more a guy thing. Right?" Still nothing. Brenda swung her arms. "Well, all right, then. Enjoy the rest of your evening."

She'd turned, ready to run, when a large hand clamped on her arm and she was dragged into Deke's house. Brenda wasn't proud of the little squeak of surprise she made. As soon as the noise came out of her mouth, Deke dropped his grip and was standing several feet away—still clutching the basket.

"Hell." He looked torn up about something. "I shouldn't have grabbed you like that. I didn't mean to scare you." He muttered some more and took another step away from her.

That's when the pieces clicked into place. Her past wasn't just the elephant in the room—it was a huge, invisible wall between them. One she intended to take a sledgehammer to straight away.

"You didn't scare me." Brenda stepped further into his living room. Although every curious bone in her body wanted to snoop through his house, she kept her eyes on Deke. He was totally beating himself up about pulling her into his house. Brenda took a step towards him. "I met one bad guy. I know he isn't like all guys. Trust me when I say he was nothing like you. If you buy a punnet of strawberries and one is bad, do you throw the rest away? No, you don't."

A little muscle in his jaw throbbed. "We aren't talking about strawberries. I'm a whole lot bigger and deadlier than a small red fruit. No one gets through what you've been through without having issues they need to deal with."

"You mean I couldn't possibly be over it and I must be terrified of all men and therefore should be treated as though I'm made of spun glass?"

The poor guy was struggling hard not to agree with her. "I know you don't get over that sort of thing."

That brought her up short. She stared into his shuttered expression. Had he been abused?

"Who hurt you?" She couldn't even imagine someone hurting Deke. Everything about him was powerful. From his fantastically overdeveloped chest muscles, to the strength in his arms, to the easy way he handled himself. He had the loose fluidity of a man who knew his abilities and had confidence in them.

"Not me. My dad beat my mum. We grew up in refuges, running every time he found us."

Brenda's heart stilled, but she didn't offer any sympathy. She knew how that felt.

"I hope you met some good people along the way. I know I have."

He frowned, clearly confused. "Aren't you going to run now that you know I was spawned by a wife beater?"

She couldn't help it—she burst out laughing. What an idiot. If your parents were the fate you had to look forward to, then Brenda should have been married with three kids by three different fathers by now.

"What's so funny?"

"Personality and morality aren't in the genes. Being predisposed to heart disease or breast cancer is. Life choices come from who you are, not who your parents were. You're no more your dad than I am my mum, and we can thank God loudly for that. Now, do you want a massage or not?"

The poor man blinked at her, stunned into silence.

"We can do it on the bed," Brenda said and she could have sworn she heard a muffled moan. "Or we can put towels on your table and you can lie on there." She eyed the piece of furniture. "Maybe the bed would be better. That table is pretty wide. I'm not sure I could reach you properly without climbing on top of you." She fluttered her eyelashes at him. "If you don't want me in your bedroom, you could open the spa and we'll use my treatment room."

Deke seemed frozen to the spot. He blinked a couple of times, then the tip of his tongue flicked out to wet his lip. "I'm not sure we should do this."

"You mean have a massage at all?"

"Aye. I'm not sure it's a good idea."

Brenda studied him for a moment, trying hard to read his mind. Nope. It didn't work. She still didn't have a clue what was going on in there. And then it hit her. The only possible reason for his adamant refusal of her gift.

"Are you worried that I'll get you naked and take advantage of you?" She pushed back her shoulders. "I'll have you know, I'm a professional and I would never do that." She paused, thinking about it. "Unless you wanted me to."

Deke actually paled. She'd either terrified the poor man, or…

It was Brenda's turn to pale. She backed towards the door. "Oh my goodness. I'm so sorry, Deke. I'll just go."

She was fumbling with the door handle when a heavy hand rested gently on her shoulder.

"Please tell me you don't think I'm into guys?" Deke said softly.

"No!" Brenda looked over her shoulder at him. She swallowed hard and took grip of her courage with both hands. "I, um, you, um." She took a deep breath. She could do this. She was brave. Mostly. "It occurred to me that maybe you weren't attracted to me and wouldn't want me joking about touching you."

He groaned. It sounded pained. There was a thud as the basket hit the floor. Brenda jerked slightly and bent to look into it, to make sure the oil bottle hadn't broken.

She looked back up at Deke. "You need to be careful with that stuff. It's a bandit to clean up."

"Brenda." He reached out and held her hand in his. She could see him struggling with something, and inwardly winced. Here it came. The brush-off. She'd been too pushy. Again.

"It's okay." She held up a hand. "I'm going to go. Football tickets are obviously the way forward." She plastered her best fake smile to her face.

"Brenda." He tugged her a step closer. His hand came up to cup her cheek, and she stopped breathing entirely. In fact, if he didn't say something soon, she would probably pass out. Knowing her, she would land face first and he'd get to stare at her huge backside again. "I've lost you again, haven't I?"

She blinked at him and he slowly came back into focus. "Did you say something?" She had to stop doing that. She was missing conversations with real live people because she was too busy having imaginary ones with herself.

"I said, I do find you attractive." His smile was tiny, intimate, soft. She loved it.

Her heart started hammering as she focused intently on him, worried she might miss something else important.

"There you are," he whispered. "I'm worried I'll scare you. I don't want to do that."

"You won't." The words rushed out and that was humiliating. Unfortunately, there was no way to save the situation and come across as less eager. All she could do was press on. "You aren't your father. You aren't my ex. You're Deke. The guy who works on new recipes all the time, the owner of a restaurant that's going to be great when it opens and the guy who poured all his money into a business that doubles as a safe haven for women like me." She wet her suddenly dry lips. "You're a superhero."

"I'm just a guy."

She totally disagreed, but she let that slide. Maybe she'd make him a cape. Oooh, maybe she could talk him into dressing up as Superman and she could be Lois Lane. Role play. Oh, yeah, she could do that.

"And you're gone again," he said with amusement.

Brenda blinked at him until her breath hitched. "You're attracted to me." She couldn't hide the slow, smug smile that broke out.

"Aye." He ran a thumb softly over her lower lip.

"Does that mean there's going to be sex in my future? Because, I have to tell you, I'm a bundle of pent-up need." Yeah, she probably shouldn't have said that either. Oh well.

Deke's head dropped and he muttered something before looking back up at her. "What am I going to do with you?"

"Oh!" She thrust a hand up in the air, as though she was in school. "I know the answer to this one. Pick me. Pick me."

"Lunatic."

She would have told him her Superman idea, but his focus was on her lips, and the heat in his eyes made her wobble. Slowly, he lowered his mouth to hers. He hadn't even kissed her yet and already she felt lightheaded. Her eyelids grew heavy. She could already feel his warmth seeping into her and knew this would be the best kiss of her life.

Or it would have been, if the spa alarm hadn't gone off right at that moment.

CHAPTER 20

Jodie was sound asleep, curled into Mitch, when his phone went off. They'd headed up to his room after dinner, and he'd been proud of the fact he'd managed to exhaust her so quickly. She stirred as Mitch reached to the table beside her to grab the offending object. It was almost eleven, and whoever was calling better have a great reason to pull him away from lying in bed with Jodie in his arms.

"What?" he barked into the phone as Jodie put a palm in the middle of his chest and pushed herself up.

She looked sleep-dazed and slightly confused as to where she was and how she'd gotten there.

"Is Jodie with you?" It was Deke.

Mitch went instantly alert. "Yeah."

Deke's relief was evident. "The alarm in the spa has gone off. I'm there now. Someone has trashed the place."

Mitch sat up, taking Jodie with him, curling her into his side. "Her apartment?" He felt her tense in his hold.

"That's worse. Lake said she forgot to set the alarm in her flat. They must have trashed that first. We only knew they were there when the spa alarm went off. Lake came out straight away. Matt arrived soon after."

"We're on our way." Mitch ended the call with a stab of his thumb.

"What?" Jodie was looking up at him, all wide, dark eyes and sleep-softened skin.

"The spa has been vandalised." He paused. "Your apartment, too."

She didn't say a word. The fury and fear at war in her face said it all for her. In a heartbeat, she was out of bed and searching the floor for her clothes. Mitch jumped up, quickly pulling on a pair of faded jeans and a t-shirt. Shoes on and he was ready to go as Jodie came out of his bathroom.

"It's probably the same yobs who graffiti-ed the building," she said, but she sounded more hopeful than certain. "They did try to break in the other night." She looked up at him. "It has to be them, right?"

"I don't know, baby, but we'll find out."

Mitch grabbed her hand and held tight, in case she pulled away, but she didn't. He needed to touch her. He hated that she lived in a world where she hoped an attack was an act of senseless vandalism rather than the alternative—a guy who'd found the women she was trying to shelter.

The drive to the spa was short. When they got there they spotted Matt's police car, along with Lake's SUV and another two cars—one emblazoned with the Benson Security logo.

Jodie was out of Mitch's car before he'd even pulled on the handbrake. She rushed over to Matt. "Did you catch anyone?"

Mitch came up beside her and put a hand on the small of her back as a gentle reminder that she wasn't alone. Jodie didn't need him taking over—she probably didn't even need his support, but he was giving it anyway.

"They were long gone by the time Grunt got here." Matt

inclined his head towards the Benson Security vehicle. "Lake and I did a sweep of the area. There was nothing."

Deke came up beside them, Brenda at his side. "I saw the tail end of a car when I ran out at the sound of the alarm," he said. "No plates."

"No plates, as in you couldn't see them, or as in they weren't there?" Mitch asked.

"They weren't there." Deke's closed face said everything. It was a whole other level of forethought to remove the plates from a vehicle before you broke into a place.

"The women?" Jodie asked her brother.

"Everyone's good." Deke held her eyes. "The vandals didn't go near the manse."

Mitch felt Jodie relax under his touch.

"You forgot to set the alarm for your apartment again, Jo," Deke said.

And Jodie was instantly tense again. Mitch could have thumped her brother.

"There's more." Lake stood beside Matt, his arms folded over his black sweater. "Grunt checked the alarm system on the spa. They tried to bypass it and they would have managed if it had been a standard system."

Mitch felt his stomach clench. "Experience?"

Lake nodded, shattering any hope Jodie may have been holding that it was a couple of amateurs from town who were taking the protest too far.

"They take anything?" Jodie asked her brother.

"Not that I can tell. They only got as far as the reception area of the spa. The computer is trashed, the desk cracked, plant pots smashed. The damage one or two people could do in a couple of minutes." Deke looked pained. "Your flat, though…"

Mitch took a step closer to Jodie and gently rubbed her back. He felt the shiver go through her, although there was no visible sign that she wasn't taking everything incredibly well.

"They would have had more time in my flat. I need to go look."

"What we need to do," Matt said, "is sit down and have a long talk. You two have been holding out on us."

A look passed between Deke and Jodie as Brenda visibly paled. Jodie nodded then turned to Matt. "Let me have a look at the damage, then we can talk."

"Brenda and I will make coffee," Deke said. "Meet at my place when you're done here." He headed in the direction of his house with Brenda close to his side.

Mitch followed Jodie. His jaw clenched when he saw that the door to her apartment had been kicked in and was hanging askew on its hinges. Jodie didn't say a word, just climbed the stairs to her home. The damage was worse than Mitch had expected. Everything that could be smashed was smashed. The floor of the open plan living, dining and kitchen area was covered in broken ceramic and glass. The table had been upturned. The wooden chairs broken. The walls had gouges in them. The glass doors to the patio had been shattered. And the smell—one look at the overstuffed sofas made it clear that someone had urinated all over them.

Jodie stood in the middle of the room, her lips thin and her face white. Her body was stiff as she checked through the rest of the apartment. Mitch followed, finding more of the same. All of her bottles emptied in the bathroom, mirror broken, sink pulled away from the wall. In the bedroom, her clothes had been shredded and there was evidence of defecation on the bed. Mitch could tell by the stiff way Jodie held herself that she'd seen more than enough. He gently took her hand and led her out of the apartment. It was clear she was in shock when she didn't object to him leading the way.

They found Grunt waiting at the bottom of the stairs. The man mountain's face softened when he looked at Jodie.

"You want me to take care of it?" he said.

Jodie stared at him for a moment. Mitch hated the blank look in her eyes. Grunt pointed up the stairs.

"Want me to clear it out?"

Jodie swallowed hard. Her shoulders straightened and she dropped Mitch's hand. There she was—the shock was passing.

"I'd appreciate it," she said.

"You want to keep anything?" Grunt used the same tone with Jodie that he reserved for his wife—as though she was made of priceless porcelain.

"Only if it clearly hasn't been touched." Her jaw clenched before she spoke again. "High in the closet, there's a box. Mementos, photos, that sort of thing. If it hasn't been touched, I'd like to keep it. Can you get someone to retrieve what's left of my hard drive? Most of my stuff is stored in the cloud, but there are still photos on the drive I'd like to save."

"No problem." Grunt stepped to the side to let them pass, pulling his phone out of his back pocket as he did so. The conversation was clearly over.

Mitch followed Jodie through the darkness to the converted carriage house. Before they went inside, Jodie turned to him, her expression pained.

"I can't live there now," she said softly, as though ashamed. "Does that make me weak?"

"Baby." Mitch pulled her into his embrace. "It's just a house. If it has memories you don't want to have, you move. It isn't about being weak or being strong. It's about making decisions that suit you. You live there or you don't; doesn't matter. You'll never be weak. You're the strongest woman I've ever met. Do what you feel is best, and stuff what anyone else thinks of it."

He felt her relax against him briefly before she nodded and stepped back. Her eyes were blazing. "Let's get this over with."

With that, Mitch followed his woman into Deke's tiny house.

"You knew about this?" Matt said to Mitch.

The town's only police presence was clearly annoyed that Mitch had known about the refuge and hadn't shared the information. Mitch didn't seem bothered by the cop's threatening tone. He lazed back in his steel-framed chair at Deke's glass-topped kitchen table and sipped his coffee. No one seemed to care that the coffee would keep them up for the rest of the night. Although Jodie knew most of them wouldn't get any sleep anyway.

"Yeah, I knew." Mitch sounded unrepentant.

Matt seemed to be grinding his teeth. He looked at Lake. "Did you know?"

Lake shook his head. He was leaning against Deke's granite-topped kitchen island. "I was digging. I'd found some threads and was ready to tug them, then this happened." He gave Jodie and Deke what looked like a look of admiration. "Not sure I would have found what I was looking for, though. This network is buried deep."

They'd just finished telling Matt, Grunt and Lake about the refuge, the network and the backgrounds of their staff. It wasn't something Jodie was comfortable doing, but Deke had taken her aside as soon as she'd walked into his house and told her they had to come clean. The break-in and the damage weren't caused by some random thugs out to amuse themselves. The person, or people, who'd done it knew what they were doing. To protect the women, they needed help. Which meant they had to trust Benson Security and the local cop. Jodie didn't like that one bit. She'd been somewhat reassured when she'd insisted that everything they shared remain completely off the record and Matt had reluctantly agreed. The local cop might know the truth, but at least Jodie was assured there wouldn't be a paper trail.

"You should have told us." Matt's anger was clear, but restrained. "Something like this, the town needs to know. We need to be able to pull together and protect you."

"Did you hear the part about how one of the women was running from her cop husband?" Jodie's own anger was building, and Matt was beginning to look like a good outlet for it.

"Fiona isn't here anymore," Matt said. "That's no excuse."

"I don't need an excuse," Jodie snapped. "These guys find people. We couldn't take the chance of leaving a trail. This network is the last resort for these women. Before they become part of it, they have already been found by their partners, sometimes several times, and none of it was good. We couldn't take the risk of information on their whereabouts leaking out."

Matt clearly didn't like what she said, but didn't argue. He couldn't argue with fact.

"What you're saying," Lake said, "is that this break-in could be related to any one of the women here?"

Jodie's gaze flicked over to Brenda, who was sitting on the sofa at her brother's side.

"There's been some trouble in London," Jodie said. "The

Hampstead Heath drop-in centre was broken into." She said to Brenda, "One of the volunteers was beaten and is in hospital."

Brenda jumped to her feet. "I need to pack." She started running for the door, and got three steps before Deke wrapped an arm around her waist and put her back in her seat.

"No," he said.

Brenda instantly jumped back up. "I have to go. I have to run. Nobody is safe with me here. Nobody."

"Damn it, Brenda." Deke scooped her up again, and this time he sat back down with Brenda in his lap and his arms tight around her.

"I need to leave," Brenda practically wailed. "You're all in danger. You need to let me leave. You don't know what Clive is capable of. You don't know how dangerous he is. He has connections, powerful people who help him get away with everything he does."

Deke held her tight, one arm wrapped around her waist, his bicep bulging with the effort. His other hand gently cupped her face. Looking into Brenda's eyes, Deke said, "No running. This is it. You stay here where I can protect you. This is your last stand." His voice was soft, but vibrated with determination.

"Last stand?" Brenda's voice, on the other hand, was hysterical. "Like Custard? That did not go well for him. I need to run."

Grunt barked out a laugh. "Custer. Not Custard." The whole of his mammoth body shook with silent laughter.

Brenda frowned at him. "To hell with American history. This is more like William Wallace, anyway. He made a last stand too, and it did not end well. Mel Gibson died. Gruesomely."

Jodie shook her head at the sight of the men in the room trying not to laugh. Idiots.

"You're done running. Look around you," Deke said. "You've got an army at your back this time. You're safe here."

Brenda looked around. "I count six people. That is not an army." She pushed at him again, struggling to get free.

"My men will step in," Lake said.

Jodie's head jerked back at his words. "We can't afford that."

Lake's eyes were flat. "I didn't say we'd charge you anything."

"We can't let you—" Jodie started.

"Yes," Deke interrupted. "We can. We will." He looked at Lake. "Thanks."

Lake gave him a manly chin lift. "Are we sure this guy is after Brenda?"

Brenda's shoulders slumped as her eyes turned glassy. "I spent months being sheltered by the Hampstead Heath centre while I recovered enough to run. None of the other women who are here had anything to do with that particular refuge."

"Still, it's a bit of a jump to go from an attack in London to vandalism in the Highlands," Matt said. "We can't jump to conclusions. One might have nothing to do with the other."

"When you're running," Brenda said, "you learn to trust your instincts, and if they say jump, you jump."

"Were you a masseuse while you were with this guy?" Matt asked, which was totally out of left field, yet the strangeness of it seemed to comfort Brenda.

"I did my training while we were married."

Matt glanced over at Lake. "Maybe it's as simple as the guy checking spas, then once he finds one he thinks might be harbouring her, he comes in and does a search. Or in this case, a trashing."

"That's still a lot of ground to cover," Lake said. "There are a lot of spas in the UK."

"Which leaves us with the fact that there's no connection between the break-in at Hampstead Heath and the damage here," Matt said wearily.

"What about new faces in town? Can't you check out guys we haven't seen around here before?" Jodie said. Invertary was small. Everybody knew each other and strangers stood out.

"There's a fishing tournament going on. The town is full of guys I don't know," Matt said. "I will bring in Rab and his mates again and hold them as long as I can. They had an alibi for the break-in the other night, but it was a flimsy one. With any luck, this is just them at it again and this time I'll be able to lock them up for a good, long time." Matt ran a hand through his thick black hair, making it stand on end. "I don't think this was Rab, though. This kind of act is usually personal, Jodie. The damage they did to your home shows a rage against you. This feels like a personal attack."

Jodie glanced at Mitch. An action that stunned her even as she was doing it, but the small smile Mitch gave her fortified her.

"I don't have any personal enemies," she told Matt.

"What about your ex-husband?"

Jodie burst out laughing.

"Sorry," she said. "There's no way Serge would have done this. He might look tough on the football field, but he's nothing like that off it. Plus, he doesn't like getting dirty when he isn't playing. He'd never make a mess like that."

"Was the divorce acrimonious?" Matt asked.

"No," Jodie said. "He told me he needed a real woman and I left. There was no fighting. In fact, he seemed remorseful and was generous in the divorce settlement." She waved a hand to indicate the property. "It was his money that paid for all this."

Matt was like a dog with a bone. "Then maybe he resents what you're doing with the money."

"Oh yeah, he's totally eaten up by his resentment as he lounges around in the Bahamas with his new pregnant wife —a former Victoria's Secret model." She hoped she didn't sound bitter, because she really wasn't. She was happy for him, plus she'd never wanted kids anyway. Yet another thing they hadn't had in common.

"I'll look into him anyway," Matt said.

"It's your time you're wasting," Jodie said. "But this isn't my ex. It's someone else. The only trouble we've had locally is from the men protesting and the graffiti artists. And the only trouble the organisation has had is at the Hampstead Heath drop-in centre. The attack on my flat may seem like it's directed at me, but whoever did it may have thought one of the other women lived there."

"Because we did." Brenda jerked upright on Deke's lap. "The other women and I stayed with Jodie until last week." Her eyes were wide. "It has to be Clive. He's found me."

Matt looked like he could use a vat of coffee to get him through their conversation. "The woman who was attacked —what kind of information would she know? What would she have been able to tell her attacker?"

Jodie cast a glance at Brenda, who looked ready to bolt. "The woman who was attacked is Susan Prentice."

"I have to leave." Brenda sounded borderline hysterical. "Susan was my support person. This isn't a coincidence. This is Clive."

"Bren," Deke said as he cupped her jaw again. "Is Clive bigger than me? Is he combat trained?"

She looked confused. "No."

"That's what I thought. He's a bully. He attacks you

because you're smaller and he's sick in the head. No matter how much rage this guy has, or how twisted his thinking, he won't get through me to get to you. That's a promise, Bren. He won't get through me to get to you."

There was silence as everyone watched hope blossom in Brenda's face. Suddenly, she burst into tears, and Deke tucked her face into the crook of his neck and held her tight. He rubbed her back soothingly as he whispered into her ear. Brenda's sobs could be heard, muffled against his chest. It was hard to watch.

Jodie turned away to give the couple privacy. Her eyes hit Mitch and the intensity in his gaze robbed her of breath. She knew, in that moment, that Mitch Harris would stand in front of her if she needed it. Jodie felt as though the ground beneath her feet shifted. Her whole life, it'd been just her and Deke. And when Deke was in the Army, it'd been her, alone. She was perfectly capable of taking care of herself, so much so that people assumed she never needed anyone or anything. To have Mitch see past that, to have him sit there, supporting her yet not taking over from her, and see in his eyes that he would stand in front of her—it was a gift beyond compare.

"Who's Susan Prentice?" Matt said, breaking her connection with Mitch.

Jodie turned her attention back to Matt. "She's been there for years. She runs the centre."

"She was the one who helped me the most," Brenda said in a choked-up voice, "after Clive."

"Susan is a strong woman, sweetie," Jodie said. "She'll make it through this."

Jodie hoped she was right. The older woman had been an inspiration to her during her time teaching at the centre. But there was only so much a body could handle and the fact she was still unconscious wasn't a good sign.

"We need details on this Clive guy," Matt said.

Jodie opened her mouth to protest the police running a search that would set off all sorts of flags.

"Give me the info," Lake said. "I'll do the digging under the radar."

Jodie nodded, relieved.

"I'm going to need background on all the women, to cover bases," Lake continued. "I'll station a man at the manse, twenty-four-seven, until we know what's happening."

"I'm here," Deke said. "You don't need to station another guy."

"The restaurant opens soon. You have your hands full. Another pair of eyes will help."

Deke inclined his head in acceptance as he continued to soothe Brenda.

"If it was someone looking for Brenda, why didn't he attack the manse?" Mitch said, drawing everyone's attention.

"Probably didn't know it was there," Deke said. "There's no clear driveway to it, no mailboxes or numbers and you can't see it from the road or the spa. Unless you know it's there, you wouldn't look for it. That's why we turned it into accommodation for the women, and like Bren said, most of them have been staying with Jodie until we got the manse ready for them."

"It would have been better if someone had attacked the manse instead of Jodie's place," Lake said. "The manse basement is set up as a panic room. They would have been fine." He looked at Jodie. "Your flat is too exposed. There are no clear escape routes if you need them. And you live alone. We need to go over your security before you move back in."

"I haven't decided if I'm going to move back in yet or not," Jodie said.

There was silence. It was tense. Jodie looked at her feet. She didn't want to see the judgment in anyone's eyes. She didn't want them thinking she was a weak, defenceless woman because she was creeped out that her home had been invaded.

"Now that you're homeless," Mitch drawled into the heavy silence, "this would be a good time for you to consider moving in with me."

Jodie's eyes snapped up to his and relaxed when she saw the mischief in them. He was defusing the tension in the room. He was rescuing her. Crazy man.

"You live in a hotel room," she pointed out.

"I can move. We'll go house hunting. Is there a real estate agent in town?"

"Nope," Matt said. "It's the internet or Fort William."

"I'll get Caroline on it," Mitch said. "She'll find us a house."

"Caroline McInnes?" Jodie said. "You're going to get your best friend's pregnant wife to house hunt for you because you're too lazy to do it yourself?"

Mitch shrugged like there was nothing wrong with his plan. "She enjoys doing this stuff."

"You expect me to move into a house Caroline picked?" Jodie didn't know why she even asked the question; she didn't intend to move in with him anyway. He was pushing this relationship forward at the speed of light. No doubt to ensure she didn't have enough time to think things through properly. Sneaky man. "I mean, do you really expect any woman to live in a house you couldn't be bothered picking yourself?"

"Face it, baby. You want to pick out our first home yourself." Mitch affected a laidback attitude. "That's fine with me. Let me know when you have one for us."

Jodie gaped at him as Deke chuckled. Brenda sat up to look around the room as she wiped her eyes.

"Is it wrong that I really want custard right now?"

"I'll make you custard," Deke told her with a grin as Matt laughed.

"I'm not moving in with you," Jodie told Mitch.

"Where else are you going to go?" the cocky man asked, and he had a point.

"I'll get a room at the hotel."

"Booked out. Fishing tournament. Remember?"

"I'll stay here with Deke."

"No you won't," Deke called as he pulled ingredients out of his pantry. The chef was going to make fresh custard from scratch, not the packet kind Jodie added boiling water to. "Brenda is going to move in here until this business is over. I need to keep an eye on her."

"You do?" Brenda said. "I am?"

"Yes."

Brenda looked around, a little bewildered, but didn't object. Probably because having Deke between her and her ex-husband sounded like a really good idea.

"That's settled, then," Jodie said. "I'll move into Brenda's old room at the manse."

Mitch scowled at her. "You can't stay there forever."

"Watch me," Jodie said.

CHAPTER 22

For some reason, Brenda thought a night spent alone with Deke in his house would be more exciting than it turned out to be. She'd imagined some snuggling—sharing a bed at the very least. Instead, he'd been hands-off and polite from the moment everyone left. He'd shown her the guest bedroom, promised to go to the manse with her in the morning to fetch her clothes and then he'd left her with a t-shirt to sleep in and a promise of pancakes in the morning.

They were back to square one. Where Deke saw her as something fragile and forbidden. The stupid break-in had reminded him that there was a dangerous nutter after her. It had also reminded him of everything that nutter had put her through. Which meant Deke was back to seeing her as nothing more than a delicate little victim. It sucked big time.

By the time the spa opened the following morning, Brenda was completely frustrated and totally annoyed with him. If she wasn't so freaking horny for the big, hot moron, she'd give up on him entirely. As it was, she was stuck thinking up new ways to make him see her as a woman again. A woman with needs. A seriously frustrated woman with needs.

"There's no way it was one of the Domino Boys," Margaret Campbell said, bringing Brenda back to the present and the realisation she was massaging Margaret a little too vigorously. "It's a damn shame about that reception area. I liked it the way it was."

The reception area had been gutted and everything dumped in the local tip. It now held a sofa that had been dragged over from the manse and a small wooden table and chair, with a laptop on it, that acted as a desk.

"I agree," Heather said. "There's no way those old men trashed the place."

Margaret had brought along Shona, Jean and Heather to "keep her company" during her session. It took Brenda about ten seconds to figure out they'd heard about what had happened and were there for a debrief. The three other women sat drinking tea and eating biscuits while Brenda worked out the kinks in Margaret's back.

Shona pointed at them with a biscuit. "Archie would have thrown out his hip just getting up the stairs to Jodie's flat and James never leaves his mobility scooter. Findlay wouldn't have done it without the other two, so that rules him out as well."

"Plus, it was malicious," Heather said. "The boys are daft, but they aren't malicious."

"They're daft, all right—did you see what's in today's paper?" Shona said.

Brenda looked over at her. "I didn't."

Shona rummaged around in her huge handbag and came out with a precisely folded copy of the Invertary Standard. She held it up for Brenda to read. The front page headline wasn't subtle. Local men tired of female oppression.

"Aye," Shona said, her lips in a tense line. "They are that

daft. Listen to what Findlay had to say." She cleared her throat before she read the quote. "'Back in the seventies, this women's lib crap bit us on the backside. Now we're biting back.'" She folded the paper and put it back in her bag. "The bloody idiots have started one of those online petitions to get equal treatment for men. We've all signed it. Let them see how they like equality when their wages are reduced to match the women's."

There was a round of nods.

"Look at the trouble they've stirred up," Heather said. "With their stupid behaviour, the Domino Boys have given permission to the yob element to act like miscreants. That's why they keep vandalising the spa. They've taken what the Domino Boys are doing and run with it."

Brenda bit her lip to stop from telling them it had nothing to do with the local yobs. It was her. She'd brought this problem to their doorstep. She was the reason they were all in danger.

"What about that nephew of Findlay?" Heather said. "I bet this was him. He looks like the kind of boy who'd take to vandalism. What's his name again?"

"Angus," Jean said.

"That's the one." Heather lowered her voice, as if anyone could hear them in Brenda's treatment room. They'd have to be standing right outside the door to listen in. "I heard he's into drugs. He could have gotten high and done it. I wouldn't put it past him."

"Aye," Shona said. "He's the one who's been writing his damn name all over town. Then he acts like Matt is a genius for arresting him." She gave them an incredulous look. "He wrote his name. Who else would have done it? The boy is an idiot."

"Dangerous idiot, though," Heather said. "Remember that time he broke into the post office?"

Jean nodded. "He cut a hole in the ceiling and dropped down into the shop. Only he couldn't get back up to escape. The staff found him asleep on the floor when they opened up the following morning, surrounded by chocolate bar wrappers. They didn't put him in jail for long enough for that, if you ask me."

"This town is going downhill with its growing criminal element," Heather said.

Margaret leaned up onto her elbows, disrupting Brenda's massage. "What criminal element? There's Angus and there's that lad Rab who comes into town with his friends every now and then. Matt gets rid of them fast enough. The only permanent criminal element around here is us lot."

"Breaking into the pub wasn't really a crime," Shona said. "It was more of a protest."

Heather reached for her handbag and pulled out her phone. "I'm going to call Matt and tell him to bring Angus in for questioning."

The women nodded, but Brenda didn't think Matt would like having his mother tell him how to do his job.

"Maybe you should just let him get on with it," she suggested gently. "It seems like he knows what he's doing." And he knew that the problem wasn't a local one, but an imported one.

Suddenly Brenda was the focus of four pairs of eyes. She concentrated on keeping all guilty thoughts out of her head and just doing her job.

"You know something." Shona pointed a finger at her.

"No!" Damn, that came out far too fast. It made them narrow their eyes at her. "I mean, I know that Matt is a very competent police officer. He questioned everyone at the spa and he seems to have everything under control." She smiled at Heather and tried to deflect their attention. "You should be really proud of him."

The women didn't buy it at all. In fact, her attempted deflection seemed to confirm they were onto something. Margaret moved out from under Brenda and sat on the padded table, pulling the sheet around her.

"You know what's going on," Margaret said. "Spill."

Brenda scurried over to the sink in the corner of her room to wash her hands. Her mind raced for a way to get out of the situation before it turned into an interrogation. "There's nothing to spill." Oh man, she didn't sound as casual as she wanted to sound. "I know as much as you. Probably."

She turned to find all the women staring at her.

"Brenda, we welcomed you into the sacred circle of knitters. We trusted you with our dangerous and illegal nighttime raid on the pub." Margaret looked over at Heather. "When was the last time we let a new member into Knit or Die?"

"Nineteen eighty-six," Heather said and cocked a thumb at Jean.

"And I had to go through an initiation," Jean said with a sniff.

Brenda felt her eyebrows climb up her forehead. "Seriously." She held up her hands. "I know nothing."

It was as though they could scent blood in the water.

"You are one of the sisters," Shona said. "That comes with responsibility. You don't keep secrets from the sisters. The first rule of knitting club is that you don't talk about knitting club. The second rule is that you don't keep secrets in knitting club. The third rule is that you always, always have your knitting sisters' backs."

"And the fourth rule is that there's always cake. Every official meeting and knitting session has to have cake," Jean added helpfully.

"I...I...I..." Hot fudge sundaes! Brenda couldn't think of

anything to tell them that would get them off the scent. She eyed the door and wondered if she should make a run for it.

"Not going to happen." Heather saw where her eyes had gone and stomped over to stand in front of the closed door. "Now start at the beginning and tell us everything."

Brenda looked at each of them in turn, took note of the pure determination set on each face and knew that if they didn't get what they wanted from her, they would drive everyone insane digging for it.

Her shoulders slumped. The women smiled at her. It was scary.

"Here." Shona dragged a chair over to her. "Have a seat and get it all off your chest. You'll feel much better once you tell us what you know. Jean, get her a cup of tea. Margaret, get the chocolate biscuits out of your bag. It looks like our girl here needs them." Shona patted Brenda's shoulder as she slumped in the seat, defeated. "Don't worry. It will be okay," Shona said.

Ten minutes later, after three chocolate biscuits and a cup of strong tea, Brenda told them everything.

CHAPTER 23

Jodie had only spent one night in the manse, but already she hated it. Brenda's old room was comfortable enough and the women were welcoming. The problem was that Jodie was used to having her own space and now she was sharing with several other people. It didn't help that she'd spent most of the night tossing and turning, thinking about what could have happened if she'd been home when the intruders had broken into her house. Even that thought wasn't as bad as the nightmares she had when she did sleep. Dreams where Brenda was battered and bleeding and Jodie was rendered helpless, only able to watch in silence. Yeah, her first night wasn't fantastic.

But it was already looking better than her second night.

"You're here to do what?" Jodie said to the four women who were standing on the doorstep of the manse.

"We're moving in," Margaret Campbell repeated before she elbowed her way inside the building.

Each of the women from Knit or Die pulled a large wheeled suitcase behind them as they entered the house.

"Don't worry," Shona said. "We brought blow-up

mattresses. Just point us to a spot on the floor somewhere where we can set them up."

For a minute, Jodie stood open-mouthed with shock as they strode into the common living area and made themselves at home. It was just past dinnertime in the house, and everyone was relaxing after the great meal Carly, the pastry chef, had made them. Patricia, the spa's skin expert, was putting her two little kids to bed, and Robin and Carly were watching TV in the living room.

Jodie shut the front door, rearmed the alarm and followed the surprise guests into the living area.

"Okay," Jodie said. "Why are you moving in? Won't your husbands miss you?"

"My husband is glad for the break," Shona said. "The rest of them are single." She sounded wistful at the thought of being single.

"We're here because women need to stick together," Jean said.

"And because you lot belong to Invertary now and no one messes with the women of Invertary," Shona said.

"And because you need bodyguards and from what we hear, the women in this house wouldn't take too kindly to a bunch of men hanging around, so we've decided to do our part," Heather said.

"Safety in numbers," Margaret said.

Jodie's heart sank as Robin and Carly's eyes grew wider with each successive reason that came out of the women.

"Brenda," Jodie said. "I'm going to kill her."

"Don't blame the wee lassie," Jean said. "We made her tell us."

Heather gave Robin and Carly a pointed look. "There's nothing to be ashamed of. Some men are just born arseholes."

"Heather!" Margaret said.

"What?" Heather shrugged as she headed to the kitchen. "It's true. I'm making tea."

"This is supposed to be a secret refuge," Jodie said. "Brenda can't go around telling people what's going on here. There's too much at stake."

"We know that." Margaret plonked into an armchair. "That's why we're here. Don't worry. We didn't tell anybody else."

"We'll be discreet," Jean said. "No one in town will even know we're here."

"How long do you plan to stay here?" Carly asked.

"Until this crap is done," Shona said. She sat in the other armchair and produced some half-finished knitting from a bag at her side. "We're here for the duration."

"Aye," Margaret said. "We're staying until this current threat is eliminated. We have experience with this sort of thing. We defended the castle against armed idiots not that long ago. We're old hands."

"Speak for yourself," Jean said. "I like to think of myself as a middle-aged hand."

Robin started to chuckle and Jodie cast her a quelling look. "You can't stay here," Jodie told the knitting women.

"Of course we can," Margaret said. "We women need to stick together and everybody knows there's safety in numbers. Plus, we've all done Lake's self-defence classes, so we can pass on some skills while we're here."

Jodie stared at Margaret for a minute before looking at Robin and Carly. Most of their shock had worn off and they seemed to be more amused than anything else. Amused and touched by the show of support.

"I don't know what to do here," Jodie confessed.

Robin grinned, but her eyes were glassy with unshed tears. "Let them stay."

Carly seemed to have problems speaking, but she nodded.

Jean noticed the emotion coming from both women and leaned over to pat their hands. "Welcome to Invertary, ladies."

At that, Robin announced she had something in her eye and made a hasty exit. Carly wasn't so restrained: she burst into tears. Jean sat beside her and hugged her, telling her that everything would be fine now the women of Knit or Die were there.

At that point, Heather bustled into the room with a tray laden with teacups, teapot and a plate of biscuits. "Everything's all settled, then?"

"Aye," Shona said. "I'll just go find Patricia and tell her she's got company in the house. We wouldn't want to freak out the wee ones."

As Jodie watched Shona leave the room, she felt her heart swell. When they'd been searching for a place to call home for the women, she never really believed they'd find somewhere that would completely accept them. Not because they were unacceptable, but because of all the secrets and how people always reacted when they found out about the women and their pasts. But she had found a home. A home that welcomed the women, and all of their problems with open arms.

And for that, she was very grateful.

CHAPTER 24

Brenda took a deep breath and peered at Deke from the corner of her eye. He was in the kitchen, trying out a recipe for the restaurant for their evening meal. He'd been polite, friendly and distant since she'd come home from work. Something she intended putting an end to as soon as possible.

"I thought we could watch a movie together tonight," she said casually as she sat on one of the breakfast barstools.

"I need to go over the details for the restaurant." He didn't even look at her as he spoke, and she noticed his shoulders were so tense that he had to be developing a headache.

"You've got time to keep me company for a couple of hours."

"No can do. But feel free to watch what you like."

There went her plan of cosying up together on the couch. She'd even downloaded a couple of really hot movies to get him in the mood.

"Can I help with the restaurant prep?" At least that way, they could spend some time together. Something he'd been avoiding since he insisted she stay at his place.

"No thanks." He continued stirring sauce.

Brenda wanted to snatch the wooden spoon from his hand and beat him over the head with it. A million suggestions ran through her mind, but none of them were suitable to break through his new icy demeanour. She was pretty sure he'd run for the hills if she suggested they shower together.

"Okay, once you've finished here, how about I give you that massage I promised and help you relax? You look tense." She kept a wide smile plastered in place, in case he turned towards her. He didn't. He focused on that saucepan as though it held the mysteries of the universe.

"I'm going to be working late. Some other time, maybe."

It was no use. He had an answer for everything, and Brenda was fed up with being subtle. Well, subtle for her, anyway.

"What's going on?" she said. "You almost kissed me, now you can't even look at me?"

His back went rock solid. She hoped he was getting a tension headache, because he was sure giving her one.

"Now isn't a good time," he said stiffly. "We need to concentrate on the danger. We can't afford to let our guards down. The kiss was a mistake."

"Fantastic. Just what every woman wants to hear, that she's a mistake. It's right up there with 'you need to lose some weight' and 'Chris Hemsworth is happily married.'"

She saw his lip twitch, but he fought the urge to smile. Stubborn monkey.

"You weren't a mistake. The timing is a mistake. We need to concentrate on eliminating the threat to you, then we can let ourselves become distracted by other things."

Brenda threw up her hands in disgust. "There will always be a threat. I live under constant threat. Does that mean I should put my life on hold forever? Does it mean I shouldn't have any fun? Shouldn't have any romance? Shouldn't have friends? Or laughter? Or sex?"

He shifted the pan off the burner and turned to look at her for the first time since she'd entered the room. He leaned back against the counter, crossed his ankles and folded his arms. He was top to toe in army green, except for his heavy black boots. She half expected to see dog tags around his neck and a machine gun strapped to his back.

"This current situation isn't forever," he said. "But we need to be smart. I can't protect you properly if I'm distracted."

He looked so calm, so reasonable, so freaking mature that it made the top of Brenda's head blow off. She slapped her palms on the counter in front of her and stood on the rung of her stool.

"I can't think properly if I'm this frustrated," she snapped. "If I don't have a decent orgasm soon, I'm going to snap and go on a rampage."

His eyes popped wide, but Brenda was on a roll.

"I should have known better than to depend on a man to help me out. I'm better off sticking to my toys. At least they don't make excuses for not touching me." She jumped off her stool and stalked towards the guestroom. "Don't worry, I'll take care of myself. As usual. And don't think I'm going to fantasise about you while I do it. That ship has sailed, mister."

She was cursing Deke's stubbornness under her breath when an arm wrapped around her waist. The next thing she knew she was sitting on the breakfast bar with Deke standing between her knees. She opened her mouth to ask him what the hell he was doing, because she was too damn angry to argue anymore. The words never came out because her face was cupped in his huge, strong hands and his lips were on hers.

He tasted delicious, like the best meal she'd ever eaten.

She moaned into his mouth as he deepened the kiss. She kissed back with everything she had, ravenous for him. Deke shifted closer until their bodies were flush against each other and she felt his hard length press against her. It felt wonderful. Her fingernails bit into his shoulders as she tried to pull him even closer. She wanted them naked. She wanted him inside her. She wanted it now.

Suddenly, Deke was half a dozen steps away, panting hard. His lips were swollen and his cheeks were red. Desire-filled eyes gazed at her as his hands fisted.

"What?" she said, feeling all sorts of dazed.

With a growl, Deke turned on his heels and stormed out of the house, slamming the door behind him. Brenda was too stunned to move. She sat on the counter, breathing hard and wondering what just happened and why he'd stopped.

A moment later, the door opened and Brenda's eyes shot to it hopefully. Grunt stood there and her heart sank.

"Deke's got stuff to do. I'm with you."

Great. Just what she needed. The human version of King Kong as her companion.

"I'll be in my bedroom." She jumped down from the counter.

Her only answer was a grunt. With each step, Brenda became more furious. And more frustrated. If Deke thought he'd dealt with this issue between them by running, he was about to be sorely disappointed. After that kiss, Brenda was certain he wanted her just as much as she wanted him. And she was going to make sure he got her.

Jodie's gratitude lasted until two o'clock in the morning. None of the younger women in the house would let the older ones sleep on airbeds, so they'd given up their comfy beds for their unwanted houseguests. That's how Jodie found herself lying on a blow-up mattress on the floor of Brenda's old room, while she stared up at the ceiling and tried not to murder Shona for snoring like a foghorn.

Shona and Jean were currently sharing the double bed, and how Jean could sleep through the noise, Jodie did not know. It was hell. Utter hell. The room was shaking from the sound. Jodie had tried to ignore it. Then she'd tried to block it out. Lastly she'd just lain there, barely tolerating it. She was counting off the minutes with each loud snore. She felt like the sound had penetrated deep inside her brain and would never, ever leave. By half past two, she knew she would have to find somewhere else to sleep. She knew this because she'd begun to fantasise about smothering Shona.

Taking the sleeping bag Shona had brought with her and her own pillow, Jodie headed downstairs to claim the couch—only to find Robin was already asleep on it. Too tired to look for a soft spot anywhere else, Jodie pulled the cushions off the chairs and lined them up on the floor. They were long enough to support her body and head, but her legs trailed on the carpet. She didn't care. She climbed into her bag, lay on the cushions and went to sleep.

Jodie woke to loud banging and a cramp in the small of her back. "What the hell?" she demanded.

"Make it stop," Robin whined from the couch.

Jodie didn't know why Robin was complaining; she looked nice and snug and comfortable.

The banging started again and Jodie's sluggish brain realised it was coming from the front door. She became instantly alert.

"Robin, wake up. Someone's at the door."

Just like that, Robin was awake and on her feet. "Is the alarm set?"

"I did it after the women came in."

"Good." Robin tiptoed to the window and peeked through the blinds to see who was out there.

Jodie watched as her shoulders slumped with relief. "It's your apprentice," she said and then made a beeline straight for the sofa, where she snuggled back under her duvet.

Rubbing her eyes, Jodie disarmed the alarm and opened the door to find a blue-headed Betty on the stoop. She had a red tartan shopping bag on wheels behind her.

"What are you doing still asleep?" Betty demanded as she stomped into the house, dragging the trolley with her. "There's work to be done."

"It's Saturday. The spa isn't open until this afternoon." In fact, it was staying open into the evening as a special promotional event. They had clients booked right up until eight o'clock. It was going to be a long day, especially on so little sleep.

"I'm not talking about the spa," Betty said. "I'm talking about self-defence. I've come to get you lot up to scratch."

Jodie groaned, just as Margaret and Heather came down the stairs. Both of them were dressed and awake. Jodie headed for the kitchen, where the clock told her it was barely eight in the morning. There was a full pot of coffee, which she helped herself to.

"What are you doing here?" Margaret demanded as she followed Betty into the kitchen. "And why is your head blue?"

"Tea," Betty barked at Jodie.

"Go to hell," Jodie snapped back, which made Betty cackle.

Shona and Jean came into the kitchen. They too had obviously been up for hours. They looked bright and well rested. Jodie hated them on sight.

"Thanks for the bed," Shona said. "I had a great sleep."

"I didn't even notice Shona was in it," Jean said. "That's a sign of a good mattress."

Jodie tried hard not to glare at them. It amazed her that neither woman seemed to notice that Betty's head was blue.

Robin staggered into the room and headed straight for the coffee. She was wearing Wonder Woman pyjamas and bunny slippers, and yet, strangely, she seemed far more normal than Betty in her tartan mu-mu. Carly and Patricia arrived next, both looking wide awake and ready for the day. They stopped in their tracks when they spotted Betty's head. With a shared look of horror, they entered the room.

"Where are the kids?" Margaret asked.

"They're watching cartoons in their room." Patricia filled the kettle as she looked out of the kitchen window. "Grunt is on duty. I'll see if he wants some coffee." She grabbed her walking stick and headed for the back door.

"Why are you here, again?" Shona asked Betty.

"I heard all about the trouble coming after Brenda," Betty said.

"Does everybody know?" Jodie asked Margaret. "Did you take out an ad in the Invertary Standard?"

Margaret gave Jodie what could only be described as a mum look. It worked, because Jodie's sarcasm dried up instantly.

"I know because I was listening at the door to the massage room." Betty was obviously proud of this, as she grinned widely after she'd told everyone.

Margaret opened her mouth, ready to tell Betty off, when the old woman held up her hand to stop her. "Before you start," she said, "you should know that I came with weapons. You need to arm yourselves." Betty opened her tartan bag and bent over it. She came up with what looked like a set of hair clippers.

"You came to arm us with hair clippers?" Jodie asked.

Betty gave her a look of disgust. "I expect more from my prodigy. This is a stun gun. I dropped by Lake's security shop on the way here and picked up a few. I wanted to bring guns, but he locks the armoury and he never gave me a key."

"I wonder why?" Shona muttered.

"When you say picked up a few," Heather said, "do you mean bought some, or helped yourself to the stock?"

Betty stared at Heather until she shook her head. Jodie took that to mean she'd helped herself.

"I don't see the point of having stun guns," Jean said. "You need to get up close to use them. It's not like a real gun or one of those Taser things that shoot out cables with arrows on the end that let you electrocute people from a distance. The chances are if you have to use a stun gun, you'd be fighting for your life. It'd be better not to get into that situation in the first place, or to shoot the bastard from a distance before he got near you."

"When have you ever used a real gun?" Shona said.

"That's not the point," Jean said. "The point is we need real guns, not toys."

"This isn't a toy." Betty held up the black object. "You hold this against a man and it will knock him out in less than five seconds. Then once he's down, you can tie him up, or kick him, or something."

"That wee thing?" Jean mocked.

Patricia walked in with Grunt following her. They had all gotten to know the taciturn giant over the past few days, and he no longer caused any tension in the house full of women. In fact, the women found his presence to be reassuring. It was generally accepted that any guy daft enough to attack the manse would take one look at Grunt and run.

Grunt nodded to the women, then came to a stop in front of Betty. He frowned. "Does Lake know you have that?"

Betty reached out, pressed the stun gun to his stomach and switched it on. It all happened so fast that Jodie hardly had time to process it. One minute Grunt was glaring at Betty, the next thing he was unconscious on the floor in front of her. There was a stunned silence as all of the women stared at the downed man. Then Betty grinned.

"See?" she said. "That's why you need a stun gun."

Nobody spoke, but shock rippled through the room. Betty reached into her bag and pulled out a tiny digital camera. She tottered around Grunt, handed the camera to Carly, then sat on the man's belly. She beamed at Carly.

"Take a picture for me," she demanded.

Carly seemed to be on autopilot, because she did as she was told.

Betty was thrilled. She took the camera back from Carly then looked down at Grunt. She had a look of speculation on her face that made Jodie's blood run cold.

"There's a rumour going around that he has a pierced willy," Betty said. "I've never seen one of those."

She reached for the zipped fly of Grunt's jeans.

"No!" every woman in the room shouted at the same time.

Margaret grabbed Betty's dress and yanked her back. Shona snatched the stun gun from her hand and Heather confiscated the camera—although that seemed a little pointless.

"What do we do now?" Robin said. "He's going to be pissed when he wakes up. Does being stunned give you a headache? Did anyone see if he hit his head on the way down? Maybe we should call a doctor or something."

"No doctor. I'm sure he'll be fine. Grunt has a history of being knocked out. He's used to it," Margaret said. She glanced at Heather. "And no police. I'm pretty sure this could be considered assault."

"I don't think there's any considering about it." Robin pointed at Grunt. "This is definitely assault."

They stared at the man mountain lying on his back in the middle of the floor. For some reason images from Gulliver's Travels danced through Jodie's brain. It wasn't delightful thinking of herself a Lilliputian.

"I think," Jodie said, "that it might be a good idea if we weren't here when he wakes up."

"You don't think he'd get violent, do you?" Patricia paled at the thought.

"No." Jodie looked at the big man. "But I don't think he'll be happy, and I'd rather not be around for that."

There was a pause before unanimous agreement. The women scattered. Jodie grabbed her phone as soon as she was in Brenda's bedroom. She called her brother.

"Deke," he said by way of hello.

"So," Jodie said. "Betty zapped Grunt with a stun gun and now he's unconscious on the floor of the manse kitchen.

We're all leaving before he wakes, but somebody should probably check on him." She took a deep breath. "Tag. You're it." She cut the call dead.

The phone rang while she was pulling on her jeans. Jodie didn't answer. She threw her things into a bag and was halfway down the drive when she heard the roar that signalled Grunt was awake.

It took minutes to get to the hotel in her car. With a sigh of resignation, she let herself in through the side entrance and climbed the tartan-carpeted stairs to Mitch's room. She mentally crossed her fingers and wished upon a star that Mitch was out doing Mitch stuff with his buddies and she would be able to dump her stuff and run. Of course, she wasn't that lucky. As soon as she swung the door open, she spotted him hunched over his laptop at the desk. His slow, smug smile said it all.

"Don't." Jodie held up a hand as she dumped her bag on the paperwork-strewn bed.

The guy seriously needed to find a house. How he could live like this, she honestly didn't know. Mitch spun in his chair, which she noticed wasn't a standard hotel issue, but was an ergonomically designed desk chair. His jean-clad legs stretched out in front of him and crossed at the ankles. His arms folded over a denim-blue Henley. The smug smile stayed in place.

"I don't want to hear about it," Jodie snapped, even though he hadn't said a word. "I just want to have a shower, get some food and get to work. Okay?" She put her hands on her hips.

All he did was grin wider and arch an eyebrow at her. With a grumble, she grabbed her washbag and stormed into the bathroom, slamming the door behind her.

Men. There was no dealing with them.

Brenda wasn't happy. She'd spent a restless night, and all of her very long workday, wondering what she'd done to make Deke run like his backside was on fire. She wasn't that bad at kissing. At least, she hadn't thought so. It wasn't like she'd had a lot of experience. She'd had exactly two boyfriends—one had turned out to be gay and the other one beat her. Not exactly a stellar track record in the experience department. Although neither one of her exes had ever complained about her kissing technique. Clive had complained about almost everything else, but not her kissing. So what had made Deke run? Maybe she'd been right the first time. Maybe he just didn't fancy her. She stopped dead as she felt the blood drain from her face. That meant his kiss was a pity kiss.

A pity kiss!

"Are you almost finished?" Jodie put her head around Brenda's door in time to stop her from having a complete meltdown.

"Just cleaning up. I'll be done in another fifteen minutes or so."

"Okay, I'm going to walk Patricia back to the manse,"

Jodie said. Patricia, their skin specialist, had a weak leg courtesy of her ex-husband, and after a long day it became worse. She would never mention it, but the women took turns making sure she had support crossing the short distance to the manse. "Lake's guy is on the door, so yell out to him if you need anything. I won't be long, and I'll lock up after you're done."

It was past nine at night and everyone was eager to get home. The special promotional event had been a huge hit, which meant lots of work for all the women. Brenda wished she was going back to her little room in the manse instead of Deke's house, which was filled with Deke's problems.

"Okeydokey." Brenda was perfectly comfortable dealing with any of Lake's security guys—especially after Grunt and Lake had explained to the women that if the men scared them in any way, Grunt would break their legs. It took a while for the women to realise they weren't joking.

Jodie hesitated and her face softened. "You holding up okay?"

Mm, what could Brenda say? That she was more worried about dying from sexual frustration because Jodie's brother was an idiot than she was about her ex getting her? No, that definitely came under the category of TMI.

"I'm okay. I hate waiting. I wish something would happen. Not something bad, just something to give us an idea where Clive is and what he's doing. Or even better, I wish Matt and Lake would catch him and this would all be over."

One look at Jodie's face told Brenda she didn't think this would ever be over.

"I'm deluding myself," Brenda said. "I know that. Unless they catch him doing something seriously illegal, he'll be free to carry on harassing us." For a minute her focus was on folding the towel in her hands. "I should leave, Jodie. Before someone gets hurt because of me."

"No." Jodie stepped into the room and placed both hands on Brenda's shoulders. "You heard Deke: this is your last stand. At least here you have people to protect you. If you leave, you'll be alone. It will be worse. You know that. You know how bad it can be when you have no one to help you and nowhere to go."

Brenda couldn't look her in the eye anymore. She nodded as she stepped away to put the towel on the shelf.

"You know it wasn't you," Jodie said. "It was never you. This is all on him."

"I know." And she did. It still didn't make any difference. Brenda still felt guilty that her poor choices put good people at risk. She should have seen how messed up Clive was before she got in too deep. She should have recognised the signs and put a stop to things.

"Stop it," Jodie snapped. "The guilt and shame are all his. All of it. You didn't ask to be hounded by an unbalanced guy. You didn't ask to be beaten. You didn't ask him to harass your friends. These aren't things you encouraged or welcomed. These guys are all the same—they start out as charmers, and once you're isolated enough not to have any support, their control slips. You can't fix them. They can only fix themselves. And the truth of the matter is that most of them don't want to be fixed. They just want to hurt. To control. To demean. To abuse. But none of that is on you. That's all on them. It's all on your ex."

Brenda blinked away embarrassing tears at Jodie's impassioned words. "Does it get better?"

"I've spent my whole adult life thinking I'm somehow to blame for how my father treated my mother. If I'd been quieter, if I'd told the teachers at school, if I'd been tidier. It's all bullshit. It didn't matter what any of us did; he would still have found an excuse to behave exactly the way he wanted to behave." Jodie stepped towards Brenda. "The guilt never goes away, but you learn to recognise it for what it is—lies. Lies enforced on us by men who hurt us."

"I'm not like you, though. I'm not strong. I have no self-defence skills. You're Combat Barbie. You're confident. Capable. Sorted. Together. If Clive came in here now, I'd cower and cry."

Jodie's eyes flashed with fury. "That's it. I'm setting up compulsory self-defence classes for all staff."

"What's that saying about trying to shut a horse in after it's already run away? This is just like that. It's a bit late to be learning self-defence now."

"It's never too late." The way Jodie's chin jutted out with determination made Brenda wonder if she'd somehow managed to survive being beaten only to die during one of Jodie's classes.

Patricia called Jodie's name, and their boss turned towards the door. "Don't knock yourself," Jodie said with her hand on the door. "You're courageous. You survived and you aren't afraid of life or men."

Once Jodie had shut the door behind her, Brenda let out a snort of derision. Nope, she wasn't afraid of men—well, apart from her ex—but men sure as sugar were afraid of her. Exhibit A: cowardly Deke Miller.

Brenda set about sorting her shelves, making sure her supplies were ready to go first thing Monday morning. She wished the task would take longer, because she didn't want to go back to Deke's place and spend another night watching him invent ways to avoid touching her. It had become humiliating.

She heard a thud coming from the direction of the reception area. Jodie was back. Brenda reached for her tote, but stilled as her hand touched it. Every hair on her body stood up. Slowly, silently, she turned towards the door, as though she had somehow developed x-ray vision and would suddenly be able to see through it. She told herself that all this talk of Clive was making her paranoid. But her breathing sped up and her palms became clammy. It was then she realised what was bothering her—the building was silent.

There were no voices. No footsteps. No doors closing. Nothing. Nothing when there should have been something. For a second Brenda was frozen, then instinct kicked in. Hide. She had to hide. Her gaze flew around the room. There was only one place. The large Alibaba basket for the used towels.

She swayed at the thought of being tucked in that small dark space. It was just like... No! No. This was different. Her hands shook. Her mind raced, options flying through her brain at lightning speed. There was nowhere else to hide and she couldn't fight.

Her mouth went dry as she stared at the basket. It was just a basket. It had holes. She would be able to see light through them. There was no lock on the outside for someone to keep her trapped. She could do this. She could. She wasn't the person she'd been. No one was forcing her to get into the basket. No one was making her sit in the dark. This was her choice. She could do it. She had to do it. Because there was someone out there. Someone moving silently through the building. Someone who shouldn't be there. She knew it. She felt it in the vibrations in the air. In the silence that was suddenly oppressive. There was no other choice. She had to get into the basket.

Now.

The basket would make noise when she climbed into it. She needed cover. There was no time to think. No time to second-guess her reactions or fears. She grabbed her phone from her bag, swiped the screen, set the alarm and placed the phone on the table. She rushed on tiptoes to the basket. Less than one minute. That's what she had to get ready. Her heart raced as she removed the lid of the basket. She placed her tote in the bottom. She couldn't hear anything above the rushing of blood in her ears.

And then her alarm went off.

Wham!'s "Wake Me Up Before You Go-Go" blared.

Brenda launched herself into the basket and pulled the lid on top of her head. It was tight, but for once her tiny frame was an advantage. She crouched, her arms wrapped around her knees, frozen in place. Any movement and the basket would creak, giving her away. She was struggling to breathe as panic fought to overcome her. It was such a small space. There was no light. The air was musty and thick. She couldn't move. She couldn't make a noise. He would hear her.

He was out there. She knew it.

It was happening all over again.

He was going to shout through the door. He was going to thump the wood. He was going to tell her what she'd done wrong this time. Then he'd disappear. Leaving her in the darkness without water or food. Leaving her locked away, hidden, terrified. Waiting. Then the door would suddenly open and the pain would start. She couldn't breathe. She wanted to scream. To run. To fight. He was coming. She knew it. The door was going to open and he'd grab her hair…

No.

There was no door.

No. Door.

Brenda scrunched up her eyes. Breathe. Just breathe. She wasn't back there in the closet. She was here in the spa and she'd chosen to hide. Her decision. Nobody forced her into the basket.

Basket. Not closet. Basket.

She felt lightheaded. There didn't seem to be enough air in the small space, which didn't make sense, because there were holes in the weave. She had to get out of there. She had to. There was no one out there. She'd panicked. She'd made a mistake. Listened to her imagination instead of logic.

And then the door opened.

Brenda stopped breathing entirely.

"It's a fucking phone. One of the bitches must have forgotten it." The voice was deep. Rough. English accent.

Brenda didn't recognise it.

"Take the phone. There might be something on there we can use." Another voice. English accent.

She didn't recognise that one either.

"She isn't here. We shouldn't have trashed her flat. Now we don't know where she's sleeping."

There was a moment's silence as Brenda's ears strained to hear something. Anything.

"Are you fucking criticising me?" It was the second man, and his voice dripped with menace.

There was a screech of tyres on gravel.

"Time to go," the first guy said.

A car door slammed.

"Out the back," the second guy ordered.

There was absolute silence. Had they gone? Was she safe? They could move around without making any noise. Were they there? In the room? Were they waiting?

Brenda's fingers began to tingle. Pins and needles. She let out the breath that had been burning her lungs. Slow. Quiet. Invisible. She had to be invisible. Dizzy. She felt dizzy. She forced herself to breathe as multi-coloured lights seemed to dance in front of her in the darkness of the basket. She couldn't faint. The noise would give her away. She had to breathe. Just keep on breathing.

A door slammed.

Brenda jerked. Froze. Panic. Had they heard? Was she found? No. No. No. No...

"Brenda!" A panicked shout. Deke.

A wave of relief washed over her, but she still couldn't move. Her head slumped onto her knees. Tears rolled down her cheeks in silence as her limbs began to shake.

"Brenda!" The door to her room slammed open.

Brenda wanted to call out. Wanted to get out of the basket, but her limbs were noodles and she couldn't speak. Not yet. A sob erupted.

Loud footsteps, then light as the lid was lifted. "Aw, Bren."

Strong hands reached for her. They grasped her under her arms and lifted her straight out of the basket. Brenda curled into Deke as he wrapped around her, holding her tight to his chest, cradling her like a child.

"It's okay, honey. It's okay," he crooned against her hair.

More footsteps, then someone skidded to a halt inside the door. Brenda pressed her face into Deke's firm shoulder.

"Is she okay?" Jodie. Tense. Fearful.

"I found her hiding in the basket." Deke's voice was a tight wire, ready to snap.

Brenda wanted to tell them she was okay, but the words wouldn't come out and she couldn't stop shaking.

"Adrenalin crash," Deke said to his sister.

"I'll get a blanket."

Brenda wanted to crawl inside Deke until she was back to normal. He was right. He was strong and big and capable and nothing could get through him. So where the hell had he been when she needed him?

She lifted her head to look at him and was vaguely aware that he was striding down the corridor to reception.

"You said you'd stand in front of me."

He winced. "I screwed up. From now on, I'm sticking to you like glue."

Brenda blinked up at him. "Does that mean you're going to stop running from me like a timid teenager?"

"Yes," he snapped.

Brenda didn't care. She wasn't intimidated. She felt wired and she wanted to talk. No, she wanted to rub herself all over Deke like a cat with catnip.

"Night-time too? Are we going to sleep in the same bed?"

"I don't think I need to sleep beside you to protect you."

"What happened to that glue?"

He sat on the reception sofa with her in his lap. She felt protected. She felt safe. She felt…horny? She wriggled in his lap. Oh yeah, she definitely felt horny. Brenda flattened her hand against his chest. So many muscles. So little time. She traced them with her fingertips.

Deke covered her hand with his. "Stop. It's just the adrenalin working its way out of your system."

"I've had adrenalin before. I've never felt like this." She'd also never felt muscles like this. How did he cook and eat all the time yet stay this buff? Surely the workouts she'd seen him do weren't enough.

A blanket wrapped around her shoulders. Deke pulled it tight, tucking it in around them, making them a little cocoon, only with their heads sticking out. Brenda became aware that they weren't alone. Jodie was standing in front of her and Mitch was leaning against the wall by the door. Lake and Grunt stood side by side, arms folded, faces stone.

"Can you tell us what happened?" Jodie clearly thought Brenda would shatter if she didn't talk to her as though she was a cowering puppy.

That was not going to happen. The last thing she needed was for the man she was sitting on to think she was even more fragile than he already thought her to be. Brenda sat up straight, her palm still flat against Deke. Skin, she thought. I need skin.

"I'll tell you what happened," she said—okay, well, maybe she shouted. Her hand slipped under Deke's shirt as she spoke. His hand clasped her wrist to stop her. She snapped her head around to face him, her eyes wide. "Seriously? You're going to stop me from touching you? Really? When everyone knows that the best treatment for shock is skin-on-skin contact?"

There was a muffled chuckle behind her.

"That's the treatment for hypothermia," Deke said.

"Then why do they recommend that premature, traumatised babies spend time against the skin of their mothers? Explain that."

"Bren," Deke started, but then he just sighed. His hand moved away. "Have at it, then."

Brenda gave him a wide smile. "You know what would really help? If you took off your shirt."

There was more muffled laughter.

"You are a total nut," Deke told her, but didn't object when she shoved his shirt up and leaned into him, her hand splayed over all those yummy muscles. His hand tightened on her hip.

"I could be your nut if you'd get your act together and stop running away," she said.

The laughter wasn't muffled this time. Deke scowled at their audience and it stopped.

Brenda turned back to everyone. "I can't believe I hid in a basket. I've been claustrophobic since Clive used to lock me in the closet. I was good at escaping, though. I'm fantastic at picking a lock. That's why the women of Knit or Die recruited me. But that's beside the point." She felt Deke shift her closer into him. "The point is that I went into the basket on my own. My choice. I did it and I didn't freak out." She beamed at everyone. "Not until Deke pulled me out, but then it was only a little freak-out. I mean, what woman isn't allowed some tears after she's spent time in a laundry basket?"

"Bren." Deke's hand tightened on her hip as his other hand brushed her wild curls back from her face. "You're hyper because of the adrenalin. We understand that. But you need to focus. You need to answer Lake's questions."

He was so considerate, so caring. He was perfect. Her heart melted just looking at him. Which reminded her that other parts of her weren't melting but heating up.

"I'm sure I could concentrate better if you were naked." She batted her lashes at him.

"Not going to happen."

"You just mean here, right? But later, you'll totally help me get over my trauma by getting naked. Right?"

Deke groaned and looked at Lake for help. Lake was doing that lip twitch thing he did when he thought he was too cool to smile.

"Brenda, did you get a look at the person who broke in? Was it your ex?" Lake said.

"No." Brenda looked at Lake as she stroked Deke's chest. She definitely felt better, more relaxed having her hands on him. "It wasn't Clive."

"Are you sure? Because we haven't been able to track him down yet."

Lake's words made her shudder, and Deke rubbed her arm to reassure her.

"I can't believe I sat in a basket," Brenda said loudly.

"It was the smart thing to do," Deke said. "Brave. Now, are you sure it wasn't that arsehole you used to live with?"

"Definitely." She shook her head. "There were two of them. They took my phone because I set the alarm to cover the noise of me climbing into the basket." She looked at Deke. "I'll never be able to listen to Wham! again after that. And thus endeth my eighties music phase." She turned back to Lake. "But it's okay. There was nothing on the phone they can use. I don't save any numbers to contacts and I delete every text and voice mail when I get it. There's nothing on there but some bad pop music and a couple of X-rated e-books." She looked back at Deke. "Do you realise how hard it is to read on a phone?"

Deke cast a helpless look at Lake. "She's going to be like this until it works its way out of her system."

"We know," Lake said.

"Know what?" Brenda said. "What's the problem? Am I doing something wrong?"

"No," Jodie said. "It's fine, sweetie. We just need to know about the men."

"Right, the men." Brenda scrunched up her nose. "There were two of them. English accents. I didn't recognise either of them. They said that they shouldn't have trashed your flat because now they didn't know where you were staying." The words sank in as they came out of her mouth. Brenda felt herself pale as she looked at Jodie. "They were looking for you."

Everyone in the room turned to Jodie. Mitch strode to her side and wrapped an arm around her waist. He tugged her tight against him. Brenda turned back to Deke.

"I know it's selfish to think this right now, what with the fact bad guys are after Jodie. But does this mean that you won't be sleeping naked beside me tonight?"

He stared at her for a moment. She couldn't read his expression, but she thought it was a mixture of bewilderment and exasperation.

"You are a complete and utter lunatic," he said with a shake of his head. Which still wasn't an answer to her question. She opened her mouth to talk, but he kept on going. "I am so proud of you. You did the right thing hiding in that basket. It kept you safe."

"I hid. I didn't call for help. I didn't fight. I hid." It was nothing to be proud of.

He clasped the back of her neck. "You got out in one piece. You got information for us. You did the right thing." He lowered his voice. "I would have gone nuts if you were hurt."

"But—"

He cut her off with his lips. They were firm against her. Firm and delicious. Brenda felt her nails curl into his abs as he deepened the kiss, licking past her lips to get her mouth to open to him. Brenda melted into him. She'd give him anything he wanted, anytime he wanted it.

When he slowly moved his head away, she looked up at him, feeling kind of dazed. "Please tell me that was a yes to full-body contact later on? Because I'm dying of frustration here."

"Nut," Deke said as he pulled her into his chest.

Brenda knew everyone was watching, but she didn't care: she rested her cheek against him and closed her eyes, suddenly very tired. In the warmth of Deke's strong hold, she felt exhaustion steal her away.

CHAPTER 27

"She's out cold," Lake said with a nod at Brenda.

Mitch followed his eyes, and sure enough, the hyperactive little blonde had crashed. He kept his hold firm around Jodie, scared to let her out of his sight, even though he knew that she was more than capable of taking care of herself.

"Never seen anyone react like that before," Grunt said, his eyes on Brenda.

"Usually people rant; sometimes they find a willing partner and work it out that way before they crash. Never seen someone yammer and proposition a guy before. Interesting." Lake looked amused.

Deke scowled at all of them as he stood, holding the sleeping woman in his arms. "I'm taking her home." He headed for the door.

"Don't forget the naked therapy part of your caregiver responsibilities," Mitch called after him and got a glare.

As soon as the door was closed, Jodie exploded. She jerked out of Mitch's arms and started pacing. "This is my fault. They were after me and they got Brenda. The woman who would struggle to defend herself against a kitten! If I'd been here, I could have kicked their backsides until Matt got here. Why are they after me? Who are they? What do they want?"

Mitch snagged Jodie as she passed him, intent on wrapping her in his arms and holding her tight until she calmed down. Of course, that wasn't what happened. Yet again he was flying through the air. He landed with a smack on the wooden floor with Jodie glaring down at him, her hands on her hips.

"Will you stop doing that? You're going to get hurt," she snapped.

Mitch lay there for a minute, waiting for the room to stop spinning. At this rate he was going to end up with concussion or permanent bruising on his spine.

"Are you trying to kill me, woman?" he demanded.

She just resumed her pacing—this time around his prone body.

"A little help?" Mitch said to Lake, who offered a hand.

"Do you have a connection to the Hampstead Heath drop-in centre?" Lake asked Jodie, who was still frothing with fury.

"I did some volunteer work there, years ago." She didn't stop pacing; this time Mitch left her to it.

"What kind of volunteer work?" Lake said.

"I taught a class. Once a week."

"Hair and makeup?" Grunt asked.

She glared at him. "Self-defence."

He grunted—it could have been with approval, but it was hard to tell.

"Did anything out of the ordinary happen while you were there?" Lake said.

"Nothing. I went in, I taught my class, I left. I didn't know any of the women outside of the class. I didn't socialise with the other staff. And I didn't have any run-ins with any men."

She stopped in the middle of the room. "It was completely uneventful."

Lake eyed her thoughtfully. "Maybe this has nothing to do with the London centre. We need to dig deeper. At least now we can eliminate the threat as being directed at Brenda. Although we'll keep searching for the ex. I don't like that I don't know where he is."

"How's your guy?" Mitch knew the man Lake had left guarding the spa entrance had been cold-cocked and knocked out for the duration.

"Embarrassed," Lake said. "Otherwise, he has a headache and some extra training to endure." He looked at Jodie. "That won't happen again."

Mitch expected her to say something about it not being Lake's fault, or that she didn't expect perfection from a bunch of guys she wasn't even paying to be there. Instead she gave him a cold look.

"It had better not," she warned.

Lake nodded and headed for the door, with his mountain-sized shadow in tow.

Mitch watched Jodie as she bubbled with rage. Rage that needed an outlet or she was going to blow. He pushed away from the table he was leaning on and held out a hand.

"Come on," he said. "We've got somewhere we need to be."

"I've got things to do here."

"No." Mitch snatched her hand, preparing himself for another flight to the floor as he did so. Fortunately, it didn't happen. "Trust me. You need this. Give me an hour, okay? We'll lock up, set the alarm and if you need to come back after we're done, I'll bring you."

"This better be worth it," Jodie grumbled as he led her to his SUV.

Five minutes later, they pulled past the guardhouse at the castle entrance and made their way up the driveway to the building. Josh was waiting at the top of the steps outside his front door. He was wearing his favourite Cookie Monster t-shirt, which had been decorated by tiny handprints made with what looked like spaghetti sauce.

"Heard you had trouble at the spa," he said once they'd climbed out of the car.

"Yeah, not good." Mitch tentatively took Jodie's hand again. "Can we use your back lawn? Jodie's a bit tense."

"I am not," Jodie said.

Josh and Mitch shared a knowing look.

"Sure." Josh waved them into the house. "What you got planned?"

"Some stress relief," Mitch said as he made his way through the wood-panelled hallway, past the carved staircase to the kitchen, dragging Jodie behind him.

"Please tell me you don't plan to have sex in my back-yard," Josh whined.

Mitch just glared at him. When they hit the kitchen, they found Caroline perched on a high stool at the breakfast bar, one hand on her swollen belly, the other clasping a pen as she went over the notebooks in front of her. A laptop sat open beside her paperwork.

Mitch kissed her cheek. "Hey, Caro, what you doing?"

"Planning. Christmas market." She smiled at Jodie. "Good to see you. I'm sorry you're having so much trouble. Let me know what I can do to help. I'd take guard duty if I wasn't so big."

"No. You wouldn't." Josh wrapped his arm around her shoulder. "First because you're a delicate woman. Second because we aren't supposed to know anything about Jodie running a secret refuge for beaten women."

Jodie's eyes snapped to Mitch. "Did you take out an ad in the paper?"

"I didn't tell him." In fact, Mitch was a bit pissed that she even thought he would betray her trust like that.

"It was Matt," Josh said, throwing their friend under the bus without even a shred of remorse. He looked at Mitch. "What you doing in the yard?"

Mitch smiled down at Jodie. "Fight club. Jodie and I are gonna spar. She needs to work off her aggression, and we needed somewhere private and safe for that to happen."

Jodie gave him a look that said she thought he'd lost his mind. "Are you insane? You could get hurt."

Josh, the idiot, started laughing.

"What?" Jodie said.

"You're a girl. Mitch is almost twice your size. Plus, we had our fair share of street fighting when we were kids." He looked at Mitch. "You better watch it, dude. Pull your punches or you'll feel bad if you accidentally hurt her."

Mitch could have sworn he saw steam coming out of Jodie's ears. Her face went a strange shade of purple and she was on the cusp of exploding.

"Let's go." Mitch yanked her towards the door, but her threatening gaze stayed on Josh.

"If you still need to get rid of some aggression after you've dealt with Mitch," Caroline said, "I'll let you beat on Josh. He deserves it after that 'delicate woman' comment."

"Baby," Josh said. "You are delicate and I like you like that. You're the princess of the castle."

"I think I'm going to vomit," Jodie said as she watched Caroline's pregnancy hormones kick in. They made the woman go all misty-eyed for her husband.

"I feel like that a lot around them." Mitch led her over the stone patio, out to the lush, grassy field.

He let go of her hand and bent to take off his shoes. Then he rolled his shoulders and hoped for the best. He took his place a distance from the small wall that encircled the patio, noticing that Josh and Caroline had come outside to watch, armed with snacks and drinks. Mitch sighed. If he didn't love this woman, there was no way he'd let Josh watch her kicking his ass.

"Come on." He crooked a finger at her. "You need this. Come beat on me."

Jodie gaped at him. "Have you lost your mind? You could get hurt."

Mitch knew reasoning with her wouldn't help, so he went for a more tried and true method of getting her to do what he wanted—he wound her up.

"I never took you for a chicken. It's one thing to throw me around when I'm not ready for it, totally something else when I expect the attack. You're worried you can't take me in a fair fight." He smirked. "I understand. We'll go back to my hotel room and work off your anger another way."

And there it was, that murderous look he'd come to know and love. She pulled off her crocs, the ones he'd bought for her, and stomped over the grass to face him.

"I won't hold back," she promised.

"Neither will I," he assured her.

"Fine, then you only have yourself to blame." With that, she flew at him.

After that, it was all kind of a blur for Mitch. He managed to land a couple of blows to her body and got her in a chokehold once. The rest of the time he was on the defensive, or on his back looking up at her. Jodie was a whirling dervish of feet and fists. It would have been amazing to watch if he hadn't been the one on the receiving end.

At last, breathing heavily, Jodie sat astride him, pressing her forearm into his throat.

"You concede?" It was a relief to see that she was breathless and had broken a sweat. The humiliation he would have suffered if that hadn't been the case would have been too much for his poor ego to handle.

"Absolutely." He had no problem conceding.

Her hold on his neck eased. She sat back and looked down at him. Thankfully, she was no longer one little ball of pent-up rage.

"You okay?" she asked.

He tried to nod, but it made his head spin. "No broken bones." Just a body that had turned into a head-to-toe bruise. In fact, he wasn't even sure he could get up off the ground.

Her face softened as she looked down at him. "If we're going to do this often then I need to teach you some better moves."

His heart clenched tight. It was the first time Jodie had mentioned a future together. Mitch fought to keep the elation he felt out of his voice.

"That would be appreciated."

She stared at him for a moment, her expression hard to read. Then she leaned forward and kissed him. It was a slow, soft tease of a kiss.

"Thank you," she whispered against his lips.

Those two words made the damage to his internal organs worthwhile.

"Unbelievable," Josh said as he came rushing over. "I've never seen anything like it. You totally kicked his ass. It was pathetic. He was so far out of your league he looked like a toddler throwing punches while holding an ice cream cone."

"Thanks," Mitch said dryly.

"You're welcome." Josh was still bouncing with excitement over Jodie. "Me next. My turn. I need to try my luck. I bet it takes longer to knock me out than it did Mitch."

"No," Caroline said, coming up beside them. "You have a concert tour. You need to remain unbruised and unbroken."

She smiled down at Jodie. "You can beat him up another time."

"Uh, thanks?" Jodie said.

Mitch grinned at her confused expression and pulled her flat against his chest for a hug. One he probably needed more than she did.

"Caroline?" he said over Jodie's shoulder. "I need a house. Can you find me one?"

Jodie jabbed him in his poor, abused ribs.

"Of course," Caroline said.

"About time," Josh said. "It's lame that you think hanging around the hotel or crashing in our spare room is a life a forty-year-old man should live."

"Forty?" Mitch almost choked on the word. "I'm nowhere near forty."

"It's right round the corner, dude," Josh said. "Denial isn't going to stop it from happening."

"You're going to be forty soon too," Mitch pointed out.

He felt Jodie begin to shake against him and knew she was struggling to hide her laughter.

"Yeah," Josh said. "But I have a house. A wife. Kids. Dude, what do you have except for your iPhone and free breakfasts at the pub? You're one of those sad guys who hits middle age and still thinks he's twenty. It makes you look older. Plus, I'm in way better shape than you are. You just got beaten up by a girl."

There was a snort from Jodie.

"Help me up," Mitch ordered her. "I'm going to kick his ass and see how he likes it."

"No problem." Jodie jumped to her feet. "Caroline, you don't happen to have a Zimmer frame Mitch could borrow?"

"Walking stick?" Caroline said, and Mitch just groaned.

CHAPTER 28

Brenda woke up snuggled beside a wall of solid muscle. She didn't need a minute to orientate herself to where she was. She knew instantly. There was only one scent in the world that smelled like cookie dough and passion—Deke. With a languorous stretch, she snuggled closer to him and rubbed her cheek against his firm chest. His firm, cotton-covered chest.

"Hey," Brenda said. "What happened to being naked in bed?"

The wall of muscle moved and Brenda found herself on her back, staring up at a sleep-tousled man. She never would have believed it was possible for him to look any better than he normally did, but in that moment, he did. Deke lay on his side, the top half of his body propped up by his elbow as he looked down at her. Brenda's heart sank a little when she noticed there was a very careful few inches of space between them.

"How are you feeling?" His voice was a sleep-roughened rumble that made her toes curl.

"I feel fine. I wasn't ill. I was scared." She batted her lashes at him as she became aware that the room wasn't dark. A faint morning glow peeked in around the edges of the curtains. "I'm not scared now, Deke."

She watched as wariness flashed in his eyes. She slumped further into the bed. Nothing had changed—he was still too scared to touch her. It seemed like the only time he was able to get over his reservations was when he was more worried for her than he was about her.

"Thanks for keeping me company last night." Brenda aimed for the same light, friendly tone she used with her clients. "I really appreciate it, but now that the threat to me is over, I'd best move back into the manse."

She turned away from him, flipped back the thin blue duvet that was covering them and moved to get out of the bed.

A large hand suddenly covered her stomach, and Brenda stopped. She looked at the hand, so much bigger and darker than hers. There was power in those hands, and skill. There was also kindness and, she thought, maybe passion.

"I..." Deke's voice snapped her eyes to his face. He was frowning. The same little look of concentration he got when he was trying to figure out a recipe and make it better. His tongue flicked out to wet his lips. "I never know if you're being honest or if you're messing around with me."

Brenda desperately worked to tamp down the hope that was building inside of her. She'd been wrong about this man before now. "I'm both. I'm honest and I tease you. You're fun to mess with."

The fingers of the hand on her stomach curled as a look of pure frustration swept over his face. "That doesn't help."

"I don't understand, Deke. Just ask me what you want to know. I'll tell you."

Dark eyes held hers captive. "Are you joking when you say you want me naked? Is it a game when you tell me you want me? When you pout for a kiss, is it harmless flirting?" He paused, searching her face for something; she didn't know what. "I don't know what's real and what isn't."

A dam of hope within her burst. Brenda couldn't stop it. No matter how much she got pushed down, there was something inside of her that made her bounce back. Something that made her hope for the best. Something that made her believe that things would get better.

"I wasn't playing with you that way, Deke." Tentatively, she placed her hand on top of his, holding him against her stomach. "It's all real. I'm not very good at flirting. I don't know how to do it properly. I tend to come off as crazy or heavy-handed."

His eyes flared with heat. "You were flirting with me?"

Brenda let out a short, mirthless laugh. "If you have to ask, I'm not doing it properly."

"So you really do want me?"

"Well, duh." Brenda rolled her eyes. Maybe there was a book on how to flirt she could buy.

"What do you want me for?"

"Really? You're asking that?"

"Bren," he growled. "Do you want a one-night stand? Do you want to use me to get past the bastard who hit you? Do you want to date? Do you want a relationship and commitment? I don't know what you want."

"Does anybody know what they want when they start something?"

He looked like the words he wanted to say were strangling him on the way up his throat. "I'm a big guy. I know how to hurt people." He seemed to realise what he'd said and rushed out a qualifier: "I'd never hurt you, though. You need to believe me. I'd never lift a hand to you."

"I know, you daft man." Brenda rubbed her hand up his arm to soothe him. It seemed to help.

"Okay." Deke took a deep breath. "I'm a big guy. Bigger than you. I can be scary. I'm worried that I'll scare you. I'm worried that..."

"That you're too much for me?"

"Aye." He looked away for a minute. "If I knew what you really wanted, what you expected from me, then I could act the way you needed and maybe you wouldn't get scared."

Damn, he was going to make her cry. Brenda came to her knees in front of him. She'd been chasing him, in her own weird way, since the day she'd met him. She'd thought it was lust, because he was so damn gorgeous it hurt her eyes to look at him, but now, she was beginning to think it was so much more. When she looked at Deke, she didn't see a way to get over her past—she saw her future.

His body was tense as he lay before her, waiting for her response. Without really thinking, Brenda laid a hand on his shoulder and rubbed at the muscle. It was on the tip of her tongue to ask him what he wanted from her. Did he want to start something important? Did he want to get her into bed and then be done with her? Did he want her to go away and leave him alone? But she couldn't. One of them had to be brave. One of them had to say what they wanted, even if it meant rejection. Brenda took a shaky breath. She could do it. For him. For them.

For the potential of being a them.

"I want you, Deke," she said, her voice shaking a little. She looked up into his intense gaze and carried on. "I want to see if we have a future together. I think we could have one. A good one. I don't want to use you to get over my ex. I don't need to. I'm over him. Trust me. Sure, I have some residual issues, like if we ever moved in together I'd have to take all the doors off the closets and replace them with curtains, but apart from that I'm totally stable and as sane as the next person. Unless that next person is Betty, then I'm way saner."

She took a deep breath and noticed that he seemed to have relaxed some. It bolstered her courage. "I've wanted you from the moment I met you." She swallowed hard. "I knew you were a good guy, just from the fact you were setting up this haven for people like me. But it was more than that." She let her hand trail down his chest. "You are so blooming hot. Seriously? Shouldn't chefs have a belly? How much working out do you have to do to keep in shape like this?"

Deke barked out a laugh, which made her realise that she had drifted off point again.

"What I mean," Brenda said, "is that I like you. As a person. And as a totally drool-worthy male specimen. But definitely as a person too. I want a relationship. Long term." She looked away and grasped at the last of her courage, laying it all out there for him, leaving herself open and vulnerable in a way she'd never been before. "I think I want forever," she whispered.

He was up on his knees, facing her before she'd finished the sentence. When she looked up at him, his jaw was firmly set with determination.

"Be sure," he ordered. "I might scare you, but I'd never hurt you. So be sure." She watched his throat work as he swallowed. "Because I want you too damn much to play around. I think that if I get you, I might never let you go. And I know how creepy that makes me sound."

Brenda hiccupped a laugh as she felt tears run down her cheeks. It seemed that all of her emotions were erupting at once. "I'm sure." She pulled her top over her head.

It was gratifying to hear Deke's sharp intake of breath, because she wanted him to like how she looked, but she knew she wasn't anywhere near as toned and fit as he was. Nope, her body was all about the plentiful curves and pale white skin.

"Bren?" He sounded shaky, and she wasn't sure what he

was asking. But hell, he hadn't run and he knew what he was getting.

With the last of her courage, Brenda reached behind her and unclasped her bra. She let it fall down her arms as she looked up at him through her lashes.

Deke nodded as though coming to some conclusion. His hands fisted on his thighs.

"Aye," he said as he looked down at her. "I'm keeping you. You're a complete nutcase, you look like Marilyn Monroe and I'm pretty sure you talk to imaginary friends, but you are so fucking perfect for me."

Brenda smiled widely and launched herself at her man, tumbling them both back onto the mattress. They rolled until Brenda was flat on her back with Deke leaning over her. He brushed her wild hair away from her face and smiled down at her. The look Brenda saw on his face made the whole world fade away. It was a soft look, an intimate one, just for her.

"I think I'm falling in love with you, Brenda Smith," he said softly.

And just like that, at the sound of those words, Brenda knew she was entirely in love with Deke Miller.

"Holy hamstrings, Batman, what do we do now?" Brenda whispered.

"I get naked like you keep begging me to do, crazy girl." Deke grinned before he reached behind his neck and pulled his t-shirt over his head.

"About time," Brenda said just before his lips met hers.

CHAPTER 29

Jodie and a very mellow Deke, who wouldn't let Brenda take more than a step from his side, had called a meeting in the living room of the manse. They'd timed it for after church, because the women of Knit or Die said they couldn't miss the service. Apparently Morag was doing the prayer, and that was always hysterical, although Jodie suspected the local baker never intended it to be. Jodie had pointed out that the Knit or Die women didn't work for the spa and didn't need to attend the meeting, and was promptly silenced by four "mum stares." The meeting was moved to the afternoon.

As Deke and Jodie explained to the group everything that had happened in the past couple of weeks, Brenda stayed welded to Deke's side. The look of pure adoration in her eyes was enough to make Jodie feel nauseated, but from the smile on Mitch's face, he was just amused. And yes, Mitch was there, because it was Sunday and he told her that couples who were dating hung out on Sundays. There were a whole lot of complicated rules for this dating thing. Jodie was glad she'd skipped that stage with her ex-husband. It was a whole lot of hassle for very little return.

"I'm sorry, Jodie," Patricia said, bringing Jodie's attention back to her staff and the reason for the meeting. "I really appreciate everything you and Deke have done for us, but I need to think about my kids." Her hands shook as she clasped them in her lap. "I think it would be best if we moved somewhere else."

Jodie couldn't blame her. Of course Patricia would be worried about her kids. The Invertary refuge hadn't turned out to be the safe, quiet spot she'd been promised it would be.

"I disagree," Margaret Campbell said. "You need to stay here, Patricia. Where we can all keep an eye on you and the children. This is your home. We won't let anything happen to you."

The other women of Knit or Die nodded fervently and Jodie wondered again why she'd allowed them to stay for the meeting. And they weren't the only outsiders who'd turned up for the "secret" meeting to talk about "secret stuff." Nope, somehow word had spread and their numbers had swollen to the point where the manse living room was starting to get crowded. The Knit or Die women were there, Lake and Grunt represented Benson Security and Matt was there unofficially as the police contact.

It didn't end there. Betty was there too. Nobody knew why, but unless they wanted to physically lift her and toss her out, she was there to stay. Plus, it was entertaining watching her laugh at Grunt after she'd managed to stun-gun him into unconsciousness. Only evil Betty MacLeod would mess with Grunt.

"I completely understand your concerns," Jodie told Patricia. After everything she'd told them about the break-ins and Brenda hiding, she didn't blame Patricia for her reaction one tiny bit. "We can arrange for you to be moved on to another safe house. I'm so sorry this hasn't turned out to be the haven we wanted it to be for you."

Patricia lowered her eyes and Jodie could have sworn she was blinking back tears. This was hard for all of them.

"I think—" Deke started, but he was cut off by the front door slamming open.

All of the alpha males in the room were instantly on their feet, ready to go into battle. A sight that was comical when Matt's wife Jena tottered into the room in her cut-off purple dungarees, sparkly rainbow tee and mile-high sparkly purple stripper shoes—in other words, wearing what she deemed to be her work uniform. Considering she worked in the local hardware store, the sight was bewildering.

"Are we late?" She ploughed into the middle of the room, kissed her husband then stole his seat.

"I brought cake." Claire, Grunt's wife, came in next. The young, very pregnant blonde smiled. "Chocolate cake."

"What are you doing here?" Grunt managed to sound irritated, concerned and loving all at the same time.

"I'm here to support the effort, baby."

Grunt didn't even argue. He just picked her up and walked back out of the house with her.

"Hell," Jena said. "She got further than I thought she would."

Kirsty, who was Lake's wife and the daughter of the leader of Knit or Die, Margaret, was grinning when she came in. "Claire gave me the cake. She said to tell you Grunt has her under house arrest."

At the sight of Kirsty, Mitch tensed where he stood leaning against the wall. "Please tell me you didn't bring…"

"I can't believe you started without me," Josh snapped as he came into the room.

"And you did bring him." Mitch slumped at the sight of his best friend.

Josh confronted the room. "You lot are prejudiced against men who don't have military training. Just because I sing doesn't mean I can't fight."

"If we let you fight and you get injured," Matt said, "Caroline will kill us. Half the time she acts more like your manager than Mitch does."

"This is true," Mitch said with a strange, considering look in his eyes.

"I wouldn't kill you." Caroline waddled into the room. "I would volunteer all of you for every single thing that I'm on a committee to oversee." Deke instantly gave up his chair for her. She lowered herself into it and gave everyone a solemn nod as the men in the room turned white—Caroline was on a lot of committees.

"You brought your heavily pregnant wife?" Mitch looked at Josh like he was an idiot.

"You try stopping her sometime, see how well that works out for you. Anyway, she needed to be here for strategy. Nobody does planning like Caroline." He beamed with pride until he spotted the chocolate cake. "Ooh, cake."

Everyone held their breaths waiting for Caroline to put a stop to Josh consuming extra calories. Instead she gave her husband an indulgent smile that shone with love.

"Abby couldn't be here," Kirsty said as she leaned into Lake. "She's having problems with the twins. Flynn said he'll be over later."

"Good," Matt said. "I need to talk to him."

"So, it's okay for an ex-footballer to come to the secret meeting, but not the singer?" Josh complained around a mouthful of cake.

He was uniformly ignored, so he settled himself on the arm of the chair his wife sat on and consoled himself with cake.

Like everyone else, Jodie stared in the direction of the

door, waiting to see who would come through next. It didn't take long for Dougal and Reverend Morrison, who was as old as Betty, to come into the room. They said hello and took up seats at the wall. When it appeared all of the unwanted and uninvited attendees were in place and no more were coming, Jodie slowly stood, put her hands on her hips and scanned the room.

"You want to tell me what you lot are doing here?" she said, her tone ice-cold.

"We're here to help," Dougal boomed. "This town sticks together. You're part of us now. We're going to help protect you. Don't go looking a gift horse in the mouth, lassie."

"Aye," Reverend Morrison said. "Say thank you and be done with it."

"That's what I tell him when we play hide the salami." Betty cackled loudly as Reverend Morrison scowled and the rest of the men in the room turned green.

"What part of 'secret refuge' was hard for you folk to understand?" Jodie asked. "You're putting the lives of these women in danger by telling everyone what's going on here."

Caroline's chin went up. "That isn't true. The more people who know and band together, the safer it will be. Now there are more people looking out for them. More places they can stay, if need be. More bodies willing to fight on their behalf." She looked at the spa staff. "You can't keep running. We want you to stay and we will make it as safe as possible for you here. You have the backing of the town council on that front too. We want this to be your home. We want you to know that you can depend on us." She looked back at Jodie. The room was so silent that you could almost hear hearts beating. "The Domino Boys are here too. They're setting up outside. They plan to watch the perimeter for anyone sneaking around."

Jodie turned to the window, and sure enough, two deck

chairs were set up at the side of the spa and two old men were drinking tea and scanning their surroundings. Jodie didn't know what to say. She looked at her brother and saw he was in the same state. The looks of pure awe and raw emotion on the faces of the women hiding out in Invertary almost undid Jodie. She cleared her throat. The gift these people had given them was overwhelming. They were putting their lives on the line to support the refuge. They were standing with the women in the house, whether they wanted it or not.

"Jodie?" Patricia's soft voice cut through the thick silence. When Jodie looked at her, she saw silent tears running down her cheeks. "I've changed my mind," she said. "I want to stay here." She took a deep breath and whispered, "Forever."

Jodie blinked back her own tears as she smiled at Patricia.

"Well, that's settled." Caroline pulled her laptop out of her bag. "Now we need a plan of action. Lake, let's start with you."

Lake's lips twitched, but when he opened his mouth, it was Betty's voice that came out.

"We need to start with weapons," she said. "Lake needs to issue everyone with stun guns and pepper spray. Maybe a gun or two." She reached into her handbag and pulled out a paper bag with a Scotch pie in it and proceeded to snack.

"I can't believe I'm going to say this," Margaret said, "but I agree with Betty. We would have dealt with the problems at the castle much faster if we'd been armed with something other than water balloons."

"Condoms," Jena coughed the word into her hand, then tried, unsuccessfully, to stifle a giggle.

As everyone argued about what was most important and had to happen first, Jodie caught Mitch's eyes over the crowded room. He stared at her with a combination of pride and relief. It was in that second Jodie realised who was behind the gathering in front of her. Mitch had called in the cavalry. These were all people who'd weathered trauma in the past. People he trusted. People he relied upon. And he'd gifted them to her. She should have been mad at his interference, but instead she felt the wall around her heart crack and wobble.

"What we need," Jena said, "is a moat, and I know how to build a drawbridge."

"No," was the unified cry as Invertary's most accident-prone woman pouted.

"Nobody would get injured. I'm real good at DIY now. Ask Matt." Jena pointed at her husband, who squirmed.

Matt looked at Lake for help.

"No moat," Lake said. "It will interfere with the land sensors."

That shut Jena down, but not before she gave her husband a look that promised retribution later. Matt seemed more amused than anything else.

As everyone continued to argue, as though each of them had an equal say in what measures they took to protect the manse, Jodie realised that they did. The refuge and the women in it had truly been welcomed into the bosom of Invertary.

Over the heads of the squabbling crowd, Jodie met Mitch's eyes again. As though the room were empty, they shared a smile that was only meant for the two of them.

The arguing stopped dead when the front door slammed open and a mobility scooter zoomed into the house.

"Right!" James waved a fist with fury. "Which one of you buggers painted my scooter pink?"

Everyone in the room stared at the bright pink scooter and the angry old man. When there was no answer, he spun the scooter around and zoomed back out. "Bloody women, running riot," he muttered as he left.

"Should we tell him about the glow-in-the-dark words that will appear on the back of it when the lights go out?" Shona asked the room.

"Probably not," Margaret said.

"I wonder if Findlay has spotted his upgraded phone yet," Jean said as she reached for a biscuit.

There was a loud shout of outrage from outside the building.

"That'll be him now," Shona said. "He doesn't sound happy. Maybe we should have bedazzled it with blue sparkles instead of pink?"

"I've just about had enough of this war of the sexes," Dougal called over the women. "I'm the one who's caught in the middle of this nonsense. Do you have any idea how stinky wet wool is? I had a toilet full of it. Not to mention that bloody sister song. I can't get it to shut off. I've had enough. As unofficial mayor of Invertary, I'm putting a stop to this right now." He stood and pointed at the women of Knit or Die. "This childish fighting with the Domino Boys will stop this instant."

Everyone stared at Dougal's red face for a few minutes and then Margaret and her cronies started laughing.

"We'll stop when you become the official mayor," Margaret said.

"I'm putting all of this in the minutes," Caroline said. "I will also make sure to minute that I've arranged for counselling and gender awareness classes for both the Knit or Die women and the Domino Boys." She smiled sweetly. "As per point fourteen, subsection three, paragraph two of the town charter, any person who is undermining the stability of the town must, by law, take part in such efforts as the town council deems appropriate to amend the situation. There is even a codicil that states the unofficial town council has these powers should the town fail to turn up and vote for an official town council. Now, unless you ladies would like to attend classes for the foreseeable future, as well as any other conciliatory measures I can arrange, I suggest you put aside your squabbles with the old men outside and undo any damage you may have done so far."

There was a stunned silence.

"What she said." Dougal pointed at Caroline.

"That's my wife." Josh wrapped his arm around her. "She's a genius." He looked like he was going to burst with pride.

Jodie noted that Mitch was looking at Caroline with unconcealed speculation. She made a note to ask him about that later. Margaret Campbell looked sheepish when she stood.

"We'll sort it out, Caroline," she said. "No need to organise any brainwashing for us."

"Mum!" Kirsty stared at her mother.

Margaret turned to her fellow knitters. "Come on, girls. We need to go sort out the men."

Four demure women left the house as Mitch sauntered up to Caroline.

"Is there really a point fourteen, subsection three in the town charter that gives you those powers?" Mitch asked.

Caroline smiled serenely up at him. "There isn't even a town charter, Mitch."

He barked out a laugh that made his eyes sparkle. Then he pulled up a chair beside his best friend's wife. "I have a business proposition for you," Mitch said, but his eyes were on Jodie while he said it, making her wonder just what he was cooking up now that involved her.

She was pretty sure, at the rate he was going, he'd have her married by the end of the week and wondering how it happened.

Strangely, that thought wasn't as terrifying as it had once been.

. . .

As the meeting degenerated into a social, Brenda looked up to find Lake standing in front of her. He didn't say a word, only handed her a piece of paper.

"What's this?" Brenda said as she stood.

She felt Deke's presence beside her a second before his arm went around her waist.

"Proof," Lake said.

Brenda was unsure why her hands trembled as she unfolded the paper. She just knew that Lake had given her something important.

Her knees gave out as she started to read. Deke caught her, easing her onto the sofa behind her as a hush stole over the room.

"Is it real?" Brenda's voice trembled as she looked up at Lake.

"Holy crap." Deke exhaled as he finished reading over her shoulder. His arms tightened around her.

"It's real," Lake said. "It's why it was difficult to find him."

Brenda looked back down at the death certificate in her hands. Clive Emerson had died eight months earlier, after a bar fight in a Spanish resort.

"It's over," Brenda whispered.

She wasn't even aware she was crying until she was sitting in Deke's lap, surrounded by the man she loved.

"We owe you," she heard Deke tell Lake. "Anything, anytime."

"Make her happy," Lake said. "That's enough."

Brenda heard him walk away.

"It's over," she whispered to Deke.

"No, Bren," he whispered back. "It's just beginning."

"You were behind this afternoon's meeting, weren't you?" Jodie asked as soon as they'd made it inside Mitch's hotel room.

"I've no idea what you're talking about."

It'd been a long day and suddenly the room Mitch had called home for the past few years didn't feel anything like home. He needed to find a house. Scratch that, he needed Caroline or Jodie to find him a house. Mitch was certain they'd enjoy house-hunting way more than he ever would anyway.

"You know exactly what I mean."

Jodie kicked off the ladybird-covered crocs he'd bought her. She'd rarely had them off since he'd given them to her and he made a mental note to get her the rest of the pairs in the set. He'd seen ones with bees on them that were cool. She'd like those.

Mitch placed the takeout bags he'd picked up on his way through the pub on the table. Neither one of them had been in the mood for eating in the restaurant and Dougal didn't do room service. Although the food was bound to be decent, Mitch still missed Chinese food. The best Chinese food he'd ever eaten was in Harlem, New York. He vaguely wondered if he could talk the owners into opening up a franchise in the Highlands.

"Are you listening to me?" Jodie seemed amused by his tired, wandering mind.

"Nope. I was thinking about food." Mitch kicked off his shoes and started unpacking the bags.

"I said, you arranged for everyone to be there this afternoon." She pointed a finger at him. "Don't deny it. I know it was you."

"How do you know it was me?" There was no way she could know it. She was fishing for information.

Mitch lounged back in his hard dining chair, wishing it was a nice, soft armchair. La-Z-Boy, that's what he needed in his new house. He'd make sure to put one in every room. He became momentarily distracted by the fact Jodie was shimmying out of her jeans. Damn, her legs were perfect. Long, lean, toned. They made him hot just looking at them. She sauntered over to the closet and helped herself to one of his dress shirts. A soft grey one that was his favourite. He watched as she slipped off her t-shirt, unclasped her bra and put on his shirt. Yeah, now he was really hot. There was no self-consciousness in any of her actions. She was simply a woman, comfortable around her man, getting ready for an evening at home. Only their home was a hotel room and she didn't acknowledge he belonged to her.

But he did. She owned him heart and soul.

"I know it was you," she said as she strolled towards him, "because it's just the kind of thing you'd do." She climbed straight onto his lap, straddling him. He put his hands on her hips and held her in place. "You facilitate things for people. It's what you do. It can be subtle, or you can throw your weight behind it, but it still has the same end goal. You smooth the path for the people around you."

"It's my job." Mitch tried to sound casual when really he was worried. Usually people didn't notice what he did behind the scenes and he was afraid Jodie would take his interference as a grab for control.

"It's more than your job. It's who you are." She put her forearms on his shoulders and leaned into him.

Mitch found himself waiting for her to cast her verdict on his penchant for helping the people around him. Okay, maybe "interfering in their lives" was a better way of putting it. She seemed to be staring deep into his eyes as she thought things over. Mitch didn't hide anything. She either accepted everything that he was, or she didn't. There wasn't a whole lot he could do to influence her either way.

"Does it bother you?" he asked, because he couldn't stand the stress of waiting for her conclusion.

"No." Jodie sounded bewildered by that. "You don't tell people what to think, or what to do—you just wait until they make their goals clear and then you go in quietly and smooth the way. Or, in the case of sorting out the protest outside the spa, you go in not so quietly, but you still sort it out."

"Some people would think that was me taking the control away from them."

She cocked her head to the side, considering. "No, I don't see it like that. You're kind of like a rock, a big, dependable rock."

Mitch wasn't sure he liked the sound of that. "I'm a big, dumb rock? Yeah, that screams sexy and smart."

Her smile cleared the shadows in the room. "You're my big, dumb rock."

Mitch froze at the words, but she didn't seem to realise what she'd said. She'd claimed him. Mitch didn't dare point it out in case she changed her mind, or worse, ruined the moment by trying to justify it.

"Okay," he said, trying to keep it light. "If I did good, where's my thank you kiss?"

"Oh, I think you need a bigger thank you than one little kiss." Her smile was an invitation to sin.

"You do, do you? How big a thank you are we talking about here?"

Jodie tugged at the bottom of his tee and he moved his arms to allow her to pull it over his head.

"Did I ever thank you for getting rid of the protestors?" Her hands were flat against his chest, mapping every inch.

He felt her touch resonate throughout his body. "No, you didn't thank me. You threatened me."

She tugged her bottom lip between her teeth and looked up at him through thick black lashes. It was a good job she had other skills, because her acting was awful.

"That's terrible. I've been neglecting you." She popped the button on his jeans. "I need to make up for it. You deserve a big, big thank you."

Mitch couldn't help the chuckle that rumbled out of him. "About time. I've been waiting for a decent thank you."

Jodie lowered the zip on his jeans, thankfully being careful to ensure she didn't snag anything important. She climbed off his knee and tugged at the waistband of his jeans. He lifted his hips to let her pull them, and his underpants, down his legs. As he sat there, naked, Jodie traced his ribs with her fingertips.

"You're bruised," she said. "I hurt you when we were sparring."

"It's fine." Mitch didn't want her to back off in any way. He wanted to be the one who gave Jodie everything she needed. Whether that was support to achieve her dreams, smoothing out her problems for her or being her sparring partner when she had to let off some steam, he didn't care what he had to do. Just so long as he did it with her. For her.

"I really need to teach you some decent moves." Jodie actually looked worried for him. "We'll start tomorrow. You don't need to train in martial arts or anything, but if we can update your skills, you won't get bruised when we fight."

Mitch liked that she'd said "when." She was talking about a future again. One with him in it. His heart warmed at the sound of it.

"Maybe I should get one of those big padded suits some guys wear for target practice?"

She shook her head. "Don't worry. I'll protect you. You don't need the suit."

Damn, but he wanted to kiss her. Badly. But this was the first time since they'd been together that she'd taken the initiative. He didn't want to ruin it and make her back off.

"Now," Jodie said in that low, seductive bedroom voice of hers, "time to thank you for everything you've done to help me."

Mitch went lightheaded as she lowered to her knees in front of him. All of the blood he needed to power his brain had rushed south and was now standing to attention in front of Jodie.

She gave him a slow, wicked smile, before she leaned forward and licked him. Holy crap, the sight of her mouth at his cock was enough to make him lose his control. She wrapped a hand around him and sucked him deep. Mitch groaned as his head fell back onto the wooden rest behind him. If there were any other thoughts in his mind, they'd been entirely erased. There was only Jodie. Jodie loving him with her mouth.

He sat there, enjoying everything she did until he couldn't stand it anymore.

"Baby," he rasped at her. "Bed." Yeah, he'd turned into a

caveman. Only able to bark words because sentences were way too hard.

She held him tight. "What if I don't want to go to bed? If I want to finish up here?"

Damn it to hell. Who was he to get in the way of what she wanted? He groaned and let his head fall back again. Her laugh was wicked as she climbed onto his lap and straddled him. Mitch slid his hands under her shirt and paused when he realised she'd removed her underwear. He slid them up satin-soft skin until he held her tiny waist.

Jodie's lips found his and her kiss was languorous. This wasn't the fiery combustion of previous sexual encounters. This was a tasting. Slow, sensual lovemaking. Mitch couldn't help but feel that she was claiming him through her touch and her intent. And he loved every single second of it.

Her lips travelled down his throat to his shoulder, kissing and nipping and tasting. Mitch sat back and let her have her way with him. There was no need to battle for control. If he had his way, this would be one lovemaking session in amongst years of lovemaking. There would be times when each of them would run the show and times when they would clash with desperate need.

"Taste so good," she said against his chest before biting into his pec.

Yeah, that was perfect. He ran a hand up her back and clasped her hair, telling her by touch to do it again. Jodie understood him perfectly and instantly complied.

"You make me crazy," she said.

He made her crazy? Mitch tugged her hair until his mouth was on hers. That was better. He could kiss her for hours and still want more. He was so wrapped up in the feeling of her mouth on his that he didn't realise what she was doing until he felt himself slide into her wetness. Jodie broke the kiss and sat back on him. She was everywhere. Surrounding him. Owning him. Completing him.

He opened his eyes, eyes he hadn't even realised he'd shut, to watch her slowly rock herself on him. She was the most beautiful woman he'd ever seen.

"Mitch." Her voice hitched as her movements became more frantic.

Mitch sat forward, pressed a hand to her back to support her and cupped her head as he kissed her. Together they moved in rhythm, punctuating the silence with moans of need and whispers of desire. At last, Jodie broke the kiss and her head fell back. She moaned as she clamped around him, making Mitch follow her into the abyss.

He fell back into the chair, taking Jodie with him. He could feel her heart pounding against his chest as she rested her cheek on his shoulder and wrapped her arms around his waist.

"Best thank you I ever had," Mitch whispered before pressing a kiss to her head.

"Mmm," was the only reply he got.

They sat there like that, Mitch holding Jodie tight to him, stroking her back until he realised she'd fallen asleep. With a chuckle, Mitch stood, taking her with him and placing her in the bed. He turned out the lights and crawled in beside her. Showers and food could wait a few hours.

He pulled Jodie into his side, until she was lying with her cheek on his chest and her arm slung over his waist. Perfect. Mitch kissed her hair and stroked her arm.

"I love you, Jodie," he whispered into the darkness before his eyes drifted closed.

In that moment, he knew it to be true. Whether it had happened the first time he'd set eyes on her, or gradually over the time they'd spent together, he didn't know. All he knew for certain was that Jodie had his heart. She had all of him. And he had no intention of ever asking for it back. Mitch fell asleep with a smile on his face. Content. Happy. Complete.

IN THE SILENCE of the dark hotel room, Jodie opened her eyes as Mitch fell asleep, his whispered declaration ringing in her ears.

CHAPTER 31

For once, Mitch woke up before Jodie. She was still out cold in their bed, sprawled across it, flat on her stomach. The shirt she'd stolen from him had ridden up during the night, allowing him a fantastic view of her luscious rear. Mitch smiled at the sight.

As quietly as he could, he got dressed in his running gear and made his way down the stairs to the hotel exit. He probably should have woken her, but he knew she had a lot to do that day—what with the restaurant opening that night—and she needed the sleep. She might be stronger than anyone he knew, but she was still dealing with a lot and there were dark circles under her eyes that only sleep would erase.

Mitch passed Dougal on his way out of the building.

"Going running?" Dougal said.

Mitch looked down at his running shorts. "Nope, going dancing."

"Cheeky arse," Dougal said. "What is it with you lads? You're always running or lifting weights or hitting something. In my day, men got their exercise from good, honest hard work."

Mitch looked at Dougal's large, round belly and wondered if his day had really been that great.

"Jodie's in my room. I'm going to run along the loch, then up to the castle. I have a meeting with Josh early this morning. Can you wake Jodie in an hour? She needs to get back to the spa. The restaurant opens tonight."

"Of course," Dougal said, but his lips thinned at the mention of the new restaurant. For years, Dougal's pub and restaurant had been the only option in town. A little healthy competition would do the man good. "Why you need to exercise before the sun even comes out, I don't know. Shouldn't you do this in daylight so you don't trip and break your neck?"

"Great talking to you, Dougal. On that cheery note, I'm going to head out." Mitch left Dougal shaking his head as he stepped out of the building.

The sun was rising over the loch and the world was painted in the blues and greys of early morning. Even though it was technically summer, there was still a nip in the air. Although he loved living in Scotland, Mitch still missed the warmer weather of his home town. He wondered if Jodie had ever been to Atlantic City and made a note to take her for a visit, if he could talk her into it. He stretched his calf muscles and then started his jog alongside the loch with only the dark waters for company.

Mitch didn't get very far before the first blow struck him.

The fist glanced off his jaw, making him stagger to the side. He spun on his heels, back to the loch and faced the men who surrounded him. Three of them. None of them had Mitch's height, but all three looked a helluva lot meaner. He quickly scanned the area behind them. They were hidden from town by a line of bushes. An SUV had been parked on the grass at the side of the bushes, out of sight of the road.

They'd been waiting for him. And there wasn't a single other person in sight.

"You're coming with us," the one in the middle said. Mitch didn't need to hear the English accent to know who he was dealing with.

The leader was slightly smaller than the other two, but they all shared the same thick brow, stocky build and square jaw. Definitely relatives. Two of them had buzz cuts; the third had a shaved head with a blue swastika tattooed on the crown. Mitch mentally catalogued the heavy steel-toe boots, the crowbar the one on the right held and the brass knuckles the one in the middle wore on his tattooed fingers. He really didn't want to get close enough to those fists to read what the words spelled out.

"Not going to happen." Mitch kept his weight on the balls of his feet and shook his arms loose. Three against one weren't ideal odds, but he'd take at least one of them out and do as much damage as he could to the other two before he'd let them take him.

"Fucking American." The leader spat in Mitch's direction.

"And here I thought you guys were only racist when it came to non-whites." Yeah, he probably shouldn't prod them.

"You need to get the fuck back to your own country and mind your own fucking business. First, we need you to do something for us." The leader nodded at the guy on the left, who reached behind him and slipped something out of the back of his jeans.

A knife.

Mitch stilled at the sight of it. A flash of memory from months earlier hit him. The feeling of a sharp blade sliding into his flesh. He shook it off. Concentrate. He had to concentrate.

"Get in the car and you won't get hurt," the leader ordered as his two henchmen stepped closer to Mitch. "Much."

Mitch was hemmed in, with the icy water of the loch behind him. He contemplated running for the water and making a swim for it, but they would be on him before he could make it to the water's edge. There was nothing else to do but stand and fight. This was going to hurt. He looked around for a weapon. There wasn't one. There was only one thing for it—he needed to take theirs.

"Get him!" the leader snapped, and they lunged for him.

Mitch dropped, threw a handful of dirt and stones in the face of the guy holding the knife and rolled towards the guy with the crowbar. Crowbar guy landed hard on his back. Mitch punched him in the throat before jumping to his feet.

A brutal blow hit him low on his back, just missing his kidney. He sucked it up and stamped on the hand carrying the crowbar. The guy squealed. Someone grabbed a handful of Mitch's hair as he bent to get the crowbar. He elbowed the guy behind him in the face, loosening his hold, and grabbed the bar. Swinging around, he hit the nearest guy behind him with the crowbar. It was the guy with the knife. The blow hit his jaw and he crumpled.

Mitch ignored the blood and lunged for the knife. A boot kicked him hard in the thigh as he got his hands on it. As he clambered to his feet, he flung the knife into the water. Crowbar guy was standing, cradling his wrist.

Mitch swung the crowbar at the leader, who cursed and ducked. The wounded guy rushed him and Mitch stepped back towards the loch. He felt a punch hit his ribs like a freight train and thought he heard a crack. He swung the crowbar at the leader, but it just glanced off his shoulder.

A heavy boot hit the back of his knee and Mitch toppled. The leader was on him and the last thing he saw was a fist with brass knuckles aimed at his head.

CHAPTER 32

The text message came through while Jodie was helping Robin to fold napkins in the spa's new restaurant. She'd been outwardly annoyed at Mitch for letting her sleep in, but secretly touched that he'd even thought to do it. When Dougal had woken her, Mitch was already gone. Running, she'd been informed by the bewildered pub owner. He said "running" the same way someone else might have told her Mitch was off having a prostate exam.

It hadn't taken her long to get ready and get to the spa, where she found it already buzzing with people. Deke was barking out orders, Brenda was soothing ruffled feathers and Robin was her usual sarcastic self. But everyone was excited about the grand opening. Even Jodie. At least, she was until the text came through.

It was three sentences: Ferguson boatshed. One hour. Come alone. The words made Jodie's world tilt, but it was the accompanying video that made it turn upside down.

Mitch.

Her Mitch.

Mitch lying on his side on a mucky wooden floor.

Hands and ankles tied. Face bloody. Eye swollen shut. Unmoving.

Was he breathing? Breathe, she mentally snapped at him. Talk. Do something. Anything to tell her he was alive. Anything.

A boot appeared and kicked him hard in the stomach. Mitch groaned and a wave of relief hit Jodie so hard that she staggered. Alive. He was alive. The screen on her phone went black.

Jodie replayed it. Once. Twice...who knew how many times, until a hand clasped her forearm to stop her. She looked up to find Deke. His eyes scanned her face and then they hardened.

"What's happened?"

Jodie handed the phone to him and watched as he played the video. His jaw clenched tight.

"Call Lake," he told Brenda. "Tell him we need him now."

Brenda's face paled, but she ran for the phone.

Jodie stood. She felt calm. Centred. She knew what she had to do. What needed to be done. "I need to find out where the Ferguson boatshed is. Betty will know. She's in the manse. I'll talk to her while I change my shoes." Mitch's crocs were on her feet. She'd hardly taken them off since he'd give them to her, but she needed other shoes for fighting.

Deke's hand shot out to stop her. "You aren't thinking of going alone, are you?"

Jodie looked at him and she knew he saw the resolve in her eyes. She knew because she burned with it. "No. I'm going in with an army. Then I'm going to beat the guy who kicked him just the way he beat Mitch."

Deke searched her face then nodded. "Talk to Betty. I'll assemble the army."

Jodie ran for the manse, where Betty had become yet another uninvited resident. The old woman was dozing in an armchair. When the door slammed shut behind Jodie, she jerked awake.

"What the hell is it now?" Betty said.

"Where's Ferguson boatshed?"

She scowled, her lined face folding in on itself until she looked like a wrinkly Shar Pei. "You woke me because you want to go boating?"

"Mitch has been taken."

Betty jerked to her feet. "You'll need backup. I'll get my stun gun."

"I need to know where the shed is. Deke is calling in backup. You need to stay here and guard the women."

Betty studied Jodie's face for a minute, trying to decide if she was being fobbed off with some busywork. She nodded, obviously deciding she wasn't. "I'll get everybody into the basement. The boatshed is on the other side of the loch, northeast of here. There's a little cove area that can't be seen until you're nearly on it. That's where Ferguson built his shed. There's no road over there. The only way to get to it is by boat."

Jodie took a second to close her eyes and breathe. If a boat was the only option, it meant that Mitch's captors would see her coming, as well as anyone who accompanied her.

"I need shoes." Jodie ran up the stairs, grabbed her sneakers and pulled them on. She tied a sheath with a small knife to her ankle and considered what other weapons she could take. In the end, she decided the knife was enough. The knife had been a gift from her brother, but she'd never used it. Her martial arts discipline was more concerned with hand-to-hand combat than weapons. That didn't mean she didn't know how to use them if need be.

When she ran back downstairs, she found Betty filling Patricia in on the situation.

"Don't worry about us," Patricia said. "Go get Mitch."

Jodie pulled open the door.

Betty called out behind her, "You teach them a lesson, lassie." There was absolute confidence in the old woman's voice. Jodie held the words to her, but focused on what had to be done.

When she arrived back at the spa, Lake, Grunt and Matt were there, as well as two more of Lake's men whom Jodie had only met briefly. Solemn eyes turned to her as she entered the restaurant.

"Matt's got a boat waiting for you," Deke said, letting her know that he already realised it was the only way to get to the location.

Jodie checked the clock in the kitchen. Forty-eight minutes until deadline. "How long does it take to get across the loch?"

"About twenty-five minutes to get to the boatshed," Matt said, before hesitating. "There are no roads over there and that area is rough woodland."

"Betty told me," Jodie said.

"I think it's best if you step back and let the police handle this," Matt said.

Jodie lifted her chin and stared him in the eye. "How will you handle it? A boat full of police and someone calling out over a loudspeaker asking them to surrender? How long will it take police backup to get here from Fort William or Glasgow or wherever they need to come from? What kind of damage could they do to Mitch in the time it took for your guys to arrive? Or worse yet, what would they do to him if they knew it was the police coming instead of me?"

Matt shared a look with Lake. It said, more than words could have, that anything Matt could do officially would be too little too late.

"We don't even know who these guys are or what they're

capable of," Matt said. "It's too risky. You go in there and the chances of you being hurt along with Mitch are high."

"I'm going to the boatshed." Jodie didn't bother to argue or raise her voice. Her mind was made up; this conversation was a courtesy. She knew there was a vast amount of expertise in the room and she needed these men at her back. But she was going to get Mitch. With or without them.

"Okay," Deke said. "What do we know?"

Lake pulled a perfectly folded map out of his back pocket and spread it on one of the tables. "The boatshed is here." He pointed to the middle of the tiny cove that was hidden behind a curve in the loch, out of sight of the main water area. "The hills behind are steep, covered in dense vegetation and forest."

"They had to use a boat?" Brenda said as she came up beside Deke.

"It's the only way they can get in or out." Lake pointed along the northern edge of the loch. "This is the nearest road. It's probable they'd have a car parked there and use a boat to get to it."

"Could we cut them off on the water as they tried to escape?" Brenda said.

"Is that before or after they kill Mitch and me?" Jodie asked calmly, but instantly regretted it when Brenda paled.

"I'll go to the manse, make sure everyone's okay there," she said.

"No," Jodie said. "I'm sorry. Stay."

Deke wrapped an arm around Brenda and pulled her to his side.

"We can't let Jodie go in there alone," Matt said.

"There's no time to get anyone in overland," Lake said. "We could run from the road, but with the terrain, there's no way we'd make the meet in time."

"Jodie can take care of herself," Deke said, making her love her brother even more. "She has martial arts training."

Lake, Matt and Grunt gave her long, assessing looks.

"You don't know how many people are in there with Mitch," Matt pointed out. "It doesn't matter how well you can handle yourself if you're outnumbered."

"Water," Grunt said, and all eyes turned to the big man. "I'm Marines." He pointed at Lake. "You're SAS." He eyed Deke. "I don't know what you are."

"Army."

"Water experience?" Grunt said.

"The basics."

Grunt nodded. "That leaves me and Lake. We go in from the water. We bail from the boat before it rounds the bend and swim in."

Lake looked at his team member. "I was thinking the same thing."

Grunt headed towards the door.

"Where's he going?" Deke said.

"He's going to get kitted out and sort my gear. As far as Grunt is concerned, this discussion is over," Lake said, as though Grunt's behaviour was perfectly normal.

"Deke and I will take the second boat and follow," Matt said.

"Engine noise," Lake pointed out.

"We'll keep our distance. You need me for clean-up. I know you like to think this is the Wild West and you're the sheriff, but it's Scotland and I'm the law in these parts," Matt said.

Lake's lips twitched.

Jodie looked at the clock again. Thirty-five minutes to deadline. "We need to go."

She caught Deke's eyes as Lake folded his map.

"Be careful," he said.

Jodie nodded—it was all she could manage. Her mind was on Mitch and on the fact she would do whatever it took to get him out of there in one piece.

"Can you drive a boat?" Lake asked as they headed out the door to his SUV.

"I'll learn." Jodie climbed into the car and watched Matt climb into his. Grunt was long gone.

If she hadn't been so wrapped up in what she was doing, she would have raised an eyebrow at the hard kiss Deke shared with Brenda before he climbed in with Matt. Brenda stood beside the two men Lake had left behind to protect the women. Her face was pale and her eyes were wide as she watched the man she cared about ride off into trouble.

Jodie wondered what her face revealed about her relationship with Mitch. Could everyone see that she would give everything she had, everything she was, to get him back safely? Could they see that there was nothing more important to her than getting to his side? Could they see that under her calm resolve, deep inside where it wouldn't distract her, she was screaming and crying and begging God to let Mitch live?

She turned her face to the window as the town zoomed past. Tiny grey terraced houses that used to belong to the workers in the old mine. More modern houses, with less personality, built on the edge of town. The large grey church at the top of the high street that dominated the town and was used as a meeting point for everyone who lived there. Two facing rows of crooked white buildings that made up the shopping centre of Invertary. And at the bottom of the street, past all the cute little shops and the large, welcoming pub, was the wide expanse of the loch.

The water glistened, a deep teal that looked both peaceful and inviting. The hills around the loch were a tapestry of purple heather and every shade of verdant green. The sky was blue with patches of puffy white cloud. It was beautiful. And it meant nothing at all. Because across that water, Mitch lay unconscious and bleeding.

No, he wasn't just Mitch.

He was the man she loved.

The man who belonged to her.

And she was going to eliminate everything in her path to get to him.

Mitch dragged himself up into a sitting position and leaned back against the remains of an old wooden chair. He winced as the pain in his torso told him he had some cracked or broken ribs. It was the least of his worries. His eye was swollen shut, his cheekbone was shooting out lightning bolts every time his face twitched and his left arm was hanging limply.

"I say we kill him now," the one with the damaged hand said. "Dump his body in the loch with Jonny." The guy stomped over to him and spat at Mitch. It hit his chest. "You killed my cousin, you fucker."

Mitch would deal with the fact he'd killed someone later. Right now, he only regretted that he hadn't managed to kill more than one of them.

"Back off, Kenny," the leader snapped from where he stood looking out over the loch. "We need him. The bitch won't talk without him."

Kenny leered at Mitch. "You hear that? Ray says I get to hurt you to make your woman talk. The day's looking up."

At least a dozen smart-ass comments flitted through Mitch's mind, but he was wise enough to keep them to himself. Instead he looked past the henchman to the leader. "What do you want with Jodie?" Pain from talking made him nauseated.

"I know what I want with her." Kenny grabbed his crotch and pumped his hips. "I'm going to do her in front of you. Then I'm going to slit your throat."

Ray's eyes were dead when he turned to Mitch. "I'm going to ask her where she hid my wife. Then I'm going to hand her over to my cousin here."

Mitch tried to fight past the pain to think logically. "Why would Jodie hide your wife?"

Ray didn't answer; he focused on staring out at the water.

His cousin had no problem sharing his thoughts, though. "Your bitch is part of that dyke team who steal women from their husbands."

It all fell into place for Mitch, a whole lot slower than it usually did. "You attacked the Hampstead Heath worker."

Kenny shrugged. "She deserved it. Bitch steals women from their men. She gave up Jodie Miller's name in the first five minutes."

"But you kept hitting her anyway." He'd have to have done for her to end up unconscious in a hospital bed.

"Ray did the hitting. I like to teach bitches a lesson another way."

"You mean you like to rape women, because you can't get it up unless you're making somebody suffer." Mitch wished he still had the crowbar, because he'd love to use it on Kenny until he cried like a baby.

A blow to the side of his head meant he saw nothing but white light for a minute.

Mitch licked his lips and tasted blood, but his eyes stayed on Kenny. "It's a good job you like rape so much. I hear you'll get to experience quite a bit of it in jail."

With a roar, Kenny's fist came up and Mitch prepared for the blow.

"Don't touch him!" Ray shouted. "Can't you see he's

fucking with you? You can hurt him when the bitch gets here."

Mitch bit the inside of his cheek to stop from telling them that he wasn't the one who was going to get hurt when Jodie arrived. She was going to wipe the floor with their backsides and paint the walls with their blood. Oh yeah, he liked that imagery. It made him feel much better.

"He's not worth it, anyway. He isn't even man enough to keep his woman in line." Kenny kicked Mitch's leg before walking over to his cousin.

Mitch shifted straighter and felt like he was going to pass out. He stayed very still. Losing consciousness again wasn't something he could afford to do. Plus, he wanted to see Jodie lay waste to his attackers.

"She doesn't know where your wife is," he said to Ray.

Flat shark eyes met his. "It doesn't matter. She'll know the next link in the chain. It took me years to get this far and I'm a patient man. I plan to keep dismantling the chain, a link at a time, until I get my property back."

He turned back to the loch. Mitch closed his eyes, only for a second. His whole body was thrumming with pain. Man, he was tired of being the beating boy for assholes and lunatics. Invertary attracted violence and when it got to town it headed straight for him like he was its lightning rod. It was getting old. And so was he. He wasn't sure his body could take much more abuse.

His mind floated as he waited for Jodie to arrive. He supposed he should have been fighting to keep her out of harm's way. If he'd been Grunt or Lake, he would have been doing everything in his limited power to protect his woman. But he wasn't Lake or Grunt, and Jodie sure as hell wasn't like any of the other women in town. She didn't need his protection. She needed his support. She needed his belief that she was perfect just as she was. She needed to know that he wasn't threatened in the least by her strength. And that's what he was going to do for his woman. He was going to sit back and let her do her thing and he was going to cheer her on while she did it.

"That's her," Ray said, and Mitch's eyes snapped open.

Kenny picked up the sawn-off shotgun that was leaning against the wall and smirked at Mitch.

"Bring her straight in here," Ray ordered. "Check the boat. Make sure that brother of hers hasn't tagged along."

"I know what I'm doing." Kenny sounded cocky as hell. "I can handle her."

Mitch smiled at the thought. That guy was so going down.

CHAPTER 33

The boat was small. It had a starter motor at the back and a steering wheel at the front. And that was Jodie's sum knowledge of the craft.

Grunt was going to steer the boat until they reached the bend before the boatshed came into view. He'd given Jodie a crash course in taking over from him. All Jodie remembered was how to slow down and steer. If Grunt expected her to moor the thing, he was going to be disappointed, because she hadn't paid attention for that part.

Lake sat at the back of the tiny boat. He was dressed in a black wetsuit and there was a backpack at his feet. The pack was sealed to make it waterproof and to protect the weapons inside it. Grunt also wore a wetsuit. Jodie knew that if they all made it through this in one piece, she was definitely going to ask him if it was custom made, because she was pretty sure they didn't come in Godzilla size.

"Get up here," Grunt said and Jodie jerked up from her bench, holding on to the rail as she made it to the wheel.

Grunt moved away without so much as a word. Jodie looked back and caught Lake's eye.

"We're minutes behind you," he said.

"I know." There was nothing else to say. They'd already discussed her carrying a weapon, but decided it wasn't worth it, as they would likely pat her down as soon as she set foot inside the shed.

Lake nodded and pulled the attached hood of his suit up over his head. Grunt did the same before giving her a chin lift, and then the two men silently slipped into the cold loch water. Jodie looked back for them and could barely make them out.

She turned and focused on steering around the bend into the cove without hitting something. As she turned into the cove, she spotted the shed. It was large, wooden and had obviously been abandoned at some point. There were slats missing on the walls and the roof was warped to the point of being unsafe. There was another boat moored off the tiny dock. It was the same sort as the one Jodie was in, only slightly bigger.

Slowing the boat, Jodie didn't even bother to try and align with the dock. Instead she aimed for the shore, cut the engine and ran the boat aground. The ripping noise that came when the boat shuddered ashore told her she'd managed to trash her transport. No matter. Mitch could buy the owner a replacement and she could use the other boat on the dock to get back to town.

As she clasped the rail at the side of the boat, ready to jump over onto the shore, a figure appeared in the doorway of the shed. Jodie stilled and stared at him. He was less than six foot tall, built like a tank, but looked to be made of more fat than muscle, and was pointing a gun at her. A sawn-off shotgun. Jodie noted everything about him, as though time had slowed. The guy's right hand was bandaged, which meant his left arm was taking the weight of the gun, but he was definitely right-handed, because that one was on the trigger. There was a blue tattoo up the side of his throat, something crudely done that screamed prison time. His hair was cropped close to his head and he wore heavy boots, probably steel-toed. Boots just like the one that kicked Mitch.

The guy sauntered towards her, clearly believing she wasn't a threat. Jodie jumped onto the shore. The guy was about four feet from her. He leered and she noticed he was missing a tooth.

"Get inside." He motioned to the shed with the gun. He was so confident that he didn't even check inside the boat.

She almost shook her head at how bloody ignorant he was. He thought she was a timid little woman who would be stupid enough to rush off alone to save her boyfriend.

Idiot.

But an idiot with a gun pointed at her back as she walked in front of him to the shed—even if he was cradling it loosely in her direction rather than aiming at her with his finger on the trigger.

"Fucking bitch," he snarled. "You're to blame for all this shit. Once Ray's done with you, you're going to make up for everything—on your knees." He sniggered, and Jodie knew they had no intention of letting her or Mitch go free.

She moved fast, grabbing the barrel of the gun and yanking it forward. The guy flew into her back. Jodie spun and kicked the side of his knee. She heard a snap as he fell to the sandy shore. Keeping her fingers straight, she jabbed him in the throat. His eyes rolled back and he fell unconscious. Jodie felt for a pulse. It was there. His breath was a rasp, but if he got medical attention soon, he'd survive. She tossed the gun into the loch and headed towards the boatshed, aware that she'd eliminated at least one threat without making so much as a sound.

The rotted wooden door creaked loudly as she

pushed it open. Jodie stepped into the dimly lit interior, scanning as she went, making sure to take in every detail in the room. There were piles of junk, rotting and moulding away. There were rat droppings and evidence that other animals had been using the building as shelter. Light shot through the cracks in the building, making streams that sparkled and danced with dust particles.

And in the middle of the floor, sitting with his legs stretched out in front of him, was Mitch. Jodie's heart stopped beating at the sight of him. She'd been fooling herself since she met him, lying to herself that she could never love again, that she didn't want a relationship with him. And all the while she'd been neck-deep in the most important relationship of her life. No more. She was done holding herself back. If Mitch really wanted her, he was going to get her. And if the damn man ever changed his mind, she would kneecap him.

Mitch was hunched over, but conscious. His undamaged eye was firmly focused on her and clouded with pain. One arm was wrapped around his ribs as though to protect them; the other arm hung limply at his side. There was blood and dirt on his face, neck, clothes.

But he was alive.

Her heart started pounding again.

She looked up from the man she loved to the guy looming over him. He was older—mid-fifties, she guessed. His face was pockmarked from acne scarring, with more scars on top of the pitting. Ones he'd obviously obtained through violence. His neck was thick, his leather jacket offered some form of protection for him and his feet were clad in the same heavy boots as the guy outside.

One of his hands was fisted in Mitch's hair. The other clasped a knife, the tip of the blade at Mitch's throat.

"Where's Kenny?" His accent was pure East London and his words held menace, but Jodie didn't recognise him.

"You mean the guy outside? He said he was watching to make sure I wasn't followed." She tried to sound timid, afraid and weak. She wasn't sure she could pull it off, but if it got that knife away from Mitch's throat, she would try. She hunched her shoulders and wrung her hands in front of her. "I didn't bring the police." She tried to sound slightly hysterical. "I swear I didn't. I did exactly what you said to do. Please." She took a step towards him, coming in on the side that held the knife. "Please let Mitch go now. I'll do anything you want. Please." She took another step towards them.

Ray didn't seem at all worried by her slow advance. He tugged on Mitch's hair. "I'm keeping hold of this fucker until you tell me what I need to know. Kenny has plans for him." He leered. "And you."

She bet he did. Pity Kenny was unconscious. She hoped he was used to disappointment, because that was all he was going to experience. Well, that and jail.

"I don't know anything," she almost wailed, managing to get two steps closer to Ray as she did so. Two more steps and she'd be within reach of the arm that held the knife. "Please, let him go. Tell me what you want, please."

"I want to know where my wife is," he spat. "You helped her. You were with her in that feminist propaganda centre. The woman in London told me you'd know where she was hiding. I want the address." He tugged Mitch's hair tighter, making him wince. "I plan to keep slicing lover boy here until you remember where you stashed the bitch. You've got two minutes to answer before I start cutting."

Jodie mentally added to the man's tally of infractions and adjusted the punishment she intended to inflict. First for hurting Mitch. Second for attacking the worker in London. Third for beating his wife.

"What centre? I don't know what you're talking about." She forced her voice to hitch as though sobbing, and took another step.

"Stop right there!" he snapped. "You know exactly what I'm talking about. The London bitch had a photo of you at the Hampstead Heath centre. I know you were there. I know you are hiding my property. I want it back."

The knife bit into Mitch's throat. He clenched his teeth as a drop of blood ran down to his shoulder. Jodie felt ice-cold fury flood her veins. Ray would pay for that, too.

"I just want to touch him. Please, let me touch him." She held out her hand towards Mitch. One more step and she would be able to grab that arm. "Mitch," she said, sobbing. "Stay with me. Please don't pass out. You need to stay conscious. You may have a concussion. Stay with me."

He gave her a look like she was mad. Jodie cast her eyes to the floor, hoping he got the message. She needed him to act as though he had passed out. To slump down.

"Please let me touch him," she said to Ray. "He's losing consciousness. I need to help him." She flashed a glare at Mitch to tell him he'd better bloody well lose consciousness as soon as she told him he would.

"Where is my wife?" Ray roared, scattering dust particles in the air, sending them into chaos.

"I don't know who you're talking about!"

"Linda Cornell. She's mine. She doesn't leave. I own her fucking life. You know where she is. Tell me or this fucker bleeds!"

Jodie still didn't know who he was talking about. The women in the centre never gave real names, and Linda was too common to narrow down.

"Linda?" Jodie tried to sound as though she was confused. "Linda is your wife?"

She inched forward.

"You know where she is. Tell me or say goodbye to your boyfriend's pretty face. Start talking. That's your last warning before I slice and dice."

"Don't! I'll tell you everything I know." She reached out and jerked her head down, hoping Mitch got the message. "Just let me touch him. Mitch! No! Don't close your eyes. Stay with me." Yes, it was over the top, but Mitch got the message. He slumped to the side, away from her and the knife.

It was all Jodie needed. She sprang forward, her left arm blocked Ray's knife-wielding arm at the wrist as she punched him hard in the middle of this chest.

"Move, Mitch!" she said, but didn't take her attention from the threat.

At lightning speed, she moved into Ray, trapping his knife arm at the wrist in a firm arm hold. Using her forward momentum, she kneed him in the groin. He grunted and bent forward. Jodie continued to push forward; using both her hands, she grabbed his knife hand and twisted, keeping his arm straight and at an angle that was bound to hurt. As she did so, she kicked Ray in the face. Hard. He fell forward, releasing the knife. Jodie kicked it away, then kicked Ray's head again, sending him flying towards the wall. He hit it with a loud crash, making the boatshed shudder and creak. Ray groaned and struggled to stand. He didn't have a chance. Jodie was beside him. One punch to his temple and he was out cold, slumped in a heap of rotting wood and rat droppings.

The whole thing happened in seconds. Ray didn't stand a chance. By the time he'd processed that she was attacking, he'd already been knocked down. Jodie turned her back on him and rushed to Mitch's side. He had rolled over and was leaning back against the remains of a wooden chair. Jodie crouched beside him and gently brushed his hair off his forehead.

"Holy shit," came a deep voice from the open doorway.

Jodie tensed, sprang to her feet and spun, ready to take on the intruder. It was only Grunt, with Lake at his side. The big guy looked stunned and impressed.

"Krav Maga?" he asked Jodie.

She nodded. Grunt grinned as he shook his head in wonder. "You didn't need us, did you?"

"No, I needed you." Jodie crouched back beside Mitch, placing her hand on his arm because she needed to touch him. To feel his warmth and know for sure that he was alive. "I didn't know what I was walking into. I didn't know how many there were. It would have been stupid not to have backup."

Grunt kept on grinning as he turned to Lake. "I like her. We need to keep her." He turned back towards the shoreline. "I'll call Matt and deal with the trash."

"If you ever want a job," Lake said with a smile, "you've got one. I'd put you on any of my teams in a heartbeat, or sort out some bodyguard work for you."

"The only body she's guarding is mine," Mitch grumbled.

Jodie smiled at him, but it was pained. It hurt to see him damaged and suffering.

"Think about it," Lake said. "You'd make a fortune."

He walked over to Ray, pulled the unconscious guy's hands behind his back and secured them. Then he secured his ankles. Jodie took the knife from her ankle sheath and cut through Mitch's bonds.

"Is it wrong that I think it's sexy that you carry a knife?" the crazy man told her.

Jodie could hear Matt's boat pulling up at the dock outside.

"Can you stand?" she asked Mitch.

"I don't know. Guess the only way to find out is to try."

"Don't worry," Jodie said as she helped him get to his feet. "If you fall, I'll catch you."

"I know, baby. I know."

His answer sent a surge of warmth through her soul. Mitch put an arm around Jodie's shoulder and she held him around his waist, careful not to touch his ribs. Together, taking small steps, they made it out into the sunshine.

Matt was standing beside the first guy Jodie had disarmed. His hands were on his hips and his expression was resigned. When he looked up at her, she saw he was annoyed.

"Do I need to have you registered as a lethal weapon?"

"I didn't kill anybody," Jodie pointed out.

Mitch stiffened against her. "I think I might have."

Matt went on instant alert. Jodie used her free hand to reach up and gently caress his cheek. He relaxed slightly.

"They came at me while I was jogging," Mitch told Matt, his voice flat. "Three of them. I managed to get the crowbar off one of the guys and hit the other one with it. I heard a crack and he went down. I don't know what happened to him because the other two overwhelmed me, but I think he might be out there." He pointed at the loch. "I missed that part because I got knocked out with a brass-knuckle punch."

Jodie winced and silently prayed that whoever hit him hadn't cracked his cheekbone.

"No sign of the third guy," Lake said as he came up beside them.

He'd dragged the unconscious Ray with him and dumped him in a heap beside his pal.

"Nothing in their boat," Deke said as he came up to them.

His smile was part approving and part relief. "You didn't get hurt," he said to Jodie.

It wasn't a question, and she knew her brother hadn't

expected her to get hurt. "Not a scratch," she confirmed and his smile widened.

"Where did you hit this guy? Shoulder, body?" Matt asked Mitch.

"Head."

There was a heavy silence as all of them looked at the loch.

"I'll need to call the divers in." Matt sounded resigned.

"Will I be arrested?" Mitch's voice was calm, but his body was taut.

"Self-defence," Matt said. "Plus, right now, we have no body and no witnesses. I don't think this is something you should worry about."

Mitch relaxed a little and Jodie took more of his weight.

"What's the damage?" Deke asked Mitch.

"I think my ribs are broken. I took a couple of kicks to my leg as well as my arm." He held up his weak left arm. "This one isn't so good. And, yeah, after the brass-knuckle punches, I'm pretty sure my face is doing a good impersonation of John Hurt's Elephant Man."

"Let's load everybody onto the boat and get you to the doc," Matt said. "I've got him on standby."

"At least I didn't get stabbed this time," Mitch mumbled.

"Well done, you." Jodie patted his head.

"Smart ass," Mitch muttered.

After the guys helped Mitch get onto the boat, Jodie sat close by his side. She didn't know where to touch him. It seemed like every inch of his body had been bruised or broken. Mitch solved the problem for her by wrapping his arm back around her shoulder.

"Thanks for coming for me, baby," he whispered against her ear.

"I'll always come for you, Mitch." Jodie closed her eyes and leaned into him, as much as she dared with his injuries.

"I know." There was a smile in his voice. "Because you can't live without me—I am just that skilled in bed."

"Idiot."

"Your idiot." It was nothing less than a declaration of commitment. She heard it ringing out in every syllable. "I love you, baby."

Jodie fought to hide the shiver that went through her at his words. They seeped through her skin and burrowed deep inside of her, until they were snug beside her heart where they belonged.

"Not freaking out?" he said.

"No more than usual."

But it was a lie. She wasn't freaking out at all. She was done fighting this thing with Mitch. She was done pretending that she could keep her heart separate. She was done making decisions based on her past. She knew she loved him—all that was left was to tell him. She looked up at his swollen face, twisted with pain, then glanced at the men who were unashamedly listening in. The words would have to wait until they were alone.

"I want a house on the loch," she said instead, and felt his body jerk. "There's a piece of land I have my eye on. I thought we could buy it and build something rustic. I fancy one of those wooden chalets you find in the Alps." She could see it in her mind's eye. The warm wooden beams, the tall windows and steeply sloping roof. "I want a balcony off our bedroom. We can sit out there and watch the sun set over the loch."

"We?" He sounded so hopeful.

Jodie looked up at him. "Are you telling me that now you've managed to wear me down, you've lost interest and are going to give up on us?"

"Us?" His one good eye looked a little dazed.

"I'm not sure this is the best time to talk about things,"

Jodie said. "I think you have concussion. Maybe even brain damage."

Mitch's arm tightened around her. "Nu-uh, you can't back out now. I heard what you said, and I have witnesses. Isn't that right, guys?"

She looked up to find Deke, Lake and Grunt trying not to laugh at her. Although they weren't trying that hard.

"He's right," her brother said, choosing to side with the penis club rather than with his own family. "I heard. You two are building a house on the loch." He looked at Mitch. "I hope you're going to marry her before you move in together. I'm worried about her virtue."

"Does that apply to you too?" Jodie said. "Last time I checked, you were setting up house with Brenda."

Deke cleared his throat. "As I was saying. Your relationship with my sister is none of my business. I'll go watch the prisoners."

"Coward," Jodie called after him as she snuggled closer into Mitch.

The grand opening of the spa restaurant was postponed for three weeks, mainly due to the fact that one of the business owners was looking after her beaten boyfriend. Also, once word spread that the loch was being searched, people set up deck chairs on the shore and watched the divers work. Morag sold pies and Dougal arranged tables outside the pub for his patrons, so they could watch the show while dining. Mitch smiled at the thought. In Invertary they made their own fun.

"Are you sure you're up for this?" Jodie had been fussing over him since he'd come out of hospital.

"I'm almost back to normal. I can see out both eyes. Look." He pointed at his face.

That earned him a smack on the chest. Thankfully, she pulled her punch. She looked up at his face, which was now a lovely mix of blue, green and yellow bruising. At least his cheekbone hadn't cracked. He was thankful for that. Not so thankful for the cracked ribs or the broken arm, but they were both healing nicely and he couldn't complain—unless it got him some Jodie attention. Yep, he wasn't above playing the invalid card to get her to give him a bed bath.

Jodie was dressed in a shimmering ruby-red jumpsuit, with wide-leg trousers and a boat-neck top that made her shoulder eminently kissable. There was a pair of mile-high black Louboutins on her feet, courtesy of Mitch. He'd found that time in a sick bed went faster when he shopped online, but only if he was shopping for Jodie. He'd stocked her up with lingerie and shoes. He was only thinking about her. Honest.

As they pushed open the heavy wooden doors to the restaurant part of the old church building, Jodie cast a glance at him over her shoulder.

"Did you look at the email the architect sent?"

"I told him it was fine with me if it was fine with you." In other words, no, he hadn't looked at the email. He really didn't care what the house they built looked like, just so long as Jodie was in it.

"You don't mind that I told him to replace the living room with a swimming pool?"

Mitch stumbled slightly but recovered quickly enough that he hoped she didn't notice. Swimming pool? Where would he kick back and watch football?

"I've always wanted a pool," he said, wondering if the house plans had a TV room. He'd have to look at the damn email after all.

"Gotcha." Jodie's smile was wide. "Although you should know that if you aren't going to have any input with the architect at the planning stage, then you can't complain about the house once it's built."

"Baby." Mitch draped his arm around her shoulders—the arm that wasn't in a fibreglass cast. "I told you my require-ments for the house. Big bed. Soundproofing for when I make you scream with delight. Giant TV. La-Z-Boy in each room. Mini fridge stocked with beer beside the TV. And one of Lake's kick-ass security systems."

"It's good to know you're low maintenance," Jodie said and Mitch wasn't certain she meant it as a compliment.

"A mirror above the bed would be good too," he added as an afterthought.

"We're not having a mirror on our bedroom ceiling," Jodie said as they spotted her brother across the crowded room, positioned behind the long counter that separated the dining area from the open plan kitchen. "It's tacky."

"I like the sound of that," Mitch said against her ear as they made their way through the room.

"Tacky?" Her face said he was clearly losing his mind.

"Our." Mitch kissed her cheek. "I like it when you say our."

Jodie relaxed into him. "You are such a soppy romantic."

"One of us has to be, baby."

"Mitch!" Josh shouted as he practically ran across the room. "You made it. It's good to see you."

Mitch endured a manly hug that meant Josh thumped his back and jolted his bruised side.

"What are you talking about?" Mitch said. "I saw you yesterday. We watched baseball and talked about your tour. It isn't like I've been in a coma for the past three weeks."

"You got assaulted again, dude." Josh was dressed in one of his signature suits for the occasion, which meant Caroline had forced him out of the Darth Vader t-shirt he'd planned to wear. He rummaged in his pocket, dug out a business card and thrust it at Mitch. "Here, this is the name of a PTSD specialist Caroline found online." He handed an identical card to Jodie. "Make him call. He needs intense therapy before he snaps and kills us all."

"Aw, I'm touched," Mitch said. "I love you too, man."

Josh held up his hands. "I'm all about the self-preservation. Get therapy before it's too late."

Caroline waddled up to them, looking every bit the pregnant Grace Kelly in a fitting pale blue dress.

"I got your email," Mitch said. "I'll go over it and let you know what I think. I've set up a meeting with our lawyers for early next week. Because of your condition, they're flying in to see us."

Caroline patted her stomach. "It isn't a condition, Mitch. It's a baby and pregnant women have been known to get on a plane, you know."

"Nope." Josh grabbed his wife's hand. "You aren't the only one who can do research. I looked it up and way more pregnant women die in air disasters than choke on chicken bones. You're staying in Invertary until you're finished cooking Josh Junior."

Caroline gave her husband a smile that clearly telegraphed she was humouring him and would do exactly what she liked.

"Are you two really going into business together, then?" Jodie's lack of faith continued to amuse Mitch. She laughed every time he talked about his partnership with Caroline. Mitch wasn't sure why. He'd known since the minute he'd set eyes on Caroline that she would be an amazing asset to have in his corner.

"Yes, we're really going into business," Mitch said patiently. "Harris-McInnes Entertainment Management."

"McInnes-Harris," Caroline said. "It sounds better."

"Harris-McInnes," Mitch said firmly. He might think Caroline was an organisational genius, but if he didn't stand his ground, she'd walk all over him.

"How about a Hollywood mash-up?" Josh said. "McHarris, or HarInnes, or Harnes." He frowned. "That last one doesn't sound too good."

"Harris-McInnes it is," Caroline declared.

Josh beamed at her. "You are going to be totally amazing as an entertainment manager. You'll be the best in the business. No act would dare give you any trouble."

"I'm glad you think that," Mitch said. "Because she's taking over the bulk of your management."

"What?" The horror on Josh's face was priceless. "No. You can't. You're my manager. She's my wife. Never the twain shall meet."

Mitch smiled at Caroline. "I'll let you deal with this. While you're at it, can you get him to stop using the word dude?" Then he took Jodie's hand and headed towards her brother.

"That was evil," Jodie said with a fair amount of pride.

"He had it coming."

Messing with his best friend was a nice side benefit of making Caroline a partner. The main benefit being that it freed Mitch up to do other things. He just hadn't decided what other things exactly. Originally, he'd thought he'd take on more singers, but now he was wondering if there wasn't something he could do to help Jodie's cause instead. He had time. He'd figure it out.

"Deke, I'm so proud of you." Jodie let go of Mitch and wrapped her brother in a hug. "The restaurant looks amazing and people seem to really be enjoying the food."

"It's the first night," Deke said. "People are inclined to like you on the first night. Plus, the night is young. There's still time for Robin to poison the table of morons who've been pissing her off all night."

They looked over to where Robin was gritting her teeth at a table full of businesspeople from out of town. It was easy to spot their condescending smiles from across the room.

"I'll sort this." Jodie was striding towards Robin before anyone could stop her.

Deke and Mitch watched her go.

"I don't think Robin needed help," Mitch said. "She strikes me as a woman who can take care of herself."

"There's no stopping Jodie when she's out to save someone." Deke looked at Mitch. "You going to marry her or just shack up in that house of sin you're building?"

"Remind me again how old you are? Because sometimes you sound like the reverend, and he's in his eighties."

"I'm mature for my age. So what's the deal? Marriage or not?"

Oh, what the hell, he might as well answer the guy. "I don't want to push her. But we'll get there. I have it all planned out." He'd had it all planned out since the moment he'd set eyes on her. Mitch had no doubt that he was going to spend eternity with Jodie, but he also knew how to play a long game.

"You're kidding, right? You've pushed her along every step of the way since you met her."

"That's why I thought I should back off for a while. Let her get used to being a couple before I make it official." Although, he didn't plan on letting her spend too much time getting used to things. He knew Jodie. At some point her thinking would take a negative turn and she might talk herself out of keeping him.

"You aren't getting cold feet, are you?" Deke glared at Mitch. "Are you planning to dump her and run?"

Mitch glared back. "Right now I'm planning to hit you over the head with my fibreglass cast. What about you? You planning to marry Brenda?"

Deke's eyes softened when he looked over at the tiny blonde. She was laughing, surrounded by the women of Knit or Die, all seated at a round table by the window.

"Absolutely," Deke said.

"Does she know that?" Mitch could push back when he wanted to.

Deke's eyes snapped to his. A fierce determination filled them. "No, but she's about to."

To Mitch's surprise, Deke put his fingers to his mouth and let out a piercing whistle. Every face in the room turned to him. He pulled out a chair and stood on it.

"Ladies and gentlemen, if I could have your attention for a moment." Deke's voice carried through the silent room. Mitch stared up at him in awe. He was doing it. He was proposing. Now. Damn it, Mitch should have done this. The opening of the restaurant was perfect for a stealth proposal.

"As you know," Deke said, "this is the opening night for my restaurant." There was a loud cheer, and Deke gave everyone a bashful smile as he held up his hands for silence. "This restaurant has been my dream for a very long time. When Jodie and I were kids, we'd talk about what we wanted to do in the future. We wanted to start our own business together and create a safe home for our mum. Mum didn't make it—cancer took her a few years ago—but we carried on with our dream and made it a reality."

Those in the room who knew about the refuge and the safe home they'd made for other women were clearly emotional.

"During all of our planning, over the years, I didn't realise that there was one huge part of my dream I hadn't thought of." He looked at Brenda. "Someone I loved, to share it with."

Brenda covered her mouth and tears trailed down her cheeks.

"Brenda Smith," Deke said, "you made my dream complete. With you in my life, I have everything I ever wanted. Please make it permanent. Please say you'll marry me."

A loud sob escaped Brenda. "Yes," she called.

"No!" Jodie shouted.

Every face that had been smiling turned in horror to Jodie, who waved a dismissive hand. "Not no to the wedding. No to you stealing my thunder. You're a bloody backstabbing limelight stealer, Deke Miller."

Deke grinned, jumped off his chair and headed straight for Brenda. "Don't listen to her, Bren. She's jealous that I was smart enough to get in first. We're still getting married, right? Because I know I heard you say yes."

"Of course I'll marry you, Deke." Brenda threw herself into Deke's arms.

"Well, that's just perfect," Jodie said. "Fine. I guess I'll have to play second bloody fiddle to my annoying brother. Okay, everybody, I have an announcement. I'm marrying Mitch Harris."

There was a cheer. Mitch was a bit dumbfounded. He was pretty sure he hadn't proposed already. The proposal he'd planned wasn't something he'd forget. It was something that would go down in history as the most epic proposal of all time. He looked at Josh as Jodie made her way through the clapping and cheering crowd towards him.

"Did I propose when I was drugged out of my mind in hospital?"

Josh shrugged, but Mitch wasn't interested in his answer anyway, because Jodie was standing in front of him.

"We're getting married?" he asked the seriously grumpy woman who was frowning up at him.

"You don't think I'd build a house with you and not marry you." She shot a look at her brother where she tried to incinerate his head with the power of her mind. "I had a whole romantic proposal worked out and he blew it."

Mitch felt like he'd entered an alternate reality. "Did you get me a ring?"

Jodie gave him a look that told him exactly what she thought of that question.

"Fine, did you get you a ring?" He hoped not. The one he'd had made for her was locked up in the hotel safe.

She put her hands on her hips. "I can't buy my own engagement ring, Mitch."

"Of course not. What was I thinking?" Mainly he was wondering what the hell was going on.

Jodie seemed to catch that he was confused, because she stepped into him and wrapped her arms around his waist. Her face softened as she looked up at him.

"I love you, Mitch Harris. Are you going to marry me or what?"

Mitch stared at the woman he'd fallen in love with the minute he'd set eyes on her. There was never any question in his mind over where they were heading. So it hadn't gone exactly as planned. He could be flexible. Especially if it meant he got what he wanted earlier than expected. He looked over her shoulder at the crowded room, full of his friends, his family. All of them grinning his way.

"I'm getting married!" he shouted.

And as Invertary cheered, Mitch kissed his girl.

six years later

For Betty MacLeod's ninety-fifth birthday, she decided she didn't want a party. She wanted a wake. It had always seemed crazy to Betty that the biggest party of her life would happen after she died, so she decided to have it before then so she could attend and hear what people had to say about her.

"I don't know why we're indulging her," Kirsty told her husband. "This is one of the crazier ideas she's had over the years."

Lake Benson pulled up the formal white socks that went with traditional Scottish dress and smiled at his wife. Almost nine years he'd had her in his life and every single minute of those years had been perfect because she was in it.

"She's ninety-five. It's a party. I don't see the problem."

"You wouldn't. You've done nothing but indulge her since the day you met her." She pointed at him. "Look at you. You're wearing a MacLeod tartan kilt when you're an Englishman. You pander to her. And who has a big bash for their ninety-fifth birthday, anyway? Why didn't she do something for her ninetieth like a normal person? Or better yet, wait until she turns one hundred?"

Lake didn't think it was the time to point out that there was nothing normal about his pet Hobbit. "She wants a party before she dies."

Kirsty scoffed at that. "She isn't going to die. Demons don't die, they just get more shrivelled and evil."

"I'll make sure to put that in my eulogy."

"You do that."

After almost a decade, Lake had given up on Kirsty and Betty getting on with each other. At best they had an uneasy truce.

"I do like you in a kilt, Lake Benson," Kirsty said.

"Even if it isn't Campbell tartan?" he teased.

"I'll overlook it this once."

He fought a smile as he watched his wife's eyes heat at the sight of him in the offensive kilt. Lake had to fight the urge to forgo the party and get his wife into bed. Kirsty blinked out of her daze and smoothed down the formfitting silk sheath she wore, which just happened to be the exact same blue as the kilt he had on. Yeah, his wife might talk a good game, but she was completely soft-hearted. It was just one of the things he adored about her.

He watched as she fitted the drop diamond earrings he'd gotten her last Christmas to her lobes. The global success of Benson Security meant he could spoil her whenever the feeling took him. And it took him quite often.

"How do I look?" Kirsty turned to him and waited for his assessment.

Her long red hair sat about her shoulders in soft waves. Lake loved her hair. It was the colour of fire and warmth. It symbolised everything she meant to him—passion and home. He also loved the scars on her shoulder and neck that she didn't try to hide anymore. They'd silvered over the years, but were still a visible reminder of the car crash that almost took her life and ended her modelling career. It was also a reminder that his Kirsty was a fighter, a survivor. Every time he noticed the scars, he felt a surge of pride at how she'd fought past the accident that changed her life. She'd taken her experience as a lingerie model and transferred it to design, becoming one of the most popular lingerie brands in the UK.

"He's doing it again," came the stage whisper from the door. "That yucky, dopey look."

Lake looked over at his eldest daughter and grinned.

"Uh-huh." His youngest nodded her agreement.

Lake pretended to frown at them and they giggled. They were gorgeous in their matching blue tartan dresses with big blue bows in their jet-black hair.

"Oh, Grace." Kirsty knelt before their youngest. "You have chocolate all over your face." She produced a wet wipe from thin air and proceeded to clean the smiling face.

"The cake fell into my mouth, Mummy," the five-year-old terror said. "It wasn't my fault."

Her six-year-old sister was wide-eyed with matching innocence and Lake suspected that the cake had fallen into her mouth too. She was just better at hiding the evidence. Lexie came over and lifted her arms to Lake, who promptly picked her up. She put her arms around his neck and smiled at him. Lexie was definitely a daddy's girl. She'd been that way ever since they'd picked her up from the orphanage in China five years earlier. A year later they'd made the trip again, this time coming home with Grace. As far as Lake was concerned, he'd picked the two most perfect kids in the world.

"I want hair like Mummy," Lexie told him.

"When you're older you can dye it any colour you like," he said.

"Lake!" Kirsty stood and took Grace's hand. "Lexie's hair is perfect as it is."

He looked at his eldest with her long, straight black hair. It was perfect. It was also just hair.

"What's the big deal? It's hair. It grows. Nothing she does will be permanent."

"She's six," Kirsty said, like it was a reprimand.

Lake looked at his daughter. "Oh no, I thought you were sixty-five."

She started giggling and held him tighter. Kirsty shook her head at them.

Grace tugged on her mum's hand and Kirsty looked down at their baby. "Will there be cake at the party?"

"I think you've had enough cake, don't you?" Kirsty said.

Grace shook her head vehemently.

"There will definitely be pies," Lake said.

Lexie nodded. "Satan likes pies."

"Lexie!" Kirsty glared at their daughter as Lake tried not to laugh. "What did we talk about? We don't call Betty Satan."

Lexie pouted, but Lake knew it was fake. The tiny devil liked getting a rise out of her mother. "Everybody calls her Satan."

"I don't care what everybody does. You don't call her that. Are we clear?"

"Yes, Mummy." Lexie looked appropriately contrite and would have pulled it off too if she hadn't cut it short by winking at Lake.

"Monsters," Kirsty said in exasperation, but there was love and humour in her voice. She looked over at Lake. "We all ready, then?"

He nodded, and Kirsty grabbed her bag from the dresser. "Then let's get this over with."

She took Grace's hand and they headed down the stairs of their waterside home to the front door.

"This is going to be awful," Kirsty said.

"No, it won't." Lake rounded their SUV and put Lexie in her booster seat. "Caroline's organising it. It will be fine."

"Poor Caroline." Kirsty secured Grace into her car seat. "We've been best friends most of our lives and I still don't know how she manages to do everything she does."

"Yep." Lake climbed into the driver's seat. "She's formidable, all right. Good job she has Josh to loosen her up."

Kirsty started giggling. "As I said, poor Caroline."

* * *

Caroline McInnes was about ten seconds away from strangling her husband and burying his body on castle grounds. Honestly, no one would blame her.

"I want to wear a suit," the infuriating man whined. "I'm known for my suits. Or my tees. I don't want to wear a skirt."

"Josh McInnes, sometimes it is very hard to believe that you are in your forties. You behave like a child."

"I'm barely in my forties," Josh said. "I've only just scraped in."

"Hey," Jessica called from her spot at the kitchen table where she was waiting impatiently. "I don't behave like him." The eight-year-old pointed at her dad.

"Good point," Caroline told her eldest before turning back to Josh. "You're worse than a child. It isn't a skirt. It's a kilt. Men in Scotland have been wearing them for hundreds of years. You can wear one for one day."

"Can't I at least wear the skirt with my vintage Mickey Mouse t-shirt? I need something American."

Caroline stared at him. She knew he argued like this deliberately. It entertained him, and normally she'd indulge his sick sense of humour, but not right now. Not when there were last-minute details to oversee to ensure Betty's wake ran smoothly.

Caroline pushed her shoulders back and stared at Josh. "You will wear Scottish dress. You will sing at the wake and you will stop annoying me. I don't have time to deal with you. I have things to do."

At once his face softened and that mischievous glint in his eye disappeared. He stepped into her and wrapped his arms around her until she was tight against him, her head on his chest.

"Sorry, baby. I'll stop being funny." He caressed her back, and she felt herself melt.

"That would be appreciated."

"You know," Josh said, "you didn't have to take on organising this party. You have more than enough to do with joint-managing my career with Mitch, running the Christmas festival and being on the town's council. Plus, there are the kids. The kids are a lot of work."

Jessica barked out a laugh. "Not as much as you are, Dad."

"Not helping, princess," Josh said. "I'm trying to reassure your mom." He looked down at Caroline. "How am I doing?"

"Great." She patted his chest and went on tiptoes for a kiss. "I just want this day to be perfect for Betty."

His lips were soft and just the touch of them made Caroline melt. He was her addiction. One she never wanted to recover from.

"I don't see why," Josh said when he pulled back from her. "She's evil. She doesn't deserve a party."

"She's Betty." Caroline sighed and stepped back from her husband. "She's a town institution."

"She should be in an institution," Josh muttered.

She was about to tell him off when their son, Jack, ran through the kitchen wearing his tiny kilt and waving a toy lightsaber. He was chased by their Labrador, who was dressed in Josh's Mickey Mouse t-shirt.

"I am going to kill that kid," Josh said and ran after the dog.

Jack started giggling hysterically as he made it into the conservatory. A game of chase began as Josh, Jack and the dog circled the furniture—both the dog and Josh had big, sloppy grins on their faces.

Caroline turned to her eldest. "You were the one who dressed the dog, weren't you?"

Jessica shrugged. "You didn't want him to wear that t-shirt. Problem solved."

Sometimes Caroline wondered if Jessica was eight going on thirty. Still, she wrapped an arm around her and kissed her head.

"Love you, darling," she told her girl.

"I know." Jessica smiled smugly and Caroline noticed that she was working on an organisational chart for her Barbies. Jessica was definitely her mother's daughter.

"Right, we need to go," Caroline announced as she picked up their toddler from the playpen in the corner of the room. Two-year-old Jonathan was her perfect child. He always had a smile, he slept beautifully and he never cried.

As Caroline smiled down at him, she wondered if baby number four was going to be a girl. She glanced at her husband, who'd announced he was done having kids after baby number three, and wondered when would be the best time to tell him he was going to be a father again.

Josh sauntered into the kitchen with his son under his arm like a rugby ball. Five-year-old Jack was swinging his lightsaber at the dog.

"We need to go," Caroline said again.

"I thought we were waiting for Mitch," Josh said.

"They sent a text. They're running late and they still have to pick Betty up."

"Late! They're playing hide the salami while I have to wear a dress. At least he'll pay for his fun by spending extra time with Satan."

Caroline smacked him on his hard abs. "Josh!"

"What's hide the salami?" Jack asked from under Josh's arm.

Caroline folded her arms and tapped her toe as she mentally challenged her husband to get out of this one. Josh, as usual, was totally unfazed.

"I said hide for the tsunami," he said. "It's when you practice safety drills in case the town gets hit by a big wave."

Jack nodded. "I knew that."

"Uncle Mitch is very safety conscious," Josh added.

"Aunt Jodie is going to teach me to beat up boys," Jessica announced as they headed out of the castle.

"Fantastic," Josh said as Caroline groaned.

Just what she needed—more violence in her house.

"I need the experience," Jessica said, "for when my brothers get older. Aunt Jodie said every time her brother annoyed her, she'd just hit him. I'm going to do that too."

"No you're not." Caroline looked at Josh for support, but he seemed impressed with Jessica's plans, so no help there. "You can't beat up your brothers whenever you like."

"How about sometimes?" Jessica asked. "Like when they're really annoying."

"No."

Josh leaned into his daughter and whispered loud enough for Caroline to hear, "I'll work on your mom if you promise never to use what you learn on me."

"I can't promise that." Jessica rolled her eyes dramatically. "You heard Mom. You're more trouble than all of us."

Josh was laughing as he fitted their children into the car.

As Caroline took her seat, she pulled out her phone and texted Deke to make sure everything was okay with the food. There had almost been a war over who would cater the party, but Caroline had solved it by letting the spa restaurant do the food and letting Dougal at the pub play host. Although Dougal was still a bit put out that there would be someone else's food served in his pub. She made a note to soothe him when they arrived at the wake.

"Mitch is right," Josh said as he climbed into the driver's seat. "Give you a smartphone and you can rule the world."

"Girl power!" Jessica shouted and Jack hit her on the head with his lightsaber.

As Josh refereed the kids, Caroline felt warmth overtake her at the sight. This had been her dream. A family of her own to love and care for and boss around. She never thought she'd have it. At one time she'd been the cold spinster of Invertary. Too scary for men to date and too plain to attract much romantic attention. Then Josh, with his crazy idea of arranging a non-romantic marriage, arrived in town and picked her. He'd told her that he hadn't meant to fall for her, but he couldn't resist. And then he'd spent every day since he proposed showing her just how much he did love her.

If Caroline sometimes smiled smugly at the men in town who hadn't wanted her, she could be forgiven. Because Josh McInnes, world-famous singer, had seen past the grey suits and need for control, to the woman inside who desperately wanted to feel loved.

"You're thinking about marrying me again, aren't you?" Josh said as turned the engine on.

"How did you know?"

"You get that dreamy look on your face and then about half an hour later, I get lucky." He grinned at her. "Keep thinking about the time I swept you off your feet. I like it."

"Idiot." Caroline reached for his hand and held it tight.

"Your idiot, baby. All yours."

And she wouldn't have it any other way.

* * *

"Really?" Dougal said from behind Deke's shoulder. "You're serving salmon appetisers for a buffet? Don't you think that's a little over the top? I mean, the woman has asked for an assortment of beef pies and custard slices for the buffet table."

Deke gritted his teeth and counted to ten. Again. It wasn't helping. His wife gave him a sympathetic look before taking Dougal's arm.

"Dougal, have a told you yet how much I love that waistcoat you're wearing?" Brenda said as she walked the man out of the kitchen. "Wherever do you get your clothes? I'd love to get something like that for Deke. Although he wouldn't look as stunning in it as you do. You have a certain flair for fashion that's sorely lacking in Invertary…"

Deke grinned after her. She was a complete force of nature. Dougal didn't stand a chance against her.

"There's nothing wrong with that salmon," Alastair Stewart said. "I caught it myself."

Once his father had retired, the award-winning fisherman had come back to town to run the fishing tackle shop they'd co-owned. In the three years they'd been back, Rainne had qualified as an accountant and set up on her own. It amazed Deke how little she looked like an accountant. She wore ankle-length tie-dye dresses most of the time and her hair had rainbow-coloured streaks through it.

"I don't think it's the fish he has issue with; it's the fact Deke is in his kitchen." Rainne appeased her husband by rubbing his back.

"Damn straight it isn't the fish." Alastair nodded.

Brenda came back into the room and stood up on tiptoes to kiss Deke. "Margaret has taken over Dougal watch."

"Good." Let Dougal's wife deal with him.

"Is anyone else here still suffering from shock at Margaret Campbell marrying Dougal?" Alastair said.

The couple had only been married a few months and the town was still reeling.

"I thought he was gay," Rainne said. "The clothes, you know? I don't think even Elton John has that much glitter and gold lamé in his wardrobe."

Brenda climbed up on a barstool that Deke had dragged into the kitchen for her and leaned on the stainless steel counter. He would have been so much happier if his very pregnant wife had stayed home instead of partying it up at the Scottie Dog. She was overdue by about a week, but everyone kept telling him that was normal for first babies. Deke didn't think anything about this was normal. She was making a child. His child. She should have been in bed. He should have chained her to the damn thing until the baby came.

"Take a deep breath, honey," Brenda said. "Everything is going to be fine."

Deke pointed a knife at her. "If you have that baby in this pub, I'm going to paddle your backside."

"Promises, promises." The siren winked at him before turning back to Rainne. "I heard that Dougal has slept with most of the women in Knit or Die."

"No." Rainne's jaw dropped. "That is deeply disturbing."

"I know," Brenda said with a grin.

The swinging door pushed open and Deke's shoulders tensed at the thought of dealing with more of Dougal's rubbish. He was relieved to see it was only Alastair and Rainne's son George.

"What is it, sweetie?" Rainne knelt down and brushed the boy's long brown hair behind his ear.

"Somebody woke Susan." His eyes were wide with false innocence, making it clear that the someone who'd woken his baby sister was definitely him.

"Okay." Rainne sighed and stood, holding out a hand for her toddler son. "Let's go get the baby, then." She grinned back at her husband. "It was too good to last anyway."

"That kid only sleeps for fifteen minutes at a time," Alastair told them. "It's driving me insane."

"I can't wait." Brenda beamed at them as she rubbed her massive belly.

In that moment, Deke wished it was only the two of them, snuggling on the couch. He'd wrap his arm around her and kiss her hair before he pulled a blanket over her legs and put on her favourite TV show for her. Yeah, he wished he was home alone with his wife and not catering a meal for the wicked witch of the Highlands.

"You are going to love it," Alastair said. "There's nothing like having kids. It's equal parts heaven and hell. Sometimes both at the same time. And"—he grinned—"it could be worse. You could be having twins. Every time I start feeling sorry for myself at my exhausted state, I think of the Donaldson/Boyle clan and life is suddenly much better."

The three of them shared a look before bursting out laughing.

* * *

"Why did we have kids?" Abby Boyle asked her husband, Flynn, for what seemed like the millionth time, as she looked out their bedroom window onto the large paddock that made up most of their backyard.

"Because you can't keep off of me and my swimmers are too strong for standard contraception," Flynn said.

"Well, one of your swimmers just cracked an ostrich egg on the goat's horns."

"What?" Flynn jumped to his feet from where he'd been sitting on the bed, pulling on his shoes. "Bloody Fergus. He's supposed to be the smart one."

"You need to go get him cleaned up while I finish getting ready," Abby said as she watched the goat run around the garden, spreading egg everywhere. "Thank goodness I haven't put him in his party clothes yet."

"I told the kids not to touch the eggs." Flynn pulled on his other shoe.

"And I told you not to bring home any more unwanted animals, but you still keep turning up with something in tow." She pointed to the rabbit hutch compound in the corner of the yard. Flynn's latest addition to their menagerie.

"To be fair," Flynn said, "technically we already had rabbits. Wild ones. I just added a few more."

"Well, seeing as at least three of them are pregnant, that few is going to turn into hundreds."

"I'll find homes for them," Flynn promised.

"You said that about the goat." She pointed out the window to the rabid animal that was currently being chased by their son. At least in Fergus, the goat had met his match. "And the alpacas, and the donkeys, and the ostriches, and the sheep, and the blind dog, and the two feral cats, and the hedgehogs, and..."

Flynn stood in front of her and wrapped his arms tight around her waist. "Have I told you how gorgeous you look in this dress?"

It was a blue silk Chanel shift dress that her mother had brought her back from Paris. Her mother had great taste in clothes and a deep need to make up for years of estrangement from Abby by shopping for her every chance she got. It was something Abby had brought up with Victoria on several occasions, until Victoria's husband Lawrence had taken Abby aside and explained that shopping made her mother happy, and it would be best if Abby just accepted the gifts graciously. So that's what Abby did, but she also made sure her mother knew she was welcome and loved even if she didn't always come bearing gifts. They had a lot of years to make up for, years where Abby's grandmother had kept them apart, and neither one of them wanted anything to get in the way of that.

Flynn nuzzled the spot on Abby's neck that made her knees go weak. "How about we lock the door and steal five minutes with you, me and that dress, before we go to this thing?"

Abby's fingers dug into Flynn's arms. She was tempted, oh so tempted. Tempted enough to ignore the fact her three-year-old was covered in raw egg and chasing a goat in his bare feet.

"Don't you want me to make you feel good, baby? I can take away your stress," he whispered against her lips, and Abby felt what little resolve she had left weaken.

"Dad!" The shout made the house vibrate.

"Damn it," Flynn muttered, and stepped away from his wife. "What?" he shouted back to their eldest daughter.

"The twins are riding the horses again," twelve-year-old Katy shouted back. "Without saddles!"

"That's it." Flynn stomped towards the door. "I'm buying a cage and I'm putting them all in it. If I'd known how hard it was to have a sex life while parenting, things would have been a whole lot different around here."

"Dad!" Katy shouted again. "Fergus threw an egg at Josie!" There was a pause as Flynn stomped down the stairs. "Oh, oh, he threw an ostrich egg at Grandma Victoria's car." There was another pause. "Dad! The twins are galloping!"

Abby couldn't help it—she burst out laughing. This was life with Flynn. Chaos filled with animals, kids and a man who was too soft-hearted to turn anyone or anything away. She wouldn't have it any other way.

Abby looked out the window as Lawrence and Flynn chased the kids around the yard—the twins were still on the miniature horses and the men's kilts were flying as they ran. It was a wonderful sight.

With a thought, Abby opened the window and shouted down to her husband, "Flynn Boyle, you're dealing with the egg mess. You brought the birds here; you can clean up your son." She eyed the clock. "And you have five minutes to do it before Matt and Jena get here."

She then stood back and watched family and animals chase each other around her yard.

* * *

"Jena," Matt snapped into the walk-in closet. "We're going to be late. Hurry up."

His wife's perfect heart-shaped backside wiggled as the rest of her was rummaging around in a huge bag full of shoes.

"Does it really matter if we're late? It's a wake and the person it's for isn't even dead yet. We could turn up next year and we'd still be early."

Matt had to admit, she had a point.

"We're supposed to be at Flynn's place in five minutes. Can't you wear one of the other pairs of black shoes you own?"

Jena gasped and he knew he'd gone too far. In the eight years they'd been together, he'd learned the hard way never to comment on her shoe obsession. Now he'd gone and blown it. His wife's back snapped straight and she spun on him. She was barefoot, but held two ridiculously high wedge sandals in her hands. She pointed one at him.

"Donald Matthew Donaldson," she snapped, "do you think I put this outfit together, to look this fabulous, only to ruin it with the wrong shoes?"

Why did women ask questions that there was only one possible answer for?

"Of course not. I can see that only special shoes would go with a dress that amazing." Seriously? What else was he supposed to say? Still, he hoped the shoes she held in her hands were the ones she needed.

Jena beamed at him as though he were a performing dog who'd finally mastered a particularly difficult trick. "This dress is amazing." She ran her hand down the sparkly black fabric that clung to her hips and thighs in a tiny bandana-style skirt. The top of the dress was a baggy, blousy thing that fell off one shoulder. It emphasised every single one of her luscious curves and made her legs look a mile long.

One landmine successfully negotiated. "You know, if you hadn't knocked down the walls in your closet, you wouldn't have had a problem finding your shoes." And there he went, stepping right onto another one.

"I had to knock down the wall. There wasn't enough space for all my shoes."

Matt pinched the bridge of his nose. It didn't help. There was normal logic and then there was Jena logic.

"Honey, the wall you knocked through took you into the bathroom." There was now a gaping hole where the wall above the bath used to be.

"I explained this." Jena stepped into the wedge sandals, one at a time, holding on to the doorframe for balance. "I thought I was knocking out the part of the wall that led into the little alcove in the hallway. I misjudged, is all. Don't worry." She patted him on the cheek as she sauntered past and into their bedroom. "I'll get it right next time."

"Next time?"

He wasn't proud that his voice came out as a desperate, high-pitched squeak. The thought of her knocking down any more walls made his head spin. The fact she hadn't injured herself making the last hole was a miracle. She didn't have the reputation as the most accident-prone woman in Scotland for nothing. Unfortunately, she was also DIY obsessed and worked at the local hardware store, so she had access to many, many power tools. Matt often spent nights awake with the thought of the damage she could do to herself at work.

"I thought you were done with closet expansion. I thought you were going to fix the bathroom wall and that was the end of it."

Her golden eyes went wide. "Then where would I keep all my shoes?"

It was on the tip of his tongue to point out that she only had one pair of feet and didn't need that many shoes. He fought the urge. There were some things that weren't worth fighting over and his wife's obsession with stripper shoes was one of them.

"How about you patch up the hole in the bathroom wall before you knock another one through from the closet? Can you at least do that?"

"Of course I can." She tossed her waist-length wavy hair and gave him a look that totally disarmed him. Fighting with Jena was pointless—he rarely won. She sauntered towards him, her hips swaying as she tottered on the mile-high heels. The sight was mesmerising. The heels brought her height up so that they were almost eye to eye. She draped her arms over his shoulders.

"I know the hole in the bathroom wall is an inconvenience,

but I promise to make it up to you." That promise in that husky American accent of hers never failed to bring him to his knees.

"I am totally wrapped around your little finger, aren't I?"

"I won't tell anyone." She kissed him. "Promise. Now, you go put April in the car while I finish up here."

Matt did as he was told, even though he didn't know what Jena still needed to do. She looked ready to go to him. Matt found their four-year-old daughter in her bedroom trying on shoes to go with her bright pink princess dress and plastic tiara. It was like looking at a miniature version of Jena, complete with matching shoe addiction. Her long, wavy, honey-coloured hair was up in a high ponytail, and if he wasn't mistaken, she was wearing lip gloss.

"Should I wear the pink ones or the purple ones?" April pointed at the glittery flat ballet pumps scattered over the rug.

"Pink." Matt was seriously done talking shoes. If picking one got him out of the house faster, he was all for it.

April tapped a finger to her chin as she considered the shoes and Matt wondered if he'd ever make it to the wake.

"I'm going to wear both!" She sat down and put a purple shoe on her right foot and a pink on her left.

Matt looked at the shoes, then at his daughter's beaming face and decided she was four and could wear whatever the hell she wanted to wear.

"Let's go." He picked her up and snuggled her close to him, breathing in the comforting scent of baby powder and milk.

Sometimes, out of nowhere, the memory of almost losing Jena and April would hit him hard and he'd find himself holding them tighter than he normally did. Thankfully for him, both of the females in his life indulged his need to know they were safe. Even now, walking down the stairs to his home, with Jena's hips swaying in front of him and April chatting in his arms, the past was close.

Jena had had a terrible pregnancy and an even worse birth. They'd been flown by rescue helicopter to Glasgow, where the doctors had fought to save mother and child. It was a miracle that he had the two of them. He'd always thought if anything was to happen to Jena, it would be from an accident. His heart had been in his throat every time she was on a construction site, or around anything electrical. He hadn't for one minute thought he'd be the cause of what would almost kill her. As soon as he got word that his daughter and wife were fine, Matt had booked himself in for a vasectomy. There was no way any of them were going through that again.

Fortunately, Jena hadn't been too mad that he'd made the decision without her. A near-death experience could make a woman particularly forgiving. It bothered him, sometimes, to think April would be an only child, but then he remembered that Flynn's kids were just across the field and Claire's brood were nearby in town. His girl had plenty of cousins near her age and would never be lonely. Now, if he could just wrap them in cotton wool twenty-four-seven, he'd feel a whole lot less stressed.

As they rounded the side of the house to their car, Matt spotted a very large delivery box. Jena squealed and ran over to it. Matt sauntered up behind her.

"Please tell me that isn't more shoes." He stared at the box with dread.

"No, it's even better. I'm putting in a dumbwaiter!" Jena beamed at him as she waited for his excited response.

Matt felt the air get sucked out of his lungs. "You're going to cut holes in the floors?"

She nodded enthusiastically. "Isn't it a great idea?"

He looked at her happy face, and then to his daughter's answering smile, and lied. "It's great."

His females were chatting away as Matt walked away from the car for a minute, telling Jena honestly that he had to make a quick call.

His brother-in-law, Grunt, picked up on the second ring. "Yo."

"I need a pick-up," Matt said. "The box is beside the garage door."

"Done." Grunt hung up and Matt smiled.

It wouldn't be the first time Jena's DIY projects mysteriously disappeared and it probably wouldn't be the last. Smiling, he headed to the car, making a mental note to buy his brother-in-law some beer to thank him for helping out, again.

* * *

"Who was that, baby?"

Claire ran her hand down Grunt's arm as he tucked his phone back into his sporran. Yeah, he'd just said the word sporran. Okay, so it was in his head, but it was still damn disturbing. The fact he was wearing one was even more so.

"Matt," Grunt told his wife.

"Matt needs another DIY project to disappear?"

Grunt grunted.

Claire shook her head. "Poor Jena."

"Poor Jena nothing," Dimitri Raast, Grunt's brother-in-law and fellow American, said. "That woman needs a keeper. She's lucky she's got Matt."

"No kidding." Claire's twin sister Megan scooped up a rice cracker full of dip from the kitchen counter. "She's lucky she's married to the town cop. She would have been locked up years ago if she didn't have connections."

Claire snorted. "Like being married to big brother makes a difference. How many times did he lock us up because we annoyed him?"

"Yeah, but we couldn't sleep our way out of trouble," Megan said.

The twins looked at each other, scrunched up their noses and said "ew" at the same time. Grunt caught Dimitri's eye and saw amusement.

"Where you two off to next?" Grunt said.

Dimitri and Megan worked for Benson Security's London office and for the past few years had built a reputation as bodyguards. They always worked the same job together and it took them all over the world.

"Australia," Dimitri said. "Some star needs a babysitter while he shoots his new movie."

"So glamorous," Claire said on a sigh.

Grunt hooked a hand on the back of her neck and pulled her to him. He knew his wife, she might sound envious, but she was a homebody. She had no desire to travel the globe like her sister. As she kept telling him, she had everything she ever wanted right here in Invertary. And Grunt was going to make sure it stayed that way.

"Not so glamorous standing around all day watching people. It gets dull," Megan said. "But we're going to dive the Great Barrier Reef this time, so that will be cool."

"I thought you were going to start a family, so our kids could grow up together this time." Claire patted her round belly.

Megan's face was soft when she looked at her sister. "Honey, you're producing enough family for all of us." She looked up at Dimitri and her eyes went dark. "We'll get there, but we aren't ready yet."

Grunt figured Dimitri was a whole lot closer to ready

than his younger wife, but like him, Dimitri would give his woman whatever she wanted.

Claire tugged her bottom lip between her teeth. "Do you think it's weird that we're having so many kids?" Her eyes filled with tears as she looked at her sister.

Grunt felt the growl bubble out of him at the sight. "Don't upset your sister," he barked at Megan.

Megan rolled her eyes. "Calm down, King Kong. It isn't me. It's hormones." Her face lit up. "That means it's your fault. If you would stop knocking her up, she'd turn back into a normal, balanced human being."

Grunt growled again.

"Knock it off," Dimitri told him. "We need to get to the pub. You can have your annual fight with Megan once this party is over."

"It isn't a party," Claire said tremulously. "It's a wake. The purpose is to celebrate Betty's life."

"I, for one," Megan said, "think that should happen when she's not around to ruin it."

Grunt pointed at his sister-in-law. "What she said."

"Yeah, well, whatever you think about it, we're on duty, so we need to get going." Dimitri grabbed his wife's hand and pulled her off the stool.

"Why does a ninety-five-year-old woman need a security team at her wake?" Megan said.

"I don't think the team are there to protect Betty from attack. I think they're there to protect the crowd from Betty," Claire said.

"And to search for weapons." Grunt was all about searching for weapons. He'd even borrowed two hand-held metal detecting wands from the Benson Security office for the occasion.

"He wants to make sure Betty doesn't bring in a stun gun," Claire said.

"How many times has she knocked you out over the years?" Megan asked with an evil smile. She knew exactly how many.

When Grunt didn't answer, Dimitri did it for him. "Six."

They burst out laughing. Claire snuggled into his side and patted his stomach. "Honey bun, if you showed her your penis, she'd stop zapping you with a stun gun."

"There is so much that is wrong with that sentence," Megan said.

Grunt wrapped an arm around his wife. "She needs to keep away from my junk."

"She's just curious about the piercing," Claire said. "I'm sure once she sees it, she'll move on to something else."

Grunt grunted. He was not amused. He was going to get brain damage from being zapped all the time. Not to mention falling down and waking disorientated and bruised. He'd been lucky. So far, she hadn't managed to get him when they were alone, so there was always someone to protect his unconscious body. There were some people you really don't want to be helpless around and Betty MacLeod headed the bill.

"Okay." Claire patted him and pushed away. "We need to go." She looked at her sister. "You all set?"

"As set as I will ever be."

Without consulting each other, the twins were both dressed in nearly identical purple dresses. The only difference being that Claire's was wider around the waist to accommodate her pregnant belly. It was uncanny the way they shared the same mind when shopping. Thankfully, they didn't share it with everything else. Grunt was pretty sure that after ten minutes alone with Megan he'd commit murder.

"I'll get the boys," Claire said to him. "You get the girls."

Grunt shook his head. "No, baby. You go to the car. Dimitri and I will get the kids."

He kissed her nose and watched her walk her sister out to their minivan. It still amused him that he'd gone from owning a Harley to owning a minivan. And a huge one at that. It had to be huge for him to fit in it, let alone the rest of his family.

"Is this the last one?" Dimitri asked as they walked into the family room.

Grunt knew he was talking about kids. The latest scan had revealed that they were having a boy this time. A lone boy. Great news after two sets of twins.

"If she wants more, she gets more," Grunt said, even though he thought that was obvious.

Dimitri was laughing as he shook his head. "Never thought you'd be heading up your own version of the Waltons. A biker gang, sure, a football team worth of kids, nope. I know twins run in the family. Hell, we married a set and their cousin Flynn had a set too. If you keep getting her pregnant, and she keeps having twins, you'll end up with about twenty kids by the time you hit fifty."

Grunt didn't see the problem. "Claire's a great mom." She was perfect and he'd kill anyone who said otherwise. "She can handle the kids."

Grunt was a traditionalist when it came to family—he did what his wife told him to do. All Claire ever wanted was to be a stay-at-home mom. Grunt saw it as his job to make sure the family were provided for and protected and that he was around to help her out. He was her support, first and foremost. In return, he got Claire. He definitely got the better end of their deal.

"Good job Lake let you buy into Benson Security," Dimitri said. "A football team full of kids is going to cost you."

As far as Grunt was concerned, they were worth every penny.

As Dimitri picked up his two three-year-old nieces, who were blonde miniatures of both their wives, Grunt nodded at his five-year-old boys.

"Time to go," he said.

Liam grunted and Sam gave him a chin lift, then they headed out of the door. Grunt followed his boys as Dimitri explained to the girls that there wouldn't be a princess at the party. As Grunt caught sight of his radiant wife laughing with her sister, only one word went through his mind.

Mine.

* * *

"I don't see why we had to pick Betty up." Mitch knew he was whining, but he couldn't help himself.

"Because," Jodie said, "there are only two people on the planet that can be trusted not to turf Betty in the loch on the way to her party. That's Lake and me."

Mitch turned the car into Betty's road. "Doesn't it bother you that you're woefully outnumbered by the people who want to off her?"

"Not particularly," Jodie said. "If I worried about what people thought of me, I'd never have married you."

"Funny," Mitch said drolly.

As the car approached Betty's house, the door opened and she came tottering out. Apart from seeming to shrink a couple of inches over the years, she looked pretty much the same as when Mitch had first met her years earlier. She was a five-foot cuboid of a woman who favoured tartan tents as dresses and had taken to wearing glittery hairnets over her non-existent hair. At least she'd stopped dying her head various colours. That was a blessing.

Mitch climbed out of the car and helped shove Betty up and into the backseat.

"Happy wake day," Jena said.

"Thanks." Betty rummaged around in her huge black handbag and came out with an unwrapped toffee. "Here, have a sweetie."

"Uh, thanks?" Jodie tossed the fluff-covered sweet out the window.

They drove down from the hills on the outskirts of town, past the rows of old miners' cottages and onto the high street. The big Presbyterian church dominated the top end of town, with its grey stones warming in the afternoon sun. The crooked houses that made up the town's main shopping street, converted into shops and businesses, had received a new coat of white paint in recent months and gleamed brightly. They passed the first Benson Security office, Kirsty's lingerie shop and Kirsty's mum's craft shop. The uneven cobblestone road made the car shake slightly as they headed to the bottom of the street and towards the loch. Today, it was a bright blue colour that enticed you to spend some time sitting at the edge of it and daydreaming away the hours.

Instead of a peaceful afternoon in the sun, Mitch turned the car away from the loch and into the Scottie Dog carpark. The old pub and hotel took up a coveted corner spot facing the loch. The carpark was crowded, but Grunt was waiting by the side door near a spot that had been cordoned off with a sign saying VIP.

"I take it back," Mitch said. "There are some perks to picking Betty up."

As Grunt moved the sign, Mitch eased the car into the spot.

"Do you think the food is ready?" Betty said. "I'm starving."

Before Mitch could get out of the car and open the door for her, Grunt was there. But instead of helping the old woman out, he reached in and took Betty's bag from her.

"Hey, give that back, you big bampot," Betty shouted.

Grunt ignored her and turned the bag upside down to empty the contents on the hood of Mitch's car. A second later, he held up two stun guns. He stared at Betty for a minute before stalking away with them.

"Don't just stand there," she ordered Mitch. "Help me pack up my bag."

Mitch let out a heavy sigh and did as he was told. Sometimes it was faster and less painful than arguing.

"Ha!" Betty said. "I'm really glad he didn't strip-search me."

Mitch made a gagging sound and Jodie smacked him on the back of his head. The thought of anyone stripping Betty in any way was enough to put him off his food for life. The side door opened and Grunt came back out holding a wand detector.

"You spoke too soon," he told the old woman.

"Arms out," Grunt ordered.

Betty narrowed her eyes. "And if I don't, what you going tae do?"

"I'm going to toss you in the loch and then go inside and have lunch." It was clear from the matter-of-fact way Grunt said it that he meant every word.

Betty held out her arms. "Bloody Yanks. The town has gone to hell since you lot moved in."

The wand beeped three times before Grunt was through. He netted two more stun guns and a pocket knife from the old woman. With a look of disgust, he took his bounty back into the pub.

"Does Lake know you've been pilfering his stock?" Mitch asked.

When Betty wasn't hanging around the spa demanding that Jodie let her do nails and dye hair—neither of which Jodie had ever let her do—she was sitting in her armchair at Lake's security shop. Apparently, she'd also been helping herself to the stock while she was there.

Betty ignored the question and stomped into the pub. Jodie grabbed Mitch's hand and pulled him inside with her.

"Don't let her get to you," she said.

"Easy for you to say. She considers you her prodigy. I'm pretty sure she looks on the rest of us as prey."

Just inside the main doors to the pub was an easel with a huge photo portrait of Betty. It made Mitch shudder to look at it, but at least she had her teeth in the day it was done. The double doors to the restaurant area of the pub had been left wide open so that both areas could be filled. At the back of the room, the small stage had been swathed with MacLeod tartan and there was another huge photo of Betty. The rest of the room was strung with tartan bunting and signs that read: We'll miss you, Betty and You were the best of us and Betty MacLeod was an unsung genius. There was no prize for guessing who'd written the text for the signs.

"This is horrific," Mitch told his wife, who looked more amused than horrified.

"Hey, Mitch, over here," Josh called out.

Mitch looked towards the platform to see that Josh was at the tables reserved for "family." Since Betty didn't have any blood relations, that meant Jodie, Lake and anyone vaguely related to them. Mitch and Jodie made their way through the crowd to the tables and plopped into their seats.

"You did a good job, Caroline," Jodie said.

Caroline smiled brightly. "I just gave her what she wanted."

"As opposed to what we wanted to give her," Josh

mumbled and got an elbow in the ribs from his prim and perfect wife.

Caroline was in full Grace Kelly mode, with her fifties dress and sleek blond bob. She made Josh look like a hobo in comparison.

"Where are the kids?" Mitch asked. It seemed like over the past few years, all of his friends had spawned. Some of them way more than others.

Mitch wasn't jealous. He was happy with the decision Jodie and he had made not to have kids of their own. It was something neither of them had ever really wanted and the decision suited them. It also meant they were free to spend time fighting for changes in the law concerning battered women. Since Mitch had obtained his Scottish certification, and Caroline had taken over half his business, he'd had plenty of time to devote to the cause. And to his wife. His wife needed lots of attention.

"They're next door in the conference room," Caroline said of Dougal's latest addition to the pub building. Basically, it was a large, empty room he tried to hire out for conferences. The fact Invertary had never had a conference didn't put Dougal off. He was of the firm belief that if he built it, they would come.

"The Sunday school teachers are running a crèche for all the kids," Caroline said. "They have games, TV, a nap area and lots of snacks. I also managed to get a whole bunch of teens to volunteer to help."

"She means she told them they would help and that's what they're doing," Josh said as Caroline frowned at him.

"What's the programme for the day?" Mitch nodded at the clipboard in front of Caroline. "When can I get home and get out of this skirt?"

"Kilt!" Jodie and Caroline said at the same time.

Flynn was at the table behind Mitch and tapped his

shoulder. "I hope you didn't wear underpants," Flynn said. "Real Scots don't wear anything under their kilts."

Mitch heaved a sigh. He pointed at his chest. "American." He sounded the word out for the idiot.

Everyone around them laughed as Josh leaned in to whisper, "You've got underwear on, right?"

"Hell yeah," Mitch said.

"Good. Me too."

Mitch stared at his best friend, wondering why unity in underwear choices had reassured him. It wasn't like they planned to lift skirts and flash each other. Mitch looked up to see Dimitri sauntering past with a tray full of drinks. He was wearing jeans.

"Hey." Mitch pointed at him. "Where's your kilt?"

Dimitri grinned. "I'm American, dude. I don't do kilts."

"Damn it to hell," Josh said. "We should have done that."

"So," Jodie said to Caroline, "the programme."

"Yes." Caroline pulled the clipboard closer. "We have a video message, a eulogy and then Betty wants to speak before the rest of the eulogies."

"Eulogies?" Mitch said. "As in more than one?"

Caroline nodded. "Five, to be exact, and then the entertainment part of the wake starts."

"I'm singing," Josh said glumly. "Betty requested I sing Elvis's 'Devil In Disguise.'"

"Could have been worse," Jodie said. "It could have been Cliff Richard's 'Devil Woman.'"

"Ooh, bad seventies song alert." Josh clasped his chest and faked a heart attack.

A murmur went through the crowd and they looked up to see Lake escort Betty up onto the stage, where a huge, red, throne-like chair was waiting. Betty took her seat, with her short legs dangling. Lake turned to the microphone.

"Lake's MCing?" Mitch could feel his eyebrows go up at

the thought of one of the town's most taciturn men being in charge of the occasion.

"Betty requested him," Caroline said.

"Well, at least he won't talk too long," Mitch muttered to his wife.

"Hello everybody and welcome to Betty MacLeod's wake," Lake said over the PA system. "As you can see, she isn't dead. She just looks like she is."

Betty cackled loudly.

"We have a lot to get through, so let's get to it. Harry and Magenta Boyle couldn't be here today because they're with their charity setting up a school in Nigeria, but they did send this message." Lake grinned. "One that Magenta obviously edited before it got to us."

The lights went out and the screen behind Betty filled with an image of Flynn's younger brother and his wife. Harry was his usual doofus self and Magenta's Goth persona was firmly in place. While Harry grinned at everyone, Magenta glared into the camera.

"Hey, Betty," Harry said. "We're sorry we can't be at your wake."

Big red letters flashed across the screen, accompanied by a headshot of Magenta. I'm not sorry.

"But," Harry continued obviously oblivious to the message his wife had added later, "we wanted to thank you for helping us to get together."

You had nothing to do with it. Don't even think about taking credit, the screen flashed.

"If you hadn't locked us in the abandoned mine together," Harry said with a grin, "we might never have become a couple."

You weren't matchmaking, the red letters said, you were just amusing yourself.

"We realise you have a bad rep around town," Harry said.

One that is totally justified.

"But we know it's just you having fun and not everyone understands your sense of humour."

That's because you have no sense of humour.

"So on this day," Harry held up a glass of wine, "we raise a glass to your memory."

I wish you were a memory.

"You definitely had an impact on the Highlands," Harry said. "Happy wake day, Betty."

To everybody who is watching, this is not a wake. It's a trap. Run now while you still have the chance.

The screen went blank and Betty's loud cackle reverberated throughout the room.

"Magenta's right. We need to go while the going is good." Mitch whispered to Jodie.

"Don't be daft." Jodie patted his hand.

"I say we run," Josh hissed.

"Stop overreacting," Caroline said. "She's just an old woman."

Jodie burst out laughing. At least Mitch's wife had some sense.

"Betty has never been an old woman," Josh said. "She's Satan in drag."

"You know, it wouldn't take much to get Betty legally removed from society." Mitch considered the old woman. "I could have her out of Invertary by the end of the week and locked up tight where she didn't bother anyone ever again."

Jodie elbowed his side while Josh nodded eagerly at the idea. Mitch gave Josh a chin lift. As soon as the wake from hell was over, he was consulting his law books. He owed it to the town of Invertary to deal with Betty. Hell, he owed it to common decency.

"It's my turn to give a eulogy." Lake arched an eyebrow as though mystified at how he'd managed to get into the predicament he'd found himself in. "I first met Betty almost a decade ago, when she conned my little sister, Rainne, into buying her old underwear shop and keeping her on as the mascot."

"Good times," Betty shouted and Lake shook his head in her direction.

Why Lake and Jodie found Betty amusing, Mitch would never know.

"Anyway," Lake said. "By the time I arrived, Betty had Rainne intimidated and the shop was going nowhere."

"Not my fault," Rainne shouted. "She's impossible to work with."

"You were too soft for the business," Betty shouted back. "You need a backbone of steel to sell knickers."

"Moving on," Lake said. "Soon after I arrived in Invertary, I realised I only had two options when it came to Betty. I either adopted her or buried her somewhere remote."

"You made the right choice," Betty told him.

"No you didn't," Josh coughed the words into his fist.

"In the ten years since I acquired my very own pet Hobbit, I've learned a few things about Betty. One, never turn your back on her. Two, check every seat for false teeth before sitting. Three, if you need peace and quiet, buy her a pie. Four, make sure she's always monitored. Lastly, five, never ask what she does with the life-sized cardboard cutouts of men she orders from the internet."

There was a raucous cackle of laughter from Betty's seat. She was the only one amused. Mainly, the rest of the room were shifting with nervous energy.

"Although Betty is hard work, she's also entertaining. I realise she isn't everybody's cup of tea, but I can honestly say my life is more interesting for having known her," Lake said. "So if you'll raise your glasses, let's toast Betty MacLeod.

She's ninety-five, she isn't dead and she's still terrifying the Highlands. To Betty."

There was a murmur of tepid enthusiasm as the crowd toasted Betty.

"Now Betty wants to say a few words before we get on with the rest of the eulogies," Lake said.

There were loud groans from the crowd, which Lake ignored. He turned to Betty, who was struggling to get out of the chair. Lake lifted her and put her on her feet. "Keep it short," he said. "There's food waiting."

"Son, this is my wake. I'll take as long as I bloody well like."

At those words, everyone in the room, including Mitch, slumped back in their seats and resigned themselves to a very long speech.

* * *

Betty MacLeod looked out over the room full of people. Most of them she'd known for their whole lives. Some of them she'd known for most of hers. She gave a finger wave to the retired Reverend Morrison, who'd come back from Spain for her wake. He was looking sexy as ever. Maybe he'd be up for a celebration party of a different kind after her wake.

"Right," Betty said as she scanned the room. "For ninety-five years I've lived in this town and barely tolerated most of you. There have been few of you with the courage and brains to interest me for very long. The exceptions are Lake here, who's like the son I never had and who is great with a gun. And Jodie there, who I consider my prodigy. I hope you'll keep this town on their toes long after I'm gone, lassie."

Jodie grinned back at her and Betty felt proud. In the past six years, Betty had tried to tell Jodie everything she needed to know about terrorising the Highlands. She just hoped it stuck.

"Now, as resident genius of Invertary, I've managed to find out a lot about the citizens over the years."

She saw people sit up straight and grinned. Aye, she thought that would get their attention.

"As this is my wake, and I don't want that knowledge going to the grave with me, I thought I'd share it with you now."

There were mutterings and Lake shook his head in resignation. Betty grinned at him. She knew her boy would get her out of there when the crowd turned wild. She just hoped he'd take her out past the buffet table so she could fill her bag with pies on the way.

"First off," Betty said, "Morag McKay. My arch nemesis."

The retired bakery owner was over at the bar with her cronies. Where the hell they all managed to get so many polyester coats, she didn't know.

"Morag McKay, leader of the morality society, spent her youth"—Betty paused for effect and watched Morag pale —"as an exotic dancer in Glasgow."

"I'm going to kill you," Morag shouted. "I'm going to turn this into a real wake."

"Let Betty have her say," Lake shouted, but he gave Betty a look that said she'd better not take things any further. Aye, like she would pay any attention to that.

"I've got photos of Morag shaking her wares that I've sent to the local paper. So you might want to organise another one of your protests outside the newspaper building. Dougal," Betty continued, "buys cheap beef and tells everybody it's genuine Angus."

"Somebody cut the sound," Dougal said. "I won't stand for this in my pub."

"Then sit down, you old bampot," Betty shouted back.

"Heather Donaldson is having a secret affair with Alastair Stewart's father."

Matt's mother gasped and Matt shot to his feet. "That's enough," he ordered Betty.

"It isn't secret," Alastair shouted. "It's just private. They're both single."

"It isn't private any longer," Betty said with a cackle.

"Lake," Matt said, "time to stop this."

Betty ignored him. She hadn't spent her life ignoring the police just to start paying attention now. It was time to mix some fiction with the facts.

"Shona McBride used to be a man," Betty shouted over the noise.

Shona shot to her feet. "I did not. I have the birth certificate to prove it."

Betty laughed. Shona would have to print it in the local paper to put a stop to this rumour and even then, she wasn't sure it would work. That served Shona right for having Betty kicked out of the women's league in the seventies. But Betty wasn't done with Invertary yet.

"The Domino Boys," she shouted, "don't really play dominoes. It's a cover for porn addicts anonymous."

Betty watched chaos break out and laughed. This wake thing was way better than she'd dreamed it could be.

"Somebody stop her," Archie shouted. "This isn't a wake; this is a slander fest. She's making this up as she goes."

Aye, she was, but there was nothing Archie could do about it. This was her wake and she'd have it exactly the way she wanted it. What? Did they expect her to suddenly turn into a sweet old lady? Bunch of pansies.

Lake started stalking towards Betty. "You're done. I warned you about behaving yourself today."

"Auch, I'm just having some fun," Betty told her boy.

Lake waved a hand at the raucous crowd. "Does this look like fun?"

Betty grinned at the chaos in front of her. "Aye, it does."

"That's it. This wake is over."

Lake made a grab for her, but Betty was ready for him. She stepped to the side, taking the microphone with her. She tottered as fast as she could towards her throne, where she'd left supplies for this occasion earlier in the day.

"You can take my life," she shouted, "but you can never take my freedom. I refuse to be silenced."

"Grunt," Lake snapped to the Yank. "If she runs your way, grab her."

Betty caught sight of Grunt stepping up onto the stage. They had her hemmed in, her exits blocked by beefcake and Betty knew exactly which one she wanted to deal with. She bent over, grabbed what she needed from under the chair and yelled a war cry into the microphone. As Grunt approached her, Betty held out the stun gun and pressed the button. He folded like a house of cards. Before anyone could reach her, Betty tossed up his kilt and stared down at him. Six years she'd been trying to see what the fuss was about and now she knew. The piercing was interesting, although it looked painful more than anything else. It was more the proportions that fascinated her.

With a wicked grin on her face, she looked out at the crowd and lifted the mic to her mouth.

"That is a big willy," she said before Lake picked her up and ran her out of the room.

As she was carted into the kitchen, where the pies were being held, she heard a shout go out.

"Brenda's water just broke! Somebody get Deke!"

Lake sat Betty on the stainless steel bench beside a tray of Scotch pies. He stood in front of her with his arms folded and a frown on his face. She supposed she should have been intimidated, but mainly she was hungry.

"Are you pleased with yourself?" he said.

The question was wasted on her. It was supposed to induce guilt. Something Betty hadn't experienced since the fifties. She reached for a nice, hot pie and took a bite. It was perfect. That Deke sure knew how to cook. These were better than Morag's pies.

"Betty, are you pleased with the chaos you caused? You went out of your way to upset a lot of people when this could have been a nice day for everybody."

Betty felt her jaw fall. "What are you talking about? This is the best wake I've ever been to. I'm thinking of doing it again next year."

With a groan, Lake turned on his heels and headed into the melee. Betty shrugged and reached for a second pie.

* * *

This is the end of the Invertary series.

I hope you enjoyed reading these books as much as I enjoyed writing them. Keep an eye out for the Benson's Boys series, as a lot of your favourite Invertary characters will be making an appearance in those.

Thanks for reading my Scottish books!

ABOUT THE AUTHOR

I'm a Scot, living in New Zealand and married to a Dutch man. I write contemporary romance with a humorous bent – this is mainly due to the fact I have an odd sense of humour and can't keep it out of anything I do! If I wasn't a writer, I'd like to be Buffy the Vampire Slayer, or Indiana Jones. Unfortunately, both these roles have already been filled. Which may be a good thing as I have no fighting skills, wouldn't know a precious relic if it hit me in the face and have an aversion to blood. When I'm not living in my head, I'm a mother to two kids, several pet sheep, one dog, four cats, three alpacas, two miniature horses, eight guinea pigs and an escape artist chicken.

www.ingramcontent.com/pod-product-compliance
Lightning Source LLC
Chambersburg PA
CBHW020919110726
47900CB00001B/219